Their breath is agitation, and their life
A storm whereon they ride.
Lord Byron

In time we hate that which we often fear.
William Shakespeare

CHAPTER
ONE

Paperwork could kill.

Nothing, to Eve Dallas's mind, reached the same heights — or depths — as paperwork's terminal boredom.

And if the boredom didn't kill you, the frustration would.

She had to survive it. As NYPSD's Homicide Division's lieutenant, she had to survive it.

But it seemed desperately clear to her, as she sat at her desk in her tiny office in Cop Central, that by spring of 2061, somebody sure as hell should have found a cure.

Didn't she deserve that when she'd come in early, and full of righteousness, to tackle it? She'd known it would be thornier than usual, but even so, she'd underestimated.

It wasn't every day she ended up taking her whole damn squad in pursuit of a contract killer. On two continents. Wouldn't have happened, she thought as she struggled with numbers, a lot of numbers, if said contract killer hadn't put a target on her husband's back.

And hers.

Since he had, the men and women who served under her, along with a chunk of cops from EDD and her commander, had stood up, stepped up, and had refused to back down.

Maybe Roarke had ordered the shuttle for the flight from New York so she didn't have to figure out how to add that terrifying expense into her budget, into her report.

Because she'd married a stubborn Irishman, and a filthy rich one.

And sure, the takedown happened on his family's farm in Clare, with his aunt and the rest of them capping it off with enough food for an army. So no chits for meals.

But the overtime. Preapproved by Commander Whitney, yes, but Christ on a spreadsheet, the OT boggled. Then she had the regs to meet for payment due on international investigations.

Paperwork could not only kill, she thought as she gulped coffee. It could kill slowly and painfully.

Once, as she worked, her partner, Detective Peabody, clumped down the hall to Eve's office in her pink cowgirl boots. And poked her cheery self into the room.

One snarl had her clomping away again.

And eighty-seven minutes after she'd sat down at her desk, Eve finished — every chit, every hour, every approved expense accounted for.

She submitted it — and woe be-fucking-tide any flat-nose in Accounting who questioned her. Then she laid her head on the desk, closed her glassy eyes a moment.

"No more numbers," she muttered. "In the name of humanity, no more numbers."

She sat up, rubbed her hands over her angular face, then back through her choppy crop of brown hair. Rising, she walked to her AutoChef, because she damn well deserved another hit of coffee.

As she drank it, she stood at her skinny window looking out at her view of New York. A tall, lanky woman, she wore good boots, smoke gray like her trousers, and the vest over her white T-shirt and weapon harness.

While her wedding ring was her only visible jewelry, she wore a fat diamond on a chain under her shirt. Both pieces Roarke had given her held equal fat slices of sentiment.

She watched the airtrams wind through a blue sky. The weather gods offered the city a perfect day in May. Sunny and seventies.

The poor bastards heading to their cubes inside one of the steel towers might not drink in much of it. But it was still there. And since she'd survived Death by Expense Report, she could appreciate it.

A good day, she thought, and tugged her window open a couple of inches.

With the kicky little breeze flowing in, she went back to her desk to see what else had piled up since her last shift.

Her communicator signaled.

She saw Dispatch on the readout.

"Dallas."

Dispatch, Dallas, Lieutenant Eve. Possible homicide. See the officers . . .

As she listened to the particulars, she grabbed her jacket off the back of her desk chair and headed out to the bullpen to get her partner.

Somebody hadn't had such a perfect day in May.

"Acknowledged. Dallas and Peabody, Detective Delia, en route. Peabody," she said, still moving, "we caught one."

Her stride hitched briefly as she blinked at Jenkinson's tie. She should be used to the detective's insane ties by now, she thought, but who got used to fat, bug-eyed yellow bumblebees buzzing over a neon-orange field?

Nobody did. Nobody ever should.

Peabody grabbed her coat and hustled to catch up. She wore curls today, her dark hair red-streaked and bouncy.

Something else Eve couldn't get used to.

"What've we got?"

"Dead body, West Fourth, two uniforms on scene. Interestingly, the nine-one-one came in from the Upper East Side. Two more uniforms being dispatched to that location to speak to the woman who called it in."

"How does somebody on the Upper East Side know somebody's dead in the West Village?" Peabody pondered it while Eve made a heel-turn away from the elevator, already crowded with cops, techs, civilian support heading down.

They took the glides.

4

"Dispatch didn't have that data."

"You got in early today."

"Paperwork. Done. Don't want to talk about it."

"McNab and I left early enough to walk in. You've got to take advantage of a day like this."

"Because, like the DB on West Fourth found out, it could be your last."

Hoping for the best, Eve jumped off the glides to try an elevator. Since she found it only about half as full as the one on Homicide's level, she squeezed in.

"Mostly we thought it was a really nice morning for a walk."

They squeezed off again on the garage level. Their footsteps echoed as they crossed to Eve's car.

"We walk a lot when we're in the field," Peabody continued as they got in the car. "But it's not the same as, you know, sort of strolling along. New York in the spring. I mean, it's just mag."

Eve pulled out into the insane traffic, the cacophony of angry horns, the bellowing ad blimps, and the farting maxibuses that was New York in the spring.

But what the hell; on Eve's scale it was mag, any time of the year.

"And hey, Mavis, Bella, and I spent two amazing hours in the community gardens the other day. We've got a nice plot going."

Eve thought of Mavis, her oldest friend — the performer, the mother, the crazed fashion plate, the pregnant-again Mavis. She could see Mavis doing a lot of things — strange things — but digging in the dirt didn't make the list.

"She's really doing that?"

"She's good at it," Peabody confirmed. "Good hands, good eye. I grew up farming, that's the Free-Ager way, but she's a natural. And Bella's so cute in her little gardening outfits. Oh, and she has a boyfriend."

"Mavis has a what? She's married, knocked up again and married."

"No, Bella has a boyfriend. His name's Ned. He's twenty-two — months. He's got all this curly red hair, all these freckles. Mavis dubbed him Adorablicious, and she nailed it. They're really cute together. His parents, Jem and Linc, are just learning how to garden. Jem's a blogger, and Linc's a biochemist."

"Is this gardening or a social club?"

"It can be both, that's the beauty." She turned her head to grin at Eve. "You'd hate it."

No question of that, Eve thought as she hunted for parking. But still.

"I planted a tree."

"You did what?" Peabody's dark eyes widened like inflated balloons. "What!"

"Roarke and I planted a tree. His idea, but we did it. Mostly. The landscaper guy dug the hole, but we put the tree in, and then dirt and whatever."

"What kind of tree?"

"There!" Spotting a space, Eve hit the lights, hit vertical, and as Peabody slammed her goggling eyes shut, punched it across the street. She dropped down between a scarred mini and a burly all-terrain with maybe a half an inch to spare.

6

"Score."

"I was going to say you should warn me, but it would probably be worse." Happy to be unscathed, Peabody got out, waited for Eve to get their field kits from the trunk. "What kind of tree?"

Eve pointed south to the crosswalk. "A crying tree, a crying something. Peach, maybe."

"A weeping peach?"

"Weeping, crying. Same thing, even though it doesn't do either. It's got little flowers all over it now, so we didn't kill it."

"That's good, but why did you plant a tree? Why do a cop and a gazillionaire plant a tree?"

"Roarke gets . . ." Sentimental, she thought as they joined the river of people crossing the street. "Ideas. We did that pond thing, so —"

"You did it? It's done? You said he was going to put one in."

"Yeah, it's done. It's nice. It's got those things that float on it."

"Lily pads?" Peabody sighed.

"Those, and like a stone sort of skirt and plants and a bench, and he decided we should plant the tree ourselves."

"Awww!"

"Social club's closed," Eve announced, and paused in front of the four-story building to get a sense.

Street level consisted of a place called Poets and Painters and a shop called Herbalists. Both had wide windows facing the street, as did the upper stories.

No privacy screens, she noted, no security bars, just glass.

She walked to the wine-colored door, between the two businesses, that accessed the units.

No security camera, standard locks.

"You could break in with a toothpick," she decided, and mastered in.

Iron steps led straight up to the second floor, where a door on the right had a decent alarm system and the double doors on the left had solid locks.

"DB's upstairs," she told Peabody.

They went up, boots clattering.

A uniform waited in the open doorway on the right. The double doors on the left stood open. At a glance Eve saw easels, stools, worktables, tools, big and small hunks of stone and wood.

She heard music pouring out of the room behind the uniform.

She held up her badge, turned on her recorder.

"Lieutenant." The uniform, female, about fifty, her short, densely curled hair tidy under her cap, stepped back. "Officer Miller. My partner, Officer Getz, is upstairs with the DB."

"Run it through."

"We'd just completed taking a complaint up the block, were going off shift when the call came in. Zero-eight-thirty-three hours. Half a block away, you gotta take it. No response at either unit on this level, and we could hear the music through the door."

Hot-tempered music, Eve thought. A lot of bass, a lot of angry drums.

8

"No soundproofing," the uniform continued. "We woke the tenant downstairs in case she had access, which she did. Hettie Brownstone. She and the DB are the only tenants other than the commercial on the street — neither of which were open at the time we arrived. Ms. Brownstone gave us her key cards to both units rented and occupied by Ariel Byrd, and complied when we asked her to wait in her apartment. We announced ourselves, entered. My partner took the second level while I cleared this one. He found the DB."

Miller shifted to glance toward the stairs. Through the wide cased opening, Eve saw the other cop standing at parade rest, the wide window at his back, some shelving flanking it.

"It's an artist's studio, sir. Like for sculpting. The back of her head's caved in. A good-sized hammer, like a mallet, is on the floor beside her, and has blood and gray matter on it — visibly. Also a take-out bag from Café Delish — that's about a block east — on the floor at the top of the stairs. Like somebody dropped it, and the fancy coffee splatted good. Two muffins inside the bag.

"We secured the scene, called it in. I went down to inform Ms. Brownstone and conduct the initial interview."

Miller glanced down at the notes in her hand.

"She's known the victim for three years, since the vic moved in. She runs a dance studio on the premises, directly across from her apartment. According to her statement, she concluded her last class at nine, locked up. She has a five-year-old kid. She didn't leave the premises, didn't hear or see anyone. She states she put the kid to bed by nine-fifteen, took a shower, and had a glass of wine while she watched some screen until about ten-thirty."

Miller looked up from her notes. "She was upset, Lieutenant, but cooperative. She stated she would speak to the investigating officers when they arrived, but had to get her kid to school. She would be back by nine."

"All right. We've got the scene. I'm going to send your partner down. I want you to check with the Poet place. They'd have been open last night. And there's cams on their door and the herb place. I want to see the feed from both."

"Yes, sir, Lieutenant."

"See what you can find out from the café, and check on Brownstone when she gets back. Inform her one or both of us will come down to speak with her as soon as possible."

"Yes, sir. Sir, I want to add, when I cleared this level, I noticed the bed, unless the victim wasn't in the habit of making it, had been used. I think used, as there are wineglasses on either bedside table, and a nearly empty bottle of Shiraz on a counter in the kitchen area."

"Good to know. Thank you, Officer."

Eve walked to the stairs — not iron here, but wood. Old, maybe original.

The male uniform, maybe fifteen years his partner's junior, met them at the top.

10

To his right on the floor, the soaked take-out bag lay in a pool of creamy brown liquid.

"Lieutenant. Miller said not to turn the music off. You'd want to keep everything, even that, the way it was when we accessed."

"Correct."

"I wouldn't have heard you coming up. I only knew you were here because I looked down and saw you with Miller."

Not ear-blasting loud, Eve thought, but loud enough to mask footsteps.

"Thank you, Officer. We've got the scene."

Standing where she was, studying that scene, Eve opened her field kit. She sealed her hands, her boots as Peabody did.

"Music off."

In the silence she looked at the victim, a small-statured female in sweatpants cut off at the knees, a sweatshirt cut off at the armpits.

Blood matted her hair, short, ink black with streaks of bright blue. "From the position of the wound, it looks like it hit slightly to the right — and she went down to the left. Came up behind her, that's clear enough," Eve commented. "She's standing there at that worktable, facing it, the window, working on that hunk of stone."

"It's marble, I think."

"Okay. She's got tools right there. A chisel, a hammer, there's bits of stone on the table, on the floor. Got the music going, the lights on. It'd be hard to see her from the street because the worktable's too far back. But she can see out if she wants."

"No sign of struggle. The coffee sack . . ." Peabody frowned at it. "Somebody starts up — most likely the nine-one-one caller, right? Sees the body, drops the bag. *Splat.*"

"That's how it looks. No obvious signs of burglary or theft up here, either. A lot of statues — finished, half-finished. A lot of stone and wood and tools. The killer comes in — we'll take a good look at the door for tampering — comes up the steps. Picks up that mallet — plenty of that sort of thing right there on that other bench. *Wham.*"

She held up a finger, circled the body. "Or possibly she's had some wine and sex with someone. And he comes up with her. They argue — or started to argue downstairs. She's done, calls for the music, picks up her tools. And in that moment when people just lose their fucking minds, he grabs the mallet and crushes her skull. Probably bashes her a couple times. Then it's: Oh shit. Or: She deserved it. And he gets the hell out."

"Her neighbor might know if she was seeing anyone."

"Yeah, we'll check on that." With her field kit, Eve crouched down, doing what she could to avoid the pool of blood. Using her Identi-pad to confirm ID, she read it into the record.

"Victim is officially identified as Ariel Byrd of this address, mixed-race female, age twenty-seven. I've got the body, Peabody. Start downstairs, start with the

12

bedroom. Let's see if we can lift some prints or DNA off the wineglasses."

She didn't need the microgoggles to examine the wound. "At least two blows from the shape, the width. And since the killer left the weapon right here, easily identified. Bagging for evidence."

She bagged it, sealed it, labeled it, set it aside. "Vic's wearing work gloves and boots and protective goggles."

Eve leaned in, angled her head to look through the goggles to the dark eyes — filmed now — that stared back at her. Then took out her gauges to confirm time of death.

"TOD, twenty-two-forty-eight. COD, blunt force trauma to the back of the skull. ME to confirm."

Since the victim was about five-three and maybe a hundred pounds, Eve didn't call Peabody to help her turn the body.

"Yeah, she tipped to the left, damage to right cheekbone where it slammed against the floor. Hard fall." She lifted the sweatshirt. "Rammed the table first, bet we've got a broken rib here. Couple of strong, hard blows from behind. The victim slams forward — but this table's bolted down so it doesn't move. Then she goes down to the left. I'm saying that's when the killer follows up with the next hit, and that turns her head so she hits the floor with the right side of her face. She's dead before she hits the floor."

Eve duckwalked back, mindful of the blood. She straightened, took out her 'link to call for a wagon and the sweepers.

Crouching again, she examined the take-out bag, used a finger to press on one of the muffins.

Still fresh, she noted, so from this morning.

She flagged the bag and contents for the sweepers.

She took a tour around the space, a dedicated work space. Tools, tarps, a mini-AutoChef, and a tiny friggie that held water and a couple of energy drinks. An easel stood in the corner holding a series of sketches.

The wood, of course, the stone. Some pieces seemed finished to her — and some delicate, some chunky and rough. Faces in the stone, a nude woman, a nude man, a couple of indeterminate sex caught in an embrace.

And in wood a dragon curled as if in sleep, a woman standing en pointe, a many-branched tree with a hint of a face in the trunk.

Most likely, Eve considered, she'd had some success. She wasn't an expert on art, but the pieces had something that clicked with her.

Either success, she thought as she started downstairs, or somebody backing her financially. Rent in a space like this in the West Village wouldn't come cheap.

She scanned the living area.

No sign of any disturbance.

A wall screen, and a sofa that looked comfortably saggy, covered in dark pink, bright blue, deep green stripes. A big, thick rug — probably in deference to her downstairs neighbor — covered most of the floor. An eating area defined by a square table in that same deep pink, four chairs, two in the blue and two in the green. Flowers in a stone — marble? — vase.

The flowers looked very fresh.

No clutter, she thought, unless you counted the art crammed on the walls. All kinds of art, some framed, some just tacked-up sketches.

She glanced in the kitchen. A single counter, and the bottle of red with maybe half a glass left. She marked it for the sweepers.

More wine, some cheese, some yogurt, some energy drinks in a refrigerator that looked as if it had done duty for a couple decades. An old AC — and she checked for last programmed.

No dishes in the sink.

She circled out and paused by the open door of a home office doubling as a guest room. Neat, uncluttered, colorful, Eve noted, with the bed made, the pillows plumped.

Someone — maybe the victim — had painted a mural on one wall, a street scene of sidewalk artists at their easels, cars blurring by.

She flagged the mini data and communication unit on the table under the window for EDD before continuing on.

The bathroom, clean again, simple. She opened the door of the mirrored cabinet over the sink to find some over-the-counter meds, organized by type. She took a moment to check the drawers and cabinet of the vanity before joining Peabody in the main bedroom.

Peabody stood, hands on hips, frowning at the room.

Two stands flanked the unmade bed, with a lamp and a print-dust-coated wineglass on each. The single horizontal window had a privacy screen — unengaged.

Peabody turned. "I wanted you to see it before I bagged the glasses. Prints on both. The vic's on the one on the right of the bed. The ones on the left aren't in the system. The lab's going to find DNA on the glasses and these sheets."

"Yeah, that's not sleep mode. Did you check the drawers in the stands?"

"A tablet, her 'link, and a sketch pad and pencils in a case in the one on the right. Nothing on the left. No calls, texts, incoming or outgoing, on the 'link since mid-afternoon. Then just a text. I recorded the number, registered to a Gwendolyn Huffman."

"What did it say?"

"Just: I'm looking forward to our sitting. The victim texted back she was, too, and the texter said she'd see her soon, and wouldn't come empty-handed."

"No time stated. Bag it for EDD. No condoms, no sex toys," Eve added. "Not here, not in the bathroom. Closet?"

"Just clothes, shoes, a couple of handbags — one day, one evening. Two rolly bags, the small inside the large. She wasn't a clotheshorse," Peabody added as Eve walked to the closet to look herself.

"But you can see she organized what she had by type. Work clothes, street clothes, one basic black dress, a couple of what I'd call fun-night-out outfits. Shoes the same way. She's got underwear, sleep clothes, workout gear, and that sort of thing in the dresser — organized by type again. One small drawer for jewelry — costume, arty, fun stuff. Everything's tidy, Dallas, and nothing looks as if anyone went through it looking for anything."

"No, not here, not anywhere else."

"It bugs me."

Yeah, it did, Eve thought, but turned. "Speak."

"Okay, so you look around the place — her studio upstairs, the living space down here — and everything's clean, really neat and tidy. Except for the art on the walls, she was a serious minimalist, and clearly liked everything clean and in its place."

"Agreed."

"No discarded shirt tossed on the little chair over there, no shoes kicked off anywhere to be put back on or put away later."

"No dirty dishes — except those glasses," Eve added. "The spread thing's folded on top of the bench at the foot of the bed, but the sheets are tangled, half kicked off. Not sleep mode. Sex mode."

"Maybe I can see leaving the bed messy — she's going to smooth it out before coming back to sleep. That's a little stretch considering how, you know, precise she was in her living style, but I don't see her leaving those used wineglasses."

"She used the kitchen AC at eighteen-ten last night to order up a single serving of chicken and rice with a side of brussels sprouts. Those dishes, and the ones from what she ordered for breakfast yesterday at zero-eight-twenty, lunch at thirteen-thirty-five, are in the dishwasher, clean. She programmed it to run at eighteen-twenty-eight."

"So maybe she didn't feel like emptying it so she could load the wineglasses, but I don't see her leaving them in here."

"Doesn't fit the pattern," Eve agreed.

"She's having wine and sex with somebody, and all signs say consensual. But somewhere along the line, there's an argument. Serious enough for the victim to get up, throw on some work clothes, and not follow pattern by tidying up. She's like: 'I'm not doing this again. We're done. Get dressed, get out. I'm going to work.'"

"Following that line," Eve said, "the dumped lover doesn't want it to be done, doesn't want to get out. And concludes the fight by bashing the victim with a mallet."

"Crime of passion," Peabody concluded. "'I'll show you who's done, bitch!'"

"Decent probability on all of that. The morgue and the sweepers are on the way. Let's have a look at the entrance door, and flag the sheets. The sweepers can take them, the glasses, and the rest."

"They're going to find DNA," Peabody predicted, "but if the prints aren't on file . . ."

"DNA being on file for the as-yet-unidentified lover is less likely," Eve finished as she opened the front door, hunkered down. She put on microgoggles to study the lock, the key-card swipe.

"Cheap crap," she muttered, "but no sign I can see of tampering. Let's have EDD come in, check it — and see if they can tell how many times it was accessed yesterday. They can check the main door downstairs, too. Possibility: One lover storms out. 'Fuck you, Ariel.' She's upstairs, music on, working. Second lover comes in. Hard to square someone without any sex toys or basic protection juggling a couple of bed partners, but maybe. Second lover sees bed, wine-glasses. Why, that bitch! Walks up, bashes her. 'That'll teach you to cheat on me.'"

"Being tidy and organized doesn't mean she wasn't a bitch, and one tangling sheets with multiples." Even so, Peabody sighed. "Too bad if she turns out to be a cheater, because I really like her work."

When she heard the steps clanging, Eve replaced the goggles in her field kit. "That should be the morgue or the sweepers. Either way, let's get them started, then go down and talk to the neighbor. She might know who the vic liked to tangle sheets with."

CHAPTER
TWO

Tall, slender, and visibly distressed, Hettie Brownstone let them into an apartment that smelled of vanilla from a candle burning on the ledge over a small electric fireplace. Unlike Byrd's space, this one didn't come within a mile of minimalistic.

Toys jumbled from a trio of stacked tubes in one corner and pillows forested the couch. A kind of cubby/tree inside the entrance held kid-size — and a few adult-size — shoes, boots, jackets, hats.

Dust catchers abounded.

"Is it true? There isn't a mistake? About Ariel?"

"No, ma'am."

Her eyes teared up, but she shook her head, gestured. "Please, sit down. I haven't been to the market — I was going to go after getting my daughter to school, but ... I have some tea, and some juice tubes."

"We're fine," Eve told her.

"Can you tell me what happened? It's awful not knowing what happened, and right upstairs from where my little girl sleeps."

"We're investigating."

Brownstone dropped down in a chair, grabbed the pillow tucked in behind her, and hugged it. "The officers I talked to didn't say, but I got the impression it wasn't an accident."

"No, ma'am, it wasn't an accident."

Now she squeezed her eyes shut. "She was so . . . blasé about security. The landlord's useless when it comes to security, to improvement. Even repairs take forever. I put the camera and security locks on the apartment myself, and I can tell you I've learned how to do some basic plumbing. Actually, Ariel showed me how to change a washer and clean out a drain. That's how we got to know each other."

"How well did you know each other?"

"We're the only tenants, both women, both single. But she's very private, and as a single mother, a working one, I'm insanely busy most of the time. We're friendly, but we don't — didn't," she corrected, "really socialize or hang together. I teach dance six days a week, and I have Tasha. My socializing consists of playdates, trips to the park, kid vids. Ariel teaches art, and works hard and seriously at her own."

"You had access to her unit."

"Yes. Ariel had a cat — Rodin. She sometimes travels to art festivals, and she asked if I'd look after Rodin, go up, make sure he had food and water, give him a little company whenever she was away. He died last winter. I completely forgot to give her the key card back. And she never asked, so it slipped my mind. I gave it to the police."

21

"Yes, we have it. Can you tell us about your evening?"

"Oh, sure." She pushed both hands through a wild mass of curly black hair. "Like I told the other officers, after I picked up Tasha from school, we came home. I fixed her a snack, and she took a nap while I taught a class in my studio across the hall. I use a monitor so I can see and hear her if she wakes up. The security on the front is worthless, in my opinion, but I can't afford to fix it myself. I keep the apartment locked if she's sleeping and I'm teaching, but I have the monitor."

"You know she's safe," Peabody put in.

"Yes." Brownstone's hand fluttered up to the top button of her shirt, twisted at it. "I don't want you to think I neglect her. It's just the two of us. Her father hasn't been in the picture since before she was born — his choice. I filed for professional-mother status for the first six months, but . . ."

"You need to work," Eve said.

"I do. I want her to know I'm supporting us, using what I have to teach. Anyway, we have a routine, and she generally conks during the three o'clock class, then we bring some of her toys over so she can play during the next class. After that there's dinner, and a walk to the park if the weather's good or whatever we're up for. Then I have an eight o'clock — the thirteen- to seventeen-year-old students. Tasha likes to dance with the kids, and they don't mind. After that, I lock up, put her to bed. Sometimes that's quick and easy, sometimes not."

22

She smiled a little. "Last night was quick and easy, so I had her down for the count about quarter after nine, took a shower. I had some wine, and started nodding off in front of the screen. So I went to bed."

"Did you hear anything from upstairs, hear anyone come in or go out of the building? The stairs are loud," Eve pointed out.

"Tell me about it. I invested in soundproofing for that exact reason. Do either of you have kids?"

"No."

"Well, let me tell you, when you've walked the floor with a teething baby, finally get her to sleep, and somebody comes clanging up the damn stairs and wakes her up, you want to murder them."

She jerked back. "I didn't actually mean —"

"We get it," Peabody assured her.

"The landlord wouldn't spring for soundproofing, but told me if I wanted to spend the money on it, go ahead. Actually, my parents paid for it. They live upstate."

"What do you know about Ms. Byrd's friends, her romantic relationships?"

"Oh, not much, if anything. I know she had students on Tuesday and Wednesday evenings, and every other Saturday afternoon. If I had a class or was going in or out of the building, I'd see them coming in. She never talked to me about anyone she was seeing."

Again, she shook her head. "I lit that candle for her. Silly, I guess, but I wanted to . . . If I'd made more time, put more effort into getting to know her, I might be able to help now."

"You have helped," Peabody told her.

"Part of me wants to shut everything down and run back upstate. I've lived in the city since I was seventeen and had a chance to study with the Company. I had dreams of being a prima ballerina. I made it to principal," she said with a smile. "And then there was Tasha. I don't regret for a single second choosing her over that dream. She is the dream. And this is the first time I've even thought about leaving. Can't do it."

She lifted her hands, let them fall. "We've made our life here, and it's a good one. But I hope to God you find who did this to Ariel, not only so I can sleep at night, but because she didn't deserve this. What I knew of her was she was a good person, a talented artist, and a considerate neighbor."

Outside, as they walked back to the car, Peabody slipped her hands into her pretty pink coat because, to her thinking, it made it more of a stroll.

"Parenting's hard," she commented. "Single parenting without the other parent involved has to be brutal. But that was a happy apartment. You could feel it."

"It'll be happier when we find out who killed her neighbor."

"Yeah, there's that."

"What do we know, Peabody?"

"Dead woman, attacked from behind, who, by all appearances had wine and sex prior to the attack. EDD will confirm if the lock was compromised, as visual exam leans no."

They replaced the field kits, got back in the car.

24

"We know the TOD, the probable COD. We know, because Brownstone comes off honest and credible, the vic was private about her private life, serious about her work. Supplemented her income by teaching two or three times a week, and was careless with her security."

"We know," Eve added, "that the vic's lover or lovers was or were discreet enough Brownstone can't confirm she had any. Potentially one or more of her students. Stay after class, have a roll, head out. She'll have the schedule and a list of students on her comp. Have EDD copy us there."

As she drove, Eve called in for the name of the nine-one-one caller, and a copy of the recording.

"Gwendolyn Huffman."

"The same person who texted her yesterday afternoon."

Considering, Eve tapped her fingers on the wheel. "Isn't that handy? Let's hear the call."

Nine-one-one, what is your emergency?

Oh, God, oh God, she's dead! She's dead. There was blood. Ariel! It's Ariel. You need to help, send help.

Over the calm, clear voice of the nine-one-one operator, the hysteria rose only higher as the caller spewed out the address.

Hurry, hurry, please hurry. God, God, I'm going to be sick.

The transmission ended.

"Never gave her name," Eve said. "They got it from the 'link number."

"She sounded hysterical, start to finish."

"If she actually saw the body in the West Village, dropped the morning takeout, then went all the way home to the Upper East Side, she had time to bank that down a little. And if she didn't see the body, how the hell did she know? Let's see if she's taken the time to work out the answers."

The building on the Upper East Side rose high and sleek, steel and glass with the curve of generous terraces on the top floors. On the street, two doormen in silver-trimmed black flanked the wide glass entrance.

Neither of them looked pleased to see Eve's deceptively unstylish DLE pull to the curb.

As the one on the left approached, Eve got out of the car, flipped up her badge.

"Leave it where I put it."

"Ma'am —"

She jabbed a finger at him, then at her badge. "Does this say *ma'am*? No, it does not. It's says Lieutenant. It says NYPSD. Leave my ride where I put it."

She strode past him, across the sidewalk, and through the glass that whisked open when she approached — and made her wonder why the hell they needed doormen.

They walked into what Eve thought of as obsessive elegance. Gold and silver abounded with some royal blue tossed in with a few cushy club chairs. Gold chandeliers dripped light; slim silver urns displayed an arrangement of twisted, gold-flecked branches.

The air, hushed and fragrant, whispered discreetly of wealth and privilege.

Two clerks, in royal blue suits, manned a curved, mirrored counter. One continued to work diligently on her comp. The other tossed his best professional smile at Eve.

"Good morning, and welcome to House Royale. How may I assist you today?"

Maybe it was petty, but Eve felt just a tiny bump of satisfaction when she held up her badge and watched that smile drop away.

"We're here to speak to Gwendolyn Huffman."

"Felicity?" He looked over at his companion, who'd stopped working to fold her hands on the counter.

"Verify their IDs, Jonathan."

"Oh, yes, of course. If I could scan your badges, please?"

After he rooted up a scanner, verified, Felicity nodded.

"We cleared two officers about a half hour ago. Clearance was delayed, as Ms. Huffman had a Do Not Disturb on her unit. Ms. Huffman's fiancé arrived about fifteen minutes before we put through clearance. As Ms. Huffman had updated her DND to exclude him, Mr. Caine went straight up."

"So you kept cops cooling heels, but let the fiancé go up?"

Felicity remained placid. "I certainly apologize, Lieutenant. However, in lieu of a warrant or a verified emergency, we're obliged to honor a resident's DND."

"What time did you come on the desk?" Eve asked her.

"Eight-thirty A.M. As I told the officers, I haven't seen Ms. Huffman this morning."

"We'll need a copy of the security feed for the last twenty-four." Eve paused, made it significant. "I can get a warrant."

"That won't be necessary. We're more than willing to cooperate however we're able. Jonathan, go to security and obtain what the lieutenant requested."

"Lobby," Eve said, "elevators, Huffman's floor."

He all but popped up. "I'll get it right away."

"We'll pick it up on our way out," Eve told Felicity. "Clear us up."

"You're cleared. Ms. Huffman is 4800, forty-eighth floor, east."

"Thanks." Eve walked to the elevators with Peabody. Two gold for west, two silver for east.

"Here's a thought." Eve stepped into the car with its gold-veined silvery mirrored walls. "Huffman's back here when she made the nine-one-one call. It came in at the same time Felicity came on the desk. So Huffman was upstairs, here. She puts on the DND, and buys time."

"She had to know cops would come," Peabody concurred.

"Unless she's an idiot, yeah. Pulls in the fiancé for a little support, maybe runs the story by him. So far, she's not making my wit-of-the-week list."

"The desk said they cleared the fiancé up, so he doesn't live with her."

"She goes all the way downtown, and early, stops for coffee and muffins for two. Why?"

"The text said a sitting."

"Yeah — no names on the texts, either, no chatty details. So, she heads downtown very early in the morning. Either the door to the vic's place wasn't secured or Huffman has access. If she has access, why? Goes in, goes up, drops the takeout, and doesn't just leave, she comes all the way back here before she calls it in.

"Why?"

Eve stepped out into a wide hallway with silver carpet. "Let's see how she answers."

Apartment 4800 boasted double doors, a palm plate, security cam, and double police locks. Eve pressed the buzzer.

The resident is not receiving visitors at this time, the computer began, **please —**

"Lieutenant Dallas, Detective Peabody, NYPSD." She held up her badge for the scanner.

After a brief hesitation, a scan, the computer advised, **Please wait.**

A moment later, the right door opened. She judged the man to be in his mid-thirties, with the sun-streaked blond hair, golden tan, and rugged good looks that said he liked to spend his free time hiking or sailing or playing tennis or some other outdoorsy thing.

At the moment he wore a three-piece navy pin-striped suit and a perfectly knotted gray-and-navy tie.

"Lieutenant, Detective." He nodded briefly, his eyes — nearly the same color as his suit — sober. "Please come in. I'm Merit Caine, Ms. Huffman's fiancé."

He led them through a small foyer flanked by potted trees with little oranges hanging from the branches, and into a wide living area.

If the lobby struck Eve as obsessive elegance, this struck her as studied elegance.

Everything perfect and perfectly matched, she thought. The soft colors and gentle curves of the furnishings, the huge antique rug — perfectly faded — the quiet art, all landscapes or still lifes interspersed with mirrors of varying shapes, the scent of roses and lilies in crystal vases, and the perfection of the view of the river outside the wall of glass. The generous terrace offered a little outdoor living with its glass table, cushy chairs, and potted flowers.

It all suited the woman curled in the corner of the pale blue sofa. Eve judged her a solid decade younger than the fiancé. Young enough, she thought, to do without facial enhancement — or expert enough with them to make it appear she had.

She'd pulled her blond hair back in a tail so her classic oval of a face was unframed. Her eyes — a soft blue like the sofa — showed signs of weeping. Delicately.

She wore white pants in a fluid material, and a flowing white shirt. Everything about her read fragile.

The two uniforms rose from their chairs. Each had coffee, but set the cups down.

30

"Detective, take the officers to the foyer, get their reports. We've got this from here," she said to them. "Ms. Huffman, I'm Lieutenant Dallas."

"I know." Her voice wavered. "Merit and I saw the vid. *The Icove Agenda*. I can't believe this is happening." She reached out for Merit's hand. "I — I told the officers, was telling them what happened. Except I don't know what happened. I just don't know."

"It's all right, Gwen." Merit sat beside her, kept her hand in his. Her left one boasted a chunky square-cut diamond. "It's going to be all right."

Ruggedly Handsome, meet Delicate Beauty, Eve thought. A perfect match.

He looked back at Eve. "Please sit, Lieutenant. Can we offer you something?"

"Just answers," she said, and sat.

"Before you start, I'm also Gwen's legal representative."

"You're a lawyer, Mr. Caine?"

"Yes, with Caine, Boswell, and Caine. While Gwen wants to help your investigation in any way she can, you understand she's had a shock."

"What kind of a shock have you had, Ms. Huffman?"

"I — well — I — I found Ariel. She was . . ." Gwen turned her face into Merit's shoulder. "So much blood."

"You were in her apartment?"

"Yes. This morning."

"What time?"

"Early. I'm not sure, but it had to be about seven-thirty. A little before? I'm not sure."

"How did you get into the apartment?"

Gwen turned her face back toward Eve, but left her head on Merit's shoulder. "The door was open a little. I could hear the music — she likes music on when she works — so I just went inside. I called up to let her know, then I started to go up to her studio. I'd brought coffee and muffins from this place she likes. I was telling her that. 'I've got lattes and cranberry muffins.' I think I said something about being a little early, maybe how she shouldn't leave her door unlatched.

"Then when I went up . . . I saw her. On the floor, and all the blood. I saw her face, her eyes. I think I screamed. I don't know. I couldn't breathe, I felt sick and dizzy and terrified. I ran out. Oh, Merit, I shouldn't have run away like that."

"You were in shock."

"Did you touch anything?"

"I don't know. The door, the railing. I don't know."

"How did you get back here?"

"I got a cab somewhere. I don't even know. I ran, I walked. I felt outside myself." She pressed her hand with its dazzling diamond to her heart. "It didn't seem real. It couldn't be real."

Eve gestured to another chair when Peabody came back in.

"How long have you known Ms. Byrd?"

"We met last fall — September, I think. It must have been September because Merit was on a business trip. I went to an art opening downtown. Ariel was one of the featured artists. I liked her work so much."

A single tear slid rather beautifully down Gwen's cheek. "I bought one of her pieces, and we talked. We just hit it off. I admired her fierce dedication to her art, but she also had a breezy side, if you know what I mean. We became friendly."

"Friendly enough for you to drop by her apartment at seven-thirty in the morning?"

"I was early, as I said. I was supposed to be there at eight, but I was excited. I'd commissioned her to do a piece in marble for Merit, for a wedding gift. I was going to do a sitting."

"Did she often leave her door unsecured?"

"I . . . I don't know. I didn't go to her place that often. We'd usually meet for drinks or to browse a gallery, have some lunch. Of course I'd been to her place, seen her work space, but I don't recall her door being unlatched before.

"She could be careless," Gwen added. "When her mind was in her work, she could be careless."

"All right. You were friends. You met her other friends."

"Not really. It's not that she's an unfriendly person, but she didn't socialize much."

"What about romantic partners?"

"She never mentioned anyone specifically. I used to tell her Merit had an adorable cousin, and I could fix her up." She smiled a little now when she looked at her fiancé. "Henry. But she'd had a bad breakup a couple of years ago, and said she wanted to concentrate on her work. Romance could wait."

"Did she mention the name of the ex?"

"No."

"Okay, why don't you tell us about your evening?"

Those soft and teary blue eyes widened. "My evening?"

"Where you had dinner, what time, with whom."

"I don't understand." Once again, she looked at Merit.

"You've established time of death," he said.

"We have. I'd like to get this out of the way, let Ms. Huffman have some quiet and some privacy."

"Do they think I could do that to her?" Eyes wide, lips trembling, she clutched at Merit. "To anyone?"

Eve shot Peabody a glance so her partner leaned in, all understanding. "Ms. Huffman, this is such a difficult time for you. You suffered a shock and a loss. Everything you tell us helps us find out what happened to your friend, who hurt your friend. Maybe you talked to her last evening?"

"No, I . . . Did I? No. We texted! That's right, in the afternoon. I texted her to confirm the sitting, and she texted back that she was looking forward to it. I was meeting with our wedding planner, Marjorie. Merit and I are getting married in July."

"Congratulations." Peabody added a smile.

"I came home after. Merit's preparing for a court case, so he'd be working late. I got restless. It was such a beautiful day. I went out for a walk, some window-shopping. I guess about six? Six or six-thirty?

34

I'm not sure. I ended up walking to the park. I'm not sure what time I got back here. Eight? Nine? Then I had a salad, a glass of wine. Two," she corrected. "And worked on some of the things Marjorie and I had discussed. Between the wine and the long walk, I was in bed and asleep by eleven."

"Did you meet anyone on your walk, buy anything while you window-shopped?" Eve asked.

"No. Oh, Merit and I texted, what, about nine-thirty?"

"About. I texted Gwen to let her know we were ordering in more food, and we'd probably be at prep for another two or three hours. Since we were taking a break, we texted back and forth for a few minutes."

"Ms. Huffman, given this morning's timeline, you didn't call nine-one-one for approximately sixty minutes after you found Ms. Byrd."

"I know. I'm sorry. So sorry. I've never in my life seen — I didn't start to think straight until I was back home, and even then. Then it hit me. I'd left her there. Just left her. I started to take a pill, a sleep aid. I can hardly believe I nearly took a sleep aid so I could just make it all go away. I started shaking all over again, and I called the police. But I couldn't stop shaking."

"You put a Do Not Disturb on your room and 'links."

"Yes, when I was going to take the pill. I nearly took it again after I called, but I just drank a soother, and I finally realized the police would need to talk to me, and I wanted Merit. I wanted Merit."

She began to cry slow, graceful tears as she huddled against him.

"I should have stayed with her." With pretty tears sliding, she turned her face up to his. "I should have stayed with Ariel and talked to the police there. I'll be ashamed I didn't for the rest of my life."

"Don't. Don't blame yourself." He brushed his lips on her forehead. "I'd appreciate if we could call this now, Lieutenant, Detective. She's had more than enough."

"We appreciate your cooperation," Eve said as she rose. "And we're sorry for your loss. We'll see ourselves out."

On the walk to the elevator, Eve asked, "Anything we didn't cover from the uniforms?"

"Not really. They'd just gotten started. They said there was some stonewalling — not clearing them up because of the DND, waiting for her legal rep. Then some crying and soothing to get through."

They stepped into the elevator, started down. "They'd started to establish the relationship, the basic timeline, then we got there."

"Okay, they didn't get deep enough into the initial interview to see the big, gaping holes in her story."

"They didn't mention it," Peabody replied. "I guess I'm going to risk wrath and say I felt some of her version had wobbles, and I always suspect anyone who can cry and look gorgeous doing it — but that may be envy. But I didn't see the big, gaping holes."

"Wait for them." Eve headed straight to the lobby desk. Before she could ask, Felicity gave her a packet, sealed and labeled.

"The copy you requested, Lieutenant. If we can be of any further assistance —"

"You can. How long has Ms. Huffman lived here?"

"For nearly four years, if memory serves."

"Does your memory include an approximation of how long she's been seeing Mr. Caine?"

"An approximation would be the best I can offer. I'd say about a year, less for his automatic clearance."

"Thanks. One more thing." She pulled out her PPC, brought up Ariel Byrd's ID photo. "Do you recognize this woman?"

"No, I'm sorry."

"Okay, another one more thing. The other shifts on the desk. I need their names and contacts."

"Of course. Jonathan, get that information, please."

Once she had it, Eve thanked Felicity again before heading out with Peabody.

Peabody waited until they were in the car. "So our wit's a suspect. I get that, it's routine. But I don't get why you're narrowing in on her right off."

"First, it just pisses me off when people lie to me." Eve judged the traffic, zipped out into it.

"The take-out bag — that holds up. The uniforms confirmed with the security feed Huffman — no need to run facial recognition now — brought the coffee and muffins at zero-seven-twenty hours."

"Yeah, that holds. And the wedding planner deal's going to hold. We'll check it, but that'll be solid enough. The time might be a little off, but it'll hold. The lawyer-fiancé's late legal prep, that'll hold. The rest of it's bullshit."

She cut west, then headed south on Lexington.

Peabody thought it over. "My bullshit detector's pretty good, but I'll cop yours is better."

"She does the wedding stuff, then goes back to her place. An hour or so later, she decides: Hey, I'm bored. She goes out for a two- or three-hour hike, into the park, window-shopping. Does she strike you as an urban hiker, Peabody? Or a woman who window-shops all that time and buys nothing?"

"Now that you mention it, not really. I mean, it's plausible. Urban strolling, in her case, head full of wedding plans. Just getting out in the air. But, yeah, a long stretch of it, alone. But she said she was home at the time of the murder."

"We'll check the feed, but she probably was, or she'll have come through the lobby and not gone out that way again. She's still a liar. Wherever she was during that three-hour stretch, it didn't involve urban strolling. Not alone."

"Cheating on the fiancé."

"It occurs to me, yeah. Add this." She flicked Peabody a glance. "A woman like that doesn't book a sitting at eight in the morning. She doesn't get there thirty minutes early. People wait for her, that's how it works."

"You don't like her even a little bit."

"She's a liar, potentially a cheat. Jury's out on a murderer, but she's checking boxes."

She cut west again, thinking it through during the fits and starts of crosstown traffic.

"She waltzes into the victim's apartment — and we'll establish when you check with the other lobby staff if the victim, her good friend, ever waltzed into hers — starts up the stairs to the studio."

"Taking time before to buy the takeout, which, yeah, now that you're laying it out, seems off, too. That's really early."

"She spots the body, drops the bag. *Splat.* Possibly in genuine holy shit, possibly to establish holy shit. Then she leaves. Backing up? A woman who can afford that apartment would most usually use a car service. But she didn't. She claims she walked around in some sort of fugue state until she hailed a cab.

"We'll need to track down that cab," Eve added. "She gets back, goes up to her place. Thinks about taking a sleeping pill. Poor me! Then, finally, more than an hour after seeing her dead friend in a pool of blood, she hits nine-one-one."

"I give you it's a long time," Peabody said as Eve nipped through a yellow light and pushed south again. "The line's going to be shock, and how different people experience it. That's not really wrong."

"She took a shower, changed her clothes, dried her hair, put on very careful makeup. Given the time it took her to get back, she did at least some of that after calling it in. Preparing. No way she went out this morning without doing her face up a lot more than what we saw, her hair up a lot fancier. And she was wearing white — a symbol of innocence. No splatter of coffee on her. And in all that, she contacted the lawyer-fiancé. She had the DND to give her more time to prep, to talk to him first, to make sure she had him with her when we interviewed her."

"She's calculating," Peabody agreed. "That sounded loud and clear — especially with the slow, perfect tears. But why go back this morning? Why go back, buy coffee and muffins first, and put yourself in the murder scene?"

"Some people like attention, and I'm betting she qualifies. More, we're going to find her prints on scene, too. Either way, liar, liar, fancy pants on fire."

CHAPTER
THREE

Eve hit the morgue first and started down the long white tunnel. Two techs stood at Vending, slurping up bad coffee and replaying the previous night's baseball game.

She aimed for the chief medical examiner's domain.

His sealed hands smeared with blood, Morris stood over Ariel Byrd's body. He wore a clear protective cape over a suit that made her think of ripe peaches. Obviously in a springtime frame of mind, he'd paired it with a shirt of the palest green and a tie precisely matching the suit. He'd wound his long, dark hair into braids, all tied back with pale green cord.

It always amazed her, would always amaze her, how anyone managed to coordinate a look so perfectly.

He lowered his microgoggles. "Young, healthy, and dead on a lovely day in May."

"I wasn't sure you'd have gotten this far on her yet."

"Not only your name on her tag, but I recognized hers."

Instantly alert, Eve looked into Morris's dark eyes. "You knew her."

"Not personally, not really. I admired her work, and spoke to her at last month's Art in the Park festival. Garnet, her daughter, and I went for a couple of hours."

Garnet DeWinter, Eve thought, bone doctor, fashion plate, and Morris's pal — platonic.

"Garnet took her card, and visited her home studio."

"Is that right?"

"She bought a gargoyle for her garden wall. It's charming."

"Did you go with her, to the studio?"

"No." Morris shifted his gaze back to the body. "This is my second time meeting the artist. A talented woman."

Eve moved closer to study the talented woman who lay on the slab with her chest open. "What else can you tell me about her?"

"Healthy, as I said. Good weight for her height and frame, and good muscle tone. A greenstick fracture, left wrist, from childhood. A common injury, and well healed. No signs of alcohol or illegals abuse. Peabody." He smiled at her. "Why don't you get something cold for yourself and Dallas from my box?"

"Thanks. Pepsi?" she asked Eve.

"That'll work." And occupy her, as Peabody disliked open body exams.

"No defensive wounds, no injuries other than the laceration and contusion on the face, from the fall, a cracked rib from an impact injury."

"Worktable."

"Yes, in studying your crime-scene recording, I agree. And of course the killing blows."

"More than one."

"Three, though the first would have done the job without quick medical attention, the second would have

42

completely sealed the deal. Forceful blows, from slightly above and to the right, which knocked her forward and to the left, sharply into the table. She's only five-three, small stature, slight build. The impact with the table — a solid table bolted down — cracked her lower right rib. She wouldn't have been conscious for the second blow, delivered as she bounced back from the impact with the table, pitched to her left. The third struck her as she fell."

"She had a lot of tools — organized. Hammers, chisels, files. It looks to me like the killer picked up the murder weapon from another worktable behind the victim, to the right side of the steps going up. Big hunk of rock on it, and a chisel. No mallet."

Absently, she cracked the tube of Pepsi Peabody handed her.

"She had company, either the killer or someone earlier. Someone she shared wine and sex with."

"Yes. She had about twelve ounces of red wine, a Shiraz, in her stomach contents. Consumed over a period of three hours to one hour prior to death. She had chicken, rice, brussels sprouts about four to four and a half hours prior to death."

"No wine with dinner. Saved the wine to drink with the bedmate. And the sex? Possible DNA?"

"The lab has the fluids to identify DNA. There was no semen in or on her."

"Condomized, but she didn't have any condoms in her apartment." Eve shrugged as she circled the body again. "Not all women do. No sex toys, no condoms. No oral birth control. Internal?"

"Not that I've found, as yet. She never gave birth to a child."

"Okay, this is a good start. I appreciate the quick work."

"I'm sorry to see such young talent snuffed out," Morris said. "Who knows what she might have created in an uninterrupted life span."

"I get what you're thinking," Peabody said when they walked out.

"What am I thinking?"

"That Gwen Huffman was cheating on her fiancé with the victim."

"It could play. Side piece way downtown. Keep her out of your neighborhood, your social circle. She knows the fiancé's tied up for the evening, the night. Sitting could be their code for a romp. She doesn't come empty-handed. The wine, the flowers. Huffman's careful. After the wedding planning, she goes home. I bet the security feed's going to show she changed. Then she doesn't have the doorman get her a cab, or call her car service. Doesn't want any possible record of her trip to the West Village."

"Walks a couple blocks, hails one. Maybe gets out a couple blocks before Byrd's place."

"There you go," Eve agreed. "Wine and flowers. We're going to have uniforms check on that because she'd have bought them close to Byrd's."

"Have some wine," Eve continued as they got into the car. "Have some sex, some more wine, maybe some more sex."

"And the fiancé texts!" Into it now, Peabody shot up a hand. "How are you going to feel when you're all soft and snuggly and the woman all soft and snuggly with you gets a text from her fiancé?"

"Irritated. More irritated right up to pissed when your bedmate answers the text, then spends time texting back and forth with you right there."

"I'm liking this now. I'm seeing this now." Because she did, Peabody wiggled a little in her seat. "Byrd's like, 'This is supposed to be our time, but you bring him here. I'm tired of being a convenience to you.'"

"And it escalates. Maybe Byrd even threatens to tell the fiancé."

"But if Huffman was home at TOD —"

"It's a fine alibi. It doesn't mean she doesn't know another way out. Fire exit, staff exit. We're going to check. You're steamed." Eve continued with the scenario. "If Byrd goes to Caine, it's over. Maybe you can convince him it's a lie, or was a mistake. But maybe he calls off the wedding, dumps you. You come home, establish you're in, find a way out again you don't think we'll think of or bother to look for. Go back, go in — because you've got a key card, you've damn well got one. Bash her head in."

"Then you go back in the morning, pick up the takeout to cover yourself, because you've realized you might have left prints. But . . . why don't you get rid of the wineglasses, the sheets?"

"Not as smart as she thinks she is." Eve tapped her fingers on the wheel. "Or, in the hard light of day, looking at your dead lover with her head bashed in really does shock you. And you run. Then, because you panicked, you have to cover as best you can. You come up with a plausible story, call nine-one-one, and put on a show."

"It's a good theory."

"But that's all it is. With as many holes in it as there are in her story. Do a run, see if her prints and DNA are on file."

Eve hunted up parking again, this time for the lab, and scored a second-level street spot nearly at the door.

"A day of miracles."

"Not if you want her prints and DNA. Which is kind of weird because both her parents — married thirty-one years — are doctors. Mother an ob-gyn, father a general surgeon. They ought to know better. Parents' prints — not DNA — on record at Mercy Clinic, where they both work — hold that, own as well as work — and where all staff are required to have prints on file. Her older sibling — that's Trace Huffman, twenty-nine — resides in Vegas, has both his on file, due to an arrest for drunk and disorderly — underage drinking — and possession of illegals when he was sixteen. Second arrest, at twenty-three, in Vegas, for simple assault. Bar fight, charges dropped.

"He goes by Trace D. Huff. He's a musician-slash-performer-slash-songwriter."

"We'll poke at the holes in Huffman's story," Eve said as they walked into the warren of the lab. "And widen them enough to get her prints and DNA."

She glanced up the steps that led to DeWinter's territory.

"Take Dickhead, see if he's got anything for us."

"I don't have anything to bribe him with."

"Use charm. I'm going up to see if DeWinter knows any more about the victim."

She found DeWinter examining what might have been a tibia from the carefully arranged bones on a worktable.

She'd contained her hair in a sleek twist and wore short, sparkly dangles at her ears. Her lab coat matched the deep pink tone of her body-skimming dress. Her shoes, a creamy white, boasted deep pink, needle-thin heels.

She studied the bone with a magnifier, had started to reach for goggles when she spotted Eve.

"Dallas."

"DeWinter."

They still tended to be wary of each other. Eve figured they probably always would.

"And what can I do for you?"

"I want to ask you what you can tell me about a victim."

DeWinter's lips, dyed to match the dress, curved. "Got bones?"

Eve shook her head. "Not this time. You know the vic."

Distress flickered over DeWinter's face. "Who's dead?"

"Ariel Byrd."

Puzzlement came first. "I don't know . . . Oh, of course. The sculptor." She set the bone down again. "I'm really sorry to hear this. How was she killed?"

"Somebody bashed her skull in with one of her mallets."

"God, people. What they won't do to each other. What can I tell you? I only met her twice. Once at the art festival downtown, and then when I went to her studio to buy a piece I'd seen in her portfolio."

"What did you talk about?"

"Mostly art." DeWinter stepped over to order a bottle of water. "Do you want anything?"

"No, I'm good."

"She was working on a piece — a small one — in the park. That's part of the draw, seeing artists work, being able to talk to them. My daughter was captivated, had a dozen questions. She — Ariel — was very sweet with my girl. We talked for a bit — Li was with us. And I skimmed through her portfolio. The gargoyle — limestone — was just what I was looking for, for my garden."

DeWinter paused to drink, to think back. "I didn't know I was looking for a gargoyle until I saw it, but it was just right. She gave me her card, told me I could get in touch if I decided on it, and come by her studio. She had some pieces in a local gallery, but most at her own place."

"Do you know the gallery?"

"Let me think." DeWinter rubbed fingers on her temple. "No, sorry. I'm sure she mentioned it, but I don't remember."

"Poets and Painters? It's street level of her building."

"Yes, that's right. Another one, too, I think. Anyway, I contacted her a few days later, made an appointment, and bought it directly from her. This saves her the gallery commission."

"Okay. Anyone else there?"

"No."

"What else did you talk about?"

"Nothing important. I asked about the types of stone, the tools. She asked what I did, the way you do. She found it interesting, asked some questions. It was all just . . . pleasant. She was pleasant. Oh, I asked if she took commissions, and she said she did. I talked about her doing a statue of my daughter and our dog, and we talked about what medium I might want, talked about our schedules. I was supposed to contact her in a couple of weeks to set it up."

"She didn't mention anything about friends, other clients, anyone."

"No. But . . ." DeWinter held up a finger. "She had these gorgeous striped tulips — like candy canes — on her table. When I complimented them, she got that look in her eye."

"That look?"

"The look you get when you think about a lover. That's how I read it anyway, but she didn't actually say: Oh, my lover brought me those."

"Got it. Appreciate it."

"If I think of anything else . . . Jesus, Dallas, she was so young, so . . . fresh, I want to say. And just a little thing. I hope whoever gave her those damn tulips didn't kill her."

"It's where you look first."

She made her way downstairs and found Peabody walking her way.

"My charm's on high today." After a little hip wiggle, Peabody tried a hair toss.

"Never, never do that again."

"You're going to want to do the same when I tell you Dickhead already had the sheets done. Two separate DNAs from fluids, both female. One from the victim, one not in the system."

"Good, solid. But I don't do the wiggle and toss."

"'Cause you've got no hips and really short hair. But inside, you're wiggling and tossing."

"No. What about the murder weapon?"

"No prints other than the vic's because, the experts say, the killer sealed up or wore gloves."

"Huh. Interesting. Some premeditation in that."

"Sweepers got some hair — from the sheets and pillowcases — and Harvo's on it."

"If Harvo's on it, we'll have the results soon." The queen of hair and fiber always came through. "We'll take a look at the security feed back at Central. Then you check the alibis, get a couple of uniforms to start looking for likely flower and wine shops. I'll write this up, start the board and book. Once we get that, we're going to want to get whatever other security feed the apartment building has on alternate exits."

"Cabs?"

"We backtrack from the drop-off — near or at the coffee place this morning, near or at the flower or wine place yesterday once we nail that down. Run the fiancé; let's get a sense."

Peabody settled in with her PPC. "Merit Andrew Caine, age thirty-six. Single, no marriages, no official cohabs. Only dings a handful of traffic violations. Harvard Law — like his father, mother, paternal grandfather. And give him a zing, graduated top of his class, and clerked for Supreme Court Justice Uma Hagger."

She glanced at Eve. "That's not shabby. Parents married — first and only for both — forty-two years. Nice run. Two sibs, one of each, also lawyers, but not in the firm. He's a junior partner at Caine, Boswell, Caine — grandfather's the first Caine, dad's the second, and mom's Boswell. He's worth sixty-three mil, resides Upper East Side, about five blocks north of his intended bride, and has a second home in Aruba."

Eve pulled into the garage at Central, angled into her slot.

"Why aren't the sibs in the family business?"

"Looking at that," Peabody said, working as she climbed out. "The sister — thirty-four — is currently on maternal leave from her position as in-house counsel for Atomic Publishing — offices Lower East — and the brother — thirty — is in East Washington, clerking for — hah, Uma Hagger."

"Okay, a lawyerly family." They crossed the garage to the elevator. "Rich, connected. Oldest son hooks up with the daughter of a rich, doctorly family."

"The American dream."

"Maybe." With some relief, Eve noted the elevator was empty. It wouldn't last, but it was a nice start. "The doctorly daughter is a dozen years younger than the lawyerly son — not enough of a spread to make him a cradle robber, but a spread. He'll make full partner in a

51

three-generation law firm within a couple years. She socializes, puts in a few hours here and there at her family's charitable foundation, so no apparent career ambitions."

"When did you run her?"

"When I was going up to talk to DeWinter, just a quick one." And here it came, Eve thought, as the doors opened, as cops shuffled in. "She put in three semesters at NYU, and has never worked an actual job. She has an annual income from trust funds that should cover her rent, but probably not much else."

At the third stop Eve muscled off the elevator.

"I'm guessing her parents supplement her income." Peabody followed Eve to the glides. "Their son's off in Vegas, but she's right here."

"And engaged to the oldest son of a wealthy, prominent New York family." Absently, Eve jiggled the loose credits in her pocket as they rode up. "At the tail end of planning what's bound to be a big, splashy society wedding. She sure as hell doesn't want it to come out she's cheating with a moderately successful West Village artist."

"If it does, it all blows up on her. Still . . . she's got the trust fund, and her parents are going to be embarrassed, maybe pretty pissed, but would they cut her off for cheating on her fiancé? Is she going to murder her lover over a possible threat to maybe rat her out?"

"You're a homicide detective, Peabody, so you know as well as I do people kill people over a shoulder-bump on the sidewalk."

"Yeah, and I could see her doing it in a fit of passion, in a moment of heat. But the timelines don't gel."

"Let's check that first, go from there. Right now, she's the one with motive, and she's the one lying to the cops."

They turned into the bullpen. Jenkinson, his tie du jour, and his partner, Reineke, weren't at their desks. Santiago and Detective Carmichael huddled together at hers. Baxter, in one of his slick suits, had his expensive shoes on his desk as he worked his 'link. And Trueheart, the young and earnest, worked his comp.

Since nobody jumped up or hailed her, Eve went straight to her office.

"Coffee," she said as she opened the packet from House Royale and took out the disc.

"Any way I can program something edible to go with that? My stomach says lunch. I can hit up Vending, but —"

Eve just waved a hand as she sat, plugged in the disc.

Peabody perused the offerings on the AutoChef menu. "You got everything in here. How about we split a ham and provolone sub? Because it's going to be actual pig meat, actual cheese if it's in here."

"Whatever."

Eve increased the speed of the vid feed until she saw Gwen step out of her apartment into the hall-cam range at eleven-sixteen. A pale pink dress, a short, three-quarter-sleeved white jacket, high, skinny heels in pink-and-white stripes, and an enormous pink purse — Eve judged it as meeting-with-wedding-planner attire. She'd done her hair in a loose bun at the nape, wore subtle but impressive jewelry in the diamond studs, a necklace with a pink stone heart outlined in diamonds, a wrist unit with a glittery pink band, a heart-shaped pink stone ring on her right hand, and, of course, her fat diamond engagement ring on her left.

"Classic, sophisticated, rich," Peabody said as she set half the sandwich on the desk for Eve — with half a side of fries (real ones!).

Eve toggled to the elevator feed.

They followed her progress down in the elevator, where Gwen smoothed her hair in the mirrored wall, checked her lip dye.

A woman with a baby in a stroller got on at twelve. Since the woman wore a gray uniform, Eve concluded nanny.

Gwen didn't spare either one a glance, then strolled out ahead of them. On the lobby feed, she went straight out the doors.

"She didn't even smile at the baby, and it's a really cute baby."

"Now you don't like her," Eve noted.

"I'm just saying. And I'm also saying this ham is the ult."

Which reminded Eve to pick up her half, take a bite.

She couldn't disagree.

She stuck with the lobby feed, watched the nanny and baby come out, pause by the desk as Felicity spoke to them, obviously prattled something at the kid, who grinned and waved the rattly thing in his hand.

Eve increased the speed until Gwen walked into the lobby from outside at fifteen-twelve. "She's got a shopping bag." Eve enhanced to home in on the shop's name. "Intimate Occasions. Probably sexy underwear. She didn't say anything about shopping, did she?"

"No, she didn't."

"We're going to check when she left the wedding planner, check when she hit the shop, what she bought."

"I'll add it to the list. These fries make the ham even more the ult."

Which reminded Eve to eat one.

They followed Gwen up the elevator, where she leaned back against the wall of the elevator, smiling smugly. Then down the hallway to her apartment.

At seventeen-fifty-five, she came out again.

"Freeze it. Yeah, she changed, but those aren't urban-strolling-and-into-the-park clothes."

"They wouldn't be mine," Peabody agreed.

Another dress, Eve thought, but this one in hot red with skinny bow straps that showed off the shoulders and a short, swingy skirt that showed off the legs. Heels, high again, but these were red like the dress and strappy to show off the pedicure — more hot red.

Bold, dangly earrings, thick gold cuffs on the wrists, and a gold handbag big enough to hold a toddler. The sophisticated bun had given way to long, shiny waves. The subtle makeup now smoked and smoldered.

"Would you call that date-night wear, Peabody?"

"Yeah, I would. And I bet she's got sexy underwear on under that dress."

"Count on it. She's bouncing. She's got that I'm-gonna-get-laid bounce to her step."

With a nod, Peabody nibbled on another fry. "McNab gets sort of a bounce-swagger. It's hard to pull off a swagger with his skinny ass, but he does it."

Rather than respond, Eve filled her mouth with ham and cheese.

"Here she comes — not between eight and nine. Time stamp, twenty-two-eleven. And moving fast this time, looking pissed."

"Definitely pissed," Peabody agreed. "Now it's a fuck-this-shit stride. Her hair's all I-just-rolled-out-of-the-sexy-bed. She didn't brush it out, and her lip dye's worn off. She'd buy a good one, so that says —"

"Her mouth did some work."

In the elevator she crossed her arms over her chest, glared straight ahead. At one point her eyes went glossy with tears, but she tossed her head, pulled them back.

She marched to her apartment. Eve didn't need audio to tell her Gwen slammed the door.

She ran the feed, kept running it to nearly midnight. But the door didn't open again.

"That's well past TOD, Dallas."

"Yeah, yeah." Eve pushed back. "There's always another way out if you want it bad enough, but I don't see her rappelling down the building. Still, I want EDD to look at the feed, see if there are any glitches. Alternately, she could have had it done. I want to see her 'links."

She ate another fry as she started on the morning feed. "Here she comes. Zero-six-forty-one. Bright and early, and she doesn't have excited face on."

"I'd call that determined. You were right about the clothes, the makeup."

"Yeah, jeans, spring sweater, hair pinned back at the sides, but loose, another enormous bag, low boots, and plenty of careful makeup."

In the elevator she pulled enormous sunshades out of the enormous bag. She checked her wrist unit, tapped her foot.

Again, she strode across the lobby without a word or glance.

At zero-seven-forty-three, she came into the lobby again. Eve slowed speed.

She didn't stride, bounce, strut, but walked very deliberately toward the elevator. "Freeze it," Eve ordered, then enhanced.

"That's not the face of a woman in shock. Shaken maybe, a little pale and shaken, but thinking. Calculating. She figured out what to do on the ride back uptown."

In the elevator, Gwen pulled off the sunshades, rubbed a hand over her heart. Eve froze and enhanced again.

"Pupils aren't dilated. No zoned-out look in them, no trembling. Not fucking shock. She's upset, but the rest is bullshit."

In the hallway, she quickened her pace, hurried to her apartment and inside.

"That's a lot of lies," Peabody commented.

"Yeah, a whole basket of lies. We'll be bringing her in, but let's get it all lined up first. Start on that list, I'll copy and send the feed to Feeney, and put the board and book together."

"On it. She didn't come out again on the night of the murder," Peabody added. "But what are the odds somebody walked in that apartment and bashed Byrd's head in an hour or so after she and Huffman had a fight?"

"They improve if Huffman asked somebody to take care of it for her. She strikes me as the type who gets people to take care of things."

CHAPTER
FOUR

Eve set up the board first. She wanted the visual.

She read the initial reports — sweepers, lab, ME — added them and the reports from the uniforms into her notes, into her murder book.

She wrote her report, then opted to copy Mira. The expert profiler might give her more insight into a person like Gwendolyn Huffman if and when she needed it.

She'd just begun a deeper dive into Gwen's background when she heard the clip coming down her hall. Not Peabody's clomp — uniform shoes.

She glanced around as Officer Shelby started to rap her knuckles on the doorjamb. "Sorry to interrupt, Lieutenant. Detective Peabody's holding on her 'link and asked me to relay the officers in the field located the flower vendor and the wineshop regarding your current investigation."

"Great."

She saw Shelby's eyes track to her board — not surprising. What surprised her was the way Shelby's eyes widened.

"Problem, Shelby?"

"I — no, sir, Lieutenant. It's just . . . I know her."

"You knew my victim?"

"No, sir, I don't believe so. I know — knew — Gwen. Gwendolyn Huffman. You have her boarded as prime suspect."

"How do you know her?"

"I . . ."

Eve had picked Shelby for Homicide because she'd judged her as solid. Nothing until now had changed that opinion. Before Eve could speak again, she watched Shelby square herself.

"Knew her is more accurate than know, sir. I haven't had any contact with her since we were, um, fifteen. I was fifteen. I think she was, or maybe sixteen. I'm sorry, Lieutenant. I'm sorry, sir, I'm a little thrown off."

Clearly, Eve decided, and gestured Shelby inside.

"How did you know her?"

"My uncle has a beach house in the Hamptons. He won the lottery."

"You're shitting me."

"No, sir, Lieutenant." A smile came and went. "Sixty-five million. Back when I was about eleven or twelve. He opened a restaurant there, too, and still works as chef. That's what he did — does — he's a chef, but he has his own place now. He has us up every summer, the whole family. For two weeks, or as long as we can manage. Gwen's family has a house there, too, and spent most of the summer there. So we met when I was about thirteen, I guess."

Shelby cleared her throat, looked back at the board. "Our brothers hung out. My brother was a couple years younger than hers, but they both played guitar, so they hung out, tried writing songs together. I know her brother plays clubs and sessions in Vegas because he's still in touch with mine."

"But you're no longer in touch with the sister."

"No, sir."

"Because?"

Shelby blew out a breath. "The summer I was fifteen, Gwen and I got to be more than friendly."

"Okay." Eve rose, moved around Shelby to close the door. "Have a seat. Watch your ass, that chair bites. How do you take your coffee?"

"Black is fine. Black is good. I appreciate it, sir."

Eve programmed coffee, considered her officer.

Shelby sat very straight. She'd done something with her hair — dashed blond through the brown. People were always doing things like that. She wore it short, shorter than Eve's own, and it suited her young, pretty face. Not a face so earnest and green as Trueheart's had been when Eve had brought him into Homicide.

No, Shelby had more edge to her.

Eve handed her the coffee, took her own back to her desk. Sat.

"Your private life is your own, Shelby. But any insight you can give me into Gwendolyn Huffman will aid our investigation. The victim, an artist, a sculptor, had the back of her head caved in with one of her own mallets. This occurred shortly after, evidence shows, she and Gwen had sex in the victim's bed. Further evidence leads us to believe they had an argument."

"I never knew Gwen to be violent, sir, not like that. Bitchy, demanding, um, manipulative, yeah."

"She called nine-one-one from her apartment on the Upper East Side. We have her statement, and the evidence supports that she traveled down to the victim's apartment-slash-studio this morning, very early. She claims she had an eight o'clock sitting for a statue, for her future husband. She arrived considerably before eight, claimed the victim's door was unsecured, and she went inside, found the body, then, due to shock, left, went back uptown before she gathered herself to call it in. More than an hour after she found the body."

Shelby took a moment, sipped at her coffee. "I think her statement is probably inaccurate on several points."

"Hey, me, too."

"Her brother's estranged from her and his parents, but he still gets bits now and then, and tells my brother, who tells me. I knew she was engaged. A lawyer, wealthy family. Unless she's dramatically changed, money and social status are very important to her. She wouldn't want her other relationship to come out. Her parents are very strict and conservative. It's more than that."

Shelby paused, drank more coffee. "Unless that's changed, too, they belong to a group called Natural Order."

Now Eve sat up straight. "Those people are crazy."

"Yes, sir, Lieutenant. I completely agree. It's not what you'd call a church, though they managed to get that status, but they sure do preach. No mixed or same-sex marriages — or relationships. Outlaw licensed companions, take women's reproductive rights back a couple centuries. No method of birth control but abstinence, and absolutely no premarital sex."

"Didn't they buy their own country or something?"

"Sort of. An island. People, rich ones like the Huffmans, helped finance that. Gwen's parents? If they knew she was seeing another woman?"

Shelby shook her head, drank more coffee.

"When I was fifteen, sir, I knew my orientation. My parents, my brother, my sister, my family, they all knew. It was just who I was, no issue. Gwen's, on the other hand, were of a different mindset."

"A different century."

"Yeah, you could say. Gwen and I got involved that summer. She made the moves, only because I was too shy. We'd sneak out at night — that my parents wouldn't have approved of — and were together. I was just crazy about her. She's beautiful, and smart, and, well, adventurous, at least back then. So into the second week of my stay, somebody told her parents. At least that's what I think, what her brother thought."

"What did they do?"

"They left. Just left. I got a text from her saying we were done. Like: Bitch, we're over."

"Nice. Nothing else?"

"No, sir. I tried texting her back, but they didn't go through. I knew where she lived in the city, where she hung out. I haunted those places for the rest of the summer just to talk to her, to figure out why she dumped me that hard. But I didn't see her again until right after school started. She went to private school uptown, and I saw her coming out of the building.

When she saw me, she, well, basically, she told me to fuck off, stay the hell away from her. I'd ruined her whole summer, but I wasn't going to ruin her life.

"Broke my heart."

"How's it doing now?"

"Oh, it healed up a long time ago. But you don't forget your first. And you don't forget when that person turns on you that way. She meant what she said. I'd ruined her summer. That's all it was to her. All I was. I got over it."

She blew out another breath. "The thing is, Lieutenant, I know you can look through heart eyes at fifteen, but we had feelings for each other. It wasn't just sex. But she cut those feelings off. She did the same with her brother. Appearances, in her world — her parents' world — they're priority."

"She wouldn't be the first to kill to maintain appearances."

"No, sir, but . . . she's more likely to lie. She's really good at it, or was. I'm betting she's even better at it now. Practice usually does that. And she knows how to play the victim. I'm not saying it's impossible, but it's hard for me to see her picking up a hammer and caving in a skull. That's, well, that's messy. She'd use tears, manipulation, charm, lies to get around anything, anyone."

"Okay, Shelby. This is helpful."

Shelby rose. "I want to say her brother? He's a good guy. He took off right after that summer — maybe during it. They cut him off, sir, in every way. Financially — at least according to him — they put blocks on his trust funds. But more than that, they just cut him off, forgot him. He doesn't exist. Not to them, not to Gwen. There's a coldness in that. It's in her, too."

"Are you going to have a problem if I put any of this into my report?"

"No, sir, Lieutenant, none at all. I'm a cop. Anything I can do to aid your investigation I'll do. No question, no problem."

"You're a solid cop, Shelby. That's why I brought you into Homicide."

"Thank you, Lieutenant. Can I ask if you'll keep me apprised of the situation when it's appropriate?"

"Already planning on it. If you need time to settle —"

"No, sir. I'm fine."

"Good. Ask Peabody to come in — and if she hasn't yet sent uniforms to House Royale, Huffman's residence, to obtain any security feed on staff and service exits, alternate exits, you and Officer Carmichael head uptown and take care of that. See Felicity on the desk."

"Yes, sir." When she reached the door, Shelby hesitated, turned back. "Lieutenant, I don't want to be a suck-up, but I want to say, I'd have related all of this information to any primary investigator or supervisor. But I wouldn't have been as comfortable doing so with anyone else.

"Thanks for the coffee."

Eve sat a moment, digesting all of it. Then began to write it up. She continued working when she heard Peabody's boots clomp in the hallway.

"I started to come back before, but your door was closed."

"That's right. Shelby had some information and insight on Huffman."

"No shit? She knows Huffman?"

"Knew is more accurate. Close the door."

Intrigued, Peabody closed the door. She contemplated the visitor's chair, and opted to stand.

"I'm writing it out, but quickly, Shelby and Huffman had a brief but intense romantic relationship when they were teenagers." Eve stopped, swiveled in her chair. "Huffman's parents found out — likely from some weasel — and broke it up. The parents are part of Natural Order."

"Jesus, those people are —"

"Lunatics," Eve finished. "Bigoted asshole lunatics. The thing is, Shelby sought out Huffman back in New York, and got kicked hard to the curb. Meanwhile Huffman's brother was and is friendly with Shelby's. They stay in touch. Huffman not only kicked Shelby, but, along with her parents, cut off the brother."

"Cold."

"Cold's one word for it. Shelby's take is while she doesn't see Huffman as violent, she is — confirming my take — an inveterate liar, manipulative, a status seeker. I'm adding to that. This is a woman without loyalty or genuine emotion. I'm going to share all this with Mira, get her opinion."

Peabody eased a hip on the corner of the desk. "Someone with those qualities could, on impulse or out of self-preservation, kill, and without much remorse, if any. But."

"Yeah, but, current evidence indicates Huffman was tucked up in her apartment at the time of the murder. New information, however, tells us the Huffmans are part of the whacked fringe group Natural Order."

"Members of which have been known to use violence. The group leadership disavows violence," Peabody added, "but."

"Yeah, but again, the violence happens. Huffman's pissed, slams out of Byrd's apartment. Maybe she doesn't secure the door. Maybe being pissed, knowing Byrd could threaten her cushy life and splashy wedding, she contacts someone she knows is capable of violence, of murder. Possibly she spins them a story — she'd be good at it — or possibly she tells them the truth, depending on her connection with this person."

"I'm liking this." Eyes on the board, Peabody nodded. "What if she contacts someone, spins that story, a little weepy, a little desperate, and asks them to go put a scare into Byrd, threaten her so she'll back off."

"Not bad," Eve considered. "It could tie in with her going back in the morning. Lattes and muffins, let's make up. Let's be friends. Sees the body, realizes things went too far. Now she has to figure out how to get herself out of it, how to manipulate the situation so she's just an innocent bystander."

"We've got her on her relationship with Byrd. I bet it's her DNA on the sheets, her prints."

"And pubic hair," Eve added. "Harvo came through."

"So did the uniforms," Peabody added. "We have her buying the wine, the flowers two blocks from Byrd's residence — when she claims to have been urban strolling uptown. The statements, from both vendors who ID'd her, is she comes in at least once a week, always pays cash."

"She doesn't want a paper trail. But she had to cobble all this together fast. She didn't have time to polish all the details. She's in this, Peabody. Maybe she swung that mallet, maybe not. But she's in this."

"Want me to have her picked up?"

Eve shook her head. "Let's play it this way. Contact her. She'll remember you as sympathetic. Request she come in to sign an official statement. Let it slip we're looking at this as a botched burglary. That'll take the pressure off her so she may not knee-jerk into tagging her fiancé. And he can't spend all day with her if he's prepping for a court case, can he?"

"Which he is, that's confirmed. He and five others worked in the conference room at the law firm until after midnight. Nobody left. They ordered food in — twice. And the wedding planner confirms the meeting with Huffman. They met at about eleven-thirty, parted ways about quarter to two."

"Which gave Huffman plenty of time to shop for sexy underwear."

"A Merry Widow — that's a kind of corsety thing — white silk with red rose accents, matching G-string, and a bottle of their Allure Me perfume. Time-stamped receipt — totaling thirty-eight hundred and change — at fourteen-forty-seven. She charged it.

"Oh," Peabody added, "she's a regular."

"Contact her. I'm looking forward to watching her try to swim through her sea of lies."

Peabody pushed off the desk. "On it. You know, Dallas, it couldn't've been easy for Shelby to tell you all that really personal stuff. She stands up."

"Agreed."

"And, I'm just saying, I love her new do."

"Do what?"

"Hair, Dallas, the pixie do with the highlights. It's a good look for her, but then it would be. She went to Trina."

"Trina? How does a uniform with barely two years on the job afford Trina?"

"Trina gives a cop discount."

"Trina gives . . ." Eve thought of the thoroughly terrifying Trina. "Seriously?"

"Yeah, a solid twenty percent discount at her salon for cops. She started it after the Ziegler investigation last December." Peabody flipped at her own red-streaked curls. "She said cops — us — stood up for her and her good friend Sima, so she was standing up for cops and making sure they looked damn good. Since Shelby was in on that in the end — Copley resisted and clocked her, remember?"

"Yeah."

"Trina gave her the new do on the house."

Peabody went out, leaving Eve frowning after her. A person could be loyal, she thought, even generous, and still be pushy, bossy, scary.

She figured that wrapped Trina up in a bow.

And, putting it aside, went back to work.

As she read over her report to refine it, an incoming interrupted. She saw Feeney's name, answered.

"Dallas."

"Shuffled your shit in," he told her. "No glitch on the security feed. What you see is what was what."

"Damn it."

He gave her a half-assed smile. He had a hangdog face with baggy basset-hound eyes. His silver-threaded ginger hair exploded over it.

She caught herself wondering if he took advantage of Trina's twenty percent.

"Bat five hundred, you're a baseball star. I can give you the five hundred."

"Victim's door."

"Yep." Something rustled, then he popped a candied almond in his mouth. "Not tampered with, but bullshit on the unsecured. Key card used to open it at zero-seven-eighteen."

"About four minutes after Huffman bought the takeout."

"If you say. Last key-card use prior, twenty-two-forty-six."

"Is that so?" Eve narrowed her eyes on her board, and the TOD of twenty-two-forty-eight. "Is that fucking so?"

"It's fucking so."

"Same card? Can you tell?"

"I can tell you it wasn't Huffman's original. Copy used, but I can't tell you if it was one copy or two copies. Might be able to if you get us the copy or copies." He ate another almond. "That's a might be."

"I'll take a might be."

"I got McNab going over the vic's 'link, her comp. Nothing much popping right now. She's got art and business stuff on the comp, and a calendar. She's got some of the dates marked with a little red heart. Including last night."

"I could use those dates. I'm bringing a suspect into the box."

"I'll tell him to send them."

"Appreciate it, Feeney."

She got up to study the board, make some additions. Once again an incoming interrupted.

This time she saw Julie Byrd on the readout. The mother, the next of kin Eve hadn't been able to reach to inform.

"Hell." She went back to her desk, answered. "Lieutenant Dallas."

"Yes, yes, this is Julie Byrd."

The woman, an older version of her daughter, looked deliriously happy.

"I had a voice mail from you on my 'link. I completely forgot my 'link this morning! My daughter-in-law went into labor and we all just rushed out to the birthing center. Such an exciting day. I just got back to my son's house. He'll be bringing Ally and our gorgeous Fiona — seven pounds, three ounces, and eighteen inches of perfect — home in a few hours. I came back to get everything ready for the homecoming and saw my 'link sitting on the kitchen counter."

"Ms. Byrd."

"Yes? Oh, I forgot to stop and buy flowers." With a laugh, the woman tapped the flat of her hand against the side of her head. "I need to run out and do that."

"Ms. Byrd, I'm very sorry. I have some difficult news."

"Oh, nothing's difficult on this day. Not after watching that precious life come into the world."

"I'm afraid it is. It's about your daughter, Ariel. I regret —"

"Ariel. Lucas — my son — said he'd contact her when I realized I didn't have my 'link. She's going to be so excited! She's an aunt!"

Never easy, Eve admitted. Notification shouldn't be easy. But some were worse than others.

"Ms. Byrd, I regret to inform you your daughter, Ariel Byrd, was killed last night. I'm very sorry for your loss."

"What? That's a terrible thing to say. I'm hanging up!"

"Ms. Byrd, I'm Lieutenant Dallas of the New York Police and Security Department. I'm the primary investigator on your daughter's murder."

"Murder? No one would murder Ariel. You can't mean any of this."

The screen blurred, then cleared again. Eve realized the woman had dropped down to sit on the floor.

"I'm very sorry."

"What happened to my baby? What happened to my girl?"

There were times you didn't lay the details on top of the weight. "We're investigating. I know this is difficult, but if you could answer some questions, it would help us find the person who hurt your daughter."

"I don't understand. Who would want to hurt her? She never hurts anyone. She's an artist. She works to bring joy and beauty into the world."

"Do you know of anyone she had an issue with, anyone who threatened her, or she argued with?"

"No. No. No. She's so involved with her work. I tell her she should go out more, have fun, but her work is her passion, her joy. Her fun."

"What about romantic attachments?"

The image on-screen swayed as Julie began to rock herself. "I know she's been seeing someone for several months now. I don't know who — Ariel's very private. But I know the woman she's involved with makes her happy. Frustrates her sometimes, but that's love, it can be frustrating. And she's so young, so young and so talented. So much left to do and experience."

The tears came now, in a flood. "Oh God, oh God, my baby. I have to come home to my baby. I'm — I'm in Atlanta. My boy lives in Atlanta, and I'm here to help with . . ."

"Ms. Byrd. Julie. I can assure you we're doing our best for your daughter, that she's in good hands. If you want to take a day or two before traveling back to New York, I can keep you informed."

"I can't leave Ariel there alone."

"She's not alone. Is there someone who can travel with you when you come back?"

"I . . . My husband . . . there was an accident. Four years ago now. He died. Now I have to tell my boy, on his happiest day, his sister is gone."

"Would you like me to contact your son, tell him?"

"No, that's for me to do." Julie swiped at her eyes, but the tears kept coming in a steady stream of grief. "Can you tell me, did she suffer?"

"No, no, Ms. Byrd, she didn't. You have my contact information, and you should use it whenever you need. I'm going to give you the contact information for the person who's taking care of her, and you can talk to him when you're ready to see her."

"Yes, please. Yes. You're a police detective?"

"I'm the lieutenant in charge of the Homicide Division at Cop Central in New York. And your daughter is my priority."

When she finished the call, Eve got a bottle of water, drank half of it down as she stood at her window. She didn't turn as she heard Peabody come in.

"The victim's mother contacted me. She'd left her 'link in her son's kitchen — she's with him in Atlanta — because they all rushed out early this morning when her daughter-in-law went into labor."

"Oh boy."

"Nope, girl. So I had to pop her shiny, happy balloon and tell her that her daughter's dead. Anyway, that's done."

Turning now, Eve ran the chilly water tube over her forehead, and the headache brewing inside.

"She doesn't know anyone — or couldn't think of anyone — who'd had issues with her daughter, or vice

74

versa. She did know her daughter had been in a relationship with a woman for a few months, was happy, occasionally frustrated. Byrd hadn't shared the name with her mother."

"Huffman's coming in. She's happy, too, and I think that's sincere because I dangled the botched burglary and added our pursuit of a suspicious character."

Eve lowered the bottle, even smiled a little. "You said 'suspicious character'?"

"It worked because, lo and behold, she suddenly remembered her good friend Ariel mentioning she'd seen a strange guy hanging around in the neighborhood."

"I'm shocked and stunned. What does *lo* mean? I get the behold, but what is lo and why is it always hanging out with behold?"

"Behold must like it because it always lets lo come first."

"That's right, it does. It's never behold and lo, and it could be. Get us a box, Peabody."

"Already reserved Interview B. Jenkinson and Reineke already have A, and Carmichael and Santiago snagged C."

"Busy day in Homicide."

"No rest for the wicked 'cause the murder cops are all over their asses."

"That we are, Peabody." Eve turned back to the board, looked at Gwendolyn Huffman's photo. "That we fucking are."

CHAPTER
FIVE

Eve had the box set and her basic strategy outlined. While waiting for Gwen Huffman to show up, she conferred with Detective Carmichael.

"Gotta look at the spouse, right?" Carmichael stood at Vending, contemplating her choices. "Especially when the spouse of the spouse is a cheating bastard who didn't know the meaning of controlling his dick. So . . . I know this no-cal lemonade's going to suck, but I can't handle more caffeine."

She punched in her code, and Eve watched — disappointed and annoyed — when the tube of lemonade slid into the slot without a hitch.

"Why is it, why, every time I try to use one of these things it rejects my order, changes my order, or bitches at me?"

"Maybe it fears you, and its chips freeze up and stutter at your approach. You want? I'll get."

"No." Eve aimed a death glare at the machine. "I won't give it the satisfaction."

"That'll teach it." Carmichael cracked the tube. "So she claims she didn't know her husband was catting around, even though we have the freaking security feed of her following him — three minutes after — into a strip bar. No cams inside, naturally, but we got the door feed. She's wearing a wig but, Jesus, we got her. Plus, she stabbed the shit out of him right inside the vestibule of their apartment building when he got home, then dragged him out on the stoop. She's still wearing the wig when she goes into the building, drags him out of the building. She takes his wallet and valuables, like we'll seriously think mugging."

"What did she do with them?"

"Threw them in the recycler, in the vestibule. Actually left a bloody fingerprint on it. And we looked at the bloody print, and thought: Hey, a clue!"

"That's why you're ace investigators."

"You got it." Carmichael tossed back her hair. Not in the sexy way, but in the get-out-of-my-eyes way Eve understood. "She goes up, cleans herself up — and stuffs her bloody strip-joint dress and wig in her kitchen recycler. How would we ever find them!"

"Criminals are mostly dumb-asses."

"It sure helps when they are. Anyway, we brought her in, broke her down. She's in Booking. Murder in the first. She'll tag a lawyer, and they'll probably deal it down to second. We're fine with that. The guy was a dog."

"Dog, dumb-ass, or not, good work. What did she do with the blade?"

"Oh, that." Carmichael showed her teeth in a wicked smile. "She left that in his crotch."

"Ouch." She spotted Huffman getting off the elevator. "Here's my dumb-ass."

"Go get her, Loo."

Back to the ponytail and minimal makeup, Eve noted. But now she wore light green cropped pants in a kind of shimmery fabric with a matching jacket over a bright white tee.

No heels, but Eve imagined the sandals with their thick wedges were fashionable.

She'd changed the red toenails for green.

She twirled her sunshades in her hand as she looked around. When she spotted Eve, she worked up a trembling smile.

"Lieutenant Dallas. I'm so glad — that's not the right word. Relieved, I'm so relieved your detective contacted me. She said you're making progress."

"I believe we are. We appreciate you taking the time to come in."

"Anything I can do to help — for Ariel."

"Understood. Actually, we can use this room right down here. I'll get you settled, get my partner and the paperwork. We don't want to keep you longer than necessary. You look like you're going out."

"Oh, no. I did have lunch with friends earlier. I just couldn't stay in my apartment, in my head."

"I can imagine."

"It's a relief, again, to do something."

"Absolutely. Excuse me, one minute. These officers have something for me."

Because she stood next to Gwen, Eve felt the jolt when Gwen saw Shelby.

"Thanks, officers. I'll take that." Eve reached for the packet Officer Carmichael carried.

"Jan? Good lord, I can't believe it! Jan Shelby." With a bright laugh, Gwen stepped forward, threw her arms around Shelby, who stood stiffly, her eyes on Eve's.

"Jan, it's Gwen!"

"Yeah, I know." Shelby eased back. "I didn't expect to see you here."

"I could say the same. You're a policewoman!"

"That's right. Sorry, I'm on duty, and I have to get back."

"But we have to get together, catch up. It's been forever. You look amazing. I just love your hair."

"Thanks. I have to get back," she repeated.

"Wow." Gwen let out the laugh again. "I think that's what they call a blast from the past."

"Do they?" Eve asked.

"Jan and I were summer friends — vacation friends — years and years ago. We were twelve, thirteen. It's such a nice surprise to see her again. She works for you?"

"She works for the City of New York."

Eve opened the door to Interview B.

"Oh!" The green toenails stopped at the threshold. "This looks so . . . official. And dire."

"Private and handy. Can I get you anything to drink?"

"I'd love a sparkling water, if it's no trouble."

"No trouble. Have a seat. I'll get what we need and we'll get this done."

She hurried back to the bullpen. "Peabody, Huffman's in B. Get her a sparkling water — a small one. I'll be two minutes." She moved straight back to Shelby's cube.

She looked at Officer Carmichael, got a slight nod.

Good, Shelby had told him.

"Officer Shelby."

"Sir."

"Would you like to observe this interview?"

"I . . . Yes, sir, I would."

"Look for tells, inconsistencies, fabrications. Note them down, write them up for me. Can you do that?"

"Yes, sir, Lieutenant, I can."

"Good. Officer Carmichael, I'd like you and Shelby in Observation asap. I'll be ready to start in two minutes."

"Get on your horse, girl," Carmichael said quietly when Eve strode away. "Our LT's counting on you."

Eve got what she needed from her office, then walked down to meet Peabody outside Interview B.

"I'm having Shelby observe. Carmichael will be with her."

"Does he know?"

"Yeah. Now let's break this lying bitch down."

Eve opened the door, put on her I'm very distracted face. "Record on. Dallas, Lieutenant Eve and Peabody, Detective Delia, entering Interview with Huffman, Gwendolyn, in the matter of case file H-5872."

"Official," Gwen said again, with suspicion in her eyes. "Dire."

"Just official," Eve assured her. "You're here voluntarily as a witness, in the matter of Ariel Byrd's murder. We need everything on record. I'm going to have you read over your statement from this morning — and you can make any corrections or additions — then initial and date each page, sign and date the last."

"All right."

"Before I do, I'm going to read you your rights, for the record."

"I don't understand."

"The lieutenant does like to cross all the *t*'s," Peabody said cheerfully. "Sometimes when it gets to court, or just to the lawyers, a witness will recant, or claim they didn't mean what they said or that the cops twisted their words and/or meaning. Dallas likes to cross those *t*'s, have everything by the book and on the record."

For Gwen's benefit, Peabody gave Eve the side-eye. "Even though it takes longer."

"Saves time and trouble in the long run. So. Gwendolyn Huffman, you have the right to remain silent."

Eve read off the Revised Miranda in pleasant, casual tones.

"Okay — see, not much time. Do you understand your rights and obligations in this matter?"

"I do, of course."

"Great." Eve started to draw papers out of a file, stopped. "Before you sign off, you mentioned to Peabody that Ariel Byrd told you she'd noticed someone hanging out in the neighborhood, someone out of place? Can you tell us about that? We can put it on record."

"Of course. Honestly, it just occurred to me when Detective Peabody mentioned you were looking for someone like that. Ariel commented, a couple of times over the last few weeks, she'd noticed some guy hanging out, walking up and down the street, and she didn't like the look of him."

"Did she describe him?"

"No, I'm sorry."

"But she indicated male."

"She did." Eyes clear and direct, Gwen gave a decisive nod. "A guy. Not all that clean, she said, and walking around, studying the buildings. She even said, like, he was casing the apartments, the shops. I'm sorry to say I fluffed it off, joked about it. People walk in New York."

Gwen looked away, worked up a tear shine in her eyes. "The idea that she was right, it haunts me."

"Did he ever approach her, try to panhandle or connect with her?"

"She never said so, and I think she would have. Or . . . I don't know, since I joked about it." She worked up more shine so tears just trembled but didn't fall. "God, maybe he did, and she didn't tell me because she thought I'd make fun of her again."

As if to give Gwen time to compose herself, Eve paused.

Peabody picked up the cue. "Why don't I get you another water, Ms. Huffman?"

"Would you? Thank you. This is all so upsetting."

Peabody took the empty tube. "Peabody exiting Interview."

82

"You can't blame yourself for not taking that comment seriously."

"It's hard not to. If I could just have a minute?"

Eve lifted her hands. "All the time you need."

Gwen took a pack of tissues out of her purse, dabbed at her eyes. The door opened again.

"Peabody reentering Interview."

Gwen picked up the fresh tube, sipped delicately.

"You never noticed him, this man Ariel mentioned?"

"No. But I didn't go to her apartment that often."

"Really?" Eve leaned back. "Yet you purchased flowers at Fruit and Flower a block and a half from her apartment numerous times, and wine at the Wine Cave two blocks from her apartment."

"I often buy wine and flowers. I may have patronized those shops on occasion when downtown. What difference does it make?"

"Here's where it makes a difference. You purchased flowers — flowers that the victim had on her dining table — and wine — the wine in the victim's kitchen — on the evening of her murder."

"That's impossible, as I wasn't downtown. I've clearly stated where I was last evening."

"Peabody, cue it up and run it. Both those vendors have security cams, and both those cams are date and time stamped. And both?" Eve pointed to the split screen that showed Gwen purchasing the flowers, the wine. "Both clearly show you. And show you wearing the dress, the shoes you wore when you were on the hallway, elevator, and lobby cam of your apartment.

"Peabody?"

Peabody made a business of looking at her notes. "You walked two blocks, hailed Rapid Cab number 982, rode downtown to the Wine Cave, where you paid cash for a very nice Shiraz before walking the half block to buy the flowers, again for cash."

"Those things, those cameras, can be manipulated."

"Sure, sure, House Royale, the flower place, the wine place, they all manipulated their security feeds just for kicks. Time to cut the crap, Gwen. You left the damn wineglasses in the bedroom."

"I don't know what you're talking about."

No tear shine now, Eve noted, but a hard gleam.

"I want to contact Merit."

"You want your lawyer? Sure, that's your right. I wonder what your fiancé's reaction will be when we tell him your DNA, your pubic hair were found in the dead woman's bed. Your DNA and prints on the wineglass beside the bed. Should be interesting."

Eve rose. "We'll step out so you can contact your lawyer."

"You just wait a minute."

"Can't continue once you say lawyer. Peabody, let's step out."

"I said wait a minute! I'm not contacting Merit yet. We'll just straighten this out. I don't want him upset by all this."

Eve stood, hand on the door. "So you don't want a lawyer at this time?"

"That's what I said."

Eve stepped back, sat again. "The record shows you waive legal representation at this time."

"And I know this without a lawyer." Gwen's lips curved, smugly. "My fingerprints and my DNA are not on file, and you can't compel me to give them to you without charging me. If you spied on me with my apartment security, you know I was in my apartment when Ariel was killed."

"But you were in her apartment between approximately six-forty-four to nine-forty-six last night. The second cab picked you up right outside her building, dropped you off half a block from your apartment."

Eve offered a smug smile of her own.

"Paying cash doesn't mean we can't track you."

"I never said I was in her apartment, and you're implying we had intimate relations. I'm engaged to be married, and I don't have intimate relations with other women. You can't claim I was or did, as you don't have my prints or DNA."

At the knock on the door, Peabody popped up. "They were set to rush it, but wow." She went to the door, took the file.

Sitting again, she opened it, grinned, then slid it to Eve.

"We do now. The prints you left on the tube of water match the prints on the wineglass — left side of the bed — the wine bottle, various other areas in the victim's apartment, and her attached studio. The DNA you left on the bed matches the DNA you left in the water bottle.

"Spit back happens to everybody."

"That's illegally obtained." Fear now, the first traces, ran over Gwen's face. "That's illegal."

"Nope, not even a little bit."

Eve rolled her eyes, kicked back in her chair when Gwen began to weep. "Oh, knock it off."

"I don't want to be here. I don't have to be here. I came in voluntarily, and I'm leaving!"

"Get out of that chair, and I charge you."

"With what? I didn't do anything!"

"We can start with lying to police officers, on the record, during a murder investigation, we can add fleeing a crime scene, and top it all off with murder."

"I didn't kill Ariel! I didn't."

"Who did?"

"I don't know! How would I know?"

"You were there, in her apartment. You had a sexual relationship with her, and had one for months."

"No, no! It was just the one time. I had too much to drink. I'm not even sure what —"

"Did you have too much to drink on May second?" Eve flipped open her file, read dates off the calendar. "Too much to drink on April twenty-eighth, on April twenty-first?" She looked up at Gwen's shocked face. "I can go on, all the way back to last fall. She kept a calendar."

"Gwen." Voice soft, eyes all sympathy, Peabody leaned in. "We're not going to be able to help you if you keep lying. We're not judging you for having an affair. Planning a wedding, a marriage, is stressful. You needed an outlet, a friend. But we can't help you if you don't tell us the truth."

Gwen turned to Peabody like salvation. "You don't understand, you just don't understand. You'll ruin my life. I didn't kill Ariel. What does the rest matter to anyone but me? It's my private business."

"Ariel's dead, Gwen. It all matters. We need to know what happened," Peabody continued, gentle as a patient mother. "For Ariel."

"What does it matter to her? She's dead. It's my life now. And you'll destroy it by saying these things. If Merit finds out, if my parents find out, I'll lose everything. I didn't kill her, so that should be enough."

"It's not," Eve said flatly. "You gave a false report, you were in the victim's apartment on the night of her murder. You returned to the scene of the crime, then fled it. Cough up the truth now, or we charge you."

"You can't charge me with her murder. I was in my apartment. You know that."

Letting her disgust show, Eve leaned back. "Here's what I know. I know the chances of you stalking out of her place after an argument and someone completely unconnected going in and beating her skull in with a hammer about an hour later are zip."

"But that's what happened!"

"If it is, you shouldn't have any problem telling the fucking truth, starting now. Last chance, Gwen, or we charge you and let the lawyers hash it out."

"You have to respect my privacy." When she crossed her hands over her heart, her engagement ring shot light. "You have to keep what I tell you private. You have to promise me."

"I don't have to promise you squat."

Both hands flew up — dramatically — to cup her own face. "How can you be so cruel!"

"Oh, I don't know, maybe because I just spoke with the widowed mother of the woman currently on a slab in the morgue. I'm done with you. Gwendolyn Huffman, you're under arrest for —"

"Wait, wait, wait!" Gwen covered her face with her hands. "All right. I was there, yes. I lied because I was afraid, and I was shocked, and I didn't know what else to do. But she was alive when I left. You know that."

"You'd been seeing each other romantically, sexually, for several months."

"It didn't start out that way. It was what I told you. I admired her work, and we became friends. She — she was so open, and free, so different from anyone I knew. She seduced me. I don't have much experience, and I'd never been with a woman. I got caught up, I admit it. I convinced myself it wasn't hurting anyone. It was just a fling, just a kind of interlude before I got married.

"She wanted more. I came to see that. She wanted more than I could give her, than I wanted to give her. I love Merit. I want to spend my life with Merit, and she knew that, but . . ."

"She threatened to tell him."

"I don't know what happened. We had wine. I arranged the flowers I'd brought her, then we . . . we were together. After, we were just talking, having more wine and talking. Merit texted me. I shouldn't have answered — I realize it hurt her feelings, made her angry, but I answered. She said I had to call off the wedding. We argued, and she became angrier, furious. I'd never seen her like that. She said she was tired of being some embarrassing secret, and if I didn't tell Merit, she would."

She paused to drink more water, then bowed her head. "We had a terrible fight about it. I said awful things to her, and she said awful things to me. She threw on some clothes, said she was going to work, and I'd better think about how I wanted this to end.

"We kept arguing while I dressed, then I stormed out. I was so upset. She knew I was going to marry Merit, she knew what we had was separate. I barely slept, and I started to think about the ugly things we'd said to each other. I didn't want it to end that way. She meant something to me. I decided to go back and talk to her, face-to-face, when we were both calm, calm and sober. I knew we couldn't be together, not anymore, but I'd hoped we could erase those awful words, be kind to each other again."

"And you wanted to persuade her not to tell your fiancé about the affair."

Eve noted the calculation, lightning fast. "All right, yes. I didn't want what had been a positive experience for me, a personal exploration, to upend the rest of my life. I'd hoped in the light of day we could both be calm, reasonable adults and part as friends. And the rest, the terrible rest, is what I've already told you."

"No, it's not." Just like, Eve thought, her latest version mixed truth and lies. "The door wasn't unsecured when you got there. You let yourself in this morning. Where's the key card Ariel gave you?"

The quick flush came from irritation on Eve's gauge, not embarrassment. "I'd forgotten I'd told you that.

Obviously I told you that because I didn't want you to know I had a key."

"Where is it?"

"I threw it away."

"When? Where?"

"This morning. I broke it in half, threw it in a recycler bin on the street."

"Where? Near her place or yours?"

"Near the wineshop, before I got a cab."

"Then you waited nearly an hour to call nine-one-one."

"I was in shock."

"But not so much you couldn't think to ditch the key card. Bullshit on shock. You used the time it took to get back uptown to calculate what to do, what worked best to protect yourself. No signs of shock when you entered the lobby, the elevator, the hallway to your apartment. We can run that feed for you."

"You don't know what I felt. You don't know my mental or emotional state."

"Sure I do. You ditched the card in an attempt to remove a connection that might be seen as too close. It occurred to you on that trip uptown someone might have seen you go in or out of Ariel's apartment. Not such a worry during the affair — just visiting a friend — but now that friend's dead, and the cops are going to ask questions."

Rising, Eve wandered the room.

"You have to be the one to call it in. You have to come up with a story that portrays a friendship — close, but still casual, and certainly not romantic. You have to have a reason for going downtown so early in the morning. You worked it all out while you came back uptown, while you put the DND on your apartment. Took a shower, removed the makeup, changed your clothes."

Pausing, Eve edged a hip on the table.

"The virgin white was a nice touch. Work hysteria into your voice when you call it in, then go over and over how you'll play it before you tag your fiancé, the lawyer.

"That sound about right?"

"Ariel was dead, and I couldn't change that. I reported it, and I looked after myself. That's not a crime."

"You'd be surprised. Who did you contact after your fight with Ariel? Who did you tell about her threat to go to your fiancé? Who did you ask to take care of it?"

"No one! Are you crazy?"

"Speaking of crazy, maybe you tagged one of your friends in Natural Order."

She didn't flush this time; she blanched.

"The order likes to target gays, the trans, the mixed race, LCs — and the list goes on. So, you tell them to meet you where the cab dropped you off, pass them Ariel's key card — because a copy of her card, like yours, was used to gain entry minutes before she died."

"That's not possible."

"It's fact. Your parents are longtime members of Natural Order."

"That's not a crime, either."

"Not yet, no, but some members have been known to commit crimes. Violent crimes. Maybe you called Daddy."

"I would never — For God's sake, why would I go through all this so my parents wouldn't find out, then tell my father?"

"You're good at making up stories," Eve speculated. " 'Daddy, I'm in trouble. A friend — oh, I made a terrible mistake becoming friends with her. I was visiting her tonight because Merit's working late. Just having some wine, some girl talk, and she — she tried to — she wanted me to — I refused, I pushed her away, and she got so angry. She's going to tell Merit I've been with her, intimately with her. She said unless I slept with her — she said I led her on all this time, and if I didn't do what she wanted she'd tell Merit I did, have been.' "

"I never did any such thing."

"Prove it. Let's see your 'link."

"You want my 'link? Fine." In a jerky movement, Gwen pulled it out of her handbag.

Eve took one look, held out her hand, turned the shining gold 'link over. "This looks brand-new. Doesn't this look — what is it? — brand-spanking-new, Peabody?"

"It sure does."

"Are we going to find out you bought this 'link today, Gwen?"

"So what?"

"Where's your old one?"

"Recycled. It had texts on it to and from Ariel, and I realized if Merit saw them, he'd wonder. It was my personal property."

"Destroying evidence. We'll add that to the list. Who'd you tag on the other 'link? Who did you tell about Ariel?"

"No one. No one. No one." She banged her hands on the table with each denial. "My parents could cut me off like they did my brother if they find out about any of this. Merit will call off the wedding."

"And those are very strong motives to kill the person who knows all of it."

"I was in my apartment."

"Yeah, got me there. For now. And for now, Gwendolyn Huffman, you're under arrest for —"

"What! You said you'd help me if I told you the truth."

"Yeah, well, you didn't. Not all of it. You've had plenty of experience, and it's debatable who seduced whom from where I'm sitting."

Eve pushed off the table. "She meant nothing to you, nobody does. At least not nearly what you mean to yourself. The door of her apartment wasn't unsecured, you weren't in shock. You calculated every step of this.

"Now you're under arrest, for leaving a crime scene, lying to the police, destroying evidence. We'll hold the murder charge for the moment, but, believe me, we're working on it."

"You can't do this!"

"Done."

"I want my lawyer."

"You're free to use your spanking-new 'link to contact him once you're booked. Peabody, would you take Ms. Huffman where she very much needs to go?"

"Happy to."

"I won't go with you!"

"Easy to add resisting to the mix," Eve said. "In fact, it would be some nice icing."

She cried now, and there was nothing pretty about it. And kept crying as Peabody led her out.

"Interview end."

Eve gathered her files. She stepped out to wait for Shelby.

She watched Carmichael give Shelby a squeeze on the shoulder, then peel off toward the bullpen.

"My office," Eve said.

"I'm not worried about anybody hearing about this, sir."

"My office is better."

But this time when they went in, Eve didn't close the door.

"Thoughts, Shelby?"

"First thought is it's an education to watch you and Peabody work in the box, so I appreciate the opportunity."

"Is that sucking up?"

"It's pure truth. You didn't need me in Observation to separate her lies from the truth when she tried to fold them together to her benefit. You nailed her there. I want to say, from my own experience, she's sexually aggressive. She likes to be in charge, so it's unlikely the victim seduced her. She was making a lot of that up on the fly, and when she does that — or did back in the day — she tends to talk faster, tap her foot. She was doing that.

"But I think she was telling the truth about her father."

"Why?"

"If there's anyone she's afraid of, it's her father. He controls everything. I know she gets money from a trust because she told me that summer she only had a couple more years before she started getting some of her own money. Money at eighteen, as long as she went to college for at least a year. An increase at twenty-one, and, if I remember right, another at twenty-five, another at thirty, or when she marries. If she gets married and has a child, the trust hits the top of the income stream."

"That sounds . . . bat-shit," Eve decided.

"It's how Natural Order works. Women are meant to have children — within wedlock. Once she does that, it's hers, free and clear. At least that's what she said back then, or thought back then. Until she hits thirty-five, it might've been, or marries and has a kid, her father controls the amount she receives annually from the trust. And as he heads it, he can cut it off, like he did with her brother."

"So if her father found out . . ."

"Premarital sex, with another woman? If he didn't cut her off completely, he'd sure as hell turn down the stream. I don't know the fiancé, but most people don't like being lied to and cheated on, so she has to calculate the odds he'd ditch her. She thinks he will, that came off as true to me."

"Yeah, me, too. We'll see if she's right, because he's sure as hell going to find out. Meanwhile, because I had plenty of probable cause before the interview, Baxter and Trueheart are searching her apartment with a duly executed warrant."

"She won't like that."

"No, she won't. That gives me a little spark of joy. She's a lousy human being, Shelby."

"She's a lousy human being, Lieutenant. My taste has improved considerably since that summer. She may try to contact me, knowing I'm a cop, knowing I was attached back then. She'd want an ally, someone who'd give her inside information.

"She'd have picked the wrong cop for that."

"Yes, sir, Lieutenant. If she makes that attempt, should I notify you even if you're off shift?"

"Bet your ass. And by my clock, you're off shift now. Go have a drink with a pal."

"Actually, the woman I'm seeing's busy tonight. I think I'll go talk to my brother. He may have some information he hasn't shared with me. He would if I asked him to."

"Fine. You handled yourself well today, Shelby."

"Thanks, Lieutenant."

Off shift or not, Eve sat to write it up. She expected Gwen would make bail within two, maybe three hours.

But they'd be very unpleasant hours.

CHAPTER
SIX

Once she'd finished, Eve put together what she'd need to work at home. She considered her commander might want an oral report the next day, and she might want to consult Mira.

She walked out into the bullpen and saw McNab sitting on the corner of Peabody's desk. Whatever he said made her partner laugh.

Eve was surprised he didn't send the general population into hysterics with his fashion choices.

Today's included tangerine baggies, a T-shirt she assumed depicted the results of a supernova with its explosion of reds, golds, and oranges. His airboots and the jacket he'd tossed over the back of Peabody's chair went for lime green.

She couldn't say why.

He'd tied his blond hair in a long tail with an orange cord. All those colors and more he'd represented in the hoops that circled his entire earlobe.

She started to speak, to tell them both to wrap it up and go home. And Roarke walked in.

More than a contrast to McNab's skinny frame inside a circus rainbow, Roarke's leanly muscled build inside the smoke-gray suit radiated power.

Then you got to the face, framed by that mane of black silk hair, and no heart could be blamed for skipping a few beats.

That face, carved by some genius god on a particularly artistic day. Those eyes, so wildly blue they caught the breath. That mouth, so perfectly, romantically sculpted, curved now, for her.

Maybe, just maybe, with another handful of years of marriage, seeing him unexpectedly wouldn't simply dazzle her.

"Lieutenant, my luck's in."

And there was Ireland, with all its magic and poetry, whispering in his voice.

"That makes two of us."

"I had a meeting, and took a chance you'd still be about."

"Just heading out."

"Yay!" Peabody said and sprang up from her desk. "We can meet up with Mavis and Leonardo."

"That's the plan," Roarke agreed.

"What plan?" Eve's head swiveled from Roarke to Peabody and back again. "I don't have that plan. I don't have time to have drinks or dinner or whatever."

"It's not that, I don't think. She has some surprise she wants to spring." Peabody snagged her coat. "I was going to tag her, tell her we probably couldn't make it, but we can. She wants us to meet up, just a few blocks from here."

"Why?" Eve demanded, and Roarke shrugged.

"She wouldn't say," McNab said. "She just went . . ." He wiggled his hands in the air. "All will be revealed."

"Fine. Fine." It was Mavis, after all. "But I have to make it quick. I'm working one," she told Roarke.

"Yes, I know."

"How do you know?"

"I spoke with Jack about it briefly."

She stopped dead on her way out. "You spoke to Commander Whitney about my case?"

"Briefly. He mentioned you were interviewing Gwendolyn Huffman, and I found that interesting."

"You know her?"

"I don't, no." He steered Eve to the elevator. "I do know her fiancé a little, and his family. They're lovely people."

"Maybe."

"Well now, you'll tell me all about it later. I've sent my car along, so I'll ride with you. We all will," he said as the four of them squeezed on the elevator.

"I don't even know where the hell we're going."

"I've the address," Roarke assured her.

"So you drive." And even if it was only a few blocks, she could start a good run on Gwen's parents. Especially the father.

And dig into Natural Order.

When they got home, she'd ask Roarke to dig into the Huffman finances — and Gwen's trust. It would help to know just how much was at stake for her.

By the time she got home — with this surprise detour — Baxter and Trueheart should have completed the search and have a report.

Gwen wasn't an idiot, but she hadn't expected a search. She may have left something in her apartment that added to the mix.

"McNab, did you finish with my electronics?"

"Oh yeah. Nothing hinky on the vic's e's, Dallas. Texts on her phone and a few tags. A lot of texts from your suspect, going back to last fall. A lot of the lot of are sexy texts if you read between the lines."

"Is that so?"

"Yeah, like, wait until you see what I bought. I'll model it for you, so you can tell me if it suits. Or, candlelight and wine? Lots of stuff like that, mostly from the suspect's 'link to the vic's. The vic had texts from her mother, her brother, her sister-in-law, and e-mails from same. Otherwise it was mostly business stuff, art stuff."

Eve breathed clear again when they made it to the garage level.

"She'd shoot photos of her work to the Village Scene, and they'd tell her what to bring in, when. That's a gallery-type place that sells arts and crafts made by people who live or work in the Village. And she had the same deal going with Poets and Painters — where she also worked a couple days a week."

"Okay."

They piled into Eve's ride, Roarke at the wheel.

"You get a sense of somebody when you read their communication, go through the pictures on their comp or 'link, go over their search history and all. She seemed like a nice person, you know? Tight with her family and all."

Eve pulled out her PPC and began to gather data on Dr. Oliver Huffman.

She'd barely gotten past the basics when Roarke drove through an open gate. A single gate, she noted, wide enough for a good-size truck, with a short drive leading to a big white brick house with a long, wide front porch.

Mavis stood on the porch. Her hair, cotton candy pink, fountained out of a topknot. She wore over-the-knee clear boots.

What, Eve wondered, was the point in see-through boots?

She paired them with a fluttery dress covered with some sort of pink posies.

When she bounced, clapped her hands, Leonardo — towering, copper skin, copper hair in long dreads — came out the black front door with Bella on his hip.

The kid squealed, then threw back her head so her blond ringlets danced, and laughed like a lunatic.

When Mavis bounded down the trio of steps, Eve noticed the boots had heels that looked as if someone had glued a clump of colorful marbles together.

"You made it! Peabody texted maybe not, then McNab texted maybe so. And you made it."

She yanked open Eve's door before Eve could do it herself, and tugged Eve's hand. "Come see, come see before I bust!"

"See what?"

"The house."

"I see the house. What is the house?"

"Ours!" Arms outstretched, Mavis spun in circles. "It's all so mag. It's all so whoa! We bought a house."

"You bought a house." A really big white brick house, with a porch, and what looked like an overgrown yard. Since it all struck as dramatically un-Mavis, Eve searched for something to say.

She tried, "Wow."

"It's wow to the ult! I know it needs work and love, and holy sh — shoes," she corrected. "Some freaking color and style. But it's just what we wanted, right, moonpie?"

Leonardo beamed at her, at the house, at the overgrown yard. "It really is."

Since Bella all but launched herself out of her father's arms, Eve had no choice but to catch her.

"Das! Das!" She gripped Eve's chin with one hand, pointed at the house with the other. "Mine!"

"Yeah, so I hear. I didn't know you were looking for a house."

"We've been talking about it since . . ." Mavis patted her belly. "Knocked up, the return. We wanted something with some yard, and big enough to grow. And something we could make ours. It's like a blank slate, and we can draw whatever we want on it. Roarke found it for us."

"Oh, really?" Eve turned toward him.

"Don't be mad. I made him swear not to tell." Mavis slid an arm around Roarke's waist. "I really wanted you to see whatever we picked once we'd picked."

"It could be a really great yard," Peabody said.

"I'm counting on you to help make that happen. Flowers, Peabody, and trees and bushes and room for kids to run. Oh, oh, there it goes."

Tears welled. Tears fell.

"Hormones, they're killing me. We gotta go in. The main part has five bedrooms — one can be Leonardo's office, if he wants. And there's a big-ass attic where he can have his workshop. There's even a basement level I can use for recording, even though I do that mostly at Jake's studio now."

The minute they hit the porch, Bella wiggled down to race inside. "Mine!"

Her little high-top sneaks sent out echoes and bounced with lights as she danced in the foyer.

Dingy beige walls showed off lighter squares, rectangles, ovals where art had hung, and the wood floor showed considerable wear and tear. But roomy, Eve figured, with its high ceilings and wide staircase.

Obviously thrilled, Bella grabbed Peabody's hand to tug her along, jabbering all the while.

The living area focused on what looked to Eve like an ancient brick fireplace. Light poured in the trio of windows overlooking the dilapidated front yard.

Eve noted the dinge, the scars, while Peabody rhapsodized over the natural light, the wide-planked oak floors.

Hanging back a bit, Eve looked at Roarke. "You pointed them at this place?"

"She has good, solid bones, a fine history, and is exactly what they wanted."

"They wanted old and decrepit?"

"They wanted old and character, some grounds, and that blank slate in or near their neighborhood. She's far from decrepit. Neglected she is, but she's a beauty who just needs some attention and imagination."

Eve narrowed her eyes. "You were going to buy this place."

"I was, yes. I had an offer ready to go when Mavis contacted me." Then he smiled. "And it seemed to me this had come across my desk exactly for this reason. Fate, darling Eve."

As Bella had with Peabody, he took her hand, pulled her along. "Come on, see the rest. Give her a chance."

They caught up with Peabody, who was now touting the joys of the woodwork, the moldings, and a window seat in what she termed a perfect study.

Eve poked her head into a half bath, and its red-and-gold wallpaper had her stepping quickly out again.

They made their way through the main floor into a huge space where Mavis spread her arms.

"I love how open all this is, right? Kitchen, the family room, the dining room, and you can just see everything."

Eve saw it, all right. A stunning display of ornate, dark cabinetry, acres of solid black counters, and weird, fussy lights hanging everywhere.

Plus, a lot more dinge.

"So iced having the double fireplace thing."

"There's a big pantry," Leonardo put in, and hauled Bella up when she lifted her arms. "We'll spend a lot of time in this space, I think."

"After it's Mavis and Leonardo-ized." With a laugh, Mavis spread her arms again. "It's ult ugly and mega sad. Roarke said it's a — what is it?"

"Gut job," he supplied.

"Gut job! We can donate the totally ugly cabinets, hit it with some color and freaking happy. We can hang in here and see Bella and Number Two wherever they are. And we have back stairs!"

She spun in a circle, then hurried toward them. "Let's go up. Whoever thought I'd live in a house with two sets of stairs?"

Because the sheer joy overwhelmed even the dinge, the dust, the scars, Eve put aside her reservations.

Upstairs, the doors read black to Eve, but Peabody instantly went into rapture again about solid mahogany, stripping, refinishing.

Big rooms, Eve thought, and lots of light again. Which wasn't so much of a bonus at the moment, as it highlighted lots of scary wallpaper.

Bella grabbed Eve's hand, then Roarke's.

"Das! Ork!" And raced into one of the rooms. "Mine!"

She chattered, danced. She seemed particularly pleased with a window seat, then the big closet, and finally tugged Roarke's hand until he crouched down to her level.

She jabbered.

"Ah, I see. I'm sure you have it right. Yes, of course, that's just the thing, isn't it now?"

Clearly pleased, she hugged him, wiggled her butt, then raced off laughing.

"What the hell was she talking about?" Eve demanded.

"I haven't a single clue, but she seemed firm on it."

With a shake of her head, Eve walked to the big window. It overlooked the back — and a lot more overgrown yard, some sort of shed or garage.

With big shady trees, she thought, a wide patio.

"I get it. I get what she sees here — sort of anyway. And I get what she wants. What they want. But, Jesus, it'll take months, maybe years to do all that."

"Two to three months," he corrected. "Most is just cosmetic."

"Seriously?"

"She's rock solid under the questionable decor and unhappy neglect."

"You'd know." She thought of the dilapidated farm in Nebraska he'd turned into a postcard on a bet.

Yes, he'd know.

"Okay, if she wants my nod on it, she's got it. But something's off. The dimensions. The west wall stops way before it should. You can see that from the outside, and that patio deal extends beyond where this house stops."

"The main part of the house. You've a good eye."

"I'd have to be blind not to see it. What's the deal?"

"Mavis's next reveal."

They went out again where McNab was talking about updated electronics, house systems for security, entertainment, business. All in a language she knew no one understood but Roarke.

And he and Roarke went into geek speak as they walked downstairs again.

"I can convert the lower level into a studio," Mavis said, "and Leonardo's got the kick-ass attic space. But I really want to show you the bonus round. Out here. Roarke, what did you say we could do here?"

"Blow out this wall, install glass accordion doors to the patio."

"That. So instead of this dink door, imagine that. And we can put a playhouse out there for Bella and Number Two, and have a garden. We can still walk to our favorite joints, and to parks and, well, everything."

"To us," Peabody said. "Because we're going to miss having you in the same building."

"Like nutso," McNab agreed, and scooped Bella up. "Gotta have my Bellamina fix."

"Nab," she said with swoon-worthy love, and kissed him.

"We like hearing that, don't we, honey bear?"

Leonardo opened another door off the patio. "We're counting on hearing it."

Another kitchen, not as big as the other, and this one so white it looked like a lab. White walls, floors, counters, cabinets.

It made up for the white with a dining and small lounging area with candy-pink walls.

"Need my sunshades," McNab said, and winked at Bella.

"Gut job," Mavis said.

"Not entirely. They're good cabinets and laid out well. I'd paint them out," Roarke suggested. "And tear up the white tile on the floor. If the hardwood doesn't run under it, I'd install it, match what runs through the rest."

"Tell them about it all," Mavis requested, "while we do the tour. You do it better."

"Well then, the owners — it's been in the same family for four generations — converted this space to accommodate visiting friends and family, and then for parents who they wanted close — but not in the same space, so to speak."

They walked through, paused at a sunny little room with a small fireplace flanked by built-ins — and dominated by floral wallpaper.

"The mother-in-law of the owner used this as a craft room."

"It's a good size for it," Peabody commented. "Sunny, and plenty of storage."

Mavis just beamed at her.

"And the living area, with more unfortunate wall coverings, and the fireplace — as throughout the house — converted from wood-burning. The basement area's finished — floors, walls — though they used it primarily for storage. A full bath down there, and potentially another bedroom. There are three upstairs, and two full baths with the master and a Jack-and-Jill for the other two."

"The woodwork's amazing. I'm so glad they didn't paint it. The high ceilings, the oak floors." Peabody sighed. "Are you going to tear down the walls, open it up to the main?"

"Too much house for us," Leonardo said.

"Rent it out." McNab nodded. "You could close off the back door if you didn't want tenants back in your yard. You got that private entrance there on the side."

"Yeah, it's nice the way the entrance faces the side. You'd get morning light in here. Do the fixes," Peabody said, "and you'd rent it out in a heartbeat. This neighborhood, all this room."

"You gotta get Dallas to do a run on any potentials though." McNab wandered the room. "You're really private back here. You want the right tenants, and the security we already talked about."

"We already picked the tenants." Still beaming, Mavis cuddled next to Leonardo, who had Bella back on his hips. "You guys."

McNab turned slowly, and Peabody just blinked.

"Some cops you are," Eve muttered. "You didn't see that coming?"

Peabody found her voice. "Oh, listen, this is beyond mag of both of you, but we are cops. We're cops and can't afford the rent on a place like this."

"You could if it's what you're paying now."

Peabody immediately shook her head. "Mavis —"

"Shut up. You, too," Eve ordered McNab. "Shut up and hear her out."

"I knew you'd get it." Tears welled again as Mavis threw herself at Eve. Tears fell again as she drew back. "Sorry, sorry. I can't. Leonardo, you tell them."

"These are my girls," he said. "The most precious things in my life. And I'm going to have another precious thing come into my life. How could I risk them? You said it yourself. It's private here, and we'd need to do background checks, and even then . . . It's not the same as apartment living. We don't want someone we don't know living here with us, sharing the

109

yard with us. We need friends. Someone we know, without question, Bella and the baby will be safe with."

"You're cops," Mavis managed. "What's safer than living beside cops? And we love you."

As if hitting a cue, Bella threw out her arms to Peabody.

"But it's —"

"Don't be stupid." Eve spoke flatly. "Because I'm going to tell them, flat out, they don't rent to anyone they don't know. Not here, behind a gate, when they're fricking celebrities with a kid and another coming. It's you or it goes empty, which is stupid. This is the perfect solution for everybody."

Tears still raining, Mavis hurled herself into Eve's arms again. Eve just rolled her eyes, and patted Mavis on the back.

She watched Peabody and McNab exchange looks, could interpret the nonverbal conversation between them. Especially when tears spilled from Peabody.

"Please, for God's sake, say yes before we drown in here."

"Peas," Bella said, and stroked Peabody's damp cheek.

"We'd love to be your tenants."

To Eve's relief, Mavis launched herself at Peabody. Somewhere in the hug, they both began to bounce, and Bella to laugh like a maniac.

"Great, that's settled. Now I have to get to work."

"Don't you want to see the rest?"

Eve shook her head at Mavis. "I've seen enough. I don't know how or why, but this place is perfect for the five . . . five-point-whatever of you," she corrected with a gesture toward Mavis. "Roarke says it's rock solid, so it is. He says you can fix it up in a couple or three months, so you can. Between him and McNab, you'll have the best security there is."

Mavis wiped at her eyes. "I've got a bottle of champagne, for everybody but me, Bella, and point-whatever."

"Pop it, enjoy it. We'll come back for another bottle once you exorcise the demon walls. So . . . congratulations all around. Sincerely."

She got out before more tears flooded. Roarke took her hand, kissed it as they walked around to her car.

"Well done, Lieutenant. And when did you cop to the big reveal?"

"The minute we walked into that science lab of a kitchen. Attached rental space, Mavis and Leonardo beaming with Peabody mooning over tiara moldings."

"Crown moldings."

"Whatever." She turned for a last look. "It really will work for all of them." When they got into the car, she looked at him. "And when did you have the idea of Peabody and McNab as tenants?"

"As soon as Mavis and Leonardo fell in love with the place. But I didn't suggest it, and they both came up with it immediately themselves. As you said, a perfect solution."

She settled back, started to reach for her PPC. Stopped herself. "I'm sorry I had to break up the moment."

"We all had the moment. Now they can bask in it together. But instead of doing whatever's next on your cop list, why don't you take this time to catch me up so I can help if need be."

"I've already earmarked money stuff for you to look at."

"And there we are. A perfect solution for us as well."

It kind of was, she thought.

She spent the time he drove uptown catching him up on murder.

CHAPTER
SEVEN

"I do know Merit Caine and his family a bit. I don't know the Huffmans, but know of them." Roarke considered as he wound through traffic. "I recall seeing the engagement announcement, and hearing a bit of this, a bit of that."

"I'd like to hear the bits."

"I'll say it's an open secret the Huffmans — the elder Huffmans — have an association with Natural Order, so some of the bits came from surprise Merit would align himself with that family."

"Money often speaks to money." She shrugged. "But my impression was he's in love with her. So that trumps the parents. What do you know about the parents — the Huffmans?"

"They're respected for their medical skills, from what I know, and, of course, for their wealth and position. But liked is a different matter. Where, again, from what I know, the Caines are both respected and liked well enough. Then again, from what I recall, the daughter's quite beautiful."

"Yeah, she's got the looks. And she's a manipulator, a bone-deep liar."

He glanced over. "A murderer?"

"She's involved, one way or the other."

"In that case, I expect the Caines will take a big step back from her, and this."

"Including the fiancé?"

Roarke braked at a light. "I have to go by my impression of him."

"That's good enough for me."

On the green, he drove on. "If Merit was unaware she was having an affair — male or female doesn't matter, it's the affair at the bottom — he doesn't strike me as the type to say bygones."

"Don't know why he would."

"Added to it, she pulled him right into it, didn't she, by calling him in as her legal rep, and lying to him."

Eve shifted to face him. "So you agree she lied to him, spun the same story she spun, initially, to me."

"Ah well, my impression again. No one knows, precisely, what goes on inside a relationship except those inside it, but my take is yes, she lied to him, has been lying to him. Using him, basically, as her beard. He wouldn't take kindly."

"Agreed. But there's more."

Roarke nodded along as she outlined the terms of the trust.

"Ah, well then, now you have it. She needs to marry to get the money, and with the Natural Order angle, she has to marry a man, a white male. Better yet if she conceives a child with him in wedlock. That sews it closed for her."

"Right? She does that, she can walk away with everything she believes she's entitled to. Caine would have served his purpose. I'd like you to look into the trust, make sure of the details — and what kind of money we're talking about."

"An entertaining way for me to spend the evening. Will you spend yours trying to suss out how the lovely lying Gwen managed to be in two places at once?"

"I've backed off from her doing the dirty work personally. But she admits tossing her 'link, buying a new one. She could have contacted someone who'd do it for her. Meet up, give said unknown subject the key card, then gone into her apartment."

"The hard edges of the order believe they're doing the righteous by harming or eliminating those who fall outside their lines."

"So she's . . ." Eve worked up a teary voice. "'I thought she was my friend! Then she assaulted me, tried to . . . I can't even say! When I refused her, when I fought her off, she said she'd tell Merit, tell everyone we'd been together. We've been intimate. Please help me. Please don't let her do this.'"

Roarke glanced at Eve as he turned and drove through the gates. "Well done, Lieutenant. Just the right amount of horror and desperation."

"She's a stone-cold bitch. Normally, I admire that. But she's the kind of stone-cold bitch who uses people, then discards them."

"Like the young, yet-to-be-Officer Shelby."

"Yeah, like Shelby. And there will be others between her and my victim. I'll find them."

"I've no doubt."

The last burst of the spring day struck the stone and glass of the house with a fiery flash of light. It flamed in the windows, struck the towers and turrets like torches.

"It hits me, six years ago — just a handy number — Mavis was doing some gigs at the Blue Squirrel and waiting tables there to pay the rent on an efficiency apartment about the size of the master closet in that place downtown. I was sleeping in a bigger apartment, sure, but not really living there. I mostly lived at Central.

"Now I'm living in a freaking castle, and she's going to be living in a big-ass brick house."

"Life can have some happy turns."

"Yeah, for some of us. Not for Ariel Byrd."

They got out of either side, met around the hood. "Think of this," he suggested. "Gwen Huffman isn't having a happy turn, either."

"Good thought."

They went in together where Summerset waited in the grand foyer with the fat cat at his feet.

"As you're both late, but unbloodied, I assume you toured Mavis's new home."

"He gets to know?" Eve jabbed a finger as the cat trotted over to rub her legs. "Bag of bones gets to know, but I don't?"

"No one's approval matters as yours does," Summerset said. "I assume you didn't disappoint her."

"Not only didn't Eve disappoint Mavis, she found exactly the right tone and right words to convince Peabody and McNab to take the rental."

"That's a fine thing for all of them." He inclined his head toward Eve. "Well done, Lieutenant."

"You'd be right at home there, skulking around the haunted wallpaper, baking in the kitchen from hell."

Because she wanted to set up her board, she left the insults there. She tossed the topper over the newel post and started upstairs with the cat bounding up beside her.

"Interesting. There's devil's food cake — but I didn't bake it in the kitchen from hell."

That got a laugh out of Roarke as he went upstairs.

"Why do they call it devil's food cake?" Eve demanded. "How does anyone know if the devil eats cake, and, if he does, is he only allowed one kind? I don't think so. I say the devil eats whatever he damn well pleases."

Adoring her, Roarke gave her butt a pat. "I can truthfully say I've never given the matter any thought. Let's raise a glass to the five-point-whatever in their new home."

"They won't be living there for months."

"Regardless."

He walked into her office, straight to the panel that opened to a generous wine rack.

Not to play favorites, Galahad gave Roarke's leg a rub before leaping to the sleep chair.

He chose a bottle, opened it, then poured two glasses.

"To friends," he said as he handed Eve hers, "who are family."

"Yeah, that's a good one." She tapped her glass to his. "But I still have to work."

"Understood. Why don't you set up your board, as you won't enjoy a meal until you have. I'll take a look at this trust."

"I don't know who set it up. I only have what Shelby told me."

"And what she told you, and you told me, is enough. Set up your board and book, then we'll have a meal."

She set up her board while he worked in his adjoining office. After circling it a couple of times, making an adjustment or two, she settled into her command center.

She opened operations, and copied her book to date.

She grabbed her 'link when she saw Baxter on the readout.

"Dallas. What've you got?"

"Shoe envy. Not for the type she's got, but the number. I can tell you Shoe Hoarder Huffman liked to live and dress in style. Under her clothes, too. A whole bunch of sexies. I believe my esteemed partner developed a permanent blush.

"She keeps a selection of high-end vibrators, but tucked away from curious eyes. But," he said just as Eve figured the search hit bust, "we got her 'link."

"The one she said she ditched?"

"She did ditch it — in her kitchen recycler. It's dinged up, but she didn't run a full cycle — and we got to it before it ran the auto. Still too crunched for us to access anything."

"You need to get that to EDD."

"Already there. Dinged up, like I said, with some bites out of it, but they should be able to get something."

"That's good. That's gold. What else?"

"No drop 'links, nothing on her comp or tablet that popped out, but they're in EDD now. The second bedroom's set up as an office, but she clearly doesn't do much in it. Plenty of sparkles in a safe, along with some cash, and a safe deposit box key."

"We'll check on that."

Roarke walked in, signaled her to continue as he went into the kitchen.

"It's in Evidence. I'm going to say that she lives cold. You can have the sparkles, the shoes, a closet full of high-end wear, and still live cold."

"Cold suits her."

"It must. But the possible payoff? Tucked away with the vibrators she had a small, unmarked bottle. As it wasn't labeled, it's not prescription or OTC."

"Illegals?"

"That'd be my guess, boss. And since it was tucked with her sex stuff, I'm figuring sex illegals. I didn't want to risk opening it, so we dropped it at the lab."

"Good. I'll check on it."

"My boy Trueheart's writing out the full report, then we're heading out for a brew."

"You earned it. Thanks."

"All in a day's, Dallas. The woman has a good fifty pairs of shoes that haven't been worn. I stand and salute."

"That's just sad," Eve said, and cut him off.

She sat back, considering, as Roarke came back with two covered plates.

"Shoes and vibrators."

That stopped him. "Sorry?"

"Gwen Huffman's place. Baxter admires her many shoes, reports she has a collection of vibrators tucked away — and a lot of sexy underwear."

"None of that sounds murderous or illegal."

"They recovered her old 'link from her recycler, so once EDD gets inside and recovers, maybe some murderous."

"How damaged?"

She shrugged. "Don't know yet, but maybe they'll recover any communications she made on the way home from Ariel Byrd's. And Baxter found an unmarked bottle of as-yet-unidentified liquid squirreled away with her sex stuff."

"Ah, well then, that may be illegals. Come, bring the wine you've barely touched, and eat."

"Shelby said Huffman was sexually aggressive, and I'm betting that hasn't changed. Sexy underwear, no surprise. Vibrators, well, a girl's gotta do. But if that's a sex illegal, who's it for? The desk clerks — we checked with all of them and none recognized Ariel Byrd. She hasn't been to Huffman's apartment."

"Perhaps she had yet another lover."

"Possible," Eve conceded.

She discovered they had roast chicken with some sort of herb stuff, slices of potatoes in a light creamy sauce and more herb stuff, and asparagus.

It all smelled pretty damn good. After a bite of chicken she decided it tasted the same.

"What if she uses it herself? Men don't get her revved, but she's got this fiancé. He wants some touch, so she needs the substance to get revved to have sex with him."

"Well, that would be a sad state of affairs — pun intended — wouldn't it now? Then again, the financial payoff's considerable."

"How considerable?" She poked her fork in the air. "You got it already?"

"It wasn't much of a challenge. As her father stands as trustee, and has disinherited his son, the daughter gets the whole pie."

"How big's the pie?"

"When she marries — and it does specify she marries a male, a Caucasian male, an American-born citizen, and one approved by the trustee — she receives one hundred million."

Pleased, Eve stabbed some chicken. "That's a pretty big pie."

"Until the time she marries, as specified, she gets much smaller slices of said pie. If and when she conceives — and delivers a child — within that marriage, she gets another hundred million."

Eve took a small sip of her wine. "It sounds like a really big bribe."

"It's precisely that. Right now, she receives a biannual income from the trust. It's generous, but, at six million annually, paltry in comparison. And if she doesn't marry by the age of thirty-five, the income is cut off."

"So, she comes by her manipulative streak honestly. And if she deviates from white, male, American?"

"The trust closes down, the income stops."

"He may be worse than she is," Eve remarked. "I haven't done a deep dive on him yet. That's next. Speculate," she invited. "Does Merit Caine know about these terms?"

"Unlikely."

As she thought it through, Eve ate some more, took another sip of wine. "She's taking big risks — seeking out at least one lover could cost her that pie. And I'm betting more. A sexually aggressive, self-absorbed woman? A bunch of vibrators isn't going to do it for her. She needs admiration, excitement. She knew about the trust way back when she was a teenager and hooked up with Shelby. The risks are part of the excitement. But she's going to pick lovers outside of her own social pool, her stomping grounds. Why be stupid?"

"So a West Village artist."

"Yeah, away from the Upper East Side, outside her social strata. She wouldn't want to run into an ex at the next gala. Lots to play with here," she decided, and speared some asparagus.

And decided to table murder for a few minutes.

"How come that house was so dingy and neglected? It's prime real estate — even I know that."

"The owners relocated, with the in-laws, to New Mexico for the warmer, drier climate. Some health issues, and the owners' daughter had moved there with her husband, and had children. They'd hoped to keep the property in the family, but their son didn't want it, and lives — for several years now — in London."

"So why not sell?"

"Sentiment. They thought to split time between New Mexico and New York, but it simply didn't work. The health issues, the difficulty of the in-laws traveling. In any case, with one thing and another, several years passed, and they finally accepted they had to let it go."

"So they finally put it on the market."

"Actually, no. I know the son in London, and he contacted me. He hoped I'd take a look at it, and consider buying it, making the necessary fixes — as he'd come out to take a look a few months ago and realized how, well, sad it had become."

"Mega sad," Eve recalled. "What did he think you'd do with it?"

"Sell it or rent it out, which I would have done — the renting out part, as it's too much of a jewel to sell. At least straight off. The only stipulation his parents had was that a family would live in it. He understood that couldn't be legally binding, but he hoped I'd respect their wishes."

"Now there will be."

"And now there will be." He topped off his wine, but Eve shook her head when he offered to do the same with hers. "I think you'll enjoy this part of it. My acquaintance's mother had some reservations about some performer and fashion designer living in the house where she'd been raised, where she raised her children."

Eve's back went straight up. "Getting pretty damn picky."

"Sentiment and family homes. Strong things they are. Mavis tagged her up, had quite the conversation, apparently with Bella chiming in. Needless to say, the woman was completely charmed, and is now happy indeed that this family would live in the home she'd loved. There were tears, I'm told, on all sides."

"One of those — what did you call it? — lovely turns in life."

"Yes."

Eve glanced back at the board. "Now I have to get back to an unhappy one. Do you have work?"

"A bit of this and that."

"If you have time between this and that, do you want to run Huffman's brother? I don't see him in this, but I'm curious about him."

"More fun for me. Cake?"

"Cake? Shit, I forgot about the cake. Now I'm too full for cake."

"Later then. No, I've less to do tonight than you. I'll see to the dishes."

"I owe you."

They rose, and he stepped to her. He brushed his hands through her hair, then skimmed a finger down the narrow dent in her chin. "I'll collect," he said, and kissed her like a man who meant it.

Jan Shelby kept her tiny apartment squared away. Though an organized soul by nature, she essentially

124

lived in one room. More than two things out of place at a time?

Chaos.

She'd inherited her small, navy-blue convertible sofa from an aunt, her forest-green chair from a cousin. She used her mother's ancient kitchen table — and sometimes actually ate a meal there. It had two mismatched chairs she — in a spurt of spatial improvement — painted navy and green.

Because it was cheaper and easier than painting the walls — the color of slowly decaying flesh — she hung signs she'd found in thrift shops. SLIPPERY WHEN WET, HELP WANTED, NO VACANCIES.

She'd never considered herself a quirky sort, but the signs amused her.

Since she had a free evening, she made herself some pasta, cracked a brew, and settled in to read on her tablet while she ate.

As far as she was concerned, the sounds of the city banging up to her second-story windows ranked as music. She loved the sounds of New York.

Since her unit didn't rate a dishwasher, she washed and dried her dishes, put them away.

She was on the point of pulling out her sofa bed, stretching out to spend the rest of the evening watching something fun and easy on-screen, when her buzzer sounded.

She flipped the switch. "Yeah?"

"Oh, Jan! Thank God you're home. Buzz me up."

Maybe it was small, maybe it was petty, but Shelby went with it.

"Who is this?"

"January, it's Gwen."

She said, "Oh." And waited two full beats before releasing the street-level door.

She went into her skinny bathroom to check out her face in the mirror over the palm-size sink.

Good enough, she decided, especially with the hair. The hair rocked. And a woman was damn well entitled to a little vanity when her first lover paid a call.

Maybe she had pulled on her POLICE ACADEMY sweatshirt in anticipation of this particular visit. A good way to remind everyone just who January Shelby was.

She took her time answering the knock, then angled to block Gwen from just strolling in.

She'd changed clothes, Shelby noted, into what she calculated Gwen saw as down-market and friendly. Distressed designer jeans and a silky white T-shirt with a thin leather jacket the color of buttermilk.

"How'd you find my apartment? Cops' addresses aren't public."

"I had to call your cousin Laurie, then she chatted at me for twenty minutes. Aren't you going to ask me in?"

"Sure, come on in."

Shelby closed the door, giving Gwen a minute (all it took) to look around the apartment. A cheap apartment, cheaply furnished, Shelby thought.

But hers.

"Isn't this . . . cozy," Gwen said in a tone that turned the word *cozy* into two words: a dump.

"It works for me. What brings you here, Gwen?"

126

"Oh, Jan! Everything is awful." The slow, beautiful tears spilled as she pressed fingers to her trembling lips. "That — that insane Lieutenant Dallas arrested me! I spent hours in a cell because she has some sort of vendetta against me."

"Lieutenant Dallas is one of the most, if not the most, respected officers in the NYPSD."

"Why? Because she married some filthy rich Irishman?"

"No." Shelby bit back the vitriol that sprang to her tongue. "Not at all."

"You don't understand what she's done to me, how she treated me. She ruined my life!"

Gwen lurched forward to throw herself into Shelby's arms, a maneuver Shelby blocked by taking Gwen's elbow. She steered her to the chair.

"Sit down. I'll get you a glass of water."

"God, I don't want water! Do you have anything to drink?"

No way she was wasting any of her meager supply of adult beverages. "Water, coffee, off-brand ginger ale."

"Never mind, never mind." Gwen covered her face with her hands. "I need help. I needed to come to someone who knows me, who'd understand."

"Understand what?" Shelby asked as she took a seat on the sofa.

"That I couldn't do all these terrible things. I had to post bail. Oh my God, when it gets out . . ."

"What are the charges?"

"She said I lied during interview."

"Did you?"

"I was afraid! I was in shock." She dropped her hands, then held them out in a plea. "I barely knew what I was saying."

"Is that the only charge?"

"She trumped up others." As if they were gnats, Gwen waved them away. "Leaving the scene of a crime, destroying evidence."

"Did you leave the crime scene?"

"Jan! I found a dead body. I ran. Anybody would. I was so shocked, I just ran."

"And destroying evidence?"

"I bought a new 'link. People buy new 'links all the time and toss their old ones. How is that a crime?"

Leaving out the key card, Shelby thought.

Shelby frowned, shooting for sober and concerned. "Those are pretty serious charges, Gwen. Do you have a lawyer?"

"Not anymore." The hand went back to her face. "Merit, my fiancé — he was representing me. He's broken our engagement. He told me I need to get another lawyer."

Shelby tried switching sober and concerned for sympathetic, and hoped she pulled it off. "That's rough."

"I don't know what to do, don't know where to turn. That woman, that horrible woman threatened to charge me with Ariel's murder. My God, Jan, my God. You know I couldn't kill anyone."

"Who was the victim to you?"

"She was a friend, and . . ." Straightening, Gwen dashed at tears. "We became close, and she wanted more. I know it was wrong, a mistake. I was unfaithful to Merit, but I had feelings for her."

128

"You had an affair with her."

"We had a relationship, one I believed was harmless, where both of us understood it couldn't be more. But she suddenly demanded more. I told that woman Ariel and I had an argument that night, and I left. I went home. She had my building's security feed proving I did, and I stayed home, but she's trying to twist it all up. And now I've lost everything. You know how my parents are. They could cut me off like they did Trace unless I can convince them this is all a terrible mistake. And it is!"

"If you left, and stayed home, I don't see how you left a crime scene."

"I went back in the morning, just to talk to her — to Ariel — calmly. That's when I found her. I just ran. I couldn't think. I had to protect myself."

Shelby let her eyes open wide. "You didn't report the murder?"

"I did. I did! After I got home, and — and could think clearly again. And I could hardly tell the police I was in a relationship with Ariel with Merit right there. I knew he wouldn't understand, that he'd turn away from me. And I was right."

In a gesture Shelby found fascinating, Gwen covered her eyes with the back of her hand.

Did she practice in a mirror? Shelby wondered. Or was it just innate ability?

"We've already sent out the invitations. I have my dress, and — and everything. Now I'm humiliated, and my parents will be furious. You have to help me."

"How?"

"You're with the police. You could do something. Look at the files or whatever and . . ."

"And what? You want me to tamper with evidence?"

Now it was Gwen who waited a couple of beats. "No, of course not. But you're right there, with the police. You'd have access." She rose to sit on the sofa beside Shelby, took her hand. And her eyes filled with pleading.

"Anything you could do, anything at all. I'd be so grateful. I need someone on my side, Jan, someone who knows the real me. Someone who knows my heart."

She pressed Shelby's hand to her heart. "I'm so frightened." She leaned in. "So frightened. I need a friend. I need you. I've missed you. Missed being with you."

Shelby used her hand to nudge Gwen back. "I'm seeing someone."

"It's only you and me here now. No one has to know."

An instant before Gwen's mouth met hers, Shelby rose. "I'd know. And since there's nothing I can or would do for you, Gwen, you're insulting us both by trying to trade sex for my integrity."

"I need help." Tears. "Can't you see how desperate I am?"

"You need a good lawyer. And if you don't want me to add offering sexual favors to a cop for information on an active investigation, you need to leave."

"That's it?" The tears in her eyes burned away with temper as Gwen shoved to her feet.

"Yeah, I'd say that covers it. I'd say sorry about your bad luck, but it's clear you brought it on yourself. And you're alive. Someone you claimed to have feelings for isn't."

"I never had any for you."

"I know."

"You were never anything but a summer diversion — the dumb bitch from the blue-collar family, with the rich uncle with no class who couldn't keep her stupid mouth shut about some careless sex on the beach."

"I guess I was dumb to get tangled up with you, but my uncle has more class in his left armpit than you ever will. And I never told anyone about you and me."

"Liar!"

"Of the two of us standing here, I think you're the clear winner of the title."

Shelby went to the door, opened it. "Get out."

"Of this pathetic shithole? My pleasure."

She actually sailed to the door. Shelby didn't think she'd ever seen anyone else pull that description off.

"And it was lousy sex."

Now Shelby smiled. "Liar," she said, and shut the door in Gwen's face.

After deciding she deserved a second brew, she carried her mini-comp from the closet to the table. She wrote it up, all of it, and sent the report to her lieutenant.

CHAPTER
EIGHT

At her command center, Eve read through Shelby's report. While she digested it, she went into the kitchen, programmed coffee and cake.

After she set it up, she went to the doorway. Roarke worked something on his desk screen.

"I've got cake. You want it in here or out there?"

"I'll come to you — and the cake. Two minutes."

She spent it studying her board.

"Ah, at the table, is it? Like the civilized."

"It looks like really good cake."

She sat, sampled a bite. "I'm wrong, it's not. It's really freaking good cake." She shoved in another bite. "Gwen Huffman went to Shelby. Dug up her address from a cousin — of Shelby's."

"So she made bail."

"She did — and though Caine repped her at the bail hearing, he didn't cough up the bail. She did." Considering, she eyed Roarke. "If you got busted and charged —"

He shot her a warning glance much like the one he shot Galahad when the cat bellied toward breakfast plates. "Hypotheticals can still be insulting."

"And still. If you did, I'd stand your bail. I'm a cop, but I'd stand your bail."

"How beautifully romantic. I, of course, would do the same for you."

"But he doesn't cough up her bail, and in fact breaks the engagement. That tells me it's very unlikely he knew or suspected his bride-to-be was having an affair while she planned the wedding, and your speculation on him hit the mark."

"You didn't consider him a suspect?"

"His alibi's solid, his background's clean. Gwen, on the other hand? She takes the time to go home after getting sprung —"

"And dumped," Roarke added.

"And dumped," she agreed between bites of cake. "Takes time to change her clothes into the more casual, takes the time to dig up Shelby's address, then goes there. Turns on the waterworks, spins a new story — slight variations from what I broke out of her in Interview, and a long way from her initial statement."

"A clever liar molds the tale to her audience."

Eve shook her fork at him, then licked it. "That's just right. Anyway, she had the affair, but both parties knew it was just sex. Ariel suddenly demanded more, threatened to expose her, and blah blah. She left out details like having and destroying Ariel's key-card copy, and claimed she just has an urge for a new 'link. How I'm a big meanie out to destroy her, and help me!"

"She becomes the victim."

"I half believe she sees herself that way. She went back to the shock — why she left the scene this morning — but added, maybe a slip, that she had to protect herself."

"Ah." Roarke toasted with his coffee. "A moment of truth."

"How I see it? Merit's dumped her, humiliation, bitch cop, parents will cut off the money stream. Help. You're a cop, you're right there, you can look at files, and so on. A lot of play on that long-ago summer, then she made a move."

Lifting an eyebrow, Roarke sipped some coffee. "That sort of move?"

"That sort. When Shelby rejected the move, said she was seeing someone, Gwen pushed a little harder, said nobody has to know."

"*Faithful* isn't a word in her particular world."

"Again, just how I see it. Shelby booted her, and Gwen went from sexy and needy to pissed off, tossed out a few insults, and left. One thing more," Eve added. "She accused Shelby of talking about their summer fling — at that time — so Gwen's parents found out. Shelby maintains she didn't tell anyone."

"Teenage romance often means other teenagers in the vicinity, doesn't it? It's unlikely it was a locked secret."

"Why tell the parents? Maybe somebody pissed at one or both of the teenage romancers. The brother springs to mind first, as sibs can get really pissed off. It doesn't actually matter," Eve added with a shrug. "I just hate blank spaces."

"I can't tell you if, at not quite eighteen, Trace Huffman weaseled on his sister, but I can tell you from

134

what I've dug into, his relationship with his parents wasn't likely any stronger or closer at that time than it is now."

"Maybe, maybe not. You don't have to like the authority figure to rat somebody out. People do it with cops all the time."

"They do, don't they? I found out a bit more on him than your standard run. It happens I know a producer who often uses him in recording sessions."

"I shouldn't be surprised. Paint me a picture."

"Talented, steady — though steadier now than he was a few years ago."

"Illegals or booze?"

"A bit of both. Nothing that kept him from working, but enough to keep him from progressing, you could say. He wanted to play music, write songs, drifted his way west, where he landed some gigs in Vegas. He's recently hooked up, personally and professionally, with another musician. The producer says she's also talented and steady, and he hopes to produce some of their music before long."

"So he's getting what he wants."

"What he doesn't want is any connection to his family, which is why he goes as Trace D. Huff, and in fact has turned down gigs in New York. He told my friend they're toxic, like a poison, and he didn't want to risk them getting into his bloodstream. He took off the day of his eighteenth birthday, so he tells it, with his guitar, a duffel bag, and the money he'd squirreled away over the previous six months by pawning things he felt wouldn't be noticed. His tennis racket, his dress wrist unit, and so on."

"So he planned it out."

"Yes, waiting until that day, as it made him legal, and because, he claims, that night his parents planned to initiate him into their cult. His term."

"Natural Order."

"He didn't give it a name, according to my friend. He contacted his parents the next day, to let them know he was alive and well, then pawned his 'link so they couldn't track him, stuck out his thumb, and kept riding it on the way west."

Yes, Eve thought, Roarke painted a picture very well.

"He worried they'd come after him."

"Apparently, so he kept moving for the first two or three years until he felt they'd decided disinheriting him was enough."

"It jibes with what I've dug up on the father."

She looked over at the board and Oliver Huffman's photo.

Sternly handsome seemed to fit, she thought. Chiseled features, pale gold hair dashed with silver, upthrust chin, chilly blue eyes.

"The parents keep their connection to Natural Order as down low as possible, but you don't have to dig too deep to find it. They practically helped start it up, along with Stanton Wilkey."

"A charismatic lunatic."

"I'll agree on the lunatic. Crazy eyes."

She pointed with her fork, then scooped up the last bite of her cake.

136

"Some people might look and see, I don't know, holy or empathic, but most every photo I studied today? I see crazy eyes."

"Cop vision, and yours is very sharp."

"Huffman senior went to hear Wilkey speak when Huffman was in college. He liked what he heard. Huffman had money, Wilkey had — we'll go with charisma — and together they had a vision. A few years later, Natural Order. Huffman marries Paula Vandorn — also made of money. I guess you could term them silent partners. Or benefactors. Or let's just go with cultists."

"I would," Roarke agreed. "By the time Trace Huffman was born, Natural Order was global, wealthy. Secretive, of course, as such things are, but always on the lookout for wealthy or influential . . . initiates."

"And by then the Huffmans were well established, had started their clinic here in New York, and were members of East Coast society. With Natural Order having a dubious reputation, they don't advertise their membership. Oliver Huffman's rep, however, is one of intolerance."

"You can see that on his face," Roarke murmured.

"Yeah, you can, can't you? He's a strict hard-liner who's been known to pass on certain patients who don't meet his criteria. He's brilliant, supposedly, at what he does, but he won't treat the mixed race — which cuts out a hell of a lot of patients. That goes for gay and trans, for a female who lists an abortion in her medical records, and so on.

"Oh, and he's deleted his son from his official ID."

"I'd say the son is better off."

"Yeah, me, too."

Studying the board as she did, Roarke reached over to rub his hand over hers. "We had problematic childhoods, you and I, so we recognize others with that same broken foundation."

"Some build their own, and some don't." Eve shrugged. "The mother only works at Mercy three days a week. She cut back ten years ago. A little more digging there? Paula lends her services two days a week, and half a day on Saturday, to the exclusive Eternal Flame clinic, which is — surprise! — owned and operated by Natural Order. Oliver also 'volunteers' there."

Roarke frowned. "I don't know this clinic."

"Small, exclusive — as in members only — and in Westport."

"So in Connecticut."

"Where Wilkey has his headquarters."

"That I do know about. The compound's largely self-reliant. Its own schools, medical facilities, greenhouses and gardens."

"And housing — including Wilkey's main residence. More digging? Several Eternal Flame clinics globally, in wealthy suburbs. It's a moneymaker, all of this. All legit, at least on the surface. So you wonder, in an organization like this, what's under that surface. And what the careful Huffmans would do to protect that, to protect their reputations, their natural order."

"As in dispose of the lover of their daughter who might expose the affair shortly before the wedding to the son of a respected family."

138

"Yeah that. Especially if they had some hope to rope some of that money and influence into their organization. It's a thought. Because somebody sure as hell killed her."

"And conveniently for Gwen Huffman." Roarke shifted his study from father to daughter. "If she hadn't gone back the next morning, if she hadn't reported it, started spinning lies, you wouldn't have connected her. Or not easily. Not with her DNA and prints off record."

"Even without, I'm going to trace the wine and flowers." Eve pushed up, paced. "Yeah, we'd have tracked those back to her eventually. But does the killer know she habitually bought those? Or knowing, think we'd look there?"

"Which means you don't think she's the killer."

"She didn't use the hammer — but that doesn't mean she isn't the hammer. She's not just connected, she's the reason.

"Pattern." She walked back to the table, sat. Then just pushed up again. "She's in trouble, so she contacts her fiancé. He comes running this morning, and he comes to her again after she's arrested. Somebody always takes care of things."

"But then he doesn't."

"Right. She can try lying to him about the affair, but it won't hold. He's a lawyer, her lawyer, and he sees the evidence. So he gets her through the bail hearing, then that's it. We're done. Wedding's off."

"So no clear-cut way to cover now. And bail isn't vindication."

He rose as well, walked to her board. He often wondered if he saw what she did. "If she goes to her parents, will they cover for her, believe whatever lies she spins? Or will they discard her?"

"She needs somebody to fix it." Eve paused to stand beside him. "So she tries Shelby. Summer friendship, summer love, nostalgia, rosy glasses."

"Rose-colored."

"Okay, fine. And a cop — isn't that handy? It's so perfect. She'll lean on that prior connection, weep, beg, play the victim, and warm it up with a little sex."

"And Shelby doesn't cooperate. What now?"

"She's got to come up with a new plan," Eve said. "But go back. Her secret lover doesn't want to be a secret. She wants more than sex when it's convenient for Gwen. Argue, fight, say hard things. Pattern."

"Someone needs to fix it for her," Roarke finished.

"Everything's on the line for her, right? She doesn't attack Ariel, not physically, but she's got connections. Connections that should be more than willing to fix her problem. Maybe we can find a communication on her mangled 'link. Maybe."

As she shook her head, Eve hissed out a breath. "Still. She didn't expect to find Ariel dead in the morning. Now that I have a better handle on her, I don't think she'd have gone back if she knew. It's more: Fix it for me, talk her out of it, threaten her, pay her off. All those make sense. And in her shallow way, she doesn't think the fix is to take out the threat."

"That fits pattern, and it's logical. Except —"

"Yeah, yeah." She turned away, realizing sometimes his ability to think like a cop irritated. "Why hasn't she rolled on whoever she contacted? Save her own skin, make a deal."

She turned back again, scowled at the board. "But that might be next. Or she might fear the fixer more than the fix she's in."

"Who does she fear? Her parents."

"Yeah, yeah." It didn't work, it didn't play, Eve admitted. "But her parents — certainly her father — are the ones she doesn't want to know she's banging it with another woman. I can't see her telling Daddy. Somebody else she's got on the string?"

Slipping her hands in her pockets, Eve shifted. "Sex is a kind of power center for her. Another lover, or former lover. Somebody she can play victim to, or try to bribe.

"Somebody," she muttered, "I don't have on the board yet. But I will."

"I have no doubt, but it won't be tonight. You're spinning, Lieutenant. Time to let it sit and brew a bit."

"I'm leaning toward someone connected, like she is, to Natural Order. And someone close enough geographically to meet Gwen, take the key, get downtown. Somebody, most likely, with personal transportation, because it's a pretty narrow window."

She paced another minute. "And somebody who'd kill without hesitation. Walk into the apartment, go up to the studio, pick up the hammer. *Bam.* No attempt at persuasion, bribery, threats. Just end it."

She turned back to Roarke. "That's not spinning, that's logic."

"It is, yes. But as you don't have candidates for that position, as yet, and won't likely get any until you squeeze Gwen a bit more, or EDD comes through, you'll be back to spinning."

"I can do a search for members of Natural Order who live within the geographic range, then filter to ones most likely to know my prime suspect."

"You can, and should. Why don't I set that up for you?"

He walked to her command center, sat, and began what would — she knew — take her three times as long.

"Of course," he continued as he worked, "it may be someone outside this range who happened to be inside it for a variety of reasons. Dinner, a meeting, work, or any number of engagements or activities."

He glanced up at her frown. "Which you've already considered."

"I have to start somewhere. I can't filter it by gender, even if it's a sexual connection. I don't know if she's bi. No condoms at her place, but her male partners may bring their own. She sure as hell doesn't want to get pregnant before the I dos. No oral birth control at her apartment, but she may opt, and probably does, for longer-term internal."

She gave Merit Caine's photo a study. "I think I'm going to have to ask the ex-fiancé a couple of very personal questions."

"Wouldn't be the first time." Job done, he rose. "And I suspect he'd be in the mood to cooperate. Now, you'll have your candidates in the morning, with a secondary list of any arrested for a violent crime."

"Money's a weapon, too. It could be somebody who needs it. She says get this woman off my back and I'll pay you."

"And, of course, I'm happy to pry into the financial business of any you select."

He took her hand to draw her out of the room. "Tomorrow. You've some debt of your own to pay off."

"I could work this another hour, then pay up."

"Let it brew."

Because she knew he had it right, she didn't argue. It needed to sit until she could look at it with fresh eyes, could think about it with a rested brain.

"The connection to Shelby, that was a lucky break. You can't count on luck, but you use it when it falls in your lap. I think I'll pay a visit to the rejected bride in the morning, too."

"If she has any sense at all, she'll have a new lawyer by morning."

"Maybe, maybe not. She's the type who thinks she's so irresistible she could lure the fiancé back with enough pretty tears."

"I believe that would take more than tears, however pretty."

"I'd say add sex, but I'm not sure about that."

"I am," he said as he tugged her into the bedroom.

"You're always sure about sex. Maybe I'm too tired."

"Want a wager on that?" He scooped her off her feet. "I'm feeling lucky."

He carried her to the big bed and, careful to miss the cat already stretched over it, dumped her. Before Galahad finished muttering and leaping off, Roarke dropped down on Eve, body to body.

Eve twined some of his hair around her finger. "Maybe I'm not in the mood."

"We'll up the wager. Double or nothing."

"What's double?"

He closed his teeth over her jaw, worked slowly around. "I have you twice." And his hand slid stealthily, skillfully between her legs.

"That's cheating."

"I call it improving the odds." He flipped open the button of her trousers.

"I don't make sucker bets." Reaching up, she unbuttoned his shirt. "And I pay my debts." Still, she ran her hand down his side. "How are the ribs?"

"They're fine enough."

No heat there, she confirmed. "They took a pounding."

"Cobbe took a harder one."

"True." Now she stroked a hand on his cheek. "And it was pretty sexy, all in all, watching you kick a contract killer's ass. In fact . . ."

Lightning fast, she scissored her legs, made her move, and reversed their positions. Then she scooted up to straddle him. "Now that you're all healed up, I don't have to be gentle with you and hold back."

He lifted an eyebrow. "You've been holding back?"

"You tell me." Bending down, she took his mouth with hers in a deep, aggressive kiss.

"Maybe you have, a bit." He started undoing her vest. "Considerate of you."

"Oh, you know me. I'm made of considerate."

More than you think, he mused, then did the same with her shirt. "Due to my very minor injuries," he began.

"You were a bruised, bloody, aching mess."

"Comparatively minor injuries. I may have held back, just a bit, myself."

"Is that so?"

He dragged her down, then rolled her over. "You tell me."

His mouth ravished hers, and his hands got very busy.

She felt the weapon harness she'd forgotten she was wearing unhook before he dragged her up to pull off her vest, her shirt. All the while spiking a fever in her blood with his mouth.

And quickly naked to the waist, she wrapped around him.

"Maybe a little."

But not tonight, he thought as he began to work his way, hands and lips, teeth and tongue, down her body. She arched for him, moaned for him when he tugged her trousers down, when he found her center.

And she erupted for him.

Now, all heated skin, both of them half-dressed, she dragged him up to fight with his belt. His breath as unsteady as hers, he closed his mouth over her breast — small, firm, her heart drumming under his lips.

She wanted the rush, the power and thrill, the crazed friction, the frantic movement of him inside her. Joined and locked and mated.

She freed him, guided him to her. Then dug her fingers into his hips as they rode each other, fast and hard. Need, all need, drowning her senses, clouding her mind.

When that need peaked, it tore through her like a gale. All she could do was hold on until he met his own.

She closed her eyes, and her body sighed under the good, solid weight of him.

"Yeah, maybe just a little," she murmured.

On a breathless laugh, he lowered his head to the curve of her shoulder. "On both sides."

"We still have a lot of clothes on — mostly on."

"And still, somehow, managed." He turned his head to press his lips to the side of her throat.

"We should probably take off the rest."

"We should."

But they stayed as they were another moment, another two.

"It was kind of sexy."

He lifted his head. "Kind of?"

"I mean when you were pummeling Cobbe into the ground. I revisited that today. I had to deal with all the paperwork."

"Ah." He kissed her again. "The downside."

"Definitely, but done, which is handy, since, you know, murder."

"You could take on an aide again, to help with that sort of thing. Shelby, for instance."

"No, Shelby's where she needs to be. And I don't want an aide. I took on Peabody because . . ."

"You put her where she needed to be."

"Yeah. It's going to work, you know. The five-point-whatever of them in that big, crazy house."

"It will, yes, and very well." He rolled away, sat up to take off his shoes.

She did the same with her boots. "You'll help them with the fixing it up and all that? I know Peabody will put her crafty-girl hat on, and probably knit a sofa or something, but the big stuff. You like that kind of thing. You're good at it."

"I will, of course."

"Good."

Still naked to the waist, she took her weapon and harness to the dresser, emptied her pockets. "Did you know Trina offers a cop discount in her salon?"

"Does she?" He turned down the bed. "That's good of her, and clever as well."

As she undressed, her mind began to turn again. "I need to check where Gwen gets that stuff done. She might have an ex or current there, or somebody she could talk into eliminating her problem. She does some work for her family's foundation — which I need to look at more closely. Maybe somebody there . . ."

Knowing her, knowing she'd start circling again, Roarke took her hand, drew her over to the bed. "You'll have a busy day tomorrow."

"Yeah. I have to check out what's in the safe deposit box. Need a warrant for that. I want to hit Merit Caine first thing, then the box, then — when I know what's in it — back to Gwen."

She got into bed, started lining up her day and the potential timing. "I can split the names from the search with Peabody. Or pull in one of the other teams if there's too many. And I want to go over all this with Mira. Then . . ."

He rolled on top of her.

"No way, pal."

"Double or nothing," he said, and slid inside her.

"I didn't take the bet."

"It was implied."

Slowly now, he moved inside her. Long, slow strokes that stirred the soul seconds before they stirred the body.

"I know this is cheating." But already soft, subtle, seduced, she moved with him.

He touched his lips to hers, then went deeper until the kiss spun out and spun out for both of them.

He murmured Irish in her ear. Some words she knew, some she didn't, and all were as seductive as those long, lazy strokes.

She all but felt her bones melt even as the drugging pleasure spread, as it quickened, as it gathered, and released.

When she finally curled against him, body limp, mind empty, she slept.

"There now, *a ghrá*." He touched his lips to her hair. "Rest that busy brain."

He closed his eyes and slept with her.

CHAPTER
NINE

When she woke, alone, Eve stared up at the fading stars through the sky window over the bed. She lived in a house, she thought, with three males — including the cat — who insisted the day began before dawn.

With Roarke undoubtedly in his office wheeling some deal with somebody on the other side of the planet, and the cat surely gobbling down breakfast served by Summerset, she considered giving sleep another shot.

But since her brain had already started to wake enough to think about work, she gave that up. She rolled out of bed, hit the bedroom AC for coffee, then gulped down its precious, life-giving properties on the way to the shower.

There, under the hot pulsing spray of multiple jets, she went over her day's crowded — and hopefully productive — agenda.

First up, check the search results. Since EDD would have Gwen's electronics, she'd have them do a cross-match with the contacts.

It wouldn't hurt to ask the desk manager at House Royale if any of those names were on Gwen's approved guest list.

She stepped out of the shower, into the drying tube. As the warm air swirled she closed her eyes and refined her moves.

It was still shy of sunrise when she walked into her closet. Sighed.

Roarke wasn't there to pick over her choices, and she had to admit that the picking over sometimes made it easier.

She went with brown pants that made her think of chocolate, and that made her think of checking on her hidden stash in her office at Central.

And made her think, unkindly, of the elusive Candy Thief. She grabbed a white shirt — always safe, in her opinion — then a navy jacket because it had brown buttons, but mostly because it was leather, and she was weak.

She started to grab brown boots, but saw the navy ones with the chocolate laces.

"Damn it."

She took the navy.

By the time she dressed, the sun had started to sneak in the windows.

Since neither Roarke nor the cat had made an appearance, she headed to her office.

She heard Roarke's voice — that don't-fuck-with-me business mogul's voice — so poked a head through the doorway.

"Hold," he said, and paused the transmission. He smiled at her, easy as sunrise. "You're up early, and looking quite put together."

"I want to look through the search results. Don't want to interrupt, just wanted you to know I was out here. I'm curious though. Has whoever's on the other end of this pissed themselves yet?"

"Possibly." His smile turned to a cold, feral grin.

"Well, when you're done scaring the piss out of whoever, I'm in here."

She started to go straight to her command center, then stopped and recalculated.

If she ordered up breakfast before he did, there would be no possibility of oatmeal or of something sneaky like spinach hiding in an omelet.

"Pancakes," she murmured, and made it happen before she got to work.

The over ten thousand members stunned her. But then Roarke had, correctly, she thought, included all the boroughs, and the near reaches of New Jersey and Connecticut.

And, being Roarke, he'd ordered secondary searches.

Just New York, just Manhattan, which cut those numbers to just under six thousand, and just over two, respectively.

Too many, she admitted — and as a cop she shouldn't have been surprised to find so many bigoted nutballs.

His search criteria for members in that geographic area with violent records dropped the number down to just over three thousand for the whole thing, and seven hundred and change for Manhattan.

She considered, drummed her fingers.

"Computer, continue search adding the following filters. First, search for violent crimes against persons

— exclude animals and property. Second, search multiple counts, all violent crimes. Third, multiple counts against persons only."

Acknowledged. Working . . .

She sat back with her coffee.

She started to swivel to study her board, and Galahad leaped on her counter. Stared, stared deeply, with those bicolored eyes.

"I know you've already eaten, so that won't work."

He stepped down into her lap. "No more food for you, tubby."

But she scratched his head as the comp announced completion of the first search.

"Display. Okay, better."

By the time Roarke came out, she had the new searches complete.

"After whoever pissed him/her/themselves, did they offer to pay you to buy their planet?"

"Manufacturing complex, not a planet, and we'll say we came to terms. Breakfast in here, is it?"

Obviously amenable, he walked to the doors, opened them to the little terrace and the dawn of a May morning. He stood there, looking out, in his pale gray suit, dark blue tie, and shirt that somehow blended both colors.

Eve paused her work, gave Galahad another rub before dumping him. She went to Roarke, slipped her arms around him.

"Now, this is a lovely way to start the day."

"Better than scaring the piss out of people?"

"Even better than that." He tipped her face up, kissed her. "I thought you'd sleep longer."

"Me, too. But I woke up, started thinking, and that was that. Gives me a jump."

"Which you've made use of already." After running a hand down her hair, he turned to the table to pour them both coffee. "What did you find in the search?"

"That there are ten thousand — and change — people who are batshit crazy in the geographical area."

"Well now, I expect there are more than that, but I wouldn't say everyone who joined Natural Order is bat-shit. People seek tribes," he said as they sat. "Justifications for their own worldview. Others are deceived or naive or simply weak in some way. And you don't have to be crazy to be bigoted."

"I'll give you that one." She uncovered her pancakes with considerable pleasure and immediately drowned them in butter and syrup.

She dumped the mixed berries she'd ordered over that.

"Anyway, the numbers narrow some with the other filters, and narrow more with the ones I tried this morning. I'm looking at about six hundred names with multiple violent offenses in New York who are current members."

"Still a considerable number."

"I'm sending it all to Feeney. They can cross it with contacts on Gwen's comp and address books and all that. If we get any matches, it won't be hundreds."

"You've considered this murder is a first offense — or the killer has never been caught before."

"Yeah, but this is an angle with high probability, so we'll test it out. Plus, I'm hoping I can make her piss herself today and give me a name."

"If anyone can. And you're going to talk to Merit."

"First on the list."

As she shoveled in a bite of syrup-soaked pancake, she saw Roarke's gaze track over. She didn't have to turn around to know that cool, steady stare stopped Galahad's pancake advance.

"I'm having Peabody pick up the bank-box key from Evidence while I go by Caine's. Then she'll meet me at the bank. Once we see what Gwen's tucked away in it, we'll hit her."

"Why don't I go with you to Merit's? I do know him, and he might be more forthcoming with a friend — even a casual one."

"Don't you have other people to intimidate?"

"Scores." He topped off her coffee, then his own. "But I've time for this."

"It couldn't hurt. You'd be sympathetic."

"I am sympathetic."

"So am I, at this point. But he's still a lawyer, and lawyers tend to shut the doors on cops. So, yeah, it couldn't hurt to have you there. If we get anything from Caine, Gwen, the bank box, Peabody and I will follow it up. If not, I think it may be time to have a chat with Stanton Wilkey."

"Mind your six there, Lieutenant," he warned her. "While he seems to be one who knows how to stay above the fray, he's surrounded by —"

154

"Bat-shit crazies?" She smiled, very much as he had earlier. "I eat them for breakfast."

"No doubt drowning in syrup. Still, let me know if you're heading to Connecticut."

She shrugged. "It won't be until later. I've got a lot to cover this morning."

"At least you're fueled for it," he commented as she finished off the pancakes.

"I've just got to finish up one thing before we go."

He glanced at his wrist unit. "Very early."

"That's tactics."

"I'll tactically deal with the dishes then before the cat tries to reach his goal of licking the pool of syrup on your plate."

When they did head out, Eve let Roarke take the wheel while she consulted her 'link.

"Peabody's set to get the key, and McNab will get started on Gwen's 'link when they get to Central." She blew out a breath. "She's going to be full of that house today."

"It's a big step for all of them."

"Yeah, I know it. But she'll probably talk me into a brain bleed by the end of shift. I can be happy for her and not want my brain to bleed."

He gave her hand a bolstering pat. "I believe your brain's tougher than that."

"We're going to find out."

He drove across town, with traffic so light it seemed like the city slept after all. At this hour, dog walkers and joggers outnumbered vehicles.

Merit Caine's home had a pretty front courtyard already in lavish bloom. The three-story brownstone whispered elegance.

Eve took a good look at it from the sidewalk.

"She'd have lived here in a couple months. My first take is she'd go for something more modern, more sleek, but I can see this. It looks like old money, and old money says status and prestige."

She started up the short walkway. "Top-drawer security," she noted. "That's one of yours."

"It is, yes."

"Tough for thieves." She glanced at Roarke. "Except you."

"Former," he reminded her. "He's well secured his home."

Eve pressed the bell beside the double front doors.

Please state your name and the purpose of your visit, the computer demanded.

"Dallas, Lieutenant Eve, NYPSD." She held up her badge for scan. "Roarke, civilian consultant to NYPSD. Police business."

Your identification is verified. One moment please.

It took a few more than that, but Merit Caine opened the door.

Not fully dressed for the day, Eve observed. Suit pants, dress shirt, but no tie or jacket. But it told her he intended to go into work.

"Lieutenant. Roarke." He held out a hand to Roarke to shake. "It's good to see you, if unexpected."

"Can we come in, Mr. Caine?"

He looked back at Eve. Though shadowed with fatigue, his eyes stayed calm and direct. "If this is about Gwen, you should know I'm no longer her attorney."

"I'm aware."

"Yes, of course you are. Aware of all of it. Yes, come in."

He stepped back into a foyer with white marble floors and an enormous chandelier with serpentine silver coils stabbed through layers of glass balls. Then he gestured to the living area, which hit the grand and sleek and modern.

Twin curved sofas in pure white held fancy white pillows. Glass and silver tables held more crystal, ornate vases or bowls.

White marble framed a long, narrow fireplace, and above it only a high blank space.

"Gwen wanted our wedding portrait to hang there. That won't happen now."

"I'm sorry for your trouble, Merit," Roarke told him.

"Apparently, I've narrowly avoided much more trouble. Sit down, please. Can I offer you coffee?"

"We're fine," Eve said, "and we'll try not to keep you long."

He sat in a silver chair. "I understand a woman is dead, and finding who killed her is — must be — your priority. I understand, too, you verified my whereabouts during the time in question — as you should, and must. You need to ask, and I'll answer before you do. I had no knowledge of Gwen's affair. Maybe that makes me a fool, but I had no knowledge, no idea, no suspicion. I never heard the name of the victim before yesterday."

"She never mentioned Ariel Byrd to you?"

"No, not before yesterday. And I believed her claim that she'd gone to the victim's apartment yesterday morning for a sitting. Why wouldn't I?"

He looked down at his hands. "I'm also aware she lied to me when she claimed, after you arrested her, that Ms. Byrd attempted to assault her. The preponderance of evidence negates that claim."

"You're in a difficult situation, Mr. Caine," Eve began.

"Merit." He looked up again. "You know far too much about my personal life at this point for formalities."

"Merit. Faced with your knowledge that she lied to you, did she tell you the truth?"

"I can't tell you what she said to me while I was still her attorney of record. I can't do that."

Since she'd expected that, Eve followed up. "Since you're no longer representing Gwen Huffman, can you tell us your opinion on the character of your ex-fiancée?"

He sent her a weary look. "She's a talented liar, or I'm more gullible than I like to think."

"You loved her," Roarke said simply.

"I did. Or I loved the woman I thought she was, even with her flaws. I actually found her flaws endearing. She needs admiration, even devotion. She needs appearances."

He spread his hands to encompass the room. "This house, for instance. She agreed to it, though that took some persuasion, and I agreed to let her furnish and decorate it. I believe in compromise. I also believe in being faithful and keeping a promise. Finding out she was unfaithful, and repeatedly, left me with no choice but to sever our relationship.

"I'm angry," he admitted. "I'm angry and humiliated she betrayed my trust, and I have no doubt would have continued to do just that after we married."

"Did you know of her, and her family's, connection to Natural Order?"

He let out a short, bitter laugh. "I'm not at all sure now I knew the real truth on that, either. She told me she was raised in a very strict household, an unforgiving one. When her brother rebelled, he was cut off and kicked out. She loved her parents, she claimed, despite all, and only kept her — distant — association with Natural Order to avoid conflict with them. When we married, of course, things could change, but until then she had to meet those requirements. Demands."

"All of them?" Eve asked.

"We were never intimate — which makes me incredibly stupid. She feared they'd find out she'd broken one of the tenets, or she'd get pregnant. If I could only wait, be patient with her, she would make it all up to me on our wedding night. I accepted this, assumed she was inexperienced, and was careful with her. I was faithful to her."

"Did you ever meet any of the other members?"

159

He spread his hands. "I don't honestly know. I've certainly socialized with her parents, been in their home. I can't claim I liked them, particularly, but they were to be my in-laws, my family. So I and my family maintained a cordial relationship. I'm not sorry that's no longer necessary."

"How did she react when you broke the engagement?"

"Since I did that after I informed her I would no longer represent her, I can tell you she reacted strongly. She demanded I reconsider, reminded me of all the plans, the humiliation we'd both suffer. She begged me to say nothing of any of this to anyone, much less her parents. When she saw I was resolute — even immune to her tears — she threatened to tell everyone I'd been abusive. That I'd struck her, forced myself on her."

Hurt ran across his face as Merit shook his head. "I saw her so clearly then. I don't know if she realized how clearly I saw her in those moments when she raged at me, promised to ruin me."

"Did she get physical at that time?"

"No, no, she didn't. Despite everything, I don't believe she could kill." Pausing, he looked down at his hands. "Maybe I have to believe that, but I do believe it."

"Did her parents, or anyone you met when socializing with them, ever approach you about joining Natural Order?"

"It was suggested that I attend an orientation. I refused. Oliver — her father — was displeased, but only said he hoped I would be more open-minded and embracing in the future. A messenger delivered a package to our offices, containing informational pamphlets, data discs, and so forth. I threw them away."

"I appreciate your time, your candor."

"I hope you find who killed Ariel Byrd, and quickly. I'd like to put all of this behind me. This house." He looked around as they rose. "We were going to live in this house, start our lives together in this house. I guess I'll sell it."

"Merit." Roarke stepped to him. "It's a beautiful home. Don't put in on the market while you're still upset, don't sell it on impulse. Give yourself a bit of time to decide first."

"You sound like my family. They said just that. I learned just how much they'd support me — and found out my sister couldn't stand Gwen."

"The house looks like you."

He turned to Eve. "Really?"

"Outside," she qualified. "It's none of my business, but if you sell anything, sell all this . . ." She waved a hand. "Stuff. Because it doesn't look like you."

"Sell all this," he murmured. "I might just do that."

"Good luck to you, Merit," Roarke said, and offered his hand. "If you need a drink with a friend, let me know."

Outside, Eve stood by the car. "She's beautiful, she's young, she plays the victim really well. Yeah, I can see how he fell for that. And I'd bet he won't fall for that kind of bullshit again.

"So. Need a ride, pal?"

Roarke gestured to a dark, sleek sedan pulling up behind her DLE.

"Okay then. See you later."

Because he wanted it — and why the hell not? — he grabbed her in for a kiss. "Take care of my cop — and let me know if you go to Connecticut."

"I'll do both."

Since she had time before the bank opened, Eve didn't mind the thicker traffic. And since parking proved impossible, she pulled into a loading zone and flipped up her On Duty light. In the relative quiet of her parked vehicle, she wrote up her notes on the Merit Caine interview.

She'd seen it before, she mused, how people could fall in love with, or in thrall to, an image. And there were plenty out there, like Gwen Huffman, who knew how to project an image.

Merit struck her as too grounded to mourn the loss of that image for long.

But maybe someone else, in love or in thrall, had killed to protect that image.

She got out of the car to join the pedestrian traffic on the block walk to the bank. Nannies or at-home parents taking babies out for a stroll, walking older kids to school — or both. People in business attire heading for the office, already checking 'links. A maxibus disgorged others, primarily working stiffs who trudged the rest of the way to whatever job paid the rent.

Some breezed in and out of delis, coffee shops, bakeries. She smelled yeast and sugar and breakfast burritos.

And there was Peabody, pink coat and boots, a small file bag worn cross-body, improbable — to Eve — red streaks in her hair. She had a take-out coffee in one hand, and scrolled something on her PPC with the other.

Eve would've bet a month's pay it had something to do with home decor.

Since Peabody remained engrossed enough, Eve walked to her, looked at the screen. And mentally awarded herself an extra month's pay when she saw the image of a home office with walls the color of chili peppers.

"Peabody."

"What!" She jolted like she'd been stunned on full. "Oh, jeez!"

"I could've stabbed you in the heart, snagged that bag, your electronics, your damn service weapon, and strolled away before you hit the ground."

"I was just looking at ideas for our new home office. We're going to share one, since we work together a lot anyway, then I can have an actual craft room and —"

She broke off when Eve just pulled open the bank door and walked inside. She badged the security guard. "We need to see the manager, or whoever's in charge of safe deposit boxes."

"You're looking for Ms. Wasser." Her voice redolent with Queens, the guard pointed. "Past the desk there, first office on the right."

"Got it. Thanks."

They walked across white tiled floors, teller cages on the left, desks on the right, to an open office door where a woman with a tumble of gray hair worked at a fake wood desk on a very slick comp.

She glanced up with sharp and shrewd blue eyes.

"Something I can do for you?"

Eve held up her badge. "NYPSD. We have a safe deposit key, and the warrant authorizing us to open it and take the contents into evidence."

Wasser gave a grunting assent, a nod, and held out a hand. "Let's see the warrant."

Peabody opened her file bag, took it out.

Wasser nodded as she read it. "Box 44. Says here I'm obliged to tell you who opened the account, who's authorized to open the box."

"That's right."

"Sec." She swiveled back to her comp. "Data on box 44," she ordered, then added a code.

"Okay then, the box was acquired May 4, 2058, in the name of Gwendolyn Anne Huffman. Hers is the only authorizing signature. Ms. Huffman has no other accounts with our bank."

"Okay, good enough. How about we open it?"

"Sec," she said again. She rose, went to a locked cabinet. Once she'd entered a code, she pulled it open, selected a key from a slot.

She finger-waved them to follow her out. She clipped across the tiles in sensible shoes that went with her no-bullshit black suit. At another set of doors, she entered a code, then opened them.

Eve engaged her recorder.

Another finger wave to lead the way into a large room with walls lined with numbered metal drawers.

She clipped to 44, slid her key into the right-hand slot.

164

"Renter's slot on the left."

Eve took Peabody's mini-can of Seal-It for her hands, then took the key from the evidence bag.

When she slid it into its slot, Wasser gave another nod. "You'd know the drill, but you can use that table there. If you need a bag for the contents, we provide them at a small fee."

"Thanks."

Wasser stepped out, shut the door.

"Let's see what we've got, Peabody."

She pulled the drawer out, set it on the table.

"Cash. Get a count of that for the record." Eve set a handful of stacks aside. "Jewelry." She opened a small black leather box.

"That looks like an engagement ring," Peabody observed. "Heart-shaped diamond, gold setting with some little diamonds in it."

"It's not the one from Merit. She was wearing that in Interview, and it makes this look like a toy."

"It's sweet though."

Eve set it aside, opened a slim box. "Necklace, little heart of diamonds."

"To go with the ring."

"Right." Eve opened a third box, long and narrow. "And a bracelet, same sort of deal."

"They're not really her style. Too sweet and old-fashioned."

"And the diamonds aren't flashy enough." Another box. "Crystal heart on a stand, engraved. 'Gwen, you'll always hold my heart. Chad. 2/14/55.' College year."

"I wouldn't have pegged her as sentimental, but she kept all this from a college romance."

Eve actually snorted. "She doesn't have an ounce of sentiment in her. File folder — hard copies and discs. Ah, we have appraisals. One for a one-point-six-carat diamond ring, fourteen-karat yellow gold setting, with point-four diamond accents. Got all the particulars on the stones, for an appraisal of eight thousand, six hundred dollars — dated 6/5/55."

Peabody and her romantic heart sighed. "That's not sentimental."

"Neither is having the rest of it appraised — necklace, bracelet. Dated 1/8/56."

"I bet he gave them to her for Christmas."

"We've got the crystal heart, too, but that appraisal's dated 2/16/55. She didn't waste time. Chad spent better than twelve large on her."

"Why's she keeping them?"

"Rainy day insurance. We've got an appraisal on her current engagement ring — 8/8/60. Easy enough to check, but my money's on him sliding it on her finger late July or early August. And she hit the jackpot. Ten carats, square cut, platinum setting, nine hundred thousand and change."

"Holy shit. I hope he gets it back."

Eve let out a dismissive grunt. "You'll snowboard in hell before she gives it up, and he's too classy to make an issue of it. She's got other appraisals — minus the pieces — that coordinate with the time she's been with Merit. Chad's out twelve K. But Merit wins the prize at over two and a half million."

166

"Maybe she has them for insurance."

"College Chad and Lawyer Merit would have the documentation and carry the insurance," Eve corrected. "You wouldn't want your intended to know what you spent."

"You're right. It's just so tacky."

"More stuff not in here, but appraised. If she bought it herself, she'd use her home safe. Baxter said she had insurance stuff in there. We'll go through it. But here's a bronze sculpture of an angel, Art Deco style, blah blah, appraisal date 1/5/61."

"Ariel Byrd's work."

"Yeah, it has the artist's name. Another Christmas gift maybe. Six thousand. Angel, my ass."

"It's all monetary value to her. Tacky and cold."

"Yeah." And greedy, Eve thought. Grasping. "Another folder, legal docs. And here's a copy of the trust. She knew the terms, and man, she got close with Merit Caine. Discs — and this one's labeled Wills — Oliver Huffman, Paula Huffman. Interesting.

"Let's bag it up, Peabody. We'll check the discs on the way to House Royale."

"I loaded in evidence bags, but I should've brought a bigger file bag."

"We'll spring for one from the bank. Start bagging, labeling, and I'll get a damn sack."

They hauled it back to the car, secured everything but the discs in the trunk.

"Run the wills," Eve ordered, "look for the major terms and beneficiaries, while I check with — it's

Felicity," she remembered. "To make sure Gwen's there. Plus I want a list of approved guests."

"Got it. Damn, I left my coffee in the bank. Can I?"

"Go."

"Want?"

"Not now." Eve contacted the desk at House Royale.

"Good morning, front desk. This is Felicity. How can I assist you?"

"Lieutenant Dallas. Is Gwen Huffman in her apartment?"

"She has a DND on her unit, and hasn't left the building since I came on duty."

"Okay. I need a list of her approved guests."

"I can tell you that quite easily. Her parents, Oliver and Paula Huffman, and Merit Caine."

"That's it?"

"Yes, it is. Instructions are, any of those three may go right up, but the desk is to inform her of their arrival."

"My partner and I will be there shortly. I need you to clear us up without informing her. We have a warrant to enter that's still valid."

"Understood."

"Thanks."

Eve clicked off, looked at Peabody.

"They're really long and complicated. I don't get a lot of it, so we'll need legal on it, but I get the bottom line."

"I'll take that."

"The son's in here only to expressly disinherit him. Whoever kicks first leaves the rest — minus some specific bequests — to the other spouse. I think that's

168

kind of normal. When they both kick, and if she's met the terms of the trust, and that's all outlined, Gwen gets their house in New York, the house in the Hamptons, her mother's jewelry, some other specific stuff, and five hundred million. Any full Caucasian child she produces, in wedlock, gets fifty mil — in trust with her in charge. Natural Order gets the rest."

"It's a lot of rest."

"If she fails to meet the terms of the trust, she gets zip."

"You could say her cold comes from the natural order of things." Eve started the car. "Let's go heat her up."

CHAPTER
TEN

The doormen didn't bother to scowl this time. In the lobby, Felicity merely nodded in their direction as she signed for a delivery at the desk.

"I've got a prenup on this disc." Peabody continued to read as they got on the elevator. "I don't know much about them, but it looks like she gets to keep any gifts — jewelry, and so on — given to her by him before or during the marriage should they dissolve the engagement or marriage."

"She'll sell that million-dollar rock on her finger," Eve predicted. "Bet your ass on it."

"She gets half of any property purchased during the marriage," Peabody continued. "If they have children, he agrees to pay ten K a month, per child, in addition to all educational and medical expenses for each child until they reach the age of twenty-one or graduate from college, whichever is later. If she chooses professional parent status with said children, he agrees to pay her an additional five, per month, per child, until they reach that same marker."

"So brew up a kid, keep raking it in, in addition to raking in the trust. She sure couldn't afford for Ariel to have a snit and blab."

Eve walked down the hallway on the forty-eighth floor. "It's a hell of a lot of motive."

She pressed the buzzer.

Ms. Huffman has issued a Do Not Disturb. Please see the desk staff in the lobby.

Eve held up her badge. "Inform Ms. Huffman the cops are at the door, and the warrant to enter and search is still in effect. We will enter the premises, one way or the other."

One moment please.

Gwen wrenched open the door.

No virginal white and subdued makeup this time. She wore bold red lounging pajamas and no makeup at all to disguise swollen, red-rimmed eyes.

"Haven't you done enough?" She nearly screeched it. "You've ruined my life, broken my engagement, humiliated me."

"From where I'm standing you did that all by yourself. We can talk about all this out in the hall. I bet some of your neighbors would love it. Or you can step back and let us in."

"What do you want?" She whirled away from the door.

"Answers that don't include lies."

"Bitches, both of you. You think you're so important because they made some idiotic vid about you? You're

171

nothing. You'll be less than nothing when I'm finished with you."

Deliberately, Eve hooked her thumbs in her front pockets. "Well, now I'm terrified. How about you, Peabody?"

"I just can't stop shaking."

"I hate you!" Gwen grabbed a used wineglass off the table, reared back with it.

"You throw that, you're back in a cage for assaulting police officers. Record's on, Gwen. You might want to pull yourself together."

On a frustrated scream, Gwen threw it against the wall instead.

Eve surveyed the shards of glass, the splatter of the swallow or so of red wine that had been in the glass.

"Boy, that'll teach us."

"This is harassment. My new lawyer's going to sue you for harassment."

"Got one of those yet?"

"I've been too upset. I've lost the love of my life!"

"Oh, cut the crap. You didn't love Merit Caine any more than you love the guy who delivers pizza."

"You don't know my heart." Gwen slapped a dramatic hand against it.

"That's not going to work. It may be good practice for your parents, but it's not going to work with us. We've just come from your safe deposit box."

Drama hit shock, shock hit outrage. "How dare you!"

"Badge, cop, warrant. We dare a lot. Getting your engagement ring appraised — and the other baubles

172

Merit gave you? That indicates greedy calculation, not heart."

"That's for insurance purposes."

"No. You have your insurance papers in your closet safe. And Merit has the appraisal, is carrying the insurance on what he gave you. Cut the crap," Eve said again. "I bet Chad never knew you were adding up the value of his heart. Or hearts, since he gave you several."

"I don't know what you're talking about."

"We should just take her in, Dallas. She's lying to cops again. The judge is going to revoke her bail, so —"

"No!" This time Gwen slapped both hands on her heart, and meant it. "I'm not going back to that horrible place. I can't."

The tears looked real this time, too, as she dropped down on the sofa, covered her face with her hands. "Oh God, oh God, what am I going to do?"

"You could try telling the truth." Eve nodded at Peabody. They each took a chair. "We might be able to help you if you do."

"You don't understand. You don't understand what it's like for me."

"I understand you're a gay woman whose parents condemn that orientation, and because of that, you had many millions of dollars riding on your marriage to Merit Caine."

"They wanted me to marry another member of the order — they had candidates."

"Names."

She looked up again with eyes drenched, swollen and red. No more pretty crying.

"I don't know — I swear it. As soon as my father brought it up I told him I was in love with Merit. We'd barely started seeing each other, but I had to do something. If I married someone from the order, it would never end. Merit hit all the qualifications, except that one thing — and my father believed he could recruit him, in time. That would be a coup."

She pressed her fingers to her eyes. "So I went after Merit, and so what? I gave him everything he wanted except for sex, and I was prepared to give him that, after marriage. My mother explained sex to me as a wife's duty. She must never, never deny her lawful husband sex. Not in the mood? Well, take a quick whiff of this, and you'll relax and feel agreeable."

"You're saying your mother gave you illegals. Whore? Rabbit?"

With the heels of her hands, Gwen rubbed her red-rimmed eyes. "Whore, I think, diluted. I don't know what with. My mother came up with the . . . formula or whatever it is. She promised it was perfectly safe, and she used it herself. What does it matter? He wouldn't know the difference."

"And once you were married, you'd get pregnant as soon as possible."

Now those red-rimmed eyes fired with defiance. "Damn right. I'd meet the terms of the trust, get my money. I deserve that money. And after a while, there could be a divorce. Merit would never join the order, I knew that. And my father would come to dislike and distrust him, so I could divorce him. I could claim he'd been unfaithful. I had time to work all that out."

"More money, from the terms of the prenup."

"I'd have earned it." Unashamed, she snapped it out. "I could move away, far enough away. I'd have to be careful, until they died I'd have to be careful. But then I'd have my life — all of it. I need money to have my life."

Eve nodded. "Time plan: get married, have a kid, get a divorce — with him to blame. Put a little distance between yourself and your parents. But there's still all that money — well over a billion with the houses you'd inherit. Why wait, when you could arrange another tragedy?"

"What tragedy?" When it hit, her eyes widened. "Oh my God, I wouldn't kill my own parents! I despise them, okay? I despise them, their ridiculous rules, their ridiculous order, but my God. If I could do something like that, I'd have done it after they sent me to Realignment."

"What's Realignment?"

Gwen held up her hands. "I need a drink. I don't care what fucking time it is."

She got up, left the room. At Eve's signal, Peabody followed her.

"I'm getting some goddamn wine, for God's sake." With Peabody, Gwen came back holding a half-empty bottle and a fresh glass.

She poured wine nearly to the rim, drank deep.

"It's one of the order's big secrets. On the island, they have a medical center, and in the medical center, they have the Realignment section. Only for blood relatives of members at a certain level or beyond. I think. That's what I think. Mostly for kids, young adults. Gay kids. They sent me there after they found out about Jan."

Bitterness hardened her eyes, her voice. "If I could kill anyone, it would be whoever told them."

"What do they do in Realignment?"

"Evaluate you, physically, whether you want them to or not."

She took a long, deep drink. The drama, the hysteria faded. Flat, bitter tones replaced it.

"They take your clothes, everything, and you wear a uniform. It says 'Deviant' on the back in big red letters. You wear a collar, like a dog. I've been told they have a section there for those who get involved — romantically — with someone of another race, or mixed race, but they keep them separate."

She lifted her shoulders, let them fall. "I don't know what they put on the back of their uniforms. You have a small room, only a cot, a toilet, a sink. And there are cameras, so you know they're watching you. They play lectures on homosexuality, the evils of it, all day, all night."

She closed her eyes, leaned her head back. "You're not allowed to speak to anyone but your counselor. That's what your jailer's called. You eat in your cell — what they bring you, when they bring it. If you leave anything on the plate, no food the next day. You shower daily in the presence of your counselor. No privacy. If you complain, object, fight back? They push this button they carry, and the collar . . ."

176

She closed her eyes, and the hand holding the wineglass shook. "It's like being set on fire from the inside.

"I learned, fast, to keep my mouth shut." She sat up, drank more wine. "They show vids that would be laughable if they weren't so awful and demeaning. You have daily counseling and prayer, evaluations, menial labor. And if it doesn't take in ten days, there's shock therapy."

She smiled, thin and hard, as she toasted with her glass. "I escaped that by seeing the error of my deviant ways in five."

Fury didn't cover what Eve felt, but she kept her voice even. "You understand all of that is illegal?"

"No, really?" On a laugh, Gwen lifted her glass. "Good luck with that. They've got cops and judges and congresspeople, more money than God."

"I'm sorry this happened to you," Peabody murmured.

Gwen met sympathy with a sneer of contempt. "Screw your pity. I know how to deal with it. I was dealing with it. I had a plan and it worked. Until the two of you ruined it. And me."

"Ariel was going to ruin it," Eve reminded her.

"No, she wouldn't have." Gwen gulped more wine. "Yes, she got pissed, yes, she threatened to tell Merit, but it wasn't the first time we'd argued about it. Maybe she was more angry this time, and it got a lot more heated. So I knew I had to end it — the relationship," she qualified. "But I knew how to get around her, and I would have. That's why I went back in the morning. I

177

knew how to play her, and if she got pissy, well, she didn't have any proof. She'd never been to my place, we never went out. I paid cash for everything when I went downtown."

"Her calendar."

"I didn't know about that. I should have," Gwen admitted. "She was a romantic. That was part of her appeal to me."

"Text messages," Eve added.

"She always left her 'link in the kitchen or turned off in the bedroom drawer. She didn't like it interrupting her in bed or in the studio. If she got pissy, I'd get her 'link, get rid of it. No problem. But when I saw her like that, I didn't think, not at first. Not about the 'link or the stupid wineglasses or the sheets or anything. I just knew I had to get out, and I had to start to protect myself.

"I didn't kill her. She was crazy about me. You can always work somebody when they're crazy about you."

"You got rid of your 'link, her key card — your copy."

"I knew damn well I shouldn't have the card — too intimate. And yeah, the messages on my 'link."

Eve started to tell her they'd recovered the 'link, but Gwen frowned into the distance. "I was going to get a new one anyway, I'd been meaning to. It started echoing."

"Echoing?"

"Yeah, when somebody called, left a v-mail or voice text, their voice would echo some, and annoy me.

People said my voice echoed, too. So I was going to get a new one anyway."

"Who has access to your 'link?"

"What do you mean? It's my 'link."

"Who could get to it?"

"I don't know. People." She gestured impatiently with the wineglass. "At a party or a club, or who knows? It's just a 'link, so I'm not paranoid about it."

"When did it start echoing?"

"A couple of months ago, I guess. I didn't really notice. I don't make that many actual calls, just texts. I ditched it, so who cares?"

"We recovered it."

"What? How?"

"Search warrant."

"You — you had people in here, going through my things?" Outrage pushed Gwen to her feet again. "You have no right!"

"Search warrant," Eve said mildly. "Warrant gives us the right. And we recovered your 'link from your kitchen recycler."

"Fine then. Good. Then you'll see I didn't contact anybody after I left Ariel."

"Gwen." Eve waited until she poured more wine. "Did you tell anyone about Ariel, at any time?"

"Jesus, no." Visibly exhausted, Gwen dropped down to sit again. "Look, I liked her, I really did, but she wasn't the one and only. I've had other relationships, and I'm careful. I have to be."

"I want names."

"Oh, for fuck's sake."

"Do you want these charges to go away?"

Slowly, Gwen lowered her glass. "You can do that?"

"If you tell us the truth, if I can clear this up, satisfy myself you weren't involved in Ariel's murder, I can have the current charges dropped."

"My parents wouldn't have to know?"

"If I'm satisfied you're truthful — and you don't hide relevant information — I'd do whatever I can to maintain your privacy."

"How far back do you want me to go?"

"To the first."

"I'm probably not going to remember everybody. I'm being truthful! I might not remember last names, or somebody I had a one-nighter with."

"Start with who you can — but first, tell me about Chad."

"Chadwick Billingsly." She closed her eyes again, smiled. Not dreamily, not fondly. Smugly. "College. I needed my parents to believe I had a solid boyfriend, a good family, one who respected my vow to stay pure until marriage. He fit. Then he asks me to marry him, and I have to say yes, and then I have to string that along awhile until I can find a way to break it off.

"I set him up, put some sleeping pills in his beer, and I paid an LC who'd lost her license to get into bed with him and take pictures. Throw those up on the Internet, and I've got a tearful breakup.

"'Daddy.'" She let those slow tears roll. "'I loved him! He promised we'd wait until we were married. And he cheated on me, cheated on me with a prostitute! Oh, Daddy, I just want to die. I can't go

180

back to college, please, please, I can't face it. Please let me stay home.'"

She shrugged. "Two birds. I hated college."

"You're a piece of work."

Gwen shrugged again. "I do what I have to do."

"Start with the first," Eve told her, "and give me as many names as you can."

After they left, in the elevator, Eve gave Peabody a moment of silence. She could almost hear her partner wrestle with her thoughts and feelings.

"You want to feel sorry for her," Eve began, "because she's a victim of horrible and ugly child abuse. And worse."

"I do feel sorry for her about that, and it's not just the Free-Ager thing, it's the cop thing, the human-being thing."

"Because what happened to her, what her parents did to her at sixteen was horrible and ugly, illegal and immoral. And she had no choice, not at sixteen. Two years later, she did, and from then until now, her choice has been to lie, to cheat, to use others, then betray them, and all for money she didn't earn. For money she'll rake in simply because she was born, and lived a life of lies and greed and betrayal."

"When you put it like that."

"It is like that," Eve said as they walked across the lobby. "It's exactly like that. Our problem here is that doesn't make her a murderer. She doesn't want your compassion."

"Yeah, I got that."

181

"She also doesn't want to accept blame or responsibility for anything." They stepped outside, crossed the sidewalk to the car. "She despises her parents, and she's got plenty of cause, but she panders to them, is willing to ruin lives and reputations — because that's what she'd have done to Merit Caine — and she'd have done everything she could to have a kid — a kid who'd be just another step to the money for her — to get what she wants."

Behind the wheel, Eve glanced in the mirror, gauged the traffic, then zipped out to join it. "What she wants is a whole shitload of money, plenty of status, admiration, and the freedom to screw people over with impunity."

"All true. And still."

"She was sixteen. Now she's not, and she's screwing people over — Ariel Byrd and Merit Caine are just the last of the line. So far. Our advantage there is she'd screw over anybody who threatens her end game, and that includes whoever killed Ariel. So, clearly, she doesn't know."

"That's an advantage?"

"Because now we know — can be reasonably certain — that well's dry. But we recovered the 'link."

"The echo. Maybe just a glitch, but maybe a tracker, a recording device."

"Maybe a tracker with a recorder. Text McNab to look for it. Somebody hears the argument," Eve speculated, "the threat, and takes Ariel out so she can't follow through. That means somebody close enough to Gwen to get to her 'link, and the key card — to copy it.

And that individual had to be in reasonably close proximity to the crime scene when Gwen left that night."

"I have a feeling we're going to spend a lot of time cross-checking names."

"I've got the list of Natural Order's members in Manhattan — live and/or work. I whittled that to any with violent offenses, and with multiples. We'll start with the shortest list, then expand as needed."

"Maybe her parents know more about her than she thinks they do — or one of them does — and tapped her 'link to keep a closer watch. Killed Ariel to cover her."

"Not impossible, but unlikely. They cut off their son without a second thought. Why would she be different? They're true believers, right? Jesus, what mother gives her daughter a derivative of Whore?"

"A sick fuck of one," Peabody decided.

"That, and a fanatic."

Peabody glanced at her 'link. "McNab's on it. Okay, maybe we track it to another member, also a victim of Natural Order who kept tabs on her. Somebody, maybe, who was in that Realignment bullshit when she was."

"Possibly. Or someone connected to someone who went through that. There has to be a closer current connection. Sure, somebody could lay hands on her 'link if she's as careless with it as she claims. But why?"

Eve punched through a light. "If Gwen gets outed, her parents cut her off financially. That's highest probable outcome in that scenario. Would all that shit-ton of money go to Natural Order on their deaths?"

"If it does, that would be a reason to expose her, not cover — for a true believer anyway."

"Or make sure she's exposed — and charged with murder. Should've followed up as an anonymous informant on that. Unless they didn't know her prints and DNA weren't on file."

"Or know her so well they were sure she'd go back and find the body?"

"Or intended to follow up — after making sure they, themselves, were covered. And she saved them the trouble."

"Natural Order gets all the pie."

"A lot of ifs here, a lot of maybes," Eve considered. "And another. Maybe the Huffmans have another relative or close personal friend, even a long-term employee, who stands to rake in a pile if the daughter's disinherited. Yeah, the cult gets the bulk, but it's that shitton of money. Both kids out, both Huffmans healthy, you've got more time to ingratiate yourself and get more."

"That's an interesting maybe. The Huffmans are only in their sixties. That leaves decades to work on increasing a share of the shitton."

"Or flip it back one more time," Eve suggested as she threaded through a yellow light just before the pedestrian crosswalk charge. "Daughter exposed and disinherited, big, juicy pie for the cult. Somebody who's killed once can do it again. The Huffmans have a tragic

184

accident, a shocking murder-suicide, whatever. Then you don't wait for the money to roll in."

"If we push at that one, it could go all the way to the top."

"Stanton Wilkey. We'll need to have a conversation with him. See if you can find out where he is. I need a conversation with Mira. She may have some insight that'll condense some of the ifs and maybes. And I want one with Billingsly," she decided. "College Chad may remember somebody she palled around with. And he deserves to know he was set up, even if I can't give him all the details."

She pulled into the garage at Central.

"Let's get started on the cross-checks," she decided. "And see if Feeney can spare Callendar or any geek to take some of the list. I'll see if Mira can squeeze me in."

Peabody continued to work her PPC as they got into the elevator. "Wilkey's heading and hosting a ten-day retreat — that's for members in good standing — at his HQ in Connecticut. So he should be there. They're only on day four."

"Good. We'll work some of the ifs and maybes, then pay him a visit."

Eve pulled out her own PPC. "I'm sending you the search results. I'll take the first twenty, you take the next twenty. See if EDD can split the rest. If not, we'll keep going."

When she switched to the glides, Peabody trotted with her.

"Any matches," Eve continued, "they're flagged for interview. Set up a broad-based search for any stories on Wilkey — you're good at that. I'll do a deep run, but we'll see what's in the gossip and society areas."

And, Eve thought, she'd contact Nadine Furst. If the hotshot reporter didn't have some details on Wilkey, she'd dig them up. And fast.

As she swung into Homicide, Jenkinson called out, "Yo, LT."

Instinctively, she glanced toward him, then slapped her hand over her eyes. "Jesus Christ!"

The tie, from knot to tail, showcased a bug-eyed, pee-yellow-beaked, wildly pink flamingo.

"Can't blame me for this one. My wife gave it to me."

"You've infected her."

"Anyways, Mira's in your office."

"Good. I need medical attention."

She turned, blinked her abused eyes clear, then walked to her office.

Mira stood by Eve's desk with a memo cube in her hand.

She wore pink, thankfully not flamingo pink, but a pale, sort of dreamy hue. The suit looked soft and springy, the heels — tiny checkerboards of pink and cream — looked painfully uncomfortable.

The cream-colored purse looked big enough to hold a potted plant.

Mira smiled, replaced the cube in her bag.

"I was just leaving you a memo. I've been reading your reports and notes. I find the case fascinating, and hoped to catch you in. Do you have a few minutes now?"

"I was going to contact your office, see if you could fit me in for a consult this morning."

"This is perfect then. I had some outside appointments, and my first in-house needed to reschedule. I've got a block free right now."

"Take the desk chair."

Since Mira knew the discomfort of the single visitor's chair, she didn't argue. She set her bag aside, sat, crossed her excellent legs.

"Let me fill you in on this morning. You want tea?"

"That would be lovely."

Eve programmed the flowery tea Mira liked, and black coffee for herself.

As Eve ran through the interviews, Mira sipped her tea. Occasionally she glanced at the board with those soft blue eyes.

"I've met Merit Caine's parents." Mira brushed back a wave of her rich brown hair, currently sun-shot courtesy of Trina. "Friends of friends, that sort of thing. I know they're both enormously proud of their children. I haven't had any contact with the Huffmans, but from your reports, and what you've told me here, I agree with your conclusion. True believers.

"They're medical professionals, educated scientists, but have chosen to discard science in favor of a fanatical, systemic bigotry. So much so they would subject their own teenage daughter to what is nothing less than torture. This, and being raised on those tenets, forced to hide or deny her own sexual identity, certainly helped mold her into what she is today."

"What is she today?"

"A malignant narcissist with sociopathic tendencies. A sexual predator — not a violent one, but an opportunistic one. She doesn't form or forge genuine relationships, she manipulates those who can further her needs and ambitions. They don't matter to her beyond that use. She doesn't love, isn't capable."

"Could she kill?" Eve asked, and Mira smiled, sipped her tea.

"Oh yes, absolutely."

CHAPTER
ELEVEN

Eve rose from where she'd eased a hip on the corner of her desk. "Could she have killed Ariel Byrd?"

"She's more capable of murder than most," Mira began. "On impulse, in the moment, in temper. Physical violence wouldn't be her initial impulse or choice. It's messy — and she would worry about being hurt herself. But in an instant or moment of rage, or fear of exposure, yes, she could."

Eve thought of the moment with the empty glass. Gwen, ready to throw it at her face. But one word of warning, possible repercussions, and she'd thrown it against the wall.

"However," Mira went on, "she calculates. She's had to, all of her life. Would she have killed, then left evidence of her presence behind? Highly, very highly, doubtful."

"Yeah, well, I circled around to that same conclusion. If she'd followed the victim upstairs, killed her in that moment of rage, she'd have started thinking. And covering. She'd have taken the vic's 'link, the sheets, the glasses. Wiped the place down. Or contacted somebody she could pay to do it."

"Agreed. She could have, as you speculated before, contacted someone to solve this problem for her — pay Byrd off, threaten her, or, yes, eliminate her. That would have to have been someone she had power over."

"Her parents are Natural Order hierarchy."

"Yes." Coolly, Mira studied the board. "And she would absolutely be capable of using that lever. She has no friends, would trust no one without having power over them."

"McNab's working on her damaged 'link. But she claimed to be glad we had it because we'd see she hadn't contacted anyone."

"Possibly another lie — they're instinct for her. But just as possibly true. Her returning the next morning fits her profile. She would manipulate her lover — whom she would soon discard — and if her lover still resisted, she'd simply steal the 'link, which she believed was the only way to expose their affair.

"She's a liar by nature, but this is truth: She's desperate for you to keep this information from her parents."

Studying the board, Eve nodded. "I believe that, no question. She gave us all the information this morning without tagging a lawyer. She can't afford to hire another lawyer, to have someone else see the evidence."

"Yes. She believed she had power over Merit Caine, and learned it only went so far. She can't put her fate into another's hands. I will say that if she'd succeeded with Merit Caine, met the terms of the trust — or manages to do so with someone else — she might consider finding a way to eliminate her parents. She's

190

capable of that sort of calculation. The money from the trust wouldn't be enough for her after she claimed it. Nothing will ever be enough."

Mira sighed into her tea. "Some of this is simply her nature, but that's been enhanced, refined by the need to pay them back, those parents, for what they put her through. And their money is a tangible way to punish them."

"It's going to come out — who she is. She's deluding herself right now that her parents won't find out, and I'm using that. She'll never get what she wants."

"No, she won't. Her promiscuity will ruin her, and her promiscuity is yet another way she's striking back at her parents. Without intensive therapy she'll never be happy or fulfilled. Regardless, I believe whatever part she played in Ariel Byrd's death was innocent — so far as innocence goes."

"Because someone has power over her, and she's not aware of it." Eve only nodded as she thought the same. "Her 'link echo."

"I leave that to those who know more about tech and electronics than I, but it's a sound theory. Natural Order has power over her, as she must remain in good standing with them, through her parents, to reach her goals. Wilkey is another malignant narcissist, and one with a messiah complex. A charismatic bigot who draws in his followers with words of harmony, peace, personal success, and contentment if they adhere to his vision of what is natural, what is order. And reject what he sees as unnatural and chaos. And often bastardizes scripture to his own ends."

Mira set her empty cup aside. "He turns a blind eye and occasionally disavows any in his membership who commit violence. That, as is what he preaches, is — I like that word you often use — bollocks. Complete bollocks."

"I'm going to try to have a conversation with him today."

Mira took a moment to consider. "He will, if you manage to have that conversation, be respectful. He's a careful man. But he will not respect your authority. In fact, it will offend him. You're a woman, therefore less by nature and biology and the grand plan. He may speak with you out of curiosity."

"You know a lot about him."

"I considered doing my dissertation on cults, with Natural Order highlighted. I decided on serial killers. I'll add that if you're right about the technology on Gwen Huffman's 'link, whoever tracked or watched her already knew her secret, and has a reason to continue to keep it. Or killed to gain even more power over her."

"Either way, it goes back to money."

"Greed and power. Classic motives." As she spoke, Mira ran the thin gold chain around her neck through her fingers.

"Though your killer is a planner, he's disorganized. He watched and waited, but then struck in an impulsive and risky manner. Evidence indicates he sealed up before entering, but if he brought a weapon, why not use it?"

"The music was on, sure, and if he had a recorder on Gwen's 'link, he heard Ariel say she was going to work.

He heard Gwen leave. But," Eve added, "that's no guarantee she'd be in the studio. She could've come down after Gwen left. Or she could've been facing the stairs instead of away, seen him come in, picked up a weapon of her own."

"Exactly so. Smarter, by far, to watch and wait near the building until the lights go out. Wait until he could be reasonably sure the victim had gone back to bed. Strike then."

"Smarter still to make it look like a break-in."

Pacing, Eve put herself into the killer's place.

"You've got the key, you've used it before — how could you resist? — so you know the locks are crap. Grab some art, some tools, mess the place up. Unless you want fingers pointing at Gwen, and if that's the thing, why didn't you place an anonymous call and implicate her?"

"Disorganized, impulsive." Mira rose. "I have to get to my office. I'd like to know your impressions if you do speak with Wilkey."

"I'll copy you on my report. I appreciate the time."

"I hope it helped. I admit, I'm more fascinated than ever."

Alone, Eve started the cross-match, adding Mira's insights to her notes as it ran.

Then she contacted Chad Billingsly.

He looked exactly like his ID shot — not always the case. Young, attractive, stylishly rumpled dark blond hair, wide-set brown eyes.

He also looked baffled when she identified herself and asked about Gwen Huffman.

"Ah, yeah, we were engaged, briefly, a few years ago. A lifetime ago." He tried a hesitant smile. "What, did she kill somebody?"

"Why would you ask?"

"Lieutenant Eve Dallas. I read the book, saw the vid."

"Ms. Huffman is, at this time, a material witness in an ongoing investigation. Your name came up in connection with her."

"Really. Weird. I haven't seen Gwen in years. Four, I guess. Maybe five. I've closed that door, you know?"

"If you could open it again, tell me the names of any of her particular friends, or enemies during the time you knew her."

"Man." He shoved his fingers through his hair. "She didn't really have what we called Trip Bs — Best Bosom Buds. I guess she was pretty popular, but it was mostly surface when you look back on it. I mean, she was beautiful and stylish and pretty much had unlimited funds, so she's going to get invited to parties and all that. But she didn't belong to any clubs or groups, hang with anybody all that much."

"Except you?"

"Yeah, well." He smiled a little, and dimples popped into his cheeks. "For a while."

"During the course of my investigation your engagement to Ms. Huffman and the circumstances of its termination came up."

"Well, shit. You never close the door hard enough. Look, Lieutenant, that was a long time ago."

194

"Understood. It would be helpful if you could give me your whereabouts on Monday evening, from nine to midnight."

His eyes widened in alarm. "Is Gwen okay? Did somebody try to hurt her?"

"She's fine, Mr. Billingsly. I'm just checking off boxes. Routine."

"Okay, Jesus. I can tell you where I was Monday. I was working on my final project for the term. Grad school, engineering. Six of us have a group house, and we're all humping it this last couple weeks. We ordered pizza from Lorenzo's — I don't remember when it got there. But four of us were at home all night. Two of us came in from the science lab about nine, I think, and scarfed up whatever was left.

"My girl and I — we share a room in the house — knocked off about one, one-thirty, and went to bed. I can give you the names."

"I'll let you know if that becomes necessary. Mr. Billingsly, I feel you deserve to know that the circumstances of your breakup with Ms. Huffman were false."

"A setup." His right shoulder jerked in a careless shrug. "I know."

"You know?"

"Yeah." He pressed his fingers to his eyes, then scrubbed his face with his hand. "This is like waking the dead or something. I never cheated on her. I never used an LC. I loved her. When you love somebody, you're faithful. It was the worst time in my life. I knew I hadn't done it, but it was right there, all over the fucking Internet. She wouldn't even talk to me, and ran home.

My friends believed me, and my family, but there were plenty . . . I'm like barely twenty, heart busted, life over."

He shook it off, literally. "Anyway, my uncle — well, great-uncle — he's a cop."

"Is that so?"

"Yeah, my mom's uncle Stu. And he believed me, and did some cop stuff and tracked down the LC. She told him Gwen paid her two thousand dollars to come into my dorm room, get naked, do the recording. How I'd be zonked out, how it was just a prank."

"Must've pissed you off."

"Yeah, it pissed me off, but more it just cut." He blew out a long breath. "Man, it cut."

"Your uncle must have told you that you could have charged Gwen on several counts."

"Yeah, and he wanted me to. But I wanted it over. It didn't just piss me off, cut me, but I had to ask myself what kind of person does that? Nobody I want to be with. I loved her, and I thought she loved me. If she didn't, and didn't want to get married, she could've said that. It would've cut, sure, but it wouldn't have humiliated me and screwed with my head.

"Anyway, I got through it, and graduated, took a gap year to get some work experience. Now it's grad school, and I met Holly. Gwen's yesterday. But she taught me a lesson."

"What lesson's that?"

He smiled again, and the dimples popped back. "It's engineering, man. Something might look bright and shiny on the outside, but the structure's what counts."

196

A good lesson, Eve thought, and added the conversation to her murder book.

She scanned her search results. Two matches in her initial twenty. She'd run those names, and remove the violent offenses from the filter.

Impulsive, Mira said. And maybe a first act of violence.

While that ran, she contacted a valuable source.

Nadine Furst came onto her screen. Her normally sharp green eyes looked teary.

"Jesus, what?" Eve demanded.

"I've just finished a tour of Mavis and Leonardo's — and Peabody and McNab's — house. Mavis is in there now with an architect, an engineer. They're starting demo tomorrow."

"Already?"

"They're Roarke's guys, already had the plans, expedited permits. She's so stupidly happy, she's dancing one minute, crying the next. It got me. It really got me."

She dabbed at her eyes. "As it happens I was about to come your way."

"Why?"

"Why'd you tag me?"

"Natural Order. What do you know?"

"I might know some of this, some of that." Now those cat's eyes turned sharp. "Was the artist who was murdered a member?"

"No."

"The killer then."

"If I knew the identity of the killer, I'd be making an arrest instead of talking to you."

"Digging then. I'd be happy to have a little tete-a-tete with some tit for tat included."

"You've already got tits, and I don't have a tat."

"Then we'll quid some quo," Nadine said breezily. "Why don't you meet me in that sweet little park between Central and Mavis's new place? That's a nice little walk for both of us."

"You said you were coming here, now you want me to meet you in the park?"

"Neutral ground, Dallas. And since I'm going to be in the studio all afternoon, I'd like to soak up a little spring. See you there."

She clicked off before Eve could argue.

Annoyed, but reminding herself what Nadine didn't know she could usually find out, she left the search running. Since, knowing Nadine, she already had the tat for the tit, or the quo for the quid, she went to Peabody in the bullpen.

"I'm going out to meet Nadine, see what she knows or can find out about Natural Order. I'll fill you in on that, on the Mira consult, and on my conversation with Billingsly when I get back. Keep running the cross-matches."

"Where are you meeting her?"

"That dinky little park a couple blocks from the new house."

"Oh, that's such a sweet one, pretty green space and the playground. McNab and I can walk right by it on the way to work once the house is finished. Mavis buzzed me that demo's starting tomorrow. I can't believe it. We're going to —"

"Run the matches," Eve finished, firmly. "Full run on any. I'll be back."

She escaped from what she knew would be a daily spewing of bubbly and, rejecting the elevator, took the glides all the way down.

It gave her time to think, but what she wanted more was information. Information she could then sift through at her desk, with a cup of coffee.

She hadn't considered Chad Billingsly as a viable suspect, but now she crossed him off the bottom of her list. And he'd given her a little more, a confirmation of what she'd already concluded for herself.

Gwen didn't make friends. She selected tools.

And in the case of Billingsly, Gwen had — finally — told the truth.

On the main floor, she took one of the side exits out of the busy lobby and hit the busy sidewalk.

Apparently, everyone in New York wanted to soak up some spring. She saw business types with jackets hooked over their shoulders by a finger or draped over an arm. Tourists gawking. Shoppers hauling bags to the next place they could buy something else.

The corner glide-cart did a brisk business selling water, soft drinks, dogs, and pretzels. The smoke pumping off the cart smelled of meat and onions. Concrete planters — too cumbersome to steal — burst with flowers.

Vehicles streaming by had their windows open to the air so the sound of traffic, of horns and curses, mixed with music — from trash rock to opera.

A woman in tiny red shorts, two white bags over her arm, glittery framed sunglasses obscuring half her face, minced along on red-and-white-striped ankle boots. She had to mince, Eve figured, as the boots had tall needles for heels.

She, very casually, held the leash of a black-and-white dog as big as a pony.

She minced right into a deli with the dog, in violation of several health laws.

Eve kept walking.

She saw a woman dressed like the Statue of Liberty hyping some joint called Lady Liberty, a guy with a moustache that drooped a good three inches below his chin passing out flyers for a fortune-teller. She spotted a woman sunbathing on a fire escape in a bikini barely big enough to avoid the indecent exposure laws.

And the several people who paused to take pictures or vids as she, well, soaked up some spring.

New York had it all.

The little park did have some green space with some short flowers running along its borders. Beside it, twice as much space held the playground with its spongy checkerboard of primary colors covering the ground.

Kids sent up a din as they swung on swings, climbed on climbing things, slid down sliding things, tunneled through tunnel things.

Parents, grandparents, nannies watched indulgently.

Strollers, carriage things lined up like cars in a lot. Some still held the bags and backpacks she assumed carried kid and baby paraphernalia.

Nadine had already claimed a short bench and sat in her off-air jeans, a blousy white shirt, and white kicks.

200

Her sunshades neither glittered nor obscured half her face.

Eve sat next to her. "It sounds like a war."

"I was just sitting here wondering how the adults know if the scream is a happy one or an I-just-broke-my-arm one. God, I love those boots!"

"They got me here. What do you know about Natural Order?"

"You might be interested to know that when I was just starting out at Seventy-Five, I planned to do an expose on them."

"Planned to?"

"It didn't work out. But I did many man-hours of research, conducted interviews. I even dug up the names of three former members. It cost me fifteen hundred dollars, and got me next to nothing, as none of them — not one — would talk to me. Even off the record. I signed up for an introductory seminar, which cost me two-fifty — and that didn't include the two grand I spent on fake ID and background to get through their security."

Nadine tipped down her sunshades. "That's out of pocket for a young, struggling reporter who wasn't on expense account. I got through the first session, the break — refreshments and chitchat — before they broke through the fake ID and booted me."

"You're better now, richer now, and have an expense account."

Nadine beamed a cheerful smile. "All true, but you'd better believe they know me. I wouldn't get through the door now. I've invited Wilkey, and his three sons, his daughter, to come on *Now* — or to give me an interview.

"Denied. They only talk to, we'll say, sympathetic reporters and/or plant positive stories through their very extensive and efficient PR. And they're exceedingly well funded."

"What did the young struggling reporter find out?"

Nadine reached in her humongous shoulder bag, took out a small tube of water, offered Eve a second.

"I gave you a solid hint of the quid. Let's have a little quo."

"Red light on the info until I clear it."

"Understood, as always."

"The victim was having an affair with Gwendolyn Huffman."

"Wait, the Gwen Huffman who's engaged to Merit Caine, about to have the wedding of the season?"

"Was engaged, was having."

"Well, interesting. That's going to leak to the society and gossip channels asap. Seventy-Five gave her a full fifteen-minute segment just last week."

"You can leak the breakup, but not the reason, and not her connection to my victim."

Nadine crossed her ankles, studied her own kicks. "That's going to leak, too."

"Sure it will, but I need to keep it plugged as long as I can. It gets out, she loses any motivation to cooperate. Now I've got her where I need her."

"Is she a suspect?"

"No, but connected. That's enough quo. Give me more quid."

202

Nadine sipped some water. "Stanton Wilkey, born in Kansas — a small, struggling farm — had three siblings. Complications during the birth of his younger sister — and the choice of no doctor, no midwife, home birth — killed the mother. Besides the three live births, she'd had at least three miscarriages. The father remarried about six months later."

"Wow, so much grief."

"Eve's curse — not you," Nadine said with a laugh at Eve's baffled frown. "The Adam and Eve one."

"She always gets the pointy end of the stick."

"Ain't that the truth. Anyway, I was able to convince the mother's sister to talk to me when I was working on the expose. She despises Jethro Wilkey — Stanton's father. That's what she claimed he called it — Eve's curse. Women are meant to bear children, birth them in pain and blood. His second wife was eighteen to his thirty-nine. Just eighteen. They married on her birthday, as her parents refused parental consent. She had two children before she ran off with them. Apparently women are also meant to do what they're told when they're told or get a good belt in the mouth."

"Did she file charges?"

"Too afraid, according to the aunt — who knows the second wife's family. Fortunately for her, Wilkey the first didn't have the money to go after her, or the two daughters she'd had with him. Word was, according to my source, he claimed the second wife had tainted blood anyway. Her great-grandmother was Native American. He married a third time — without benefit of a legal divorce — but that wife and the baby she carried died in childbirth."

Nadine scooted around so she and Eve sat face-to-face.

"Stanton Wilkey and his siblings were raised by this man. He was a white supremacist, a misogynist, and a religious fanatic. His version of religion. He was also a raging alcoholic, an abuser who refused to send his children to what he considered government facilities — schools, hospitals. He homeschooled them with his twisted vision of history, science, and so on. They never saw a doctor, had inoculations, screenings, dental care."

"Okay, yeah, I know the type."

"He died from a diseased liver when Wilkey was sixteen. His sister, fourteen, had clearly been sexually abused. Child Services placed her and Wilkey with the aunt — the two older sons were eighteen and twenty, so legal age. Stanton Wilkey took off, but the aunt was able to get the sister into therapy. She eventually became a therapist herself, has never married, lives quietly. She wouldn't talk to me, and I didn't push there."

Nadine gestured with the tube. "Your turn."

"One second."

Eve spotted the thief — early twenties — in his running shoes, with his battered brown shopping bag as he loitered around the strollers. He'd casually unzipped one of the backpacks when he saw her coming.

He ran. She ran faster.

She grabbed his arm, blocked his punch, then kicked his legs out from under him.

"What the hell, lady!"

"Lieutenant." She held him down, a knee to his chest, and flashed her badge.

"I didn't do anything. I'm just walking here."

"Why did you run?"

"I wanted some exercise."

She noted the shopping bag was empty, which meant he'd already passed on his latest haul, or was just starting the day's work.

"You're sloppy. If I run you, I'm going to find priors, maybe a parole violation. You're going to get a break because I'm busy, and since you're sloppy, the next cop that busts you won't be so busy. But listen, and listen real careful."

She leaned down, shoved her face into his.

"My friend brings her kid to this park. If I see you anywhere near this area again, I'm going to bust you for exposing yourself to minors."

"What!" His eyes popped wide to goggle. "I never did! I never would!"

"You're exposing them to a half-assed street thief right now. Get gone. Stay gone."

She stood. He ran. With a shake of her head, she picked up the shopping bag he'd left behind, then stuffed it in the nearest recycler before she went back to the bench.

"How did you make him?" Nadine wondered.

"He's loitering around a playground with no kid — not watching them, so I figure not a pervert. But watching the adults, and easing his way toward the bags the adults are brainless enough to leave unattended. So thief. Anyway."

She gave Nadine the basics on the murder, on Gwen's relationship with the victim, and the cover-up.

"She could have contacted somebody, had them do the murder." When Eve simply leveled a stare, Nadine sat back. "Which you've already looked into. Oliver and Paula Huffman — I don't know anything about them except they're doctors, rich, and were giving the bride away. They're members of Natural Order."

Nadine rolled that around. "They don't know their daughter's gay?"

"She was caught as a teenager with another girl."

"So they know. Listen, Dallas, there are rumors — or were when I tried to break into this — of conversion centers."

"Realignment centers they call them, according to Gwen. Her parents sent her to one, on the island Natural Order owns."

"That's criminal," Nadine murmured. "Except maybe it's not, in the legal sense, as Utopia Island has sovereign nation status, and its own laws. Listen, I've got to get to the station. I'll dig up my research, send it to you, and I'll dig in some more. I want this exclusive, Dallas. Wilkey's a lunatic. I didn't have the chops to expose this before. My chops are bigger and sharper now."

"You help expose all this, I'll give you an exclusive one-on-one."

"On *Now*. It's important, Dallas, and a full segment on *Now*, with my audience, it has reach."

"Done."

Before Eve could stand, Nadine put a hand on her arm. "Wait. I was coming to Central to give you this."

She reached in her bag again, pulled out a book. "Hot off the press."

"*The Red Horse Legacy*" Eve read. "Talk about lunatics."

"It's not out for another ten days, but you get the first copy. Who knows how many more they'd have killed if you hadn't rooted them out?"

Eve merely grunted. "Your name's bigger on this one than on *The Icove Agenda*"

Smiling, Nadine fluttered her lashes. "Is it? I didn't notice." She shouldered her bag and rose. "Ten days and it launches, and I start a very intense book tour. We're going to close your case, expose Wilkey and his sick order, and report it all on *Now* before I leave. We'll do that because we're the smart girls."

"That's order of priority." Eve got to her feet. "Close the case, expose Wilkey, blather about it on-screen."

"We wouldn't have had this conversation if you didn't know I understand the priorities."

"You got that right."

"And I got something else." Grinning, Nadine wiggled her shoulders. "I got my next book."

CHAPTER
TWELVE

As Eve walked back into Central, her communicator signaled with a message to report to Whitney. One glance toward the banks of elevators had her taking the glides.

When she reached the commander's office, she found his door open and his admin's desk empty.

He sat at his desk, broad-shouldered, wide-faced, his close-cropped black hair shot with gray.

He still had the eyes of a street cop, and she had reason to know he still carried those instincts. It made him, to her mind, well suited for command.

He read something on his desk screen while a glass of dank green liquid stood at his elbow.

Eve rapped her knuckles on the doorjamb.

Whitney glanced up, gestured her inside.

"Lieutenant, I've read your reports on the Ariel Byrd investigation. Any further progress since your morning interviews with Gwendolyn Huffman and Merit Caine?"

"I consulted with Dr. Mira."

Eve ran through the salient points while Whitney nodded, and while he scowled at the glass on his desk.

"Following that, I had a conversation with Nadine Furst."

He glanced up. "While Nadine's a reliable and ethical source, this investigation leans hard into sensitive areas."

"She'll hold the information I gave her, sir, and gave me more than I gave her."

"Such as?"

Again, he listened, this time sitting back as he took in the information.

Through the window behind him, Eve saw an ad blimp lumber over the city. Across its fat body flashed some hype for spring sales at the Sky Mall.

"And she's willing to turn over her notes and research on Natural Order?"

"I'd say the word is *eager*, Commander. She's got her teeth in it. She was less experienced, likely made some mistakes, and they booted her out. She hasn't forgotten that. Clearly, she wants another shot."

"She may have been lucky to have been considered a nuisance rather than a threat, and only got the boot." He gestured to her. "What have you got there?"

No way out of it, Eve thought. "It's her book, Commander. An early copy of her book on the Red Horse case."

When he crooked a finger, Eve stepped to the desk, handed it over.

"You vetted this, I assume."

"Yes, sir. It's accurate. Maybe dramatic in parts, but accurate."

He arched his eyebrows. "Infecting people with an airborne virus that causes hallucinations, making them murderous or suicidal qualifies as dramatic, I'd say."

He handed it back, picked up his glass. Set it down again.

"My wife went to a workshop."

Carefully, Eve said, "Yes, sir."

"On health, nutrition, longevity, mind-body connectivity."

Being an experienced investigator, Eve studied the green gunk. "I see."

"The workshop led to another workshop and classes, which have resulted in what you see here. Her recipe — more accurately her concoction — of raw fruits, vegetables, vitamin supplements, herbs, and Christ knows into ten ounces of questionable liquid to be consumed once daily — midday, apparently."

She felt sincere and sharp pity. "And you're supposed to drink that?"

"I'm on my second day of my first week's supply. To be dispensed by my admin, whom she ordered to make it so."

Anna Whitney, Eve thought, had a long and steely reach.

"I didn't see him at his desk."

"He's at lunch, undoubtedly something he can actually chew. However."

He lifted the glass, then angled his head. "I have more if you'd like to infuse your body, mind, and spirit with antioxidants and superfoods?"

"Thank you, sir, I'll pass."

"A lesser man would order you to drink so I don't suffer alone." Instead he took one heroic gulp. "Have a seat, Dallas."

She figured she understood the Whitneys' Marriage Rules included drinking gunk, but didn't have a clue why he hadn't dismissed her after her update.

She sat.

"As your investigation has connections to Natural Order, its membership, and Stanton Wilkey, I reached out to the FBI. They have investigated Natural Order — as has Homeland, Interpol, and others — for a number of years. The feds have successfully prosecuted individual members for violent crimes, though they have never successfully tied those acts to Wilkey or any of his family."

"A cabbage rots from the head."

It took him a minute. "A fish, a fish rots from the head. Cabbage is already a head. But yes, I agree. I've learned the FBI put an agent undercover into the membership. It took considerable time and resources. My information is the agent had begun to work his way up. Ten days ago, he went silent. He hasn't reported in, hasn't returned to the apartment used during his assignment or to the workplace used in his cover."

"He got made."

"That is the conclusion and the fear. This was an experienced agent whose cover was meticulously created. The assistant director, who spoke frankly with me, states this isn't the first operation to go south. Witnesses — former members — who spoke to law enforcement or the media often recant, are deemed unreliable due to illegals abuse or other issues. Or simply disappear.

"Your investigation offers a new angle," he continued. "A prominent family who appear mainstream now involved in a murder that, it turns out, appears motivated by the daughter's affair with another woman. It provides a new pressure point. Due to that, the FBI is willing to share their accumulated data on Natural Order in exchange for the NYPSD providing them with the data on the investigation."

Another quid pro quo, Eve thought. It seemed to be the day for them.

"I plan to attempt to interview Wilkey today, Commander. Straightforward," she added. "Routine due to the nine-one-one caller's connection to his group. I don't plan to include Gwen Huffman's affair with the victim, though that will leak. She's deluding herself that she can keep that locked up, as too many people already know."

"Will she testify, once it leaks, to the forced treatment she received on the island?"

"It depends on if she sees any personal advantage. And I hope to convince her of just that. I'll add protective custody to that if she agrees to testify, Commander. A safe house. She won't like it, but if she's afraid enough, she'll take it."

"See that she is afraid enough. And watch your six with Wilkey. He didn't get where he is by being easily led."

"Yes, sir."

"Keep me fully apprised. Dismissed."

When she rose, he picked up the glass again.

She heard his muttered "Sweet Christ, Anna" as she walked out of his office.

When she swung into Homicide, into the smell of cop coffee and overseasoned veggie hash, she said, "Peabody," and kept going.

Peabody, the remaining pocket of hash in one hand, a diet cherry fizzy in the other, hustled after her.

"Grabbing some lunch at my desk. You were longer than I figured."

"The commander wanted a briefing."

"I caught up with your consult with Mira from your notes."

"Good. Saves time." Eve dropped the book on her desk and hit the AutoChef for coffee.

"Oh, Nadine's book! It looks mag. And, you know, important. Look, she signed it to you. 'Dallas, My partner in crime. Nadine.' Oh, oh, and she dedicated it to us! All of us. She's got all our names here, everyone in the division, and Roarke, too. And Whitney, and everybody who was on that investigation. 'For their valor,' it says."

That drew Eve to the desk to read over Peabody's shoulder. "Okay, she gets points for that. Now close that, because she gave me more than a book."

She filled Peabody in.

"If Nadine has research, it's going to add. And she'll dig more now."

"Yeah, she will." Drinking coffee, Eve sat on the corner of her desk. "The fact they made her so fast means they do some heavy screening on potential members. Whitney had more."

While Peabody washed down the hash with fizzy, Eve outlined her briefing with Whitney.

"Jesus, Dallas, if they actually took out a federal agent . . ."

"They're hiding something big. The Realignment center's big, but if it's located inside a sovereign nation, the NYPSD can't do much about it. Interpol, maybe."

"Proof — not just speculation — but proof — it exists, that people — and minors — are forced to undergo all that? It's going to turn most people hard against them."

"Yeah, and a lot of those people would have deep pockets. Still, bigger than that, I think. Or if not bigger, just more."

"We've got a few possibles on the searches and matches," Peabody told her. "One match from Gwen's list to a woman who works as a potter in SoHo with a connection to Natural Order. Her brother was a member."

"Was?"

"Whereabouts unknown — for two years now. There's a guy, Tribeca, a member in good standing along with his wife. He's also employed by Natural Order as a VP in their Social Media Outreach department. Three assault charges, all in his twenties. He's thirty-five now, and no bumps for six years. He was a patient of Oliver Huffman. He has three children — ages five, three, two, all delivered by Paula Huffman. His wife has professional mother status."

"Okay. So they're all tight."

"The last is East Village, female, current member — member for eight years. She's a professional mother of four — one set of twins — married to another member, a microbiologist, for seven years. Gwen listed her as her first. She's twenty-eight, so a few years older than Gwen. One arrest right after she turned twenty-one. Aggravated assault, which she claimed was self-defense. Charges dropped — and a quick run on the public defender who got them dropped? A member of the order."

"Good work. We'll find more, but this is good work. Let's go talk to all three before we jump over to Connecticut to tackle Wilkey."

"He may not see us. We'd be out of our jurisdiction anyway. Should I let the locals know we're going to the HQ?"

"What are the odds Wilkey made sure he has at least one officer inside the local PSD?"

"Really good odds, now that you say it."

"He may not see us, but if we try to make an appointment to talk to him, or alert the locals, he'll know we're coming. Let's not give him too much time to prepare."

Eve paused in the bullpen. "Peabody and I are in the field, likely through the end of shift. Anybody needs anything —"

Reineke shot up his hand with a "Yo!"

Eve tried, really tried, to ignore his flamingo-pink socks as he swung his feet off his desk. "Just need you to sign off on this."

She scanned the paperwork he offered, scrawled her signature with her finger on the tablet. Then looked at him.

"Do you seriously coordinate your socks with the ties?"

"It's the little things, boss. It's the little things that add some ups to your day."

"Anything else, contact me. Peabody, let's go."

"It's kind of cute," Peabody commented as they hit the glides. "The socks and ties. I mean, sure, Jenkinson's ties are mongo bad, but so mongo they're kind of endearing."

"They make my eyes sting."

But since she'd just signed off on a case they'd closed, a very nasty slice and dice, she'd give them their ups.

"We'll take Tribeca first. Professional mother of three under the age of six is probably home."

"That would be Marcia Piper — spouse of Lawrence. Age twenty-eight. She was a model — very successful in advertising, billboards. They're both Caucasian."

"The women, especially, get married really young."

"Yeah, that's a pattern I'm seeing," Peabody agreed. "Early to mid-twenties. Another pattern is having a child inside the first year to year and a half. Then professional mother status or some sort of work connected to the group."

"Follows." Eve considered as they worked their way down. "Women are made to have and raise kids, serve their husbands as well as the order. The younger they are, the easier they are to indoctrinate — if they didn't grow up in a Natural Order family — and manipulate."

"Wow. I'm digging back — and she's just gorgeous. Being gorgeous and photogenic earned her six and a half to seven million a year the last couple years before she got married. Now, with her PM status and what her husband makes with New Order, they pull in less than a quarter of that. Not chump change, sure, but a lot to give up. Not just the money, but the career, you know?"

"Using your face and body to shill products? Probably not on the approved list for women." When they reached the garage, Eve gestured to Peabody's PPC, took a look at the woman she hoped to interview.

"Yeah, she's got the looks. It's probably not approved to model half-naked, either."

With sun-kissed red hair flowing to her waist, Marcia Piper wore nothing but strategically placed black straps as she posed — pouty lips, slumberous eyes, milk-white skin, and the slim, angular body models sold.

"Plug in the address," Eve told Peabody as they got into the car.

After she had, Peabody continued to read about Marcia's modeling career. "She traveled all over the world, and talked about moving into acting. Then bang, that's that."

Pondering it, she sat back. "I can see giving it all up if you just want to be a mom, or you burned out on all the travel and hype and all that. You fall in love, and everything changes for you. A lot of women choose that — men, too — and focus in on making a home, raising kids."

"But she fits the pattern. Meet the guy, join the order, get married, give up everything outside that."

"Yeah. I guess we'll find out which it is."

Peabody paused to glance at her signaling 'link.

"McNab. No texts, e- or v-mails, no calls or contacts on Gwen's 'link after her texts with Merit Caine."

"That's looking like a rabbit hole. What about a tracker? Did he find anything?"

"He did, and he's working on extracting it. The 'link's chewed up some, and he doesn't want to damage the tracker. He's working on it."

"Good enough," Eve decided, and drove to Tribeca.

The Pipers had a skinny post-Urban townhouse in a row of skinny post-Urban townhouses. Someone had tried to cheer theirs up by painting the door a bold blue and adding window boxes full of flowers to the windows that flanked it.

At the moment, Eve could see someone in one of those windows spraying something on the glass and vigorously rubbing it.

With only a handful of cars on the block, she found a spot easily and pulled to the curb.

Regularly spaced trees, tall and slim, ran along the sidewalk.

"Not what you'd call a pretty or bustling neighborhood," Peabody remarked. "But it's really clean and really quiet."

"Barely feels like New York."

Eve saw another woman scrubbing her front stoop as if she would shortly dine on it, and another with a kid

218

in a pack on her back carrying two bulging cloth bags into the house next-door to the Pipers'.

"What do you bet this whole block is members? It's uniform, cleaner than clean. Nobody's hanging out or strolling along on a really nice day."

Peabody looked around and hunched her shoulders. "That would be just creepy."

"Yeah, it would. I bet it is."

The woman in the window stopped, stared when Eve and Peabody walked toward the blue door.

Distress ran over her face. Not curiosity, not irritation, clear distress.

And, Eve thought, she looked like the tired ghost of the woman in the black straps.

She wore an oversize striped shirt over black workout pants. She'd hacked off what seemed like a yard of that red hair. What was left she'd dragged back in a tail.

The bones were still there, Eve noted, that foundation of beauty, but rather than luminous, the skin looked pallid; instead of bold, the eyes carried shadows.

Rather than knock, since Marcia clearly saw her, Eve just held up her badge.

She saw fear first, then Marcia rushed from the window. The door, after several locks disengaged, burst open.

"What is it? What's wrong? Did Larry have an accident?"

"No, Ms. Piper. I'm sure your husband's fine. We're here about another matter."

"What do you want?"

"We'd like to come in."

"Why? My children are upstairs napping. This is nap time, it's nap time. I have housework to finish before they wake up."

"We'll try not to take up too much of your time."

"I don't let strangers into the house."

"Ma'am, we're the police. You can contact Cop Central and verify that."

"I don't know you. I'm not letting you into the house when my children are sleeping."

"All right. Maybe one of your neighbors can answer some questions about you and your husband."

Fear shot back. "I don't want you talking about me and Larry with the neighbors."

"We'll talk to you, or talk to them."

"Five minutes. Just five minutes."

She struck Eve as nervy as a woman holding a hot wire. Jerky movements, anxious glances toward the stairs.

The living area was as shining, sparkling clean as the windows. Not a single toy in sight, not a trace of kid debris. The air smelled like an orange grove in full bloom.

And clearly, under the oversize shirt, Marcia was carrying number four.

Marcia gripped her cleaning solution. She didn't invite them to sit. "What do you want?"

"We'd like to ask you some questions about Natural Order."

"I don't have to talk to you about that. We have freedom of religion."

220

"No, you don't have to talk to us. Our information is you've been a member for about eight years. Prior to your marriage you had a modeling career."

"I repented that."

"Repented?"

"I don't have to talk to you about that. I have children. Children need and deserve a mother devoted to them, one who makes a home, keeps it clean and ordered and happy, makes them healthy meals, who helps to teach them the true way."

"The Natural Order way?"

"We're used to outsiders spreading lies. I want you to go. I have to finish my housework. I have dinner to prepare. I have children to tend to."

"One more question. You know the Huffmans? Drs. Oliver and Paula?"

"Dr. Paula Huffman is my obstetrician. She's helped me deliver healthy children into the world."

"Your husband knew Oliver Huffman prior to your marriage, as Oliver Huffman performed a minor surgical procedure on him."

"What of it? They're excellent doctors and good people. We're blessed to have them in our lives."

"Your husband was a member of Natural Order when you met."

Marcia's eyes darted toward the window she'd just cleaned as if expecting to see someone staring in.

"My husband showed me the way. My husband saved me from a life of debauchery and uselessness. He fulfilled me, and he provides for me and our children."

"You've got bruises on your arms, Marcia. Did he put them there?"

Her already pallid skin lost all color. "How dare you! Get out, get out of our house." With those same jerky moves, she marched to the door, flung it open. "If you don't leave, I'll tell my husband. He'll deal with you."

"Feel free to give him my name. Lieutenant Eve Dallas." Eve walked to the door. "Do you know where he was Monday night? From about nine to midnight."

"My husband was here, in his home, as he is every night. Go away!"

She slammed the door.

"She's not right," Peabody murmured as they walked back to the car. "She's on something."

"Yeah. A little chemical help to keep her going, and a lot of indoctrination to keep her firmly in the fold."

"She looks so tired. And she has to be about six months pregnant. She needs help, Dallas."

"We can't help people who don't want help." She got back in the car. "Larry stays on the list. A man who'd put marks on his pregnant wife shouldn't have too much trouble killing. Protecting the Huffmans maybe, removing a threat to Gwen so she could go right on and marry the proper type, and the type with plenty of money."

"Which they'd hope would eventually flow into New Order."

"Maybe not probable, but possible. Let's hit the East Village."

"Idina Frank, spouse Anson. She's twenty-eight. Prior to marriage, she was a teacher, elementary level.

222

Four kids, ages five, four, and two-year-old twins. The husband's forty, a genetic researcher employed by Natural Order. They're African-American."

As Eve drove, Peabody probed a little deeper.

"Jeez, Dallas, she was orphaned at the age of eleven when her father killed her mother, then himself. No relatives willing or able to take her, so she went into the foster system. No criminal other than the assault. The husband's got a bump for assault, too — four years ago. No time served. It looks like a pushy-shovy that got heated."

"Older husband, lots of kids, short amount of time. Same path. Let's see if she's as whacked-out as Marcia."

The neighborhood didn't resemble a zombie enclave. The street offered some shady trees — some litter, which made it feel normal. Duplexes, townhomes, a few restaurants taking advantage of the weather with offers of outdoor seating.

The Frank house fit right in with its old, faded red brick, white doors. It had a short green area inside a decorative gate with some flowers adding cheer and color.

A toy lawn mower sat by the stoop.

The stoop held a mat that read: WELCOME TO CHAOS.

"Four kids," Peabody commented. "Sounds right."

"Good security." And through the open windows Eve heard bright, chiming music and methodical banging.

She pressed the buzzer.

223

Rather than a computerized response, the door opened.

A woman with a glorious explosion of hair, wearing black sweatpants and a pink tee that read WOLF MAMA and carried a long yellowish stain down the center, stood with a big-eyed toddler on either hip.

She looked a little frazzled, and the big dark eyes she'd passed to the toddlers, tired. But she smiled.

"Adult human females. I'm sorry to say I don't have time to buy whatever you're selling. Try two houses down. My neighbor loves a bargain."

"We're the police, Ms. Frank." Eve held up her badge. "We'd like to come in and talk to you."

"Police." Idina gathered the kids closer. "Did something happen? Is there trouble in the neighborhood?"

"No, ma'am. We're investigating another matter. Your name came up as an acquaintance of Gwendolyn Huffman."

"I see." Idina's face went carefully blank. "I haven't seen or spoken with Gwen in years. I'm not sure how I can help you."

"If we could come in."

Idina stepped back.

The methodical banging came from a little girl on the floor of the living area banging a spoon on a pot to the beat — sort of — of the chiming music generated by a somewhat smaller boy who punched bright buttons on a cube.

A laundry basket sat on a table with most of the laundry in it folded. More toys scattered.

224

"Sasha, Harry, you mind the twins while Mommy talks to these ladies."

She set down the twins, who immediately made their toddling way to the scattered toys.

Idina walked through and into the big kitchen/lounge area, where she could keep her eye on her brood.

"I was just eighteen, working toward my college tuition in the fall, when I met Gwen. I had a job with a family as a kind of baby-slash-dog sitter. Take the kids and dog to the park, feed them, entertain them, tidy up after them, that sort of thing. And I went along with them for their two weeks at the beach."

"The Hamptons."

"Yes, that's right. I met Gwen. We were friendly. Then the two weeks were up, and I came back with the family. I haven't seen or spoken to her since."

"She states you were her first."

Idina took a quiet breath in, let a quiet breath out. "I suspect I was. She was also mine. Euphemisms are important here," she added, with a chin nod toward the kids.

"Understood. Who ended the friendship?"

"It just ended. We weren't serious friends, if you know what I mean. Experimental friends. I was in a sensitive time in my life where I had made the decision never to marry or have children. I assume you know why."

"Yes."

"Then this family, this job. The kids, the dog, the happiness. I was young and torn and I met Gwen. She was engaging, wanted a friend, so that happened. Then it ended, and I went to college and thought, for a while, I could satisfy my love of children by teaching them. Then I met Anson. I don't know what that brief, experimental friendship so long ago could have to do with the police now."

"Were you aware that Gwen and her family were, and are, members of Natural Order?"

"Not back then, no. Of course I know now, as Anson and I are members."

"And you've had no contact with her?"

"None. I'm pretty occupied, as you see. Becca, baby, we'll fold the rest later," she called out as one of the toddlers began pulling laundry from the basket. "Oh well. Is this about Natural Order, or Gwen, or what?"

"Gwen is a material witness in a homicide investigation."

"Oh my God. Jasper, share those blocks with your sister." Idina shoved a hand over her hair. "Someone's dead?"

"Yes. We're looking at any possible connection to Natural Order."

"Okay, okay, give me a minute. Juice tubes!" she called out with incredible cheer that caused a small stampede into the kitchen.

She snugged the toddlers into some sort of seats that attached to the counter, and the two older kids at a tiny red table. They hooted, shouted out preferences, banged while she got the tubes and little bowls of tiny crackers or cookies, or something kid friendly.

"That'll hold them for a few minutes." She moved out of the kitchen into the lounge while the kids

226

slurped, chattered, and made an unholy mess with the contents of the bowls.

"I have to be very careful here. I have four children to think of. My husband has his career as well as our family to think of. We've been planning how and when to ease out of the order. Anson had his reasons for joining, and he was my reason. But since the kids."

She glanced back at them.

"It doesn't reflect who we are now, our beliefs, our values. At the same time, the order puts food on our table, and they can be . . . proprietary."

"That's a word," Eve said.

"He's looking for another job, even if we have to move out of New York. We love this house, this neighborhood, but we'd move if that was best for our family."

"Have you had trouble, threats?"

"No, absolutely not. And I'd tell you. For them." She watched the kids toss tiny crackers at each other. "They're our world. And if one of them, if all of them fell in love with someone who doesn't look like us, or has the same gender, they'll still be our world. We can't be in the order and know that. Anson, he's a lab rat — a really good one. He'll find another job. And when the twins are old enough, I can go back to teaching. We'll be fine."

"Would your husband talk to us?"

"He would, if necessary. He's not inside the circle, if you understand. He does his job, he comes home to his family. We don't do a lot of socializing, not with other members. That's overlooked, as we have four children.

227

But Sasha will start school next fall, and she'll be expected to attend one approved by the order, and begin weekly instructions."

"What kind of instructions?"

"On the tenets of the order." Her chin firmed. "We're not going to allow that, not with our kids."

"Are you afraid, Ms. Frank?" Peabody asked her.

"Apprehensive. If Anson and I feared for our kids, we'd already be gone. We're not important enough to be afraid. Gwen would be, I think," she added.

"If you become afraid, or if you need help, if you think of anything that might aid our investigation, contact me." Eve drew out a card.

Idina studied it. "Was the person who died a member?"

"No."

"Is it terrible I'm relieved to hear that?"

"No," Eve said again. "Talk to your husband, and if he has any information that may help, any small detail, please contact me."

"We'll talk tonight, after the kids are in bed."

"You have a beautiful family, Ms. Frank," Peabody told her.

"They're a mess," she said cheerfully. "But they're my mess."

They let themselves out so Idina could deal with her mess.

"Can't see it." Peabody shook her head. "Can't see any pertinent connection there. She's so normal."

"People who join cults or do the weird often seem normal. But I agree. The thing with Gwen was a sad and needy teenage thing. Anson might have looked at her due to the order, and she might have looked at him as a kind of stable father figure. But that's not the whys now."

"I hope they get out without any trouble. That's a happy house." Peabody glanced back at it as she got in the car. "You can tell. Just like you could tell the one in Tribeca was anything but."

"We'll see what the potter in SoHo has to tell us."

CHAPTER
THIRTEEN

"Savannah Grimsley," Peabody read as they pushed through traffic. "She's twenty-six, a potter who works at the Village Scene — one of the places Ariel Byrd sold her art. She also works as an art model. Shares her loft with Vance Bloot — another artist. Roommates, not cohabs."

"The brother?"

"Keene Grimsley, age twenty-four — twenty-two at the time of his disappearance. He joined Natural Order at eighteen, while at college, dropped out of college at twenty to work for the order in IT. He's been missing since June 12, 2059. His sister filed the MP on June 15."

"Other family?"

"Parents, divorced. Mother, remarried, living in Jersey City; father, remarried, living in Delaware. Maternal grandparents, Sag Harbor; paternal, divorced, both living out of state."

"No connection to Natural Order with the other family?"

"None that shows."

As she drove, Eve rolled it around and around. "Tribeca, the Pipers — he's higher up, and she's shaky.

So they're planted on that strange block where wives are kept under control. The Franks, not so high up, have more space. I'm betting there are other quiet little enclaves where the equivalent of upper middle management get planted."

"I have to say again, creepy. Add that an IT guy — like the missing brother — works with data. You wouldn't have to be especially high up to find a way to access sensitive data, or data you're not supposed to have."

"Or having worked with said data, have a change of heart."

"Or that."

Spring in the Village brought out the street artists, and the tourists who occasionally shelled out enough for an artistic souvenir of New York.

Since the parking sucked, Eve considered a lot, then opted for a loading zone and her On Duty light.

Instead of trying the buzzer on the door between Café Vegan and a place called the Modern Witch, she mastered through, and walked with Peabody up the narrow stairs.

"Fun neighborhood." Peabody admired the chalk mural of flowers and vines running up the staircase walls.

"If you like tofu and witches."

"I like good witches, and tofu's not horrible if you know how to cook it. She's 2A."

And straight off the stairs to the left.

The same artist, Eve assumed, had painted figures of a man and a woman on the door. The woman at a potter's wheel, the man at an easel.

Music pumped against the door from the inside.

Eve buzzed. Buzzed again. On the third try, she distinctly heard someone yell, "Fuck!"

But the door opened a couple minutes later.

The woman who opened it said, "Fuck," again. Then added, "What the hell?"

Eve held up her badge. "Lieutenant Dallas, Detective Peabody. We'd like to talk to you about your brother."

Irritation leaped to hope. "You found Keene."

"No, I'm sorry. We're investigating another matter. We're looking for connections."

"Two years, two years of nothing. Goddamn it. Is this Natural Order crap?"

"We'd like to talk to you," Eve repeated.

"Screw it." She gestured them into a tiny living area. Tiny because a double art studio took the bulk. She had her potter's wheel, tools, worktable on one side. The other held easels, canvases, painter's tools.

She plopped down on a sofa.

She hit about five-three, Eve gauged, though the pink-streaked blond hair bundled and twisted on her head added another couple inches.

She wore a splattered apron, a sleeveless shirt, and shorts cut off at the knees with a pair of work boots as splattered as the apron.

She had long hazel eyes, a long thin nose, a wide mouth, and managed to look exotically bohemian.

She pulled a tube of water out of her apron pocket as she eyed them.

"Do I have to go through the whole thing again?"

232

"We're aware your brother went missing on June 12, 2059. Peabody."

"The report stated you had no reason to believe your brother would just take off, break contact with you. And in fact had spoken with you the night before his disappearance. And, as far as you could tell, none of his belongings had been taken from his apartment."

"Somebody'd been in there. I said that, too. Keene's messy, but he's messy in a certain way, and this was different. I can't be sure if anything was missing because he had a shitload of electronics — that was his thing. And there's no fucking way he'd have left all of it behind. There's no fucking way he wouldn't get in touch with me, especially with what we'd been talking about the last couple weeks."

"Which was?"

"Natural Order. I mean, Jesus, he finally woke up, he finally got his head on straight. He told me he found out some shit that really opened his eyes."

"What shit was that?"

"See, that's the thing." Savannah gestured with the tube. "He wouldn't tell me. I thought he was being paranoid, okay? He leaned that way, which is one of the reasons he got sucked into that freaking cult. He said he couldn't tell me, it was for my own safety. How he was going to put it all together and put it all online so they'd be exposed.

"He didn't trust the cops," she added. "He didn't trust the media, either, so he was going to take care of it himself."

Pausing, she rubbed the heel of her hand under her eye, and smeared some clay on her cheek.

Somehow it only added to the bohemian.

"Look, I thought he was just on one of his tears, but I was so glad he was getting out of that cult shit, I went along with it."

She took a drink. "The night before he went missing, he came over, all juiced up. Actually, I think literally juiced, which is, again, why I thought he was paranoid. He told me he only needed another day or two, then it was going to blow wide open. And he figured once it did, he'd be famous, and make millions from telling the story. It was, I thought, Keene stuff. That's the last time I saw him."

She set the tube down. "I tried to tag him the next day, but his 'link was dead. I thought he'd shut it down or whatever. I tried a couple more times, and finally went over there. His neighbors said they hadn't seen him. I finally got worried enough to go to the cops."

"His supervisor at Natural Order claimed he quit on June 13, via email." Peabody again referred to her PPC. "According to the report, the email was sent from one of your brother's devices."

"They disappeared him, that's what they did." Long eyes hot, she jabbed a finger at Peabody. "I don't care what you say."

Eve pulled Savannah's attention back. "Do you know any of his friends or associates from Natural Order?"

"No. Keene and I barely spoke after he joined that crap. He tried, at first, to convert me — that would be the word. To, like, renounce my way of life for the true way. Jesus Christ, I'm gay and he's preaching at me about how that's unnatural. My roommate, my best pal, is mixed race. Keene wouldn't even speak to him. He wouldn't come over here. And then he came back. He was coming back.

"I think they killed him. I think he got caught trying to get to whatever turned him around. And I think they killed him. He had issues, okay, he had some serious issues, but he wouldn't just take off like this."

She shook her head fiercely, but her voice wobbled. "He just wouldn't. Even when things were at their worst, he'd tag me on my birthday, on Christmas."

"Has anyone from the order contacted you?"

"He had me listed as his next of kin. They sent me his final paycheck. Fuckers. I went out there once — to where he worked in Connecticut. They wouldn't let me in. I wanted to see where he worked, to talk to somebody, but I couldn't get past the gates. The place is a frigging fortress. They don't want you in, you don't get in."

"Tell us about your relationship with Gwendolyn Huffman."

"Gwen?" Savannah's eyebrows winged up. "We hung out for a while. What's she got to do with it?"

"Are you aware she's a member of Natural Order?"

"Well, that's bullshit. She's gay. You can't be a member when you're gay. We hung out — intimately — for a couple months. Then I introduced her to Ariel, and that was that. If you want to talk about Gwen, talk to Ariel — Ariel Byrd. I think they're still a thing. But Gwen didn't know Keene. I never talked to her about Keene. We had sex, but we weren't serious about it."

235

"You and Ariel Byrd were friends?"

"Yeah, sure." Savannah shrugged. "I mean, we're not tight or anything. We're both artists, and show our stuff at the same gallery. We hung out a few times — not intimately. Gwen went to an art show with me, and I intro'd them. I could see right off that was that. No big deal."

"I'm sorry to inform you Ariel Byrd was murdered the night before last."

"What?" Savannah lurched up from her slouch. "Come on!"

"You run in the same circles, as you said, but you hadn't heard?"

"I . . . These are my two days off, my work-around-the-clock days. I haven't left the apartment. I turn off my 'link. My roommate's in Ohio for a few days for his great-granny's hundredth birthday deal. She was murdered? Are you saying Gwen killed her?"

"No."

"But she's with the order? I never saw it, never . . . We didn't talk a lot. I knew she was slumming — rich uptown girl having a fling with a SoHo artist. No problem. But I see, if that's the way of it, why the sex had to be so secret. I just figured she hadn't come out yet."

Everything about her went hot and tight. "You think she had something to do with Keene?"

"No." Peabody walked over, sat beside her. "But we're investigating Ariel's murder, and we'll do everything we can to find out about your brother."

"It's those fuckers. Somehow, with both of them, it's those fuckers."

236

You're not wrong, Eve thought.

They walked down, out onto the sidewalk, and stood a moment in a world simply teeming with life.

"A missing brother — and we may never find his body — a missing FBI agent — and same goes. And a dead woman. Common link. Natural Order."

Peabody remained silent while they walked to the car, while Eve plugged in the route for Wilkey's HQ.

"I'm going to ask McNab if he can run a search on missing persons, accidental deaths, homicides of members. Say, for two years. And keeping it to New York, New Jersey, and the area of Connecticut where we're going now."

"That's a good thought, Peabody."

"You had it yourself."

"I did, which is why I'm saying it's a good thought. Tag him now, see if he can start it. We'll correlate it with whatever data we get from the feds."

"I know she said she thinks they killed him, but part of her — most of her — still hopes to find him."

"Yeah, I know. We'll get her some answers. That's all we can do."

Stanton Wilkey came to prominence shortly after the end of the Urban Wars while people, still reeling from them, worked to rebuild. While those bitter from them stewed in anger.

He spread his word primarily on college campuses, where young, questing minds sought answers, solutions, and an order many had seen ripped to pieces.

Most who listened disregarded him as a bigoted lunatic, or a joke. But there were always a few, and a few could become many.

He promised a utopia, where there would be no wars, no strife, no struggle. Where each, cleaving to their own kind, would prosper. His fundamentalist and extreme religious views turned many away.

But there were always a few.

It was, he claimed, the mixing of races, diluting their purity, their culture, and the toxic freedom of unbound sexuality, the stain of homosexuality and prostitution, the ambition of women emasculating generations of men that led to war, to strife, to struggle.

He spoke of children, so innocent, so helpless, so neglected by mothers who failed to nurture in their quest for money and power.

As the few became many, he built his order. A small, rented building in the city, a quiet home in the suburbs.

On-screen appearances that led to crowded auditoriums. Seminars that led to retreats. All for a price.

He built his order, and his wealth, step by step.

Eve knew all this when she drove up to the gates of his Connecticut compound.

The walls, a good ten feet of natural stone, stretched a couple of city blocks on either side of the entrance with the wide iron gate flanked by sturdy pillars.

She'd noted the security cams at various points, and imagined the reinforcements included motion detectors, shockers, and infrared.

Beyond the gate, the road split in three directions: straight, right, and left. Trees, flowering shrubs, perfectly landscaped gardens broke up the expanse of green lawns. She spotted buildings of rosy brick or creamy white, all fronted by more trees and flowers.

Just inside the gate sat an actual gatehouse, white like the walls, with a peaked roof and one-way glass windows.

A human voice spoke through the speaker embedded in the pillar.

"Natural Order is closed to visitors. If you wish information on Natural Order, please visit one of our outreach posts. Have a peaceful and fulfilling day."

Eve held up her badge. "Lieutenant Dallas, Officer Peabody, NYPSD. We're here on police business."

A man stepped out of the gatehouse. Tall and burly in a dark suit, he walked to the gate, waited.

"Okay. Sit tight, Peabody." Eve got out of the car, walked to the gate on her side.

Ex-military, she thought. Not just the high-and-tight brown hair, but his bearing, his dead-eyed stare.

"This is Connecticut."

"We're aware. I believe Mr. Wilkey would like to be informed of an active investigation involving one or more of his members, and would cooperate with the authorities before too many details of that investigation and the connection to Natural Order become public."

"You expect to show up here without going through channels and speak to Reverend Wilkey?"

Eve gave it a beat. "Yeah. Maybe you could ask him if he'd rather we go through channels, get a warrant, bring him into Central in New York for interview rather than do this here and now. Discreetly."

"Reverend Wilkey is in afternoon meditation."

"Great. Well, when he gets out, be sure to tell him NYPSD attempted to speak to him here, get his cooperation on record before this all blows up in the media. You have one of those whatever days yourself."

She turned, took two steps back to her car.

"You can wait in your vehicle while we check to see if Reverend Wilkey is available."

She just nodded, and to be pissy, leaned against her car instead of getting back in.

She watched two people walking on what she assumed were paths between buildings.

A woman came out of one building followed by about a dozen kids in knee-length navy shorts and white shirts. She, in her navy skirt, white shirt, navy blazer, crossed to a bench under one of the trees.

The kids — all white, she noted — sat, neatly in two rows, on the grass facing her.

The gatekeeper came back out.

"Pull inside the gate and then over to park."

The gate opened, a slow, silent sweep.

"This place already gives me the creeps," Peabody muttered.

"I think it can get a lot creepier."

She parked as instructed.

"Please place your weapons inside your vehicle, then secure your vehicle. A cart will transport you to Reverend Wilkey's residence."

"My vehicle is secured, and our weapons stay with us."

He smirked at her. "Weapons are not permitted in the compound."

"Do those include the one on your left hip, the second on your right ankle?"

He stiffened. "I'm security."

"Hey, so are we. Our weapons stay with us."

She had a dead-eyed stare of her own. With it she saw temper burn across his face.

As an electric cart hummed toward them, he turned on his heel and marched to it. It stopped just far away enough Eve couldn't clearly hear the conversation — though she did catch the gatekeeper's bitches before the driver — Hispanic, early forties, light brown uniform — waved the air in a chill-it-down gesture and drove the rest of the way.

"Lieutenant, Detective, welcome. I'm Cisco. Why don't you take a seat in the back? I'll take you to Wilkey House."

They got in, and the cart took the road to the left. Eve glanced back to see a second man come out of the gatehouse and join the first in studying her car.

She figured they planned to bypass the security, do a search, try to access data from her nav system, her comm.

Smiling to herself, she settled in. They were in for an unpleasant surprise.

She saw more buildings now, and a half court behind one of them where a group of boys — all black — played some round ball. Red shorts, white tees.

Beyond stood a small chapel-like building with stained-glass windows and a little fountain burbling out front. A statue of Wilkey stood over the water, arms spread in benediction.

Yes, creepy.

More buildings, then a screening of trees before another wall, another gate.

A compound within a compound, she thought as the gates slid open.

The house, bride white, the carved white pillars rising across its expansive covered front porch, reminded her of pictures of plantations in the old South. Trees spread shade on the manicured lawns. Gardens flourished in a kind of regimented march of color.

A woman in a flowy floral dress and a wide-brimmed straw hat busied herself weeding it along with the two young girls flanking her.

None of them looked over as the cart rolled by.

Three stories, and Eve decided she'd term it palatial. Another porch spanned the second floor, and both porches had deeply cushioned chairs, iron tables, urns of flowers.

By the way the sun reflected on the windows and glass doors, she recognized one-way glass.

Eve and Peabody got out opposite sides when the cart stopped.

"Someone will escort you inside. I'll be available to transport you back to the gate when you're ready. Enjoy your visit to Wilkey House."

Even as the cart rolled away, the right side of the double white doors opened. A woman stepped out.

242

She wore a light blue suit, quietly and conservatively cut, with low-heeled shoes. Though she looked older, Eve knew Wilkey's daughter, Mirium, was twenty-four.

The older came from the cut of the suit, the dull brown hair worn in a thick roll at her nape — and the look of profound annoyance.

She tried to mask the last as Eve and Peabody started up the spotless white stairs to the porch.

Her welcoming smile didn't hit sincere.

"Lieutenant Dallas, Detective Peabody. I'm Mirium Wilkey. On behalf of my father, welcome to our home. My father will join us as soon as possible. Since it's such a lovely day, we'll sit on the veranda."

Without waiting for an assent, she led the way to the cushy chairs around a round table.

"I serve as my father's personal assistant and domestic staff manager. Is there any way I can help you today?"

"Have you been in New York recently?" Eve asked. "Say, Monday night?"

"Monday?" Blue eyes, as quiet as her suit, turned contemplative. She reached up absently to toy with the little pearl stud in her ear. "I was on campus — as we say — Monday, as I have been all week. We're holding a retreat. I do have a pied-a-terre in the city, as we often have business in New York."

Two women came out onto the porch — one in her late teens or early twenties, the other nearer sixty. Both wore navy skirts, white shirts buttoned to the neck, with small navy bows at the collars.

The younger set out glasses filled with ice while the other poured a golden brown liquid into them from a pitcher.

Neither spoke, smiled, or lifted their eyes.

As the younger set down Eve's glass, she dropped a grimy little twist of paper in Eve's lap.

Eve moved her hand over it as the older poured the liquid.

"Herbal sun tea," Mirium said. "We grow our own herbs, and of course, abstain from caffeine. You'll find this quite refreshing."

She neither spoke to nor acknowledged the other women. They slipped back into the house like ghosts.

Eve slid the twist of paper into her pocket.

"And your father? Was he on campus Monday night?"

"Of course. He's in retreat. Perhaps if you tell me what brings you to us, I could help."

"A woman was murdered Monday night."

Mirium lowered her head, shook it. "The taking of a human life. Is there any stain darker on the human heart and mind? But I don't know how that brings you to us."

"Did you know Ariel Byrd?"

"I don't recognize the name." Mirium lifted a hand, this time to the single strand of pearls at her neck. "Was she a member? I can look at our files to check that if you need —"

"She wasn't a member. The woman who found her body and reported it is. Gwendolyn Huffman."

"Gwen?" She actually clutched the pearls now. "Oh, how terrible for her!"

"You know Ms. Huffman."

"Yes. Since we were children. My father and her parents have been friends for years. I need to contact her, offer my support. We limit outside contact during retreat, including any electronics, but I can request a dispensation for this. Poor Gwen."

"Yeah, poor Gwen." Eve glanced around. "Obviously she didn't participate in this retreat."

"No. She's to be married very soon, and is very tied up in the plans. Hopefully, Gwen and her husband will join us for our retreat in the fall."

"You know her fiancé?"

"Merit? Yes. Not very well, but the order is very involved with charitable organizations, as are the Caines and, of course, the Huffmans."

Mirium produced a tight little smile. "I'm afraid there's little I can tell you that you'd find helpful. The Huffmans are, I'm sure you know, exemplary people. We value them. I'm very sorry Gwen had this dreadful experience, but this is the sort of secular business we shut out during our retreats."

"Your father may be more helpful."

"I don't see how, as he's been in retreat for several days. I don't want to waste any more of your time, so . . ."

As Mirium trailed off, Eve watched Wilkey walk out of the trees. He glided — he was good at it — to the woman and the two young girls weeding.

He paused to speak to them. Both young girls smiled up at him, but Eve noted the woman kept her head down, and clutched their hands even after Wilkey continued on.

Mirium got to her feet as Wilkey started up those grand white steps.

"Lieutenant Dallas, Detective Peabody, Reverend Stanton Wilkey."

She said it in a way, as he stood basking in the light at the edge of the porch, that made Eve wonder if they were expected to rise and take a knee.

Not going to happen.

CHAPTER
FOURTEEN

He made an impression, Eve supposed. Tall, lanky on the edge of thin, with his lion's mane of white hair waving to his shoulders. His eyes of clear and crystal blue beamed what she supposed others saw as benevolence.

He had a thin, scholarly face. As the house had made her think of a plantation, his face made her think of paintings of ancient saints and martyrs.

She considered that very deliberate.

He wore white — cotton pants, a long white shirt, and white loafers. He had long, slender feet, long, slender hands.

When he spoke, his voice came deep and soft, like a velvet cushion.

"Welcome to my home. Forgive me for keeping you waiting."

He didn't offer his hand to shake as he approached the table, but set one on his daughter's shoulder.

"I trust Mirium has made you welcome until I could accommodate your unexpected arrival. Thank you, Mirium."

Softly delivered or not, the words rang with dismissal.

Mirium's lips twitched tight before she smiled.

She started to step back.

"It would be helpful and save time if Ms. Wilkey stays now." Eve looked directly into those crystal-blue eyes. "We don't want to take up any more of your time than necessary."

"How kind of you. Please sit, Mirium."

He'd barely taken a seat himself when the two women were back. The glass, the ice, the pitcher, the pouring. The younger risked the briefest flick of a glance at Eve.

"Since communications are forbidden" — Eve let that hang an instant longer than necessary —" it would be difficult for word to get out of the compound or in. We're here to do both."

"I assume this is of great import."

"Anyone needing help from the police I consider of great import."

She assumed — hoped — her message was received as the two women returned to the house.

"Ariel Byrd requires that help now."

"You said she —" Mirium caught herself. "I'm sorry to interrupt, but you said she'd been killed."

"We're Homicide, Ms. Wilkey. Ariel Byrd needs our help to bring her killer to justice. Her family needs our help to give them that justice and some sense of closure."

"We aren't separate from the world here," Wilkey began. "During retreats, yes. We separate ourselves in order to feed the spirit, clear the mind, rededicate the heart. But we are part of the whole, and anyone's death at the hands of another diminishes us. How can we help you find this justice?"

"Did you know Ariel Byrd?"

"I know so many — this is a blessing in my life — but her name doesn't sound familiar."

Peabody took out her PPC, brought up Ariel's photo.

Wilkey sighed. "To help, I must break a vow. But a life is worth more than a promise to abstain from devices."

He looked carefully at the photo. "So young, poor soul. She doesn't look familiar. Is she part of the flock, Mirium?"

"I don't believe so." She started to say more, then folded her hands and kept her silence.

"She was not. But the person who found her body and contacted the police is. Gwen Huffman."

"Gwendolyn." He let out a quiet sigh. "This is tragic for all involved."

Time for some careful editing, Eve thought. "Ms. Huffman and Ms. Byrd became friendly when Ms. Huffman admired Ms. Byrd's art."

"An artist?" Now he smiled his benevolent smile. "A gift given to offer beauty."

"Ms. Huffman arrived at Ms. Byrd's apartment early Tuesday morning, for a sitting. A wedding gift for her fiancé."

"Merit Caine, yes. Gwendolyn's parents and I have been friends for many years. She will be a lovely bride, and I'm sure a dutiful wife."

Not anytime soon, Eve thought. "When she arrived that morning, Ms. Huffman states the door was unsecured. She heard music the victim often played when working and, calling out, went inside. She discovered the body. On-scene exam and the medical examiner's exam confirms Ms. Byrd's time of death as ten-forty-eight the previous evening."

"Tragic, as I said, and shocking. We will, of course, do whatever we can to comfort and support Gwendolyn and her parents at this difficult time. But I fail to see how we can help you."

"I'm unable to share further details of an active investigation with you. I can only tell you that certain aspects, individuals, and areas of that investigation imply a connection between Natural Order and Ms. Byrd's murder."

His long gaze mixed sorrow and pity. "I don't see how that's possible. We abjure violence. Natural Order is dedicated to spreading peace. We would not and could not take a life, even in defense of our own."

"The victim was a lesbian of mixed race. Two other things you and your followers abjure."

He simply kept his gaze — and oh yeah, Eve thought, plenty of crazy in it — locked on Eve's face.

"We do renounce and denounce such misguided choices, as these false freedoms create discord, strife, and violence. But violence to those so misguided is not the answer."

At Eve's glance, Peabody once again consulted her PPC. "Sir, there have been numerous incidents of violence since the inception of your order perpetuated by members. I have a long list here. I can refresh your memory on those incidents."

250

"No need." He waved the PPC and Peabody away. "These unfortunate and tragic incidents were perpetuated by those equally misguided, those who twist the tenets of the order for their own means. We renounce and denounce them as well."

He opened his arms, much like the statue, as the velvet voice continued.

"True order promotes peace with the embrace and strict adherence to the natural." He lifted his hands, palms up. "Peace, harmony, a natural balance in all, for all. We educate, reach for the soul and spirit as well as the mind."

"And how do you deal with those who twist or break your tenets?" Eve reached for Peabody's PPC. "Like James Burke, Wayne Marshall, and Cody Klark, who set fire to a church in West Texas during a same-sex marriage ceremony, killing three, seriously injuring twelve? That was just last year, so you might remember it."

He lowered his hands, folded them. "I do, and remain appalled. We leave it to the secular authorities to mete out punishment. The law of the land must be followed and respected."

"The law of the land states that individuals of the same sex can marry, that individuals of different races may marry — and has for decades in most of the civilized world. The law of the land states a lot of things your tenets claim as aberrations."

"While we believe these laws are misguided, violence is never the answer. Education," he insisted in that same eerily soft voice. "Spiritual guidance and support."

"When you teach these things as tools of evil or abominations or whatever terms you use, you can't be surprised when those who follow those teachings attack those who don't."

He opened his hands now — soft hands, well-manicured, Eve noted. "The human condition, the choices some make in the name of good, doesn't surprise me. It saddens me, as it saddens me when some make the choice to embrace the unnatural, to choose the crooked path. The woman you speak of made those choices, but I will mourn her death. I will pray for her to be forgiven, pray for her immortal soul."

"Okay. And your whereabouts Monday night, during the time in question?"

"Here, at home. I led a seminar after the evening meal, then retired to my rooms to meditate and pray."

"What time were you meditating and praying?"

"By nine, certainly. No one leaves the compound during retreat."

"And your wife?"

"My wife isn't well, I'm afraid, and is unable to join this retreat. She's in treatment."

"Where?"

"Utopia Island. We hope she'll be well enough to join us soon."

"You have three sons. And where are they?"

"Samuel and Joseph are also here, in retreat, along with their wives and children. My youngest is with his mother, at my request. As we're unable to communicate over these ten days, I needed to know one of us would be there, with our beloved. Aaron would never leave his mother during her illness. And my sons, their wives and children, my daughter would never leave the compound, therefore breaking their vows."

"You have really good security, which I assume includes electronic surveillance, alarm systems — and gates are electronic."

"Yes, exceptions necessary for the safety of those inside the compound. I'm sure you're aware we often receive threats, violent ones."

"With that exception, it would be easy to verify no one left by reviewing the security feed for Monday."

Wilkey glanced at his daughter, nodded at her.

"The security feeds are overwritten routinely every twenty-four hours. We wouldn't have Monday's by this time."

"Our EDD would be able to analyze and perhaps locate the overwritten data."

"Father, may I speak?"

He patted her hand. "Of course, Mirium."

"My father has given you a great deal of his time, and during his rest period. We've been cooperative, and answered your questions even when they edge toward insulting. Now you imply we're liars or worse. Much worse, and ask us to turn over our property — our security and privacy. You have no warrant, and no cause."

Wilkey patted her hand again. "My daughter is quite right. We've cooperated, and though we didn't know this woman, we'll pray for her, and for her family. But now I must prepare for my next session. We wish you a peaceful and fulfilling day."

He rose, walked to the front doors, and went inside.

"Cisco will transport you back to the gate." Mirium pushed to her feet. "I wonder if you would so relentlessly pursue someone who'd murdered one of us, since you so clearly hold us in disdain."

"We've pursued the killers of people we've held in a lot worse than disdain." Eve got up. "And we've put them in cages. That's just what we'll do with the person who killed Ariel Byrd. Thanks for your time."

Eve walked down the steps with Peabody.

The woman and the young girls had finished weeding the front section. Eve spotted them around the side of the house, still on their knees, still meticulously pulling whatever wasn't supposed to be there out of the flowers.

The cart rolled up.

On the silent ride back, she saw the basketball players had left the court. A group of adults — white again — practiced yoga on a green lawn. She saw two Asian women leading a group of six Asian kids — green shorts for them — toward a playground.

Peabody nudged her with an elbow, so Eve looked in the opposite direction.

High school-age kids, Eve noted, in a circle, legs crossed, eyes closed, the instructor in the center of the circle.

Hispanic. Brown shorts.

Their driver, Eve thought, Hispanic, attached to security. The two guards at the gate, Caucasian. Different sections then for different races. Segregation in the workforce, in the school, with women, as far as she'd seen, regulated to domestic and teaching areas. Including Wilkey's daughter, who served as his "personal assistant" and staff manager.

While no fan of small talk, Eve knew how to use it in an interview.

"So, Cisco, right? How long have you worked here?"

"Eight years at headquarters, ma'am."

She didn't bother to correct the *ma'am*. "Beautiful location."

"Yes, ma'am, it is."

"No hardship, I'd guess, to stay on campus during the retreat. Does staff have housing right here, too?"

"We do, but not all staff is required to remain on the compound during retreat. That would cause a hardship for many families, and also put a strain on the housing and service facilities."

"Yeah, that makes sense."

A stupid little lie then, and so easily debunked.

"Our schools and medical facilities are second to none," he went on, like a membership pitch. "We grow most of our own food, some here in the compound, and, of course, on our farms. By feeding the mind, the body, the spirit, we help lead the world to peace and prosperity."

"How long have you been a member of the order?"

"All my life. My parents joined the faithful before I was born."

"And they live here, too?"

"Oh, no, ma'am. They're part of our farm system, in Iowa."

System, Eve noted. "So they aren't attending the retreat?"

"Farming is rewarding work. My wife is part of our farm system here. She can be proud to know she helps feed the faithful."

He pulled up beside Eve's car.

"I hope you enjoyed your visit."

"It was illuminating," Eve said as she hopped out of the cart.

"An enlightened mind and spirit lead to order."

"So do truth and justice."

When Eve got into her car, when the cart rolled silently away, the guard came out of the gatehouse.

From his scowl she deduced he hadn't enjoyed the theft-repellent shock that had likely knocked him off his feet when he'd tried to break into her DLE.

She did a three-point turn as he opened the gate, and decided her deduction hit the mark when he shot up his middle finger.

She found that a bright side to an ugly visit.

"They color-code them!" Peabody exploded. "They color-code them by race! Did you see that?"

"I've got eyes, Peabody."

"Every group of kids I saw was color-coded and segregated by race. Jesus Christ, Dallas, and they're all just fine with that? And that woman with the two little girls, doing all that weeding. I didn't see anybody else out there, and it would take hours and hours to weed all those beds. Did you see that? Did you see? And those women who came out with their stupid tea? They didn't even look up, heads bowed like — like slaves in their damn color-coded uniforms."

256

Eve let Peabody rant. It was a damn good rant, and she wanted some distance. Enough to be certain nobody tried a tail.

"And that cart guy? His parents are in the farm system? 'System'? And his wife, too. And he was proud of it! I wanted to punch him in the head. I wanted to punch them all in the head. That fucking fuck Wilkey with his holy bullshit."

When she satisfied herself they were clear, Eve pulled into the parking lot of some fancy suburban shopping center.

"What? Why are you stopping? Are we going back to punch them in the head? Can we kick them in the balls, too?"

"If only." Eve hitched up to pull the twist of paper out of her pocket.

"What's that?"

"It's what the woman dropped in my lap when she set out the glasses for the stupid tea."

"I didn't see that. I was sitting right there."

"I'm willing to bet she practiced." Carefully, Eve twisted it open, did what she could to smooth it out.

I am Ella Alice Foxx
5/6/43
Brooklyn, New York

"Run the name with that birthdate and birthplace, Peabody."

"On it. Why didn't she write a message?" she added while she got to work. "You know, like 'Help' or something?"

"If somebody finds this, she maybe gets a slap for it, but she can say it's just her name. Just a personal reminder of her name. She adds a message, that someone knows she's trying to communicate with the outside."

"I've got no one with that name born on that day in Brooklyn."

"Leave out the location."

Eve got out, took an evidence bag from her field kit, and sealed the note inside.

"Nothing, Dallas," Peabody told her when Eve got behind the wheel again.

"Run variations. Search for the name Foxx in Brooklyn in that year." As she spoke, Eve pulled out of the lot. "Try her full name using the birth year without the month and day. Spread it out."

Eve called up her in-dash, contacted Detective Yancy.

The police artist answered quickly, and Eve heard the sound of cranky New York traffic.

"Are you off shift?" she asked him.

"Not yet. I'm uptown, about to work with a wit. Some asshole tried to snatch her kid. Kid kicked him in the balls, and they both got a good look at him. I'm going to them because the mom's pretty shook. Apparently the kid's feeling just fine."

"I need you to work with another wit after that. I'll clear the OT with your lieutenant."

"Who's the wit?"

"Me, potentially Peabody. I'll explain later. Give me the address where you'll be and I'll send transpo to bring you to my house."

"I'm only going to be a few blocks from your place. I can get there. I know where it is. I was at your Christmas party."

"Right. Text Peabody when you're done. I'm heading there, but I'll clear you in if we're not back."

"Copy that."

"I'm not getting anyone with the full name that fits, Dallas. On a national search I get some Ella Foxxes, some Alice Foxxes, but nobody in that age range. I'm getting results for the last name in Brooklyn, residents in that year."

"Copy to my home unit. Contact McNab, and let's have EDD do a search. Tell him to come to the house."

Eve went back to the in-dash. This time Roarke's face filled the screen.

"Lieutenant, heading back from Connecticut, are you?"

"Yeah, and I'm bringing cops into the house. I'll hit the details later, but I had a woman pass me a note with her name, birthday, and birthplace. Nothing pops on a search."

"Data in the system can be altered."

"Exactly, which is why one of the cops is going to be an e-geek. I thought you might want in on that."

"As it happens I would. I'll be on my way home myself shortly."

"I'll send you the data, and see you there."

"McNab will head out as soon as he's wrapped at Central. He's finishing up testing out the echo deal on the tracker and 'link."

"They recovered enough of it."

"It was pretty mangled, but . . . He went into ultra-geek mode, so I cut that off. He'll bring the results with him, and he'll fill us in, and dig into Ella Foxx. Why wipe her data, if that's what happened?"

"She doesn't want to be there. She didn't write that note yesterday. She's been carrying it around for a while now, looking for her chance. She doesn't want to be there, but she obviously can't walk out."

"She's eighteen — if that date's right. Just, but eighteen and legal. If she's being held . . ."

"Walls, security, cams, close supervision. Maybe she walked in there on her own at some point, but she sure as hell believes she can't walk out again. She won't be the only one. You wipe her data so she doesn't exist outside those walls."

Like she hadn't existed, Eve thought, outside that room in Dallas, or the other ugly rooms her father had locked her in.

"The woman doing the weeding. She was afraid, she was afraid of Wilkey. The kids weren't, but she was. This Ella and the other woman with the tea?" Eve continued. "Mirium didn't even acknowledge them. Like they were droids, or more, just invisible. You say things in front of people you just don't see that you wouldn't say otherwise."

"You think she — Ella — might know things."

"I think she knew cops were coming so she had that note handy. I think Mirium was plenty pissed to have to deal with cops on her own — what was it? — veranda, and likely said so. What else has she, or others, said in front of the invisible?"

260

"And they lied. They might consider some of the staff as no big, but they said specifically nobody goes out during retreat. And the cart driver said some staff does. We already knew that because Marcia Piper said her husband works at the HQ and was home Monday night. Either she lied or they did about that one."

"He was home long enough to put those bruises on her. They looked pretty fresh."

"They lied about that to get rid of us. Nothing to see here," Peabody muttered. "But how do you wind it all back to Gwen Huffman and Ariel Byrd?"

"I don't know yet, but we're damn sure going to find out."

"Dallas, we have to get Ella Foxx out of that place."

"Yes, we do."

"We could send some officers to Brooklyn — work with the locals — and interview any Foxx still living there who was there during the birth year. It's a start."

"If you were connected to someone who took off, went missing, whatever, you'd file a report, so we start there. But I can promise you Savannah Grimsley still looks at her brother's data now and again. Just hoping he's updated it."

"Yeah, you're right."

"Reach out to Brooklyn anyway, check on missing persons. Do the same in the other boroughs. Let's be thorough."

Maybe they'd find one, Eve thought as Peabody got to work again. Maybe. But she doubted it. They'd wiped her data because nobody would notice or care. Because they could.

And they'd made her invisible.

Wasn't it another kind of murder? You could still breathe, walk, talk, eat, sleep. But you no longer existed because someone killed your identity.

When she finally reached the city, when she finally reached her own gates, Eve felt a knot of tension loosen in her guts.

"There's nothing, Dallas, no MP reports filed on Ella Foxx, Alice Foxx, Ella Alice Foxx. Just nothing. But maybe we should start interviewing —"

"What if her parents, her family, whoever had control of her are members? True believers who shoved their daughter into that place before she had a choice? What do you think will happen to her if we ask questions, hit on the right people, and word gets back to Wilkey and the order?"

"For her own parents to do something like that to her, to trap her that way, to let her just not exist and be afraid, not be able to ask for help? It's so hard to imagine what kind of people would do that to their own kid, their own family. I just can't —"

It hit her, quick and hard. "I'm sorry. God, that was stupid. I'm wound up, but that was stupid. I'm sorry."

"Don't be. It wasn't normal for me, it's not normal for her."

Eve pulled up at the house, sat a minute. "She took a risk dropping that note in my lap, so I'm going to say she wasn't shoved into the group, or joined the group, as a kid, not too young anyway. I'd never have done that, looked to a cop for help, because he'd drummed it into me that the cops would hurt me, throw me into a hole, in the dark. But she knows better."

Eve got out of the car, let out a long breath. "We're not going to let her down."

She walked in to a looming Summerset and the waiting Galahad. "Lieutenant, Detective Peabody. I'm informed we're expecting other members of the NYPSD this evening. I'll send them to your office as they arrive."

She started straight upstairs with the cat trotting beside her. Then paused, looked back. "You were in Dublin at the end of the Urbans, and after. Any rumbles of Natural Order?"

"They gained no foothold there. I did have my own contacts, however, and there were murmurs about them. I regret to say I and many others considered them no more than a flash in the pan. We were wrong."

She nodded, started up again.

"Detective Peabody, may I say your hair is quite fetching."

Peabody grinned back at Summerset. "Yeah? Thanks."

She had to quick time it to catch up with Eve and the cat.

"What the hell flashes in a pan?" Eve demanded.

"I . . . don't actually know."

"See? See? That's why that kind of stupid saying doesn't make any sense."

"Now I have to look it up." Peabody pulled out her PPC as she followed Eve. "Oh, oh, it's from flintlocks — you know, muskets — and they had these little pans for the gunpowder. And if it went off without the bullet or the ball thing, the gunpowder just, well, flashed in the pan."

"And that makes it make sense?"

"Well, sort of. Not really," Peabody decided.

Eve turned into her office. "Update the board. I'll do the book. Get coffee or whatever if you want it."

"I'm coffee'd out, and hoping you have low-cal fizzies."

As Peabody headed into the kitchen and the AutoChef, Eve sat at her command center.

"Score!" Peabody called from the kitchen. "And there's Yancy — he's just finished. He'll be here within fifteen."

Peabody came out with a fizzy for herself, a black coffee for Eve.

"I'm looking at this board," Peabody said as they worked, "and the connections between the Huffmans and Wilkeys. It goes back. I'm sort of surprised the families didn't arrange for one of the Wilkey sons to marry Gwen."

"You don't expand your membership or your treasury that way. They wanted the Caine money, and hoped — more assumed, I think — Gwen would draw Merit into the order."

"And all the while, she planned to use him to hit the terms of the trust, then set him up so she could divorce him with their approval and support."

Eve glanced up, frowned. She knew all that, had gone over and over that. But something new wanted to click.

264

And Yancy came in.

"Hey, Peabody. Dallas."

"Hey, Yancy. How'd the wits do?"

He paused by Peabody and the board to answer her. "Solid as it gets. I ran facial rec on the sketch while I was there, and *pop!* They confirmed ID. Pedophile, on parole after doing fourteen years in. He's out three months and tries to snatch a twelve-year-old girl walking home from band practice after school. Her mom's looking in a shop window three feet away. Kid yells, kicks his nuts. Mom screams, grabs kid, pervert takes off limping. I got word on the way over, we already picked him up in his flop."

"Nice work."

"The kid gets the credit. She says her mom taught her the move."

He shifted his gaze from the board to Eve.

Peabody might term him ultra-dreamy, with his mop of curly dark hair and handsome face. But he was, Eve knew, a solid cop. He had a way of easing small details out of a witness, a way of relaxing them into remembering more, then merging those details into a face.

"So." He smiled at her. "First time for us. Have you ever worked with a police artist as a wit?"

A lifetime ago, she thought. At eight, broken and battered and terrified. She'd been gentle, too, as Eve knew Yancy could be. But that traumatized little girl hadn't remembered a single detail of her father's face.

It was simpler to hedge.

"They brought a couple into the Academy for training, had us witness a mock attack, then set us up to describe the attacker to the artist."

"How'd you do?"

"I did okay."

"I bet. I'm ready when you are." He glanced around. "How about we use the table there, by the doors?"

"That'll work. Do you want coffee?" Eve asked as she rose.

"I'd rather have one of those fizzies."

Peabody tipped hers side to side. "This is low-cal."

"Skip that part. Make it lemon if you've got it."

"You guys set up. I'll get the fizzy."

"You want to fill me in?" Yancy asked Eve.

"Roarke's coming, and McNab. I'd rather brief everybody at once."

"Okay." He took off his satchel, then set it down to open it.

Peabody delivered his fizzy while he set out his tools.

"Grab a chair, Peabody. We both got a good look at her."

"Subject's female." Yancy nodded.

"Female, eighteen, Caucasian, ivory skin. Triangular face, on the thin side. She's lost the fresh of eighteen. It's strain, it shows. Hollows in the cheeks, not deep, more like somebody who's lost weight in the last couple months. Oval, double-lidded eyes, blue-green tending toward blue. A little wider than that," she told Yancy as he sketched. "More oval."

She paused for coffee.

"Nose is thin, but not sharp. She had a stud in it at one time, I could just see the piercing. Right side."

"Missed that," Peabody murmured.

"You were on her left. Just a little wider on the nose. Yeah, that's good. Wide mouth, wide with a full top lip, a slight overbite. Eyebrows, forgot the eyebrows."

Eve closed her eyes, brought them back. "Thick, slight arch, medium brown — long lashes, medium brown. Ears close to the head, triple piercings on both. Two in the lobes, one up in the cartilage. Lobes a little longer than that."

Roarke came in, silent as a cat. He caught the drift, said nothing, and continued to her command center to get his own coffee.

"Medium brown hair, length undetermined. She wore it pulled back, and from the thickness of the roll at the back of her neck, I'm going to guess about Peabody's length, maybe slightly longer."

Eve studied the sketch. "Bring the mouth in a hair, and a little fuller on the bottom lip, a little more narrow on the forehead."

As Yancy made minute adjustments, Peabody shook her head.

"That's her. That's excellent."

Yancy looked at Eve. "Any changes?"

"No, that's solid."

"You make my job easy."

"Not done yet. Second woman, Peabody. Take it."

"Oh, shit."

"Relax." Yancy gave her his easy smile. "This won't hurt a bit."

Eve left them to it, and head-nodded Roarke into the kitchen.

"I'm going to go over all this when McNab gets here so I only have to say it once."

"All right." He leaned in, kissed her. "You'd object to that once we're in cop mode."

"I'm still in cop mode. I don't know how long this is going to take."

"Understood. Just tell me this before we begin. What did you think of Stanton Wilkey?"

Eve bared her teeth. "I want to bury the bastard."

"All right then. Let's get started on making that happen."

CHAPTER
FIFTEEN

When they stepped back out, Eve saw Yancy guiding Peabody through the process. Giving them room, Eve listened, nodded in approval.

Her partner rolled into it.

"Mirium Wilkey," Eve murmured to Roarke. "Wilkey's daughter. She said she had a place in the city. How about you find that for me?"

"Happy to. I'll just use your command center, as you're itching to add some details to Peabody's description."

Okay, maybe, but . . . "I want her to do it, and she's doing better than okay."

Roarke took her chair anyway as she began circling the board.

She heard McNab's prance approaching, and stepped out of the office. He pranced beside Feeney.

"Didn't expect you."

"I gave the boy a ride, and I didn't want to miss all this."

"I sure as hell can use you. Peabody's working with Yancy, so keep it zipped, Detective."

"Got it."

"Go get coffee, fizzies, whatever the hell. They're close to finished."

While they headed in and straight to the kitchen, Eve wandered to the table to look at the sketch.

"What have I missed?" Peabody asked her.

"Not much. It's solid."

"But something? Yancy really takes you back, but I feel like I'm not right there."

"Her complexion's a little more sallow, and she has some sag under the chin."

"That! The sag!"

"The eyes are good, except she had little pockets — not bags, just little pockets — under them. And she got a deep line between her eyebrows when she concentrated on pouring the tea. It's left a more shallow one from pulling her brows together over the years."

"I keep reminding myself not to do that." Peabody rubbed her fingers between her eyebrows.

"That's her. That's good. She's about fifty — looks older by a few years. No work, no makeup, but about fifty if you factor that. You can run facial rec on this one, Yancy."

"Not the younger one."

"You can try it, but they wiped her data, so it's next to zero you'll hit anything. I want to see if they did the same with the older woman."

"I'll run it now. Nice working with you, Peabody. You got sharp skills."

"I'll brief everybody while that runs." Rolling into what felt like real progress, Eve turned. "Everybody grab a seat."

"You can brief over pizza," Roarke said. "Your troops need a meal, Lieutenant."

She wanted to object, maybe would have, but he'd said the magic word.

Pizza.

"Fine."

"McNab, help me set up a table. Peabody, would you order up what suits?"

"I'm all over it and back."

"Hit," Yancy allowed, and had Eve moving back to him and looking over his shoulder.

"Let's get it up on-screen."

"I'm not on your system."

To solve that, Roarke stepped over. "If you wouldn't mind?" With Yancy's assent, Roarke took his portable, synched it, and threw the data to Eve's wall screen.

"Okay, here's Gayle Steenberg," Eve began. "Age fifty-two, Caucasian, married to Carl Steenberg, age fifty-five, since 2034, two offspring, both male. And the residence listed for the last fifteen years is Natural Order's Connecticut HQ. Employed by Natural Order as a domestic-slash-domestic trainer at an annual income of a hundred and twenty-five K."

She caught the scent of pizza. Okay, fine, she thought, she could eat. And she had to bring everyone up to date before they could really dig in.

"Go ahead, set up the food. I'm going to start a deeper run. I want to find out when she joined the order, if her husband and offspring are members. Yancy, if you need to take off, you're clear. If you want to stick, I'll fix it."

"I'd like to help find her — the first one. I'd like to know who she is. And there's pizza."

"You'll earn it." She went to her command center, set up the runs.

When Roarke came over, kissed the top of her head, she was too engrossed to be embarrassed. "Come, grab a slice with your team. You'll be the better for it."

"It's more of a team than I figured on, and I think we're going to need to add to it before this is done."

While she worked, they set up a long table to hold several pies, the plates, the soft drinks, fizzies, coffee. They'd expanded the table where she and Roarke usually had dinner, brought in chairs.

He'd told her before they'd remodeled how it would work when she had a team at home. And, as usual, he'd been right.

Right now everyone talked at once while they stuffed pizza in their faces, guzzled drinks. And somewhere along the line, Roarke had shed his tie, his suit jacket.

He didn't look like a cop, but he sure looked at ease with them.

She grabbed a slice, and, moving back to the board, took a bite before she began.

"I'm going to start with Ariel Byrd."

Roarke watched her while she ate with one hand, gestured to the board when necessary with the other. Facts, evidence, timelines, names, and connections all laid out in brisk cop-speak.

Commanding, he thought, she managed commanding even with a half-eaten slice of pepperoni pizza in her hand.

He watched the others as well. Peabody, nibbling slowly on her slice to make it last while she listened. McNab, already on his second slice, tapped his airboots to some inner rhythm.

Yancy, whom Roarke assumed had come in only tonight, ate with one hand, took notes with the other.

And Feeney, taking a pull from a cream soda, kept his eyes on the board, ate absently as Eve did, putting things together, Roarke concluded, as Eve had.

She went back for more pizza as she moved into her interviews, beginning with Tribeca.

"My sense is that entire block, a good two dozen townhomes and duplexes, is occupied by members. We'll verify that, and verify if the order itself owns the real estate."

"They do." Roarke glanced up from his PPC. "As I've just checked that for you. Those twenty-six residential properties — double that for occupancy, as each is a duplex — are owned by Utopian Estates, a real estate and development arm of Natural Order."

"Gotcha another." A tiny drop of sauce plopped on Feeney's shit-brown tie as he ate and worked. "Just a quick scan, but I don't find a single nine-one-one call, not for cops, medical, fire, on that block in the last twenty-four-month period. I can look back more, but it says something."

"Yeah, it does," Eve agreed. "It says if they have any problems, they handle it internally or tag up somebody from New Order to handle it."

"Creepy," Peabody put in. "The whole block had a seriously creepy vibe."

273

"The Pipers pay three K in rent, which is very low for the location and square footage I see. Lawrence Piper, a vice president of the order's social media division at their headquarters, has an annual reported salary of six hundred and thirty-two K. There's more there," Roarke added. "Unreported bonuses perhaps, considering the vehicle he owns, a vacation property and boat, and what I'm seeing here at — as Feeney said — a quick scan, a taste for the finer things."

"Keep the rent low, keep them in line, hold the block. We had a different vibe, different take with Idina Frank in the East Village."

She ran them through the interview. Roarke listened even as he did multiple runs and searches on his portable.

He added the Grimsleys to his list when she got to SoHo, but he'd already satisfied himself on a few points.

He'd refine them, considerably, he thought, with more time.

When she outlined the visit to Natural Order and the Wilkeys, the mood changed. McNab's boots stopped tapping; Feeney's face went cop blank.

Yancy paused in his note-taking to study the faces on the board as if to imprint them.

"I want to take a minute, if that's chill." McNab stood when she finished. "Can I open those doors?"

"Yeah, go ahead. I guess we can all use some air after that."

"They start them at age five." Yancy consulted his notes. "That's what Idina Frank stated. At age five kids

274

are required to attend an approved school and begin indoctrination."

"Correct. It probably starts younger, but that's official and regimented. We've got threads," Eve continued, "leading from Byrd's murder to Natural Order. A lot of threads but no strong knots to tie them to it. We've also got a federal agent who infiltrated and has gone dark, a missing person who, according to his sister, began gathering data to expose some aspects of the order. And we have Ella Alice Foxx, who, by all appearances, is inside those gates against her will, who had her identity wiped."

Eve crossed over, took a tube of Pepsi, cracked it. "Feeney and/or McNab can brief us on the recorder placed in Gwen Huffman's 'link, but the questions are: Who put it there, and why? To track her, certainly, and whoever did knew about the affair and her orientation. Did this individual kill Byrd to protect Huffman from exposure? If so, why — who stands as protector and why? Natural Order gains more if she's cut off by her parents, but they'd risk embarrassment. Her parents are longtime, prominent members about to put on a big society wedding and merge with another prominent and wealthy family they hope to draw into the order."

"So do they take the money now, let the Huffmans deal with some humiliation, have the daughter cut off? Or," Roarke continued, "do they guard their investment, look to the future? It's a bit of a gamble, but the Caines are worth quite a bit."

"They're going to cash in either way, right?" Yancy looked from Roarke to Eve. "And you factor in they eliminated a lesbian — it's not hard to see how they'd justify that. And mixed-race, too. So, well, two strikes."

"That's how I see it. The killer planned enough to plant the recorder, but the murder, that was spur of the moment. Cold, but impulsive. The timeline tells us that. Bitch is going to screw up this merger. That's what it was to them, a merger.

"Beyond the racism, the bigotry, the misogyny, and all the rest, Natural Order's a big, fat business, and its business is money, power, and control."

"It's kids, too." McNab stepped back in. "That's the future, guaranteed. Huffman's been groomed for this, right? She's been caught once being herself and re-a-fucking-ligned. She's been smart enough to play along, and greedy enough to. But her purpose, according to this goddamn cult, is to marry the rich white guy and pop out some rich white kids. Their dad, their grandparents are more likely to go along once there are kids. Even if not, the kids are going to have trust funds, that's the culture. But you can't get there if Byrd rings the bell."

"We have to tie that thread to the order, and knot it tight. The order has big piles of money, and big piles of money buy lots and lots of lawyers. They're going to have some judges, some politicians, and, I hate to say it, some cops on their rolls."

"They do have considerable wealth," Roarke said. "Still, a great deal of it's tied up in real estate. The Tribeca properties, for instance. The rent doesn't quite cover the taxes, the maintenance. There's depreciation, of course, and other ways, but they take a loss on those

276

properties. And I've found a handful of others nationally that do the same."

"The cart driver said they have a farm system."

"They have several farms, ranches, orchards, which provide much of their food and resources. I'll look deeper, but they don't seem to be particularly profitable. They provide housing, schools, services for their laborers and staff at minimal rates. Laborers are also paid at minimal rates."

"When did you get all this?"

"I ran some searches while you were briefing. Shallow at the moment, but enough to give me a sense."

"And your sense is they're losing money with all this?"

"They are, yes, but then if you want your personal vision to spread, you need teachers to teach that vision, schools and facilities where your natural order is enforced. Someone farms the land, and that puts a little in his pocket, but he's a roof over his head, doesn't he? His children have a free, private education teaching the values — so to speak — he subscribes to."

She could see it, yes, Eve thought she could see the overall plan. Sort of, to her mind, a long and intricate con.

"But how do you sustain that — and accumulate enough money to buy a freaking island — if you're plowing your profits into the ground?"

"They make up for it, and quite well. Members are required to tithe twenty percent of their income. I suspect, once I scratch a bit more, I'll find fees. Very likely quotas to be met, and deductions when they're not. It's very likely many of their wealthier members agree to bequeathing large sums to the order in their wills."

"They don't have to pay someone like Ella Foxx, do they?" Eve asked. "She's no one. They'd have more no ones. Slave labor."

"And with all that, Wilkey spends lavishly on a personal level. Several homes, two private shuttles, a jet-copter, a yacht — in his name. His older sons each have their own shuttle, and two homes each. The younger lives in the house at HQ and/or on Utopia Island, according to his data."

"The daughter said she had a place in the city."

Roarke angled his head. "There's nothing in her name, but I'll look into it further. Their official data lists their annual salary at about ten million for Wilkey, three-point-six for his older sons, one-point-two for the younger, and the daughter in the mid-six figures. None of those will be near to accurate."

"So maybe we can toss tax evasion and fraud in there when we bag them. Okay." She took another turn around the board. "McNab, what can you tell us about the recorder on Huffman's 'link?"

"The 'link was damaged in the recycler, so we had to work around that. Lucky for us, the internals, including the tracker, held up with minimal damage. The tracker with recording features is illegal, unauthorized. No ID number so not law enforcement or military, as it's required. I'm going to say no for the spooks and their kind, too, because it just wasn't good enough. It's decent, but it's not that caliber. And that's why it got the echo. It was breaking down. You'd get audio and video — probably clear for the first while, then the vid would get blurry, the audio echoes."

"Can you estimate how long it had been in use?"

"I'd give it about a year outside, about nine months inside. I'm figuring that on the amount of use. Huffman used the 'link for texting and calls, and that's it."

"Nine months to a year." Eve nodded. "She got engaged to Caine last summer, and she met Byrd last fall. It fits. All right, Ariel Byrd's our priority. But right up with her are Keene Grimsley and Special Agent Anthony Quirk, both missing, and it's not a stretch to presume dead. And Ella Alice Foxx, alive and we presume being held against her will. They're tied together, so we make those knots.

"Peabody, use my auxiliary and start compiling everything you can on Wilkey's two older sons, their wives. I'll take the daughter, the youngest son, and the mother. Yancy, how about you do the same with Gayle Steenberg? She's going to be Ella's trainer, her immediate supervisor or whatever benign term they use for keeper in there."

"I've got my portable. I can do a run on her, her family on that."

"Great. You want coffee or whatever, there's an AutoChef and a friggie in the kitchen. Feeney, Roarke, McNab, I need Ella Foxx's data."

"We'll get it." Feeney scratched the back of his neck. "Might take some time, but Roarke's got what we need in his comp lab here."

"Roarke, the more I know about Natural Order's and the Wilkeys' finances the better."

"It's like music to my ears. I'll set that up on auto in the lab while we find young Ella."

"Let's get to it."

Eve settled in, tuned everything else out.

She started with the mother.

Rachel Leigh Wilkey, nee Charles, Caucasian, age fifty-one.

Pattern, Eve thought. Twelve years younger. And married, she noted, for thirty-two years.

She skipped over the offspring, as she already knew, scrolled down to education. And as she expected, Rachel Charles had been a student — Montana U in Missoula — when Wilkey, the roots he'd planted with Natural Order already dug in and spreading, came to town. From a ranching family, she noted, one with an impressive dude ranch as well as a working one. Wealthy then, and wealthy still. Rachel had a brother, older, who'd joined the family business.

She'd studied animal husbandry before she'd dropped out to marry Wilkey.

Six weeks, from what she could put together, after he'd come to her college.

Didn't pop a kid out — like McNab said — right off though, did she? Eve shut her eyes, did the math. Nope, it took a couple years. The second, right away, but then a four-year gap, then another four years.

Interesting.

She dug down into medical records, then sat back.

280

"Peabody?"

"Huh? What?"

"Have you looked at medical records on the oldest sons?"

"Not there yet."

"Look now."

"Sec." A moment later, Peabody frowned. "I'm not finding any. I mean none. Not sealed, just nothing."

"Yeah, I've got nothing on Wilkey's wife after their marriage thirty-two years ago. The standards up to then, then nothing."

She swiveled to face Peabody. "Their own hospitals, clinics, doctors, and so on. So no records. Not of injuries, illnesses, meds, treatments, in her case, childbirth. Or possible miscarriages or fertility treatments."

"He said his wife was ill, and on the island in treatment."

"That's right, but what sort of illness, what sort of treatment?"

Eve did another quick search. "Her parents and her older brother are alive and well on the ranch in Montana. Maybe they're members, maybe not. I'm going to find out. I'm about to have a conversation. If you need quiet, I'll take it elsewhere."

Peabody sent Eve an amused look. "Dallas, I work in the bullpen."

"Right." She used her desk 'link, contacted Montana.

A man with a short, graying beard and a big-ass cowboy hat filled the screen. "New York City? How 'bout that? What can I do for you, Dallas, Lieutenant Eve?"

"Mr. Charles?"

"That's right. Morgan Charles."

"I'm investigating a case, and during the course of the investigation I've found some potential connections to Natural Order."

Everything about him went sour, his eyes, his mouth, his voice. "We don't have anything to do with those crazy fuckers — excuse my language."

"My data states your sister, Rachel, is married to Stanton Wilkey, who is the head of the order."

"I know it. I've been sick about it for better'n thirty years. It doesn't mean we've got anything to do with it. And I don't much want to talk about it."

"I'm sorry to bring up difficult feelings, Mr. Charles. Could you tell me the last time you saw or spoke to your sister?"

"More than twenty-five years ago, when they brought their traveling circus to Bozeman. I took my wife and my two kids — had one more after, but two at that point — to see her. I wanted to see my baby sister, to talk to her, to try to mend some fences."

"I see."

"Do you?" His mouth stayed so tight, a muscle began to twitch in his jaw. "You might see better if I tell you my wife, the love of my damn life, the mother of my children, is Cherokee."

"Yes, I do."

"And what does she say to me, my own sister, in front of my beautiful wife and boys? She tells me my

282

marriage isn't recognized and my children aren't legitimate. Until I restore order to my life, she won't see or speak to me again. That she'll pray I find my way back."

"I'm very sorry."

"I took my family home, and that's been that. I don't know how that son of a bitch turned my sister into that person I met in Bozeman. I never told my parents about it, they had heartbreak enough. I'd appreciate if you'd honor that."

"Yes, sir. She would have had children herself at that time."

"Two boys, another on the way. My wife said how hard it must be to have three kids so close together, and that's maybe why she looked so sickly and tired out."

"Would you remember what year this was?"

"Happens I do — or can figure — since you ask. Our oldest had his third birthday right before we went to Bozeman. So that would've been November of '35 . . . Why?"

"Just a detail. I realize these questions are personal," she began.

"You aim to tie that son of a bitching Wilkey to some crime in New York City? Put his ass in prison?"

Though Eve chose her words carefully, she kept her eyes directly on his. "I'm pursuing all avenues in my investigation."

His jaw loosened as he nodded. "Yep, yep, I got a cousin who's a sheriff around these parts. I know the lingo well enough. There's a chance of it, ask away."

"Did or does your sister have money of her own? I mean hers to access?"

"She had access to her college money when she took off with that son of a bitch, and she yanked it out before we could do a damn thing about that. Then what does she do? I still pray she wasn't in her right mind."

Heat rolled into his face, fired in his eyes. "She has a lawyer contact our folks. She was to get a share of the ranch when she turned twenty-five, and a bigger share when they pass. The lawyer said she wanted the cash equivalent now. They said no, and the next thing you know she's suing 'em for it."

His jaw didn't tighten again, but he looked away, took several seconds to gather himself.

"They were going to fight it, but it ripped them to pieces. Tore the heart right out of them. Their own child doing that, for money. They settled it. Wasn't going to give them the share she'd've gotten when they were in the ground, fuckers — Sorry."

"Mr. Charles, I've rarely heard the term used more accurately."

"Appreciate it. They offered five and a half million, and she took it. She's never once come to see them, written to them, called them, their own baby girl. Not once in all these years. I don't know what that man does, Miz Dallas, but he turned my sister into something she wasn't. He does that to people."

"That he does, Mr. Charles."

"Is my sister . . . is she in trouble, too?"

"I don't think she's involved in the matter I'm investigating. I appreciate, very much, your taking the time to answer my questions."

"If you have any more, would you come back to me, and not my parents? They're feisty enough, but they're getting up there. And this is a hole in their heart. Their girl gone, grandkids they've never met. It's a hole."

"If there's anything else, I'll come to you. I won't contact them."

"Thanks for that. I gotta get on. But hey, do you know that New York cop they made that clone vid about?"

"Actually, I . . . Yes."

"Sure hope you're as good as she was in the vid and nail that son of a bitch's ass to a splintery wall."

Peabody stopped working when Eve clicked off. "You let him get away with calling you Miz, not just because you didn't want to interrupt the flow, but because, jeez, who wouldn't feel for that guy? For his family."

"Just another reason I want to nail Wilkey's ass to a splintery wall. She was pregnant, and there's no offspring on record of that year or the next. Or until Mirium Wilkey in March of '37. So either she miscarried or had a stillbirth, or the child died. And I'm betting that happened with her more than once."

"Kids guarantee the future."

"And he'd want a lot of guarantees."

She turned back to her screen.

"Why isn't the daughter married to some rich dude by now?" Eve wondered.

The click that Yancy's arrival interrupted clicked again.

She started her next run.

CHAPTER
SIXTEEN

Money, Eve thought as she began looking more deeply into Mirium Wilkey's background and data. Was it all about money? Always a core motive for murder.

She'd lived most of her life without it, or with just enough to get through. She'd gone hungry as a child, yes, but that had been a result of cruelty and neglect. She'd never developed a thirst for wealth.

But that didn't mean she couldn't understand it, and its sometimes lethal power.

Roarke had the thirst, and most of it a result of the cruelty and neglect in his own childhood. He'd stolen to survive, then to quench the thirst. But rather than being driven by that lethal power, he'd held the wheel.

He'd never killed for gain.

Had Wilkey? Every instinct said yes, oh yes, he had. Maybe, just maybe, not with his own hands. But with words, with his deliberate, calculated, decades-long spread of intolerance, distrust, cool-blooded prejudice delivered behind the mask of faith.

He'd raised his flock by giving them not just excuses to hate the other, but the right. He'd certainly raised his children by the same methods.

Three sons, one daughter.

The daughter received her primary education in Natural Order schools — no surprise there. She'd earned an MBA from Unity University, Natural Order's online college. Another degree, same place, in hospitality and a third in computer science.

Were those directives from the father, Eve wondered, or Mirium's own interests and ambitions?

And even with those three degrees, she'd been relegated to serving her father and running his household.

According to her data, she owned no property in her own name, earned a salary considerably less than even her younger brother. Her job title: domestic manager.

"I bet that grates," Eve muttered.

Would it grate to know she'd be expected to marry a man approved — maybe selected — by her father? Then produce a child every year or two?

Or would that suit her own ambitions?

After another thirty minutes of searching, scanning, absorbing, Eve got more coffee. She put her boots up on her command center and studied the board.

Studied Mirium Wilkey's ID shot.

A young, not unattractive woman who presented herself as plain, wore clothes even Eve recognized as dowdy and unfashionable. An educated woman with three degrees and a substantial income, who owned nothing.

Her older brothers owned homes, vehicles, held important-sounding titles.

But not the daughter.

"It's got to fucking grate. Peabody."

"Yeah, I'm about to send you the highlights."

"Tell me this. Where did Wilkey's sons go to college?"

"Stanton Wilkey University."

Eve turned her head from the board to look at Peabody. "Where?"

"He built a small, private college on Utopia Island. All three went there. The youngest just graduated. I took a closer look at it. It's males only, and only accepts students who've graduated from approved schools."

"They can do that?"

"Private island, private school. Ninety-six percent of the graduates go on to work in what they call the Natural Order Network."

"Huh. Computer, search for any and all female-only universities and colleges connected to Stanton Wilkey or Natural Order. Global search."

Acknowledged. Working . . .

"You're doing the daughter. Where did she go?"

"Online. Two bachelor's degrees and an MBA from his online college."

Search results show no college or university on-planet with those parameters.

"Because women don't need higher education," Eve concluded.

"Plus, it might give them ideas. He let his daughter get those degrees — but not in a social or open setting

— because he can use her. I found some photos of her online, with him. Sometimes her mother or her brothers are in them, too. Mirium's always in the background. She looks like staff because that's essentially what she is."

Eve drank some coffee. "Wouldn't that bug the shit right out of you?"

"Me, yeah. But it's the way she was raised, it's what she's been taught."

"Wouldn't you say the woman we spoke to today on that veranda deal could think for herself? Even had a sense of power and authority?"

"Yeah, I would. Until her father joined us."

Eve lifted a hand, shot a finger at Peabody. "Exactly. He masks bigotry with benevolence. She masks intelligence with subservience. I think they're both liars."

She looked over at Yancy. "Got anything interesting?"

"I think so, here and there."

"Why don't you come over here, bring a chair?"

He brought the one he'd been sitting on, and his portable.

"I'm going to let this other Wilkey stuff stew back here for a while." She waved her hand at the back of her head. "Give me what you've got on Steenberg."

"Okay, she and her husband didn't join the order until they were in their late forties. She worked as a domestic, he had a small handyman business. This was outside of St. Paul. Financially they were underwater more than above. What I put together is Carl Steenberg did some work for a member, and over the course of

289

the job, the member talked up the order. Steenberg already belonged to Freedom Warriors — that's been taken down, but it was a white nationalist group in the Midwest back then — so it was preaching to the choir."

"Are you still synched with the screen?"

"Yeah."

"Put Carl Steenberg up there. I like the visual."

When he had, Eve saw a hard-eyed man in his upper sixties, going jowly. Gravel gray hair in a severe buzz cut.

"Split screen Gayle Steenberg and keep going."

"They look like the mean version of *American Gothic*" Peabody commented, and Yancy laughed.

"They really do. I have to figure the member sponsored the Steenbergs, because that's one way to get into meetings and seminars, and they couldn't afford the orientation and screening fees required otherwise."

"Sponsored?"

"I set up a fake account and filled in a questionnaire on their website," Yancy told her. "The orientation and screening fees are pretty sticky, but they waive the orientation fee if you're sponsored by a member in good standing who's been in for a minimum of three years."

"That's good work, Yancy. Good thinking."

He shrugged. "You get curious. Six months after they joined, Steenberg closed his business, and they went to work at a Natural Order center — maintenance for him, domestic for her. A few years later, they packed up, moved to Kansas. They worked on the order's Heartland Farm, and their kids went to the farm school. Five years after that, they moved to the HQ in Connecticut.

"Their kids didn't."

"What happened there?"

"The address I got for both kids, at the time of that move, was back in St. Paul. Maternal grandparents. Both had reached eighteen, so the Steenbergs couldn't legally stop them. Both still live in that general area. The oldest one's a cop with St. Paul PSD."

"Is that so?"

"It's an hour earlier there, so I went ahead and reached out. Detective Leroy Russ — both of them changed their last name legally to their grandparents'. I'll have it all in the report, but to sum it up, he said his father was a vicious brute, and his mother no better. And Natural Order's full of the same, along with lunatics, assholes, dumb shits, and other colorful terms."

"I take it he didn't enjoy his time with them."

"Counted the days. He said he would have left when he hit eighteen, but couldn't leave his brother. The minute the brother hit, they walked off the farm, stuck out their thumbs, and rode them back to St. Paul. He says he still remembers how his grandparents cried when they saw him and his brother at the door."

"Any contact with the parents?"

"None. He said if we need anything from him to ask. He and his brother had to put it all in a box, but he'd open it up if we needed him to."

"This is good information. Peabody, anything nearly that interesting on the Wilkey brothers?"

"I'm sorry to say, no. Their official data's pretty straightforward — except for no medical, like the others. I got more from media searches, which pretty much shows the two oldest as entitled, and not really bright, jerks.

"They both had big society weddings — on the island. Both their wives are members, and come from membership families. The oldest heads the order's European HQ, based outside of London, and lives there with his family. He travels a lot. The second son heads up what's called Global Networking, is based outside of East Washington. He clearly has political ambitions, has a lot of followers on his social media rants about how our rights have been stripped away, a lot of anti-immigration, anti-gay, anti-everything, really, but his own views. Plenty of his media followers are there to punch at him, but there are plenty who agree."

She glanced at her notes. "They both have law degrees, but since the island's university isn't recognized by the American Bar Association, they can't practice here. Oh, and for fun? They like to hunt. They have the money and the connections to go to these preserves overseas where they can shoot genetically engineered animals."

Her eyes went teary. "Genetically engineered animals can still feel. They kill them, then they pose with them."

"Take a break. Walk around, get a fizzy."

"I'll walk around, get some water."

When Peabody got up to go into the kitchen, Yancy turned to Eve.

"I'm not Homicide. I like my work. That's not true," he amended. "I love my work. But if and when you go to take these people down, I'd like to be part of it."

"Done."

She got up herself, but only to walk to the board. "I agree with Detective Russ, and we'll do everything we can to break this apart. But our priorities remain Ariel Byrd, Keene Grimsley, Special Agent Quirk, and Ella Foxx.

"It's money," she said. "And it's power — protecting those. Money and power they used to spread and perpetuate an ugly vision."

She heard the geek squad coming back, and hoped McNab's burst of laughter meant success.

"We're good," McNab announced when he pranced in. "We are damn spanky good."

"Data now, brag later."

"You'll have it." Looking pretty pleased himself, Roarke strolled over to swipe a fingertip down the shallow dent in her chin.

He had his hair tied back, his sleeves rolled up.

"But now we've earned a beer."

"We're on duty."

"Are you?" Roarke looked deliberately at his wrist unit. "Are you really?"

"Your house, your case." Feeney slid his hands in his baggy pockets. "But I still outrank you."

"Hell. One beer. McNab, I want whatever you got on-screen."

While he set it up, Roarke came back from the kitchen with two bottles in each hand, and Peabody, steady again, brought the other two.

"Figured we'd be on this half the night." Feeney took his beer, then a nice long pull. "But not only are we damn good, but they did a half-assed job of it. Maybe three-quarter-assed job, but not a full-assed job. Figured nobody'd bother looking into it. Why would they?"

"Why indeed?" Roarke handed Eve her beer, and rubbed an arm on her shoulder. "When she had, essentially, no one."

"There she is," Yancy murmured when Ella's ID shot popped onscreen.

Eve saw young, defiant, and sulky. In the official ID her hair, a reddish purple with bright blue streaks, exploded around that pretty young face. She had a tiny red stud on the right side of her nose, multicolored studs in her ears.

"Parents, Cokie Crosse, deceased last February — OD — and Zeek Foxx, deceased in April of 2059, shanked in prison, Florida."

"As you can see," Roarke began, "she was tossed back and forth quite a bit in her young life. Into foster care, back to the mother, into juvie, foster, and so on. Picked up as a runaway, for begging without a license."

"Picking pockets at sixteen," Eve added.

"A girl has to eat, after all."

"Last known address Stone Tree House, not in Brooklyn. Here in the city."

"It's a halfway house." Feeney took another pull. "She wasn't eighteen when she went in, but her caseworker signed off. It's in the data. Jane Po, Child Services. She's got employment listed, too. Fast Break Café, and she graduated high school with a GED — and damn good grades."

"Why didn't Po look into this when she didn't show up, at the halfway house, at work? Let's find out."

Before Eve could stride to her command center, Roarke took her arm. "Eve, not tonight. It's past midnight."

"Crap. Crap. Okay, Peabody, get her address. We're going to take her first thing in the morning."

"She's on Beach — 528 Beach, apartment 302."

"Meet me there, eight hundred hours. Nobody filed a missing persons, nobody looked and saw her data wiped? Why?"

Absently, she drank beer. "They dyed her hair, took away her personality, but they didn't get her. Not all the way."

"We have to get her out, Dallas." Peabody leaned into McNab and looked a little teary again.

Tired, Eve decided. They were all tired, and burnout could follow if she didn't call it.

"That's the plan. It's not going to be tonight, probably not tomorrow, but we'll get her out. I need those financials, Roarke."

"You'll have them. I've accumulated quite a bit already."

"All right. Peabody and I will talk to Po first thing in the morning. I need to meet with Whitney, and coordinate with the feds. I have to give them what we've got. We hit Po, and we hit Foxx's last place of employment. See what we see.

"We'll brief by noon tomorrow, that'll include the financials. Whatever you have, send them in."

"So, I'm not invited?"

She'd expected that. "You want to brief and be briefed, be there. Noon, unless I need to reschedule. This was good work, everyone. Damn fucking good cop work. Now get out. Go home."

"I'll get you transpo," Roarke told them.

"Got my own ride." Feeney handed Eve his empty bottle. "You take care of the kids." Then he lifted his chin at Ella's photo. "Reminds me of you."

Eve's jaw dropped. "What? I never looked like that in my life."

"It's in the eyes, kid. In the eyes that say I'll kick your ass if I need to."

He gave her a little shoulder punch and headed out. "See you at noon."

She frowned at the screen while Roarke arranged for a car and driver.

And when the rest of the cops herded themselves out, she turned to Roarke.

"I don't see it."

"I do." He kissed her temple. "And it will give me great pleasure to help get her away from there. Now come to bed, Lieutenant, you're as tired as the rest of your cops."

She let him lead her out, but couldn't let go. "Just give me some highlights on the financials so far."

"He spends lavishly on himself. I think many of his faithful will be disillusioned when that comes out. Fine wines, art, furnishings, the jets, the homes, and so on. And, of course, he's tucked more than a bit away in offshore accounts, under assumed names. And, as I told you before, the order itself is heavily invested in property. They do make profits — the medical centers, the membership fees, merchandizing."

"Merchandizing?"

"His oratories, his books, meditative music, that sort of thing."

"What's he really worth?"

"I'll have that for you tomorrow, but I can safely say not as much as he'd have people believe."

He turned her deliberately toward the bed where the cat opened one wary eye, then nudged her down to sit.

When he bent to take off her boots, the gesture, combined with fatigue and that late-night beer, made her smile.

"It's been a hell of a day."

"That it has."

"You were right about calling it. My brain's going to mush."

"Turn it off for a bit then." He tugged her to her feet.

Easier said, she thought, but unhooked her weapon harness.

By the time she'd undressed, he'd turned down the bed. When she slid into it, she felt her body go: Ah.

"You'll be up before dawn anyway." Another ah as she curled into him. "Organizing world domination and cop consultant duties. Wake me up."

"All right. Sleep now."

And she did, curled between him and the cat at the small of her back, until her communicator signaled. Blown fully awake, she snatched it from the bedside table.

"Block video. Dallas."

Rather than the flat-voiced Dispatch she'd expected, the voice was hesitant.

"Lieutenant Dallas, this is nine-one-one operator Harris. I realize this is irregular, but there's a woman on the line who insists on speaking only to you."

"Who is it?"

"She won't give her name, sir, and her number's blocked. She sounds desperate. I can attempt to trace her location if you can keep her on the line."

"Put her on."

Roarke called for lights at ten percent before he got out of bed.

"Ma'am, I have Lieutenant Dallas for you. Lieutenant?"

"This is Dallas. Who's this?"

"Oh God, thank God." This voice wasn't hesitant. Desperate, yes, but Eve recognized terror with it. "Will you help me? Something terrible's happened. I know something terrible happened."

"What happened?"

"I need to get away. I have a little boy, and I need to get him away. I'm pregnant, I need to get us somewhere safe. Please help me."

"I will help you." She took the coffee Roarke offered. "But I need to know where you are, what happened. What's your name?"

"You can't come here. They watch, I know they do — and I know how that sounds. I'm going to get my little boy and what I can carry and leave, but I don't have anywhere to go. I waited until all the lights were off, but I'm afraid someone will see us when I leave. I saw you today. I saw you and I recognized you, and . . . It was like a sign. I need your help."

"I'm going to help you. Are you in immediate danger?"

"No. My husband's not here. He's at the retreat. But Marcia, next door — they took her away. Do you have somewhere safe I can take my son?"

"Yes. Tell me where you are. I'll take you both somewhere safe."

After a quick sob of relief, the voice rushed on. "Please don't come here. They'll know if you do, and I'm afraid they'll find me. I'm going to walk out with Gabriel, he's only ten months old. I already packed some things, and I waited, and I'm going to carry him and get out. It's the only way, believe me."

"Okay. Walk two blocks west." Shutting her eyes, Eve brought the Tribeca neighborhood back in her head. "Then walk a block north. It's going to take me about twenty minutes to get to you, but I'll meet you and I'll take you to a safe place."

"Thank you. Thank God."

"Keep your 'link open. Operator Harris?"

"Lieutenant."

"Stay on with the caller. Ma'am, what's your name?"

"I'm Zoe."

"Zoe, Operator Harris will stay on."

Roarke, already dressed in jeans, a thin gray sweater, brought clothes out of Eve's closet.

As she spoke, Eve wiggled into underwear, soot-gray trousers. "Stay calm. Take only what you absolutely need. I'll be there as soon as I can."

"Please hurry. I'm so scared."

"Talk to Operator Harris. You're not alone."

"I'm right here, Zoe," Eve heard Harris say as she shrugged into the shirt Roarke handed her.

She muted the comm. "Tribeca," she told him.

"The car's already around front. I contacted Dochas while you spoke with her. They'll be ready."

"Great." She hooked on her weapon harness, grabbed her badge, her 'link, the rest of her belt and pocket debris.

He'd ordered a black, four-door sedan. However sedate it looked, Eve knew he could make it move.

"Something happened to Marcia Piper. I need to get this woman and kid to safety, to Dochas before we check on that. She's probably right about people watching. That block had that kind of feel."

He made the sedan move.

"It's near to four in the morning," Roarke commented as he punched speed out of the sedan. "It seems her best chance to leave unnoticed. Christ Jesus, she sounded terrified."

"Harris will keep her steady. She's trained for it. If Zoe follows through, she should be on the corner of Moore and Greenwich. But at the rate we're going, we may beat her there."

New York hit its quiet pocket. Some cars zipped now and then. A block-long white limo streamed by with a couple of women standing, arms outstretched, in the sunroof.

Eve heard their "Wooooo-hoooo!" carry boozily on the night air.

As Roarke barreled south, she saw a man in sweatpants walking a dog about the size of a large rat. The man had a poop-scoop sticking out of his pocket and shuffled behind the dog like a sleepwalker.

Roarke avoided the endless party at Times Square and kept to the quiet, nearly empty streets where he could let the car fly.

When he circled to the corner, no one waited.

"Stay in the car," Eve told him. "I'm going to walk in her direction."

"She sounded sincerely terrified, Eve, but there's no guarantee this isn't a setup."

She merely opened the jacket he'd pulled out for her to wear, exposed her weapon.

Still, she'd gone no more than a yard when she saw a woman, a bulging bag on one shoulder, a toddler on the other hip, doing her best to run.

She'd seen her before, Eve remembered, carting the kid on her back and market bags in both hands.

"Zoe." Eve held up a hand when the woman stumbled to a halt, didn't quite hold back a scream. "Lieutenant Dallas. Let me help you."

She stepped forward to take the bag. The woman shook as if sheathed in ice. "The car's right around the corner. The man behind the wheel's with me. He's with me, and we're going to keep you safe."

To get her moving again, Eve put an arm around her waist. "Just a little bit farther." Gently, Eve took the 'link out of Zoe's hand. "Operator Harris."

"Right here, Lieutenant."

"I've got her now. Thank you for your assistance."

"Glad to help. Zoe, give Gabe a kiss for me. Operator out."

"She — she sang to him. He cried when I woke him up, and she sang to him. Are you taking me to the police station? If he finds me there —"

"No."

Zoe shook harder when Roarke got out of the car. But he only smiled and opened the back door.

"He's with me," Eve repeated. "You're safe."

"Am I going to jail?"

"No. Trust me now, Zoe. You trusted me enough to call me, to ask for help. Trust me to help you."

"He said the police would take me to jail and I'd never see Gabe again."

"He lied."

Still shuddering, Zoe cuddled her son and climbed in the back.

"I'm going to sit in the back with her," Eve said.

Nodding, Roarke waited. He saw the little boy look at him with sad, sleepy eyes.

When he got behind the wheel again, Eve shifted, started to speak to Zoe. But the woman pressed her face to Eve's shoulder and wept, wept, wept.

Saying nothing, Eve put her arms around Zoe, and Roarke drove her to safety.

CHAPTER
SEVENTEEN

When they arrived at Dochas, two women stood at the door. One Eve judged as mid-forties, the other about a decade younger. Both dressed casually and wore sympathetic smiles.

"Welcome to Dochas," the older one told Zoe. "You're safe here."

"What is it?" Zoe looked around in wonder laced with fear.

"Home as long as you need it."

"You have a very sleepy little man there." The younger one pumped up her smile. "And so handsome. It's Gabriel, isn't it? I'm Natalie, and this is Gracie. Would you like to go up, get him settled in your room?"

Zoe just wrapped tighter around her son.

"I need to talk to Zoe. Maybe we can do that down here. Zoe, why don't you let Natalie take your bag up to your room? You need to trust me," she added when Zoe stayed frozen.

"It's hard," Gracie said softly. "It's hard to trust when you've been so afraid. Did you know Lieutenant Dallas and Roarke built this house, this lovely house, to keep women who've been afraid safe? Women and their children."

Eyes still wide and wary, Zoe looked around again. "There are other women here, and kids?"

"Yes, and they're all safe. Why don't you come in here with your sweet boy, and you can sit and talk to Lieutenant Dallas? Nat can take your bag. How about some coffee, or tea?"

"I can't have coffee, thank you. I'm pregnant."

"And how far along are you?" Gracie asked as she gently led Zoe into a pretty parlor.

"Seventeen weeks." When the baby started fussing, Zoe jiggled him. "I think he's hungry. He's not used to me waking him up like this, and —"

"Are you nursing?"

"I'm starting to wean him. My husband wants to wean him, but —"

"It would be a comfort to you both now with all this upheaval. Sit here now and feed your baby. Some tea for you? A nice soothing tea. Lieutenant, Roarke?"

"Coffee's good. Black for both of us, thanks." Eve sat across from Zoe.

"I'll give you a hand with that, Gracie." Roarke stepped out.

"This is your house?" Zoe asked Eve.

"No, it's your house, and the others who come here. Why don't we start with your full name?"

"Zoe Metcalf. I was Zoe Brown before I got married."

"When was that?"

"Two years ago."

"You're a member of Natural Order."

"Yes. No. Yes." Tears leaked as she shifted the baby. She unbuttoned her shirt, and smoothly flipped a flap on her bra. The baby latched on like a leech. "Harley said I had to join so we could get married. So I signed the papers, and we got married, and he brought me to New York."

"From where?"

"From Ohio."

"How old are you, Zoe?"

"I'm twenty-one — or I will be next month. I thought it would be wonderful to be married, and exciting to live in New York. But it's not. I'm only allowed to go to the store or to one of the neighbors'. I can only take Gabriel to the park if one of the other women goes, too. Once I took him by myself, and Harley found out. He got so mad."

"Is he violent with you?"

"Sometimes. Not bad, not like Mr. Piper with Marcia. Harley just slaps or takes away a privilege." She stroked the baby's cheek as he kneaded her other breast and stared up at her. "I can watch one hour of screen a day, or read for one hour, as long as all my housework is done."

She looked down, continued to stroke her baby's cheek. "It's not right. I know it's not right. But they watch — some of the other women on the block. Gina — she lives across the street — she told me once they get extra privileges if they report infractions. She tried to leave once, but they caught her. She had a black eye after. She used to laugh a lot, but not anymore."

"What's Gina's full name?"

Zoe looked up again. "Can you help her?"

"I'm going to try. What's her name?"

"Gina Dawber. She's the one who told me how to get a little money from the marketing. Every few times you go, you take something back you haven't opened or used, and ask for cash instead of credit to the debit card. Harley always checks the debit card when I go, but if you just return some cleaner or something, get the cash, you can start saving."

Smoothly, she shifted the baby to her other breast. "I saved, and put the money in one of Gabe's diapers — a clean one," she added with the first hint of a smile. "Harley doesn't change Gabe. That's a mother's job. I bought the clone 'link, and hid that, too. We're not allowed to have our own 'link."

Gracie and Roarke brought in tea, coffee, some muffins that looked freshly baked.

"Look at that little angel, sound asleep now." Gracie trailed a finger over Gabe's down of brown hair. "He's got your jawline, and your nose. Would you like me to take him up, settle him in his crib? I raised two of my own," she added.

She walked over to a small screen sitting on a table. After tapping some buttons, she gestured. "That's your room I've programmed on, and his crib right there. You'll be able to see and hear him. I'll sit in the rocker right by the crib, and when you've finished your talk, I'll come and bring you up to your room."

"You'll stay with him? He's a good sleeper, but . . ."

"It's a new place, and if he wakes he'll want his mama, won't he? Don't worry, I'll bring him straight to you if he wakes."

306

"Thank you." Tears welling again, Zoe lifted the baby toward Gracie. "I don't even know what to say."

"Not to worry." She settled the sleeping boy on her shoulder. "Bless you," she said to Roarke, then turned to Eve. "Bless you both."

When Gracie carried the baby out, Roarke stepped back again. "I'll just be in the next room."

"You don't have to go," Zoe told him. "I recognize you, too. I've seen you both on-screen, when Harley watches the news. I'm better now, I think. I feel better. Oh, look! She's putting Gabriel in his crib. He's a good sleeper. He's so sweet. I couldn't stand the idea of him growing up in that house, in the order. And now with another." She pressed a hand to her belly. "I couldn't bear it."

"You're very brave."

Zoe shook her head at Roarke. "I've been afraid nearly every day for almost two years. But I saw you today, Lieutenant Dallas. I saw you and the other policewoman next door at the Pipers', and I thought, It's a sign. It's a sign that it's time, that there's someone who can help. And still I didn't do anything."

"You called for help."

"Not until after . . . Marcia."

"I need you to tell me what happened. You said they took her away. Who took her?"

"Mr. Piper came home. He doesn't have to stay at the compound for retreat like Harley does. Because Marcia's not well, and they have children, and he's a VP and all. It was quiet. It's always quiet on the block at night. I put Gabe to bed at eight. I couldn't settle. I was trying to think what I should do, how I should do it. And then I heard them."

"Next door?"

"Yes. I had windows open, and I guess Marcia did, too, so I heard them. He was shouting at her, calling her stupid and swearing at her. I could hear him hitting her, and her crying. I put my hands over my ears. I sat on the floor with my hands over my ears but I could still hear them."

When she picked up her tea, her hand shook again.

"It's happened before. It happens a lot. The kids used to cry when it happened, but the last few times, they stay quiet, and I thought about them with their hands over their ears like me."

She breathed out, drank some tea. "He just screamed at her, horrible things, and I could hear thumps and crashes, things breaking or falling over. It was worse this time than the other times. I kept hearing something — her, I think — hit the wall. The shared wall between our houses. Then it stopped. At first, I thought, Thank God, it's over.

"I felt sick. I was afraid to close the windows in case he heard and realized I'd heard him beating her. I went upstairs, and I couldn't settle. I told myself to go to bed, just go to bed and I'd figure out what to do in the morning. Then I saw the van drive up."

"What kind of van?"

"I don't know. One of the order's. Black, I think, and no windows. I turned off the lights in my room. They — two men — got a kind of stretcher on wheels out of the back and went next door, and with the windows still open I heard voices. Not what they said, they weren't loud enough. And I needed to stay back so they didn't see me looking. I saw, oh God, I saw them roll the stretcher out. They had her covered, they had her in a kind of bag, so I couldn't see, but I know it was Marcia. It had to be Marcia. He killed her. He killed her."

Zoe covered her face with her hands.

"What time was this, Zoe?"

"I guess about nine-thirty, or maybe ten. I think maybe ten. I was going to get the 'link I'd hidden and call nine-one-one, but they drove away."

"Did you see a license plate?"

"No, I'm sorry. I thought, What if I call and the order comes here? What if Harley was right, and the police came and put me in jail? Then, not long after the van left, I heard him talking to the kids. I heard the kids crying, so I tried to see. He loaded the children in his SUV and drove away. And right after, like a minute after, another van came, a bigger one."

"Black again, windowless?"

"Yes. People got out of it. I think four or five. They wore, like, coveralls? I think. And had their hair covered. They rolled these, like, trollies out of the back of the van and into the house. They were there at least two hours, probably more. I could hear machines, like big vacuums or something, and once or twice one of them came out with a big bag and tossed it in the back of the van."

Cleaners, Eve thought. Crime-scene cleaners — the order's cleaners.

"Then they loaded everything back up, and left. I thought, he killed Marcia, and they're making it all go away. Like it never happened. What if Harley did that to me? What would happen to Gabe?"

She looked back at the monitor as if to assure herself he stayed safe.

"I sat in the dark, in case they came back. I waited in the dark until all the lights were out on the block. Then I waited more, just in case. I packed what I could without turning on any lights. Then I waited some more because I was too afraid to get the 'link. Then I went in to check on Gabe, and I just sat and looked at him sleeping for a long time. And I thought, no, no, he can't be here, can't be part of any of this. He's my baby, and I have to protect him. So I finally got the 'link, and called nine-one-one. I begged Operator Harris to let me talk to you."

"You did the right thing."

"If I'd used the 'link earlier . . ."

"You couldn't help Marcia. It was too late to help her. But what you've done now, what you're doing now is going to help others."

"Gina?"

"Yes. Did you get a look at any of the people who came — either van?"

"Sort of, yes. Maybe."

"Would you work with a police artist?"

Her shoulders pulled in. "Do I have to go to the police station?"

"No, he can come here. You can trust him, too. You should get some sleep." Eve stood and dug in her pocket for a card. "You can contact me at any time. I want you to tag me after you've gotten some sleep,

310

when you're ready to work with Detective Yancy, the police artist."

"Okay."

"Do you have family in Ohio?"

"My parents, my sister, but I don't want to contact them." Reaching out, she gripped Eve's hand like iron. "I don't want anyone from the order to hurt them."

"Are they members?"

"Oh God, no. It's just that they might send somebody there to see if I went there, or if they know. Harley might not want me back after this, but he'll want Gabe. Please don't let him take my baby away from me. Please don't —"

"Look at me." Eve leaned forward until their eyes met on the same level. "Nobody's going to touch your son. I'll get protection for your family in Ohio, and I'll let them know you're safe."

"Thank you, thank you. I've been so stupid."

"No, Zoe, you've been abused, and there's a world of difference."

"And what a fine mother you've proven to be already." Roarke stood. "Gracie's coming down for you."

"Thank you, so much. Lieutenant Dallas, would you tell my family I'm sorry, and I love them?"

"I will."

The minute they stepped outside, Eve pulled out her 'link and tagged APA Cher Reo.

Reo groaned. "Come on, Dallas. It's not even six A.M."

"Warrants, I need them. Now. Piper, Lawrence — I'll send you his salients — Murder One."

"Who'd he kill?"

311

"His pregnant wife. Beat her to death. I need a warrant to enter, to search and seize at the crime scene." She rattled off the address. "Where I'm heading now. And I need you to start working on warrants to get me and a team — probably NYPSD and FBI — into the Natural Order HQ"

"Whoa, whoa." The video popped on to show Reo jumping out of bed in red sleep shorts and a white tank. She shoved a hand through tousled blond curls. "I know you're working on a murder with connections to Natural Order, but —"

"They're holding a woman, Ella Alice Foxx, age eighteen. I believe Natural Order not only transported the body of Marcia Piper and sent cleaners to deal with the crime scene — eyewit on both — but that Lawrence Piper is holing up in their HQ. Accessory after the fact should get me a damn warrant."

"I'll get you the first two fast. The third's going to take some doing and some time. We need to coordinate there. I'll come into Central and we'll start working on it."

"Let's work fast."

She clicked off, then did a search on Piper.

"Lucked out. The SUV's in his name. If he had it through the order, this wouldn't be so easy."

She issued an APB on the vehicle, then a BOLO on Piper.

She kept working until Roarke pulled up at the address he'd heard her give Reo.

"Quiet," Eve observed. "Real quiet. You want to bet Zoe wasn't the only one to hear the screaming and pounding?" She pointed across the street. "Unit on the left, that's Gina Dawber's. We're getting her into Dochas, her and her kids, if she'll go. No vehicle out front. I bet the fuck of a husband's at the compound."

"Could be some carpooling involved."

"Could be. Here comes the warrant. Let's get inside. This dead zone's going to start waking up soon. I want a look around before the sweepers get here."

"I'll get your field kit."

Once they'd sealed up, Eve tried her master on the front door. When it didn't budge, she shrugged at Roarke.

"Over to you."

"I can't decide if I'm proud or revolted they use one of my systems."

"Pretty sure they're using your stuff at their HQ."

"Then I'll choose revolted."

It didn't take him long. When he nodded, Eve switched on her recorder. "Dallas and Roarke entering premises, duly authorized warrant."

Because you never assumed, she drew her weapon. She shoved the door, swept.

"This is the police. We are authorized to enter. Lights on full."

They flashed on to the same pristine foyer she'd seen before. She'd expected that — had already smelled the chemicals and solutions used to clean.

"There was a vase of flowers there. Gone now, probably fell over and broke. Small table missing from there. Lamp missing, a couple of pictures in frames. That's the shared wall."

She crossed to it, frowned. "I think that's fresh paint, and something else."

Curious, Roarke stepped up, sniffed as she did. "I don't smell anything but the paint."

"No, more this way."

He shifted, sniffed. "Ah, that's drywall compound, fast-drying compound. Someone patched this wall, very quickly, very efficiently."

"Yeah, she'd hit — her head would hit — right about here. *Wham, wham, wham.*" Eve mimed banging someone against the wall. "Head wound, lot of blood. And from the pieces that are missing, probably a lot across the floor as he punched, shoved, smacked her from one end of this room to the other. Ending here. Here's where she dropped. Either dead, or he finished her. Maybe strangled her. She'd have been out anyway."

"Head wound, like Ariel Byrd. Maybe, maybe. I sure as hell can squeeze him there once I have him."

With Roarke she toured the house, found every room — even the kids' rooms, immaculate.

"Creepy," she decided, and tried another door. "Locked. No, my turn." She nudged him aside when he started to step in. "Give me the picks."

He did, then watched her defeat the lock. "Now my heart swells with pride."

"Not as slick as you, but not bad." When she opened the door, called for lights, she grinned fiercely and rubbed her hands together.

"The asshole's home office. Look at all these e's. Social media guy, so yeah, lots of e's. Feeney's gang is going to have some fun."

314

"I could start having fun myself if you like."

She glanced at her wrist unit. "I've got to deal with the sweepers when they get here, and meet Peabody at Jane Po's at eight."

"You can authorize me to poke a bit."

"I can have uniforms get this stuff to EDD."

He gave her a sorrowful look. "Always spoiling my fun."

"You've got solar systems to buy. There's your fun."

"I've canceled the lot for today. I took care of that when I went out with Gracie. I'm invested, Eve. More than I already was. Now I've seen firsthand how what we built at Dochas can work. I've seen it before, but not like this. Not from the call for help. And here, I see what can happen when there's no way to help."

"Okay." She nodded, glanced back at the office. "All yours. And since you're sticking for now, maybe you can do some transporting. If I can talk Gina across the street into leaving, you could take her and her kids to Dochas. I'm not going to have time unless I reschedule meeting Peabody."

"How about this? I'll have your vehicle brought here, use the one outside. If you convince Gina, I'll take her first, then come back to play with this."

"That works. I'm going to walk over there and see what I can do with her now. Before the block wakes up. I'll keep an eye out for the sweepers."

When Eve walked outside, she noted a few lights had come on in some of the townhomes. Including the one across the street. And she caught movement in one of the upper windows — there, then gone.

She stepped to the door, pressed the buzzer. It took three tries before the door opened.

The woman, early twenties, had dark hair still tousled from sleep. She wore long cotton sleep pants, a plain white tee. She had a kid, somewhere around Bella's age, to Eve's best guess, on her hip, and another, a girl of about three, clinging to her leg.

"Ms. Dawber?"

"Yes." Though her voice stayed soft and pleasant, Eve saw raw fear in her eyes. "Is there a problem?"

"Yeah, there is." Eve held up her badge. "NYPSD. Did you see or hear anything from the Piper home last night?"

"No."

Lying, Eve thought. Fear lying.

"Is anyone else in the house, Ms. Dawber?"

"No. Just me and the kids. My husband is at work. I'm sorry I can't help you, Officer. I need to start breakfast for my children."

"Lieutenant. Lieutenant Dallas."

Something flickered over the woman's face at the name.

"I'm sorry. May I see your identification again?"

This time Gina studied it.

"Zoe Metcalf heard and saw something last night and contacted me."

What came into Gina's eyes now burned at the fear. And that was hope. "I don't understand."

"She took your advice on tucking a little money away whenever she could and used it to buy a clone 'link. She called nine-one-one and worked her way to me.

She and her son are safe, Gina. I can take you and your kids to her, to safety."

"Take the baby." Gina literally thrust him into Eve's arms. "Lollie and I can't leave the house, but take Westley. Please take him away from here."

Eve struggled with the baby as he flailed and cried and reached for his mother. "Why can't you leave the house?"

"House arrest." Gina hiked up her left pants leg to reveal an ankle tracker. "He put one on Lollie, too, just to make sure I toed the line. He'll have one on the baby before much longer."

"We'll get it off."

"No, no, it's programmed to shock if I tamper with it, if I leave the house without permission or an authorized companion. I could take it, I could, but Lollie's just three. Please. Come on, baby, don't cry now."

Eve yanked out her 'link. "Roarke, I need you across the street now. We'll get it off, deactivate the shocker. You need to trust me."

"You don't understand what these people are like, what they can do."

"Yes, I do. Take him back." Eve pushed the very unhappy baby back at Gina. "See the man coming over? Nobody, absolutely nobody, has a better hand with electronics."

She swung around to Roarke. "Tracker on the woman and the girl, with shockers."

"On the child?" Roarke masked the quick outrage, then crouched down to examine the one on Gina's ankle. "Ah, I see. Well now, nothing to this at all. It's not only old tech, but basic as it comes."

"But he said —" Gina broke off, shut her eyes. "He told me it was state-of-the-art. New tech, and unbreakable. He's a liar, but I believed it. Do mine first, please, just in case. When I tried to get mine off before, it knocked me out."

"It won't now. I've already disengaged the shocker. Just another moment here, and . . ." He unlocked it, started to hand it to Eve.

"Let me get an evidence bag."

Knowing Roarke, she jogged back to the sedan. He made sure she had a field kit in every vehicle. She got two, jogged back.

He talked in that musical voice, soothing as a kiss on the brow, to the child as he disengaged her tracker.

"I don't like it," the kid told him, with her bottom lip poked out.

"Who would like such a thing? And there you are, darling. You won't have to wear it ever again."

"Ms. Dawber —"

"Don't call me that." The look Gina shot Eve scorched. The fearful woman had vanished.

"Gina. Get what you absolutely need, and we'll get you and your children to safety."

"We don't need a damn thing but each other. We need to go now, right now. Some of the rats will start waking up. We don't need anything from here, don't want anything from here. Please."

"Change of plan," Eve said to Roarke. "Do me a solid, get the sweepers started, and contact Feeney, get

318

him and McNab here. Gina, does the man who put that tracker on you have an office in the house, electronics?"

"Yeah, locked room. I tried to get in. I paid."

"We want those confiscated, too. I'll get them to safety."

"Done. Let me help you."

He picked up the little girl, who seemed fine with it.

As they got the kids in the back, Gina looked up the block. "That's the head rat."

Eve watched a woman, early forties, flying brown hair, run out of a house.

"Can she contact Natural Order?"

"No, even the rats don't get communication privileges."

With a fierce smile, Gina shot up a middle finger.

"God, that felt good. Let's go please. Let's go." She jumped in with her kids.

"I'll tag you as soon as I get her there," Eve began.

"I've got this here, just go."

As Eve got behind the wheel, he strolled a few feet in the running woman's direction.

She turned on her heel and ran back into her house.

Yeah, he had it.

"Okay, Gina, you're safe now. And I've got some questions."

"Just let me — It's okay, Westley, we're going to see Gabe." She cuddled both kids, closed her eyes. "We're going away from here to see Gabe and Zoe. I didn't think she really had it in her. Thank God for her. Thank God."

Since Eve hadn't yet done a run on Gina, she went directly to the source.

"How long have you been married to . . ."

"Steven. His name's Steven, and is it married if you were drugged and forced to say I-fricking-do?"

"No." Tougher every second, Eve noted, and fury had replaced any fear. "How long, and how did they get to you?"

"We're in a car, driving away with a cop. I didn't recognize you, but I recognized the name because Zoe told me about you. She'd seen you on-screen. Steven doesn't believe women and children should be contaminated by watching screen. Four years ago. I was seventeen, in some trouble. Street kid, foster kid. I was working my way up to straightening my ass out, living in a halfway house, and this recruiter interviewed me for a job."

"Hold on, you were in the system? You had a caseworker?"

"Yeah, Jane Po."

"Hold that thought." Son of a bitch, Eve thought, and tagged Peabody. "Meet me at Dochas, asap."

"Feeney just tagged McNab and said Roarke —"

"Developments. Get to Dochas. I'm on my way there now."

She broke off, contacted Officer Carmichael. "Officer, contact Officer Shelby. I want the two of you to sit on the woman at this address." She relayed it quickly. "Jane Po. Just sit on the address, and when and if she leaves, tail her. I'm sending you her photo and data now."

"Yes, sir."

Since he wore a T-shirt instead of his uniform, she realized she'd gotten him out of bed. "As soon as you can, Carmichael.

"One more," she told Gina, and sent a text to Whitney, Mira, and Jenkinson.

Rapid developments on Natural Order matter, including co-operating wits. Will brief at Central in ninety minutes. Request FBI inclusion in same, Commander. Request your presence, Dr. Mira. Require all available officers and detectives in my division be present. Jenkinson, coordinate same.

When Eve finished, Gina simply stared. "This is really happening."

"Count on it. We're nearly there. I'm going to have a lot more questions."

"Lieutenant Dallas, I've never considered cops friends of mine, but if you can get my kids somewhere those very-bad-word-to-say-in-front-of-children can't touch them, I'll kiss you on the mouth."

Eve flicked a half smile in the rearview mirror. "Answering the questions will handle it fine."

CHAPTER
EIGHTEEN

At Dochas, the children were lured away with toys and breakfast, and promises to see Gabe and Zoe as soon as they woke up. To ensure privacy as the house began to stir, Eve sat with Gina in an office where Gina gulped coffee.

"I haven't had coffee in four years. Four years. God, I missed it. Nothing caffeinated, nothing carbonated — house rules from the asshole. I don't have to say his name anymore. He is now and forever The Asshole."

"Jane Po. Did she set you up with the recruiter?"

"Yeah. She talked about my progress, and this opportunity to work, entry level and all that, but I'd get training and the potential for advancement. I was really grateful she'd arranged this interview."

"Where did you meet the recruiter?"

"At Stone Tree, the halfway house. She talked about training for marketing and public relations for this global organization. It all sounded so frosty. I was going to turn eighteen and figured I had to make a choice between getting my ass in gear or living on the streets. I thought I was getting my ass in gear."

"What happened?"

"She said I'd passed the initial interview, and with Po's recommendation, she could take me to the next phase. She said it turned out there had been an opening, and if I wanted to fill it, she'd take me to her supervisor for the next phase. I jumped on it."

She broke off at the soft knock on the door. Natalie poked in.

"Sorry to interrupt, but I thought you'd both like a little breakfast. The kids are eating like horses," she assured Gina. "Lollie is a firecracker, Gina."

"They couldn't smother that personality, and they tried. I don't know how to thank you."

"Eat some breakfast. As soon as your partner arrives, Lieutenant, we'll send her in."

"Thanks. Appreciate the food and coffee.

"What happened next?" Eve asked when Gina dived into the scrambled eggs.

"She had transpo. I got right in. You know, I was a street kid, but I never sensed anything off. I thought I was so damn good at that. She had coffee in the car — dosed. It had to be dosed because the next thing I knew I was waking up in this room. No windows, one door, and this other woman sitting on a stool. She said she was Mother Catherine, and I was now a member of Natural Order. She would teach me to be faithful. I was groggy, scared, pissed, and when I tried to get out . . .

"She had a shock stick and knew how to use it. I didn't see anybody but her for I don't know how long. A couple of days, a week."

After a long breath, she picked up her coffee again.

"I had to eat when and what I was told, or shock stick. She'd run this bullshit propaganda about the order on-screen for hours. They restrained me and took me into a medical-type place. I got a physical, if you can call it that. Oh, I had a couple of tats — they took care of that. It hurts having tats removed."

Though the sudden influx of caffeine probably added to Gina's rapid recitation, Eve topped off her cup.

"Thanks. Anyway, a lot of it blurs. A lot of drugs pumped into me, a lot of shock-stick therapy."

Gina paused and closed her eyes for a moment. "I've never tasted anything better than these eggs in my life."

"Freedom tastes pretty great."

When her eyes welled, Gina used the back of her wrist to dry them. "Yeah, it does. You get it. So . . . one day Mother Bitch brought in a white dress, told me to put it on. It was my wedding day. I got a punch in, one good solid punch before she shocked me, and they drugged me."

"Do you need a break?" Eve asked her.

"No. No, it's good to get it all out. So, now I'm in a chapel — pretty, like a vid, with me in this long white dress and a veil. Stained-glass windows, flowers, a lot of people. And The Asshole's standing at the end of this aisle. They walk me down it, one on each side of me. The head guy — I find out later that's Wilkey — he's, like, the preacher, and he marries us. They make me marry this guy twice my age I've never seen before, and swear to obey him, to conceive children with him, to serve him and subjugate myself to him."

324

She stopped, held up a finger while she closed her eyes, took careful breaths. "Then they take me to another room — nicer, windows, no Mother Bitch. I'm half out of it, but I still try to fight back when these two women undress me, and he comes in. They hold me down for him, Lieutenant."

Tears leaked out again. "Maybe that was the worst thing of all. These women, they held me down while he raped me. I didn't fight much, but —"

"Rape is rape."

"He raped me every day, every night. He called it our honeymoon. He actually called it that. He brought me flowers, and candy, and sometimes wine. I could go outside for air, to walk, as long as he was with me. I knew better, I did, but he started to feel like he was okay to me. They came in, took blood, and did a test. A pregnancy test. Positive."

She breathed out. "Can you turn the recorder off a minute?"

"Sure."

"I didn't want to be pregnant. I didn't want a baby. If I'd had a choice, I wouldn't have gone through with the pregnancy. I was barely eighteen. He'd raped me. I was a prisoner."

"That's nothing to be ashamed of, Gina. They took all your choices away."

She breathed out again. "Okay. You can turn it back on. Everything changed when I got pregnant. Better food, smiling faces — like I'd learned a really complicated trick, you know? And The Asshole only wanted sex once a week. I got to go outside more. I had to take all these classes, not with Mother Bitch, but Mother Sweet Smile — ah, Mother Deborah. Child-rearing — the Natural Order way — cooking, cleaning, gardening. Lots more propaganda bullshit — you learned to say what they wanted you to say."

"That's how you survive."

"Yeah." Gina swiped away the tears, managed to smile a little. "You get it. Then The Asshole told me we were moving into a house of our own, and as long as I did what I was told — exactly — and kept a clean house and all that, I could live outside the compound. We moved to Zombie Town with our own version of Mother Catherine in Mother Rat."

"Her full name?"

"Barbara Poole. Her asshole's Vince."

"Did she ever assault you?"

"No. I mean she slapped me a couple of times when I talked back."

"Assault. You're filing charges."

"I am?"

"Yeah, you are." She gave Peabody the come-ahead when her partner appeared at the door, then picked up her 'link. "Reo, I need you at Dochas."

"I've got a meeting in —"

"Cancel it. I've got two women in-house now with their three minor children. And a fucking bevy of charges on Natural Order. Kidnapping, enforced imprisonment, torture, rape, assault, assault and battery."

"Does this tie to the Piper case? Because that's the meeting."

"It does. I've got a briefing at Central in . . . shit, forty minutes. I need to get this ball rolling. Peabody, get Yancy in here now. Reo, we have to move fast — smart but fast. I've got the block locked off, but word's going to get to their HQ eventually."

"I'm on my way."

Eve clicked off, turned back to Gina. "APA Reo's going to review this recording — I'm going to copy her on it. And take your statement, yours and Zoe's. She's going to file charges against all the people you mentioned."

"They said they'd take my kids."

"Nobody's going to touch your kids. Peabody, this is Gina — it's not Dawber."

"No. No, thanks for that. Thanks. It's Mancini."

"Gina Mancini. Gina, why don't you take a break? Maybe Zoe's up. You can hang with your kids, check out what rooms they have for you here."

Gina rose. "Can you really do this? Can you really arrest them, make them pay?"

"Yes, I can. And I will."

As Gina went out, Eve held up a finger, tried a run. "No Gina Mancini of her age in New York — that's where she was living when they took her. We've got a Gina Dawber, but the data prior to her bogus marriage is equally bogus."

"Bogus marriage?"

"Drugged, forced, raped. Fuck, it's uglier than we thought. One of them killed Ariel Byrd, and that opened a crack into the whole sick system. The social worker's part of it. Jane Po. I've got Carmichael and

Shelby watching her. I don't want to move too fast. We pick her up, she tags a lawyer, they know we know."

Peabody plopped down. "What the hell happened after midnight?"

"I'll brief thoroughly at Central."

She gave Peabody the essentials.

"Listen to the recordings. I need to keep moving."

Eve stepped out, and, following the sound of banging and hooting, found a kind of playroom. All three kids ran around like maniacs while the two mothers huddled together, smiling.

"You got her out." Zoe leaped to her feet. "You said you would, and you did."

"Here's what I need. The police artist is coming in. I need Gina to describe the recruiter and this Mother Catherine. Zoe, I need you to describe any of the men you saw last night. Gina, what did you see last night?"

"Westley's teething, so he was fussy. I didn't hear the fight — Zoe told me a little just now — but I saw the vans pull up. I saw the men get out. One of them's a doctor or medical, I think. I know I saw him at the compound. I can describe him."

"Good. I need you both to file charges when APA Reo gets here." She glanced back and both women just stared at her. "Here's Detective Yancy now. You were quick."

"I don't live far."

"Gina, how about you go first? You can use the office we were in before. Zoe's got the kids, right, Zoe?"

"Oh, sure. I'm so happy to see them. So happy, Gina."

They hugged, swayed with it. Then Gina popped up. "Let's do this. I really want to do this."

Eve led them back. "Peabody, they need the room."

"Hey, Yancy." Peabody's lips curved, but the smile didn't reach her eyes as she picked up Eve's recorder and came out.

"I didn't get far," she told Eve. "But far enough to see where it was going. Po? She's supposed to help people."

"We'll have her picked up, charged, have a team move in on the halfway house — there's bound to be some of Natural Order in there, too. We need to coordinate, all of it. It's going to take time and a shit-load of manpower."

"We have to conclude Marcia Piper's dead."

"We'll see what the sweepers find, but it leans that way. We're going to find more people who've been taken or held, or Realigned. More people, even, like Gwen Huffman, who were secretly tracked."

"If they had that sort of response to the Piper house, they've responded before. Cleaned crime scenes before."

"Yeah. Organized, ready. You give somebody that kind of power over somebody else? You're going to have more bodies to clean up. Who reports it? Nobody. And you just wipe their data, if you haven't already. Hell of a system."

Eve turned when Natalie led Reo in.

"Good. Natalie, sorry, but I need another private space."

"No problem. Moira's due in shortly, but you can use her office. I'll explain what I can when she gets here."

"It would help if APA Reo could speak to Zoe. She's watching the kids."

"I'll take over there, and send Zoe up. Oh, good morning, Desi. Would you mind showing these ladies Moira's office?"

"Thanks, but I know where it is."

Eve started upstairs. "I copied you on the two interviews," she began.

"I started listening to them on the way here. Well, to the first one. Zoe Metcalf."

"I've got to get to Central, so I'm going to leave you to handle things here. Gina, the second recording, is working with Yancy in an office downstairs. I need warrants."

She rattled several off, enough to make Reo's eyes widen. "And you're going to get me that warrant for their HQ, Reo. You're going to have plenty to get that warrant. You're going to get me an arrest warrant for Stanton Wilkey."

"On what charges?"

"You'll have a slew of them, trust me. We're going to spread that out to his sons, his daughter, and to every so-called husband and a few of the women on that block in Tribeca. We're going to clean up after these people — a social worker, a halfway house, and that won't be limited to New York. That's not how they operate."

"Let me talk to your wits first. I heard enough on the first recording we can put out a warrant for Lawrence Piper. If for nothing else at the moment, for compromising and leaving a crime scene."

"Issue it, but I don't want to use it yet. It's going to be about timing. To take them down, to break the back of this fucked-up cult, we need to time it perfectly. Come into Central when you finish here, or at least tag me."

"Count on it." Reo smiled easily when Zoe came up the stairs. "And this must be Zoe. I'm APA Reo, Zoe."

"Natalie said you needed to talk to me, and she'd watch the kids."

"They'll be fine with her."

"I know." Zoe nodded at Eve. "Everyone here wants to help. Everyone here is so kind. It's like I was inside a terrible nightmare, and now I've woken up in such a nice dream."

"We're going to talk in here, okay?" Reo opened the office door.

"Tag me," Eve repeated, then started back down. "Book a conference room," she told Peabody. "We're going to need the space. We'll head in now, get it set up. Listen to the recordings. I need to think, and you need to catch up."

Peabody used earbuds to give Eve quiet, and sat grim-faced as she listened.

When Eve pulled into Central's garage, Peabody took out the ear-buds. "I didn't finish, it's a lot. But I'm damn well caught up. They've been running this — I don't have a name for it — for decades."

"Probably didn't start out this way. It grew. It got greedy. It got arrogant, and it started to believe, really believe, its own bullshit. How are you going to propagate the world without women, pregnant women? Each to their own race. You can't have people of the same sex getting together — no organizational growth that way. You want young, healthy women with a lot of childbearing years in them. Not enough to make it profitable, to spread the word? You start 'recruiting.'"

"Then you have, like, a pecking order," Peabody continued as they got on the elevator. "Like we saw at the compound."

"And you have someone valuable, like Gwen? Good genes, deep pockets, loyal members? You do what you have to do to keep her in the fold. Realignment. If that doesn't work, you watch her, protect your investment, do what has to be done. You've just got to get her married and pregnant, and, affairs aside, she's willing to go along with that for the money and status."

"Piper's a good choice for that. He's violent, and he's deep in the loop. Impulsive, like Mira said. He killed his pregnant wife because she talked to us. It had to be because she talked to us and told him, Dallas. Or someone else on the block told him."

"Agreed. But I don't think he killed Ariel. Company man, that's what he is. They rarely act on their own. If he had orders to take her out, he'd have messed her up first. I see him as a fist guy. Could be wrong."

Because she stayed in thinking mode, she managed the elevator clear up to Homicide.

"Start setting up. I need to do some check-ins. We got a room?"

"Conference room one."

"Get plenty of chairs. I asked Whitney to bring in the feds. We're going to want them. We're crossing out of our jurisdiction for this."

They split off, and Eve turned into the bullpen. Apparently rolling out Jenkinson early didn't spare the tie.

Today's was a sunburst of yellow with a multitude of fiery red squiggles.

She literally felt her eyes shake in their sockets.

"Got Santiago, Trueheart, and Reineke in the break room getting coffee. Rest on their way, boss."

"Good, conference room one, twenty minutes."

"We gonna bust some ass today?"

"That's the plan."

"My favorite plan in the world of plans."

She couldn't disagree.

She got coffee, started to tag Roarke. Her incoming signaled from him before she did.

"I'm at Central," she said.

"As I am — in EDD. We have some work here, but you'd want to know Piper, the social media VP, has thousands of names, IPs. He has what appears to be the membership list — the global one. Or those who sign up for alerts. Only a handful of females there."

"Including someone like Paula Huffman?"

"Including and like, yes. He has considerable correspondence as well. Some's encrypted, but we'll deal with that. We've found the social media is also segregated. That is, it's designed for specific race groups and programmed to send to same. No mixing there, for the most part. It's inclusive only when Whitney himself adds a message."

"Get whatever you can get in the next fifteen. You all need to be at this briefing. Conference room one."

"I'll pass that along."

"See you then."

She pushed at the sweepers next, got an in-progress report from the head sweeper, and added it to her briefing list.

She put everything she needed together with minutes to spare.

In the conference room she saw Peabody had done her job, and well.

"EDD got a little fresh data, nothing earth-shattering, more part of the whole. The sweepers, on the other hand, got blood."

"Marcia Piper's."

"Hers and his," Eve confirmed. "It took a deep-level sweep — the order cleaned up really well, knew what chemicals would disguise or eliminate most of it, and they were pretty thorough. But the problem for them was the hole the vic's head put in the wall that they needed to patch up. It looked all clean and shiny, but the sweepers knew where to look, and they got blood, some gray matter mixed with the compound they patched with.

"And Larry — the fuck? He washed up in the kitchen sink — they know that because the cleaners polished that up, including the drain. But when he changed his clothes, the blood on the old ones, just a trace, transferred when he brushed against the bedroom closet door. Inside the door. Cleaners missed it."

"Our guys are better than theirs," Peabody said.

"Damn straight. No sightings of his vehicle from the APB I put out. He's in that compound."

"We sure as hell have probable cause to look for him there."

"And we will. I need to check with Carmichael and Shelby."

Cops started to filter in while Eve walked back into the hall, checked in. And took time to speak to Shelby, ask a few more questions.

She broke it off when she saw Whitney heading her way with a fed she knew, with one she didn't.

"Commander, Special Agent Teasdale."

"Lieutenant. I look forward to working with you again. This is Special Agent Conroy. He's well versed on Natural Order."

"Tony Quirk is a friend of mine." A well-built man in his early forties, Conroy held out a hand. "We worked on Natural Order the last two years. He went in, as I'm mixed race and wouldn't qualify."

"I've read your reports, and his. I want to say that the murder of Ariel Byrd has blown this open."

"I hope to hell we can close it, and it's not too late for Tony."

"We've gathered considerable information just in the last few hours. We're going to close it. If Special Agent Quirk is alive, we'll find him. We're waiting for EDD.

APA Reo will join when she's finished interviewing two new witnesses. A police artist is also working with those witnesses. I haven't had time to write this up. It's moving fast."

"I'll take you in," Whitney said to the agents. "We'll get some coffee."

"I'll be in shortly, Commander. I've got a communication coming in. Dallas. What've you got?"

"A damn good wit," Yancy told her. "We've got the recruiter — Gina said she'd never forget, and she didn't. I got good enough for facial rec, and we've got her."

"Show me."

When he did, she just nodded.

"You don't look surprised."

"I'm not, but you just nailed it shut. I need to start the briefing, but I need you to finish there, get all you can. I'll read you in when you get here. You're in this, Yancy, all the way."

"Understood, and I'm good here until it's done."

She needed Mira, she thought. And even as she thought it, Mira hurried down the corridor in her perfect pale blue suit, pale blue heels with their blue-and-white needles.

"I'm so sorry. Traffic."

"You're fine. I'm waiting on EDD, and any other data that comes through in the next two minutes."

"Eve, you look exhausted."

It surprised more than irritated because she felt revved. "No, I'm good."

"There are shadows under the shadows under your eyes."

"I'm good," she repeated. "Here's Feeney and Roarke. Get a seat, and we'll get this started."

"I got McNab and Callendar in the lab," Feeney said, brisk now. "I put them on the Dawber e's. They already hit on what's listed as potentials. Women, Dallas. Girls — sixteen to twenty. Either in college or in trouble. Halfway houses, college campuses, foster homes, street kids. He's got a list of those he refers to as recruits."

"And names of finders — they call them finders," Roarke said in disgust. "Jane Po's on there in the New York system."

"This is good, this is perfect. Be ready to brief on that."

"He needs to go into a very cold cage for putting that shocker on a child."

"We're going to put him in one," Eve assured Roarke. "We're going to put a whole bunch of them there. Go get a seat, get coffee. I just need a minute to organize my thoughts."

When she'd had her minute, she walked in. Cops milled, drank coffee, studied the board.

So many places to start, she thought, but she looked at the board. She knew where, who, and why.

"Take a seat," she ordered. "This is going to be long. Ariel Byrd. This didn't start with her, but her murder is the turning point. We're going to get justice for her, and when we do, we're going to take down not just her killer, but the culture that fostered it."

She took them through the murder, Gwen Huffman, the Natural Order connection. From there she wound her way to the block in Tribeca, the missing brother, before asking the feds to brief on the missing agent.

Baxter's comm signaled at the end of that portion.

"Sorry, LT, we caught one."

Whitney signaled for Baxter to hand him the communicator. "I'll transfer it, and any others for the duration of the briefing."

Rising, he stepped out to handle it.

Eve stepped back up, continued with the interviews and observations in Connecticut, and onto Ella Alice Foxx.

She had Feeney brief on the EDD input in that area.

"They wiped her out." Carmichael studied Ella — Yancy's sketch, the ID shot — on the board. "Just disappeared her. Her caseworker, the admin from the halfway house, didn't file reports? Doesn't pass the stink test."

"No, it doesn't. Which is why Officers Carmichael and Shelby are watching Jane Po at this time. We have more evidence she's complicit in this, which I'll get to."

"Pick her up now," Jenkinson commented, "her first tag's to whoever she's working with."

"Correct. We have good reason to believe she, in coordination with the halfway house, is funneling young women, potentially young males as well, to Natural Order. She may be a true believer, it may be for money. It could be both."

"It's certainly for the money."

She glanced at Roarke when he spoke.

"You have something."

"I had a bit of time during the transfer of electronics and so on, so I had a look at Po's finances. It would be unusual, I'd think, for a social worker — without family money behind her — to own a vacation home on the South Carolina shoreline, and have a bit over ten million in a pair of tucked-away accounts. Then there's the jewelry she has insured — she's fond of canary diamonds — in the amount of six million or so."

"Yeah, that's unusual."

"It was a cursory search," he added, "but with a little more time I could find when she had influxes of money. Which you could, very likely, tie to those disappearances."

"I just bet. Good work. You can add the staff at the halfway house there and we'll pin who she's working with.

"Shortly before zero four hundred this morning —" She broke off when her 'link signaled. A glance showed her Nadine on the display.

"Sorry, this could be relevant. Roarke, take over with this area, as you were there. Peabody, if necessary, brief on the subsequent interviews."

She stepped out. "I'm in the middle of a briefing," she told Nadine.

"And I assume that briefing is on Natural Order. I think you're going to want to include what I've got."

CHAPTER
NINETEEN

"Spill, but make it fast. Things are moving here. Wait, where are you? Are you on a shuttle?"

"I'm shuttling back from a source, a hot one, Dallas. I pushed on an angle, and it paid off. Rachel Wilkey — Stanton Wilkey's wife. Things weren't adding up. Number of pregnancies, timing of them, number of children."

"Yeah, I hit on that."

"Pursuing that, I found she went incommunicado for long periods of time, and, pursuing that, I tracked a source that led to a source, and while her medical records are buried in Natural Order and not documented anywhere else I can find, there are ways and means to persuade people to cough up information."

"Cut to it," Eve demanded. "I'm pressed here."

"Rachel Wilkey had three difficult pregnancies that resulted in live births, five miscarriages, and, the big one, a hysterectomy in 2037 — which is three years before Wilkey's youngest son, Aaron, was born."

"She's not the bio mother."

"Medically impossible, and, pursuing that, I hit the very, very hot."

"Is Paula Huffman her OB?"

"Oh yeah, and Huffman had an OB nurse-slash-midwife who not only attended Rachel Wilkey, but spent a couple years in the compound medical facilities. My information is Rachel nearly didn't survive the birth of her daughter, was emotionally unstable, but became pregnant within the year, miscarried, and shortly after that, underwent an emergency hysterectomy.

"Following this, a young woman — unidentified — was brought into the facility and impregnated with Wilkey's sperm."

"Okay." Eve began to pace. "That follows. That's a pattern I see coming."

"The OB nurse was assigned to tend to her. She was kept isolated. She was basically in prison, Dallas. She wasn't there willingly, wasn't pregnant willingly. The OB nurse assisted in the birth. They took the baby, and she never saw the bio mother again."

"But she saw others."

"Right, you've got it."

Eve paused by the conference room door, where she could see the board. "Yeah," she said. "I've got it. Keep going."

"Some, impregnated like this one, others who'd been shipped in, married off — against their will — who either came in for the birth, or the nurse assisted Huffman in home deliveries. The nurse was a member at the time, was given a bonus of a thousand for every successful birth."

Money, Eve thought, it always wound back to the money.

"Dallas, male members paid Natural Order upwards of twenty grand — at that time — for a woman between the ages of eighteen and twenty-four, of their specific race."

The outrage in Nadine's voice began to rise, and Eve resumed pacing.

"Healthy women who passed medical and mental screenings. These members were awarded five grand for every successful birth. Money was paid out to whoever shipped these women in, most of them unwilling or unknowing, where they were trained — and you can read that tortured — to live by the rules, were married, whether they wanted to be or not, by Wilkey, then given to some asshole whose job it was to plant his fucking seed in her so he could get his bonus and propagate the damn world."

"You've got the OB nurse? She'll attest to this?"

"She's dead. Killed herself about ten years ago. I've got her sister — and I'm not giving you her name at this time."

"For fuck's sake, Nadine —"

"I gave my word, Dallas, so just hear me out."

Though she cursed inside, Eve nodded. "Keep going."

"The nurse got documents to the sister, begged forgiveness, begged her sister not to expose this until her own children were of age. The nurse got the children out, sent them to her sister along with the documents, then hanged herself."

"I need those documents."

"My source is willing to let me turn them over and break this, as long as I keep details, any details that will lead to her and the kids, out of it. She changed her name, and theirs, moved out of the country. But I found her, so they could find her. She's afraid for them, and I don't blame her."

Nadine held up a finger, then took a long sip from a water glass.

"This is human trafficking, Dallas, enforced slavery, turning women into breeding droids. I can't begin."

"I know what it is, and we're going to take them down. All the way down. Get me the documents."

"I don't want to send them electronically. It's going to take me at least another hour to get to you, but I'm coming to you first. And now, I don't care what the hell time it is, I'm having a serious drink."

"You did good, Nadine. Think of that."

"Working on it."

Eve settled herself, then stepped back in. Peabody was winding it up, so she let her finish.

"We've got these bastards," Baxter muttered. "We've got Wilkey and his lunatic faithful up, down, sideways."

"We just got more. Nadine Furst has uncovered a source, with documentation, that exposes a decades-long system of abductions, human trafficking, enforced slavery, rape, enforced impregnation."

"A reporter?" Conroy surged to his feet. "We can't have a reporter in this."

"Nadine Furst's integrity is unquestionable," Eve shot back. "If it was only about the story, she'd be on her way to her studio to break it instead of here to turn over that documentation. She wouldn't have contacted me to relay the information, she'd have broken it on air."

"If she leaks any of this before —"

"She won't. It's just that simple."

Turning away, Eve dismissed him.

"Dr. Paula Huffman performed a hysterectomy on Rachel Wilkey three years before the birth of Aaron Wilkey. Subsequently, Huffman impregnated an unidentified woman, against her will, with Wilkey's sperm. Nadine will be bringing in documentation from a medical who assisted in these procedures, and in others. Others like Gina Mancini, who were kept in the compound against their will, tortured, forced into bogus marriages, and raped and impregnated.

"There will be other facilities like this, and the island is certainly used for this. People like Po are paid to provide the healthy women, the medicals are paid a bonus for live, healthy births. The men pay for the women who will be forced to become wives, and are given a bonus for every live, healthy child produced. So that marriage fee is an investment."

"It's a long con." Fascinated and appalled, Roarke gestured to the board. "A kind of pyramid scheme founded on bigotry with women and children as the bricks."

"That nutshells it," Eve agreed. "This is how Wilkey ensures his ranks of faithful grow, and races don't mix. He has his Realignment centers to deal with homosexuality. And he and his order profit."

344

"What do they do when it doesn't take?" Santiago wondered.

"My guess, slave labor. You don't get off the island, out of the compound, away from the farm system. More people than Ariel Byrd have been murdered to protect this organization. More people than Keene Grimsley and Special Agent Quirk have gone missing.

"To ensure the flock increases, Mirium Wilkey, the daughter, acts as recruiter in this region."

"Of course she does," Peabody stated. "I should've seen it."

"She handles the staff at the compound, serves as her father's PA. No titles like her older brothers. No big house, no luxury travel. Just a pied-a-terre — as she called it — in the city, and that's not even in her name.

"Yet she's the one bringing these women in, seeing to it Natural Order thrives. Before too much longer, I imagine, she'll be expected to marry someone approved by her father, and start pumping out babies. Maybe, just maybe, she'll keep what little power she has now. But maybe not. She needs to keep things status quo as long as possible — and ensure money keeps flowing in."

"All the work," Peabody commented, "none of the credit."

"A pisser," Eve agreed. "Roarke will go over Natural Order's financial position, but their cash flow isn't a rushing stream. If she keeps the money — and women — coming in, continues to be useful as she is to her father, she can postpone the rest. Natural Order, and therefore Mirium, made a hefty investment in Gwen

Huffman, and will be heavy beneficiaries. As long as she married Merit Caine, produced a child, and fulfilled the terms of her trust.

"When Ariel Byrd threatened that return on the investment, she had to be eliminated."

"But . . ." Peabody frowned at the board. "They don't get any real return until the Huffmans die. They're in their sixties. Just middle age."

"She plans," Mira said. "Long-term."

"Yeah, and she doesn't plan to end up with a brood of kids." Eve referenced the board. "Get Gwen married — to someone her father wants in the faithful. I'm betting she maneuvered Gwen into aiming for Merit Caine. You can bet she's accessed their medicals to be sure there are no reproductive issues. Gwen wants the marriage and the kid — for her own ends, so she'll work for it. Terms met, and all you have to do is eliminate the parents."

"Long-term planning." Mira nodded. "Bide her time."

"A tragic accident," Eve speculated. "A staged murder-suicide. I bet she's got a plan in the works for that."

"Yes, she would think well ahead," Mira agreed. "She's had to plan and plot all of her life. She's female, and therefore less. To rise up, she has to continually find ways to offer more — the recruiting, serving her father's needs. All while learning all the ins and outs of the order's business."

"Wind back?" Santiago rolled a finger in the air. "The terms of the will, right? If Gwen Huffman fucks it up, the order gets more. A hell of a lot more."

346

"Too far away, and too easy to change." Roarke held up his hands.

"Sorry."

"No, that's just it," Eve told him. "The Huffmans cut off their son, yes, and probably would do the same with the daughter. But what if they didn't? Another trip to Realignment, maybe, another delay, and Mirium's pushing the end of acceptable time for marriage and kids."

"She would have known Gwen when they were children." Mira angled her head. "Known about her being sent off and why. Could she have been in the Hamptons at the time the parents learned of Gwen's orientation?"

Eve smiled, nodded. "Not only could, but was. A long weekend with her parents, her younger brother — or half-brother, and I assume she knows that, too, and has ideas on how to use it. I think she learned the benefits of spying then and there, and the power of it. She saw Gwen, told her father, and Gwen's sent away. I bet she got a nice little reward for it."

"Her father's approval and trust, if nothing else," Mira agreed. "It lifted her up, made her useful. No doubt she found other infractions to report over the years. Telling him about Gwen might have been impulse, might have been true belief, but the reward? It mattered to her. And yes, Gwen's a focus now. A kind of personal investment. But with the terms, if she tells now, Gwen's no longer of use."

"Protect the investment. Maybe she even covers for Gwen a few times. But Ariel's a real threat, and can blow up all those careful plans. The killing itself, impulse and rage. Up to then, she had things worked out. And Gwen messes it up again by going back in the morning."

Eve walked back to the board. "She's not worried about Byrd now. How would we tie her to the murder? She's never met Byrd, can claim she was in the compound at the time of the murder. Can see that dozens swear to it."

"But she wasn't," Peabody said.

"No. She was at the house her father lets her use, really only a handful of blocks away from Ariel's apartment. Listening. She may have had a pickup — another recruitment scheduled — or planned to do some research on a new prospect."

"She'd like having time in the house, her own space." Mira re-crossed her legs. "Come and go as she pleases, dress as she pleases. Taste the freedom."

"Nothing tastes better," Eve said, thinking of Gina.

"She'll lose all of that if . . ."

Mira looked at Eve, got another nod.

"If she doesn't have a way to take over Natural Order."

"Kill her dad?" Even after all the rest, Trueheart looked shocked at the idea.

"Kill him, or, more likely, blackmail him. Turn it over to me, or I burn it to the ground. She needs the time, the money, more opportunities," Eve added. "But I saw a cold, hard, ambitious woman who slipped on the good-daughter mask.

"They're buying and selling human beings she helps find and abduct. Killing means nothing."

"We gotta take them down." Jenkinson jabbed a finger in the air.

"And we will. But they're not just in Connecticut, not just in New York. There are other facilities, their farm system, and, essentially, their island."

"Kick an anthill, the ants scatter. Some of that's going to happen however right and tight we do this."

"Baxter's right on that. We're not going to get them all, so we focus on essential areas. Utopia Island — sovereign nation aside — human trafficking, torture, slavery, those are all high crimes globally and off-planet. Abernathy with Interpol should be willing to assist and coordinate there."

"I'll contact him and his superiors," Whitney told her.

"It has to be a coordinated op. Hit one area too soon, and more ants scatter from another. The farm system here in the States. I haven't looked hard and close at that, but the FBI has data, and we use that, look hard and close and outline the operation on that. Jenkinson, you and Reineke take that, outline an op and be prepared to brief on same by . . ."

She glanced at the time, saw her day whizzing by. "By fifteen hundred."

"Lieutenant." Teasdale drew Eve's attention. "I can have the task force that headed up our intel in that area take that assignment and be ready to brief."

"That would be helpful. Will the FBI implement the operation on the farm system?"

"If the operational plan is deemed workable, has a high probability ratio of success, yes. I'll read my director into this information as soon as this briefing concludes."

"Good. I'm keeping my officers on Po, but will not pick her up until all ops are outlined and ready to implement. Meanwhile, we'll get a search warrant for Po's residence, her e's. It's probable she has useful information there. We will identify the Natural Order contact or contacts at the halfway house, and that's likely part of Po's useful information.

"Santiago, Carmichael, you'll take that search. Feeney, can you send an e-man with them?"

"You got it."

"If she comes back before we're ready, I'd rather not tip her off. You keep the search tidy. We get a warrant for the Wilkey residence downtown. Baxter, Trueheart, and another e-man, Feeney. Same requirement. Do a heat sensor first, make sure it's unoccupied."

"If she's in there?" Baxter asked.

"Let me know. We'll find a way to get her out. The Huffmans' residence — Jenkinson and Reineke. Warrants, searches." She spotted Yancy in the doorway.

"Sounds like you're winding up. Didn't want to interrupt."

"You're not, and not quite winding. Special Agents Teasdale and Conroy, Detective Yancy, police artist. You get any more faces?"

"Yes, sir, six more. Solid. I let them work together on the third. Sometimes one wit will remember some detail, and it sparks one in the other."

"Add the sketches to the board."

"Do you want the official ID with them?"

This time she grinned at him. "Do that."

"You got six out of six facial recognition?" Conroy puffed out his cheeks. "That's damn good."

"Damn good wits," Yancy said as he added the sketches.

"Yancy's damn good," Eve added. "Take it, Yancy. You'd have run them on the way here."

"Yes, sir, I did. In the first group — first arrival at the Piper residence — the witnesses identified Dr. Oliver Huffman." He glanced back at Eve, saw again no surprise. "You've probably already briefed on him."

"I have, yes."

"Okay then, in the second group to arrive — the cleaners — the witnesses identified William Henley, Caucasian, age forty-nine, ex-army corporal. Dishonorable discharge, details sealed."

"We'll get them," Whitney said. "Continue."

"He lives in Brooklyn. Married Amber Johnstone, age forty-six, mixed race, in 2037. Two offspring, both female, ages eighteen and fifteen. Divorced 2046. Ex lives with the daughters in Tennessee. Married Wendy Livingston, age thirty-two, Caucasian, in 2049. Five offspring, two female, three male, ages eleven, ten, eight, five, and three, respectively.

"Henley is employed by Natural Order as security."

"Peabody, start looking at Livingston's background. Keep going, Yancy."

"Third, second group, Wendell Phiffer, age twenty-six, Caucasian. Resides Lower West. Single, no registered cohab. He's employed by Purity Labs and Research as a forensic specialist. Parents, Francis and Lydia, married 2034 — he was thirty-eight, she was twenty. Francis is employed by the same lab, Lydia has professional mother status. Wendell is the oldest of six siblings, ages twenty-four, twenty-two, twenty, and twins aged sixteen."

"Peabody, closer look there, too."

"Four is the midwife, described and ID'd by both wits. She attended the birth of both of Gina's kids, and Zoe's Gabe. They both stated she acts as midwife for the block. In case of a difficult pregnancy, the woman's taken to Mercy so there's an OB in attendance in the last few weeks, but they have no ID there, as neither of them needed the OB."

"That's going to be Paula Huffman, I'm betting, or an associate if she was elsewhere. Who's the midwife?"

"Hester Angus, age forty-three, Caucasian, resides on that same block in Tribeca."

He relayed the salient data while Eve studied the face. It all fit pattern.

"Five, the one called Mother Catherine. Freaking torturer. Catherine Duplay, age sixty-two, Caucasian. Resides at HQ, along with her husband, Dudley, age sixty-two. Both employed there. They list her as educator, he's maintenance. Two offspring: male, age twenty-seven, female, age twenty-three. Both offspring live in Indiana, both were placed with their paternal grandparents by Child Services when they were fourteen and twelve. Details sealed."

"We'll get that, too," Whitney said.

"Both are single, neither have criminal, both are employed — he teaches, middle-school level, she works at the restaurant owned and run by her grandparents. Owned and run for forty-five years."

"They got away," Peabody murmured.

"And last, Deborah Beyers, age thirty-six, Caucasian, married Lloyd Beyers, age forty-eight, five offspring, thirteen, eleven, ten, seven, and five. Also listed as educator. She's the one, Dallas, who trained Gina on child-rearing, housekeeping, and all that. Lloyd's an IT guy. They all live in the compound."

"That's good work, Yancy. That's damn good work. We'll fill it in."

She turned to the room. "Commander, if you can get those details, every one helps. Peabody, get as much background as you can on all identified individuals. Roarke, it's your system on the compound, and very likely on the Wilkey residence in the city. Give Feeney all you can, start with the easy one, the residence, so we can start the search. Then I need the weak spots on the compound."

"You've got drone and satellite imagery of the compound," he said. "I can use that, and likely find a way to access plans and blueprints."

"Good luck there." Conroy shrugged. "We've tried that route."

Roarke only offered an easy smile. "Well then, I'll try winding there another way, see what I can find. Let me confirm the security on the house here, then we'll get your people set to bypass it without any alerts."

"Do all that. Everybody, get to work. Yancy, with me in here, and I'll roll this together for you. After that, you can rotate teams, assist wherever needed.

"Operational briefing in here, fifteen hundred."

"Is there a room we can use?" Teasdale asked.

Whitney rose. "With me. I'll set you up."

While cops headed out, Roarke went to her. "You could use an hour's downtime."

"Maybe. Can't have it." She glanced around, made sure no one stood within earshot. "It's what he was going to do to me. Sell me. Over and over again for sex, sell me. We break them, then the downtime."

"Then eat something."

"I will. You, too. I have to finish with Yancy. Nadine's on her way."

"I'll have what you need."

You are what I need, she thought as he left the room.

"Okay, Yancy, you know most of it, but let me catch you up."

When she finished and sent him to the bullpen, Reo walked in.

"Took awhile. I had to go back to the office, have a sit-down with my boss. First thing, you've got warrants — all but the one you want on the HQ."

She held up a hand before Eve could speak.

"And we're working on it. You and I need to nail this down, hard down, so we can move on that."

"I've got the hammer: docs coming in proving Natural Order, Wilkey, his daughter — who I'm also going to charge with Ariel Byrd's murder — have engaged for a couple decades or more in human trafficking, rape with the intent to impregnate, slavery, torture at their HQ, on their godforsaken island, and very likely other locations."

"That's one hell of a hammer, Dallas." Sitting on the edge of the conference table, Reo took a moment. "You have documentation, statements, wits?"

"Documentation, including a statement from Paula Huffman's OB nurse — now deceased, self-termination — who not only witnessed, but participated. The Huffmans are going down, too. Both doctors are in this, and Oliver Huffman has been identified entering the Piper residence on the night of her murder."

She paused, tapped a finger on Yancy's sketch, then Huffman's official ID.

"Okay." Reo took out her notebook. "Okay. Don't stop now."

"We have Marcia Piper's blood and gray matter on that charge. I'll be charging her husband with her murder, and I have solid probable cause he's hiding inside HQ."

"That's a big-ass hammer and a whole lot of nails. Let's put it together so I can get warrants. I'm going to hit Vending first. All I've managed to eat today is half a bagel and I'm starving."

Eve considered Vending. "Don't go there. There's a way to transfer the menu on my AC to the one here. Peabody can do it, and I want her in this anyway. We've got more, Reo. We have a whole bunch more nails. I'll get the search and seizures started. Hold here."

She hustled back to the bullpen. "Heads up. We have warrants on the Wilkey New York residence, on the

Huffmans' residence, and their clinic. Get them, get the residence searches started. We hold on the clinic. Timing. We have warrants for Jane Po's residence — her office will, again, wait. So will the halfway house.

"Move on the rest. Peabody, transfer my AC menu to the conference room, and get there yourself, with whatever data you have so far."

Even as she turned, Nadine stepped in.

"Good," Eve said. "Out here."

She walked out to the hallway.

Nadine wore a pale green shirt, untucked, yoga-type black pants with high-top green sneaks and a black leather jacket.

Not camera ready, Eve decided.

"Reo's in the conference room, and needs to be updated with what you have, and some of what we've dug up since I saw her this morning. I have a board up, a very full, complex board loaded with data. It has to be said, nothing you see or hear in that room leaves that room until I give you the go."

"It shouldn't have to be said between us."

"It has to be said," Eve corrected. "Listen, I slapped back an FBI agent for questioning your integrity about an hour ago. I should get some points for that."

"You do. And okay, I get it has to be said. Just as I have to say, out loud, all of this is off the record until you say it's back on. It's been a really long twenty-four or so for me."

As she studied Eve's face, Nadine pursed her lips. "For you, too, I'd say."

"The next twenty-four are going to be a lot longer, a lot harder for a lot of sons of bitches. So are the multiple, consecutive lifetimes in cages going to be long and hard."

"Let me help you put them there."

"Let's get started."

With a sigh, Nadine paused at Vending. "I need a boost, even something from here. I've been too busy to grab more than a bagel."

"Bagels seem to be the choice of the day. I'm having food sent in."

"Great. You know," Nadine continued as they walked, "a couple of days ago, walking through that big, crazy house with Mavis, I felt so damn up. Just knowing, seeing, good things happen to people I care about. And now?"

She shook back her streaky blond hair. "I know there's a lot of ugly in the world. You and I make our living off the ugly. But — hell, Dallas, a long twenty-four."

"We're about to carve away a lot of ugly. Have a seat."

"Been sitting, need to move a little. Hi, Reo."

"Nadine. Love those sneaks!"

"Thanks. Me, too. Did you hear Mavis and Leonardo bought a house?"

"What? When? Where?"

Eve held out a hand. "Documentation before you start chatting."

Nadine took a box of discs out of her enormous bag. "They're labeled, and I reviewed every one of them. Just a few days ago, and just a few blocks from here," she told Reo. "It's this old, big, crazy place with an

357

attached multilevel unit. Peabody and McNab are taking it."

"What? Wow!"

While they chattered over houses and friends, Eve set to work organizing the discs for display on-screen.

"I've got this," she said as Peabody came in. "Get the food going."

"What are the possibilities?" Reo wondered. "I swear I can't face another salad."

"How about a burger?"

"Don't toy with me, Peabody."

"Got burgers. Cow."

Reo just closed her eyes. "It's a whole new world. Medium rare? Side of fries, and why not go for broke if this is really happening. Tube of Pepsi."

"I'm doing exactly the same." Nadine sighed again, but this time with pleasure.

"Got you covered. Dallas? What do you want to eat?"

"What? Whatever."

"Burgers all around! I'm down a whole size."

"I knew it!" Nadine walked over to Peabody, circled a finger to order a turn. "I knew it."

"Really?" Thrilled, Peabody did another turn. "You noticed?"

"Of course I did. Congratulations."

"I won't hit burgers and fries often, but I'm celebrating a little. My pants aren't loose today because they're new, and a size down."

"And they look mag," Reo told her. "I love the little strip of navy piping down the sides. Cute, and leg-lengthening."

358

"If we've completed the socializing portion of the program, maybe we can turn to murder, abductions, torture, and human trafficking."

"They go so well with burgers." Reo sent Eve a bright smile. Then she closed her eyes again. "Oh my God, smell them!"

Peabody set it all out, complete with condiments, napkins, glasses full of ice. Eve found herself surprised her partner hadn't come up with a centerpiece of flowers.

"Now this is what I call a lunch meeting." Reo dug right in.

"Nadine, tell Reo what you told me, then we'll view the documentation."

Reo managed to eat and take notes while Nadine spoke.

"It would help to have the name of your source."

"I can't give you that."

"I know where you stand on it, but the fact is, the sister — if all this is true — will be in those documents as OB nurse. We'll have her name."

"My source changed hers, changed the children's names, and moved out of the country. You can, as I did, dig it up and find her. She knows that. She's afraid, as anyone would be, of reprisals if their names and locations go public."

"When and if we identify them, when and if we need her testimony, we will, absolutely, keep her identity out of it."

"We're not going to need it." Since it was there, right in front of her, Eve took a bite of burger. "I'm telling you, we'll have enough to put them away without her direct testimony."

Reo swept a fry through a little pool of ketchup. "I hate to give up a nail. But we'll see."

"On-screen. First doc is the medical files on a female identified only as Candidate A. You see her age, race, hair and eye color, height, weight," Eve continued as she displayed the file. "Various tests, blood work, gyn exam, dental screening, and so on, and the doctor's notes certifying Candidate A as a healthy subject, a strong candidate for insemination. It's signed Dr. Paula Huffman, with the date.

"Next is the nutritionist's evaluation and recommendations for diet and pre-insemination vitamins and supplements. Peabody, run a search on the nutritionist. We're going to want a warrant there, too."

"Already running it."

"We then have files signed by Karyn Keye, nurse practitioner, obgyn. These track Candidate A's ovulation cycle for a period of six weeks, the hormone treatments to increase chances of implantation during that same period. Huffman also signs off on the recommended date for insemination."

"No proof here that the candidate was unwilling."

"Wait for it," Nadine told Reo.

"Don't have to wait long. Here are evaluations on emotional state — we want the name of the shrink run, Peabody — and the medications used to assist Candidate A in maintaining calm."

Reo picked up her glass and read. "'Candidate A remains resistant, but her demands to be released have decreased. Mild depression is being treated. Hormone therapy has, of course, added to mood swings. We will continue talk therapy as well as closely supervised exercise, including the allotted time out of doors. Restraints remain necessary.'"

Reo took a long drink. "And there we go."

"This file," Eve continued, "documents Huffman ordered a mild sedative on the insemination date, as well as restraints. She repeated the process on the next day to increase probability of conception. Then we have the OB nurse monitoring for forty-eight hours before she administered the pregnancy test. Positive.

"More files follow the exams and monitoring of the pregnancy, the nutrition, prescribed exercise, medication."

"Jesus, look at the shrink report. She's Patient A now," Peabody said. "'Patient A has embraced her pregnancy and is very cooperative. She refers to the fetus as "my baby," talks of the names she's chosen, and has moved into a calm and somewhat dreamy state in her thirty-first week.'"

"We move to the birth. Huffman again has her sedated, not out, just a mild sedative. She induces labor — that's control again. You've got all the birth stuff, the progression of labor — lots of the OB nurse's notes and initials over a ten-hour period. Then the data on the delivery, male, length, weight, the screenings — a healthy baby boy. Pass the fucking cigars."

"Then they took the baby," Nadine put in. "Monitored her for the next forty-eight when she became Resident Female."

"Is there any documentation on what they did with her?"

"Young," Eve pointed out, "healthy pregnancy and birth? I'm betting they kept her there as a breeder, or sold her to some guy. There are more like this — I scanned — and we can go through all of them."

"I'll need to," Reo affirmed, "but for now?"

"For now, there are several with names — first names — ages, races, recruiter name, location of contact. And the name of the husband, his status in the order, his profession. Date of conception, whether it was by natural means or insemination."

"Wilkey donated his sperm. I know I'm jumping ahead," Nadine said, "but it applies here. If the husband's wasn't viable, Wilkey's was often used."

"What a generous guy," Peabody muttered.

"There's more documentation from the clinic the Huffmans run here in New York," Eve continued. "Files on females, physicals prior to conception, monitoring of pregnancies, and so on. The same for the facilities at HQ.

"Then there's accounting. Once she decided to cut ties, this nurse was as thorough as she could manage. I skimmed a bit, and clearly we're going to match some if not all of the names with payments to Natural Order, to the Huffmans, to the medical staff. We've got a spreadsheet — Wait."

She zipped through until she brought it up. "See there. Names of candidates, date of contact, recruiter, payments. Marriage payment on the profit side, right? Medical fees — Natural Order splits those with the husbands — then the payment — the bonus — for each live, healthy birth."

"Buying babies. I can work with that, too."

"Thought you could. It's all there, Reo, payments for young females, deductions for medical fees, training fees, housing fees, and so on. The bonuses. And for another bonus?"

She switched data. "Our unidentified source managed to get her hands on some of the records from the island's Realignment center. Names again — or subject numbers — dates, treatments — which is what they call torture. All of these records jibe with Gwen Huffman's statement on her experience with same.

"And you have a few files on success rate, failures, mortality. Assignments and destinations. Clearly some of these people are kept on the island as laborers. As slaves, or as forced breeders."

Eve paused, smiled thinly. "I'm sending all this to Abernathy at Interpol. That should get their asses in gear."

"I'm going to get your warrants, Dallas."

"Fucking A."

"I need copies of all of this, and we'll review it all, make our case for those warrants. You've got the FBI on this, so I want one of them in the offices."

"I'll make that happen."

Reo tipped her wrist to check the time. "We have to talk details. Our wits ID'd Oliver Huffman and others at the crime scene. They ID'd Mirium Wilkey as their so-called recruiter, Po as the conduit. And I'll get those warrants. I'll sure as hell get one for Lawrence Piper, for Stanton Wilkey. I need why you want to arrest Mirium Wilkey for the murder of Ariel Byrd."

"It's a long, convoluted story. But I'm right."

"Then I'm glad I went for red meat." Reo paused for a fry. "Tell me a story."

Once she had, Reo packed up her things. "I'm going to need a solid two hours, maybe three."

"Figured that. I need at least that, so it works."

"I'll be in touch. And I'll be riding along when you take the HQ."

"I'm fine with that."

"Nadine, as a representative of the prosecutor's office, I want to say we're grateful for your help, your integrity, your cooperation. We won't forget it. As your friend, I want to say, baby, you fucking rock."

"Right back at you."

"When this is wrapped — on your end, Dallas — it's going to be wild on mine. Can't wait! Oh, I'm going to tag Mavis tomorrow — too busy today — and get over to see this house. Yay, Peabody, another big congratulations."

"Thanks. I haven't even had time to look at the tile samples Mavis texted me. She wants me and McNab to pick them out, and the paint colors, and just all of it. It's going to be so much fun! When," she added because she caught Eve's stare, "this is all wrapped."

"I want to see everything. I'll be in touch," Reo repeated, and left.

Nadine lingered over the last of her Pepsi. "So, I'm betting there's no possible way I can get a ride-along on this."

"You win the bet. But the NYPSD joins the PA's office in extending their gratitude."

"That and your AC will get me a really delicious burger."

"It's also going to get you a tag when we have the Wilkeys, the Huffmans, Piper, and others in custody. And I can't legally stop you from being in the vicinity of Natural Order's HQ — a solid two miles away, Nadine."

Nadine smiled into Eve's eyes. "Got it."

"When I do tag you, you break the story, Nadine. Break it hard, break it wide."

"What was it you said to Reo about the warrants? Oh yeah. Fucking A. Then a follow-up one-on-one with you for broadcast, followed up by a full segment with you, possibly Reo, possibly the special agent in charge from the FBI on *Now*"

"Agreed."

Nadine set her glass down, rose. "It's a little disappointing when it's so easy."

"I know, right? People don't get that." Eve smiled. "At this time, in this place, Nadine, Reo said it. You fucking rock."

"Well, well, I'll take my kudos and let you get to it. One thing — and it's in this room, so off the record. Are you actually hitting them tonight?"

"I'm looking at it. A lot of coordination goes into it, so I'm hoping for maybe somewhere around zero one hundred."

"Okay then, I'm taking my kudos and going home to catch a nap. You look like you could use one yourself."

"I'll sleep after I fill some cages."

"Later, Peabody, who looks mag and is going to have mag new digs. I'll wait for the tag."

"They noticed I lost weight."

"Jesus, Peabody, of course they noticed. They have eyes."

"You noticed?"

"I also have eyes."

"You never said." Peabody threw her arms in the air. "I mean, a whole size!"

"If I commented on it, you'd want to talk about it. Like you are now."

"That's true. I can't deny it. I'm putting new pants and new digs aside. You didn't ask me to brief them on the data you asked me to dig."

"Reo has enough. Copy me. You've got members' names from this data who paid for human beings. Dig on them, copy me. And I want names and data from every resident on the Tribeca block."

"We're hitting that, too?"

Eve looked at Gina's and Zoe's photos on the board. How many more, she wondered, like them? "We're hitting that, too."

"We're going to need more warrants."

"Once again? Fucking A." She signaled to get moving. "Feed it to me, and I'll whittle it down for Reo and those warrants," she continued as they walked back. "If you need help with it, get a uniform. Pick two now to relieve Carmichael and Shelby. I'm pulling them back in."

She went straight to her office and hit the coffee before sitting down to access Peabody's data.

Rather than loading it all on Reo, she broke it down into bites that justified warrants — searches, arrests, both.

She contacted Officer Carmichael — now his usual spit and polish.

"The subject is in her office, now, sir. She's been to the halfway house, spent about an hour inside, made two stops on the way back we assume were home checks. She got some Thai takeout and walked back to her office."

"Stick with it. I'm sending relief to your location. I need you and Shelby back here once they arrive. Grab food if you need it. It's going to be a long day."

"Copy that, sir."

While she waited for more data from Peabody, she brought up information on the Huffmans' medical clinic and the Natural Order lab. Handily the websites listed the names and qualifications of several medicals and techs.

She started her runs, pumped more information to Reo.

A really big anthill, she thought, and yes, they'd lose some in the scatter. But if they played it right, they'd get the bulk, the influencers, and break the back of the order.

Then once Nadine, and the rest of the media, got their teeth in it?

Game over.

She looked up when Teasdale came to the door.

"I got your memo requesting I attend the meeting at the PA's office."

"It would be very helpful."

"I'm on my way there now." As always, Teasdale radiated calm and efficiency. "Agent Conroy will be sending you the intel we have on the farm system as soon as possible. I'm authorized to tell you the bureau is fully prepared to join the NYPSD and Interpol in this operation. While the bureau welcomes your input and will coordinate with you, given the multiple states and jurisdictions involved in the order's farm system, we will take that area of this operation."

"Not only is that no problem for me or this department, I was counting on it. My only caveat is timing. We have to coordinate the timing."

"Very well understood. Question: Do you actually plan to launch this multiagency, global, many-armed operation tonight? Essentially within hours?"

"Around ten, eleven hours for the main hits, yeah. It has to be now, Teasdale. If we delay, a lot of ants are going to have deserted the hill before we kick it. We can't keep Mancini and Metcalf's rescue under wraps much longer, so we have to hit the block in Tribeca today. Cops have been inside the Piper crime scene. We've only got time because the neighborhood women can't communicate, but it only takes one person coming home from work or one person figuring out how to get word to HQ to blow it up before it begins."

"You've got eyes on that block."

"I do. Anyone coming in or going out gets picked up. But we can't hold it indefinitely."

"Again, understood. Bureaus are, after all, bureaucracies, and as such and by nature, their wheels roll slowly."

Teasdale might look like a bureaucrat in her FBI suit — and she might actually be one, Eve thought. But Eve knew she was also solid law enforcement.

"I appreciate you convincing those wheels to move fast."

"I'm glad to have a part in it. And in the interest of time and speed, I'll let you get back to work."

Eve was deep into that work when Roarke came in.

"I've got what you need on the HQ."

"All of it?"

"Drone and satellite views of the compound, various blueprints — even such a place must follow building codes, procedures. These may, of course, have changes not reported, but you'll have the sense. And more, I think, as I have the schematics on their security system."

"Yours, right?"

"It is, yes, and they spared no expense. You're a bit limited in here to view it as a whole, but I can set it up."

"Let's take it to the conference room. Reo's getting a mountain of warrants," she told him as they headed out. "Teasdale's at the meeting there, and let me know the FBI's all in, and will handle the hits on the farm system. I've got cops on Po, the halfway house, and on the Tribeca block."

"Busy day. The electronics from Dawber and Metcalf are in house and being gone over minutely. I was on this area so I can't tell you precisely, but there's a lot of movement and a great deal of fizzy consumption in EDD right now."

"That's a good sign."

"Give me a minute or two to set this up. Did you eat?" he asked.

"I had a burger."

He paused, and looked mildly annoyed. "A burger? Why didn't I think of that before I had that very dubious sandwich from Vending?"

"Damn good burger. You want coffee?"

"I've had a tankerful, and most of it cop coffee. I'll take water, thanks."

She opted for water herself.

"Here are your drone views. Better, I think, than the satellite imagery."

When he put them on-screen, she slipped her hands in her pockets, studied them. "Big place."

"Slightly more than forty-two acres. Some of the buildings, such as the main house, were already there when purchased. As were these smaller houses you see here, here."

He used a laser pointer.

"Like a small neighborhood. Staff housing — high-level staff. Those low-rise apartment-type buildings, that's for the working stiffs. Roads all over, except that farming area. Are those cows? Why are there always cows?"

"Milk, butter, cheese, I'm thinking."

"They've got the farm system for that, but yeah, easy access. And I bet for training. You've got to keep training in all areas. Apartments, houses here and here, too. Segregated, that's what. You've got your sections. White, black, Asian, Hispanic, like that, and all well away from the grandeur of the main house. Woods to the east, shielding the main house property and gardens."

She moved closer. "Okay, okay, you've got a stream running through the woods, and that chapel-type building. Other buildings — medical, schools."

She held out a hand for his pointer.

"There and there and there — schools, we saw students. Playground areas. I'm betting some sort of storage buildings — see those loading docks? You bring in supplies there, log them in, divide them up. Very self-contained, very tidy. What it is? It's freaking Wilkeyville. His own town, and he's mayor and sheriff and supreme ruler."

"The blueprints have more detail. Let's have a look."

They went through them, the main house, three floors, five bedroom suites and two home offices on the second floor, what was billed as a media center on the lower level with a kitchenette, full bath, guest room. A bonus room, two bedrooms, two full baths spread out on the third. Dining room, breakfast room, kitchen, living room, study, powder room, large pantry, and laundry facilities on the main.

"Media center, maybe — and I bet a setup to record his bullshit media. But bonus room, my ass. It's not on here, but I'm betting that's where he sticks in-house staff. He needs live-in staff. What if he wants a snack at midnight? Some female type has to take care of that."

She went over the staff housing, exits, egresses, the educational complexes, the medical facility, the ware-house with loading dock. Then held up a hand to pause on the next building.

"No way that's more storage. No loading dock, and the doors aren't wide enough. It's got a full basement — for what? I'll tell you for what."

She felt the anger rise in her and had to firmly, deliberately tamp it out. Emotions had to wait.

"That's where they keep the people they abduct. No windows, not one window on the plans. If I were setting it up, this is how I'd do it. Windowless, limited exits and escape routes. Have your lab and shock therapy, testing in the basement. You could fit plenty of barred rooms in there, and a place for staff to meet or take a break, have some lunch before they go back and jab somebody with a shock stick.

"That's the prison."

"I'm going to agree with you on that."

Knowing her, he not only felt her fury, but shared it. And, knowing her, he kept his tone as cool as hers.

"It's tucked too far away from everything else to serve efficiently as storage," he added. "And the schematics on the security system add weight to that prison."

"Bring them up. I think my eyes are about to bleed." She closed them, but when she opened them again she still saw a lot of lines, graphics, incomprehensible terms and figures. "I'm going back to coffee."

"I'll join you there, and explain this to you. I have more covering the walls, and that prison building, still more on the main house, and so on. It's a very complex and comprehensive system. In addition to alarms throughout, there are motion sensors in some areas, alerts should anyone attempt to jam or hack the system."

"Okay."

"Oh, there's more." He said it cheerfully, like someone about to start an entertaining game. "Lights, sirens. The walls are outfitted with a shock system.

372

This, and more still, would be over and above any human or droid patrols."

She handed him coffee. "Here's what we're going to do. You know the system."

"I do indeed. Or, more accurately, the systems, as there are three systems combined — intertwined, and in layers. It's very well done."

"You're not going to explain it all to me or we'll be here for a month. What you're going to do is look at this — the systems — and the main house, to start, like it has a zillion hot white diamonds inside, and you want them. You're going to figure out how you'd get in, get to every one of these buildings, and steal the shit out of them."

His lips curved slowly. "Well then, wouldn't that be fun?"

"It's just you and me here, ace. Find the weak spots, and be a thief."

He studied the schematics, and his smile only spread. "I can do that."

Before he started, his 'link signaled. "Ah, that's perfect as well. I have the security schematics and the blueprints from the island community."

"How'd you find time to get those already, and what we've got going here?"

"Delegating. Summerset — and don't snarl — handled this."

"I want to snarl, but I can't because we need it. How'd he get it — Don't tell me." She quickly waved even the thought of it away. "Just send it to Whitney.

He'll get it to Abernathy, and we'll hope they don't ask too many questions."

"There's always an answer that will suit if necessary. You'll feel better knowing that since the block in Tribeca wasn't actually built by Natural Order, Feeney's team is getting those blueprints. My system again, so the security's easy to access. You'll have that shortly.

"Now." He rolled his shoulders. "Hot white diamonds, is it?"

"Zillions."

"I've always been fond of them." He sat down at one of the computers, rolled up his sleeves. Tied his hair back. "If I can build it, I can break it. It starts with the walls."

She'd spent nearly her entire career as a murder cop. She'd never chased down a master thief unless a murder was involved. And had never considered, exactly, what went into planning a theft of a highly secured building — much less multiple buildings.

Apparently at least some of it involved math. What looked to her like really big math, like calculus or physics.

Before it gave her a headache, she left him to it. She took the other computer and began her own calculations, her bare outline of multiple operations, and timing, and coordination.

All assuming Roarke got them over, through, or around the wall.

"That's that then."

She looked up. "What? You're in?"

"That's the wall, and all attached alerts, alarms, deterrents, and so on. You've the gatehouse there, and the best solution would be to just shut it down. Shut down its communications, power. If a guard or guards are inside, well, you'll have to deal with them."

"We can do that."

"Look here now. I'm highlighting what I'd consider the best areas to breach the wall. Climbing it's going to be the best of the options, at least until we reactivate the gate from the gatehouse. But I'd stick with a very small number going over and in. I'd want to be over and in before I start shutting down other areas. It needs to be done layer by layer, sector by sector."

She didn't need to understand his math to get the picture. "Can you show and equip other teams of two — three tops, with one an e-cop — how to take down levels? If you and I go over here."

"You and I?"

"That's right. We go here, front gate, deal with the gatehouse, move on. Other teams go over at your designated points. We start working our way in, shutting things down as we go."

"All right, I see it. I always kept my . . . team, we'll say, on the very small side, so I'll adjust for expanding that."

"I need how many we can get inside on the first stage, how long to shut those layers — all down — so that we can spread out to every area. My focus, off the bat, is the suspected prison, the main house. But we need to hit it all."

"Let me work out the how, then I'll give you numbers and times."

She had enough to start putting some meat on the bones of her operation. Yes, she could flesh it out now, could start to see.

Using a highlighter, she tried different routes in from the breach points he'd chosen, began assigning buildings and structures to each team — with backup coming in as the system shut down.

She lost track of time, building layer by layer as Roarke broke layer by layer.

He rose, put a hand on her shoulder, then kissed the top of her head. "I believe I have it. A bit more refining to do, but I can give you some times and some numbers."

"I'll take them."

"From point of entry, each team — I'd keep that to two each with an e-man for three — must — absolutely must — go no more than fifteen feet from the wall. Go fifteen and an inch, they'll set off the next layer with motion detectors."

"Got it."

"From that point, it will take them about four minutes, unless I can shave that down more than I have, to take down the next section. Fifteen feet at a time, Eve. No more, not a toe over."

"Slow and steady."

"Aye, slow and steady. When a team reaches these apartments, these houses, this building — do you see where it's going?"

A slowly shrinking circle. "Yeah, yeah, working that slow and steady in."

"They can adjust the jam. I can have them execute a series of codes — so you must have those e-cops — that will shut down the systems on those specific buildings."

"Then they can keep moving, keep jamming, keep shutting down while the backup comes in behind them."

"That would be your part of it to calculate."

"And I can do that."

"This doesn't factor patrols."

"I'll have that handled, keep going."

"Each building will have locks, and those require yet another series of codes."

"Okay."

"As you'd expect, both the prison and the main house have more layers."

She nodded, as she had expected. "Top e-man on the prison, you and me on the main house. It's going to take more than an hour, closer to two to shut it down, and to move in the takedown teams."

"I'm going to work on that, but I doubt we can do it all in less than an hour or seventy-five minutes."

"Slow and steady's fine with me. The main house is going to be one of the last to shut down the way it's situated. But by then, we'll have backup. We go in, and now the takedown teams pour in. I can see how I can work it."

She considered. "When all law enforcement's inside, can you reactivate the wall?"

"That would be the easy part."

"Good. Ants can't scatter if they can't get out of the hill. And here's another question."

She asked, rejected, accepted. He refined; she fleshed out.

And when she felt she had it solid, she went to her commander, coordinated with Abernathy, then with Teasdale, then with Reo.

CHAPTER
TWENTY

With Roarke back in EDD, working out any kinks with Feeney, she sat down at her desk to think, to pick at any flaws. Boots up, coffee in hand, she flipped through the various stages of her many-pronged operation on her wall screen.

Baxter tapped on her doorjamb. "Want good news, boss?"

Since he carried evidence bags in his hands, Eve swung her boots off the desk. "Have you got something in there that nails Mirium Wilkey to Ariel Byrd's murder?"

"How about three nails, like motive, means, opportunity?"

"Those work. Let's have it."

He set the bags on her desk. "Can I get in on that?" he asked, and gestured to her coffee.

"Go." She rose, unsealed the first bag.

"Trueheart's writing it up, but I figured you'd want to see this part of it. That's a copy of recordings we found on the comp in her home office. Audio and video. They go back ten months, and some of them are, we'll say, intimate. My young partner may have a permanent blush."

"From Gwen Huffman's phone."

"She labeled them, date, time, content — very organized. We got recordings of the originals for the record, since we couldn't bring anything in. The last one's dated the night of Byrd's murder. It's got the romance, the sex, the texts from Merit Caine, and the ensuing argument — pretty heated — between Byrd and Huffman. You've got Huffman storming out, and subsequently calling for a Rapid to pick her up. Pickup a couple blocks from Byrd's residence."

Since he'd previously experienced the bite of her visitor's chair, he stood and drank his coffee.

"She wiped her security feed for the night in question, from twenty-two hundred to twenty-three-forty-five."

"Covering her leaving to kill Byrd, returning to clean herself up, then leaving again to get to the compound for cover. We need EDD on that."

"Done. Trueheart took the original disc straight up. We had to risk she wouldn't look at that if she goes back to that location."

"That's the right call. Feeney will find the wiped data."

"She kept the key card, LT. We left it, but recorded it. She had it in her desk drawer. We found data on Byrd on her comp — copied that, disc in the next bag. Her background, her financials, her contacts. And a recording of Byrd's apartment, inside, room by room."

"She plans. Wanted to study the space in case."

"Dallas, it looks to me like she was working out a way to snatch Byrd up, transport her to Realignment."

"Huh. Sure, of course she was. Money in the bank."

"It looks like she planned to keep Byrd on the island. There's a lot more in the other bags on Natural Order, procedure, finances. And financially, we probably need an accountant but it looks to me like they're not exactly hemorrhaging money, but they're oozing it."

Eve nodded. "Jibes with Roarke's take."

"And Mirium felt the same. She's got calculations on how to generate more income. Gwen Huffman's a big factor — blackmail."

He raised his eyebrows. "I'm not telling you anything you hadn't figured there."

"It's money. It's planning for the next stage. Blackmail's more insurance."

"Then there's the senior Huffmans — and she has a copy of their will. She's got documentation on her recruitment angles, names, locations. She pins Po and a Michael J. Harstead at the halfway house as feeders. And there's a Denise Wexford at the Good Samaritan Shelter as another of her feeders."

"We'll pick them up, all of them. A few hours yet, but we'll get them all."

"On the family front? She's got files on her brothers. Evidence the older one dips into the membership fund, and the next one has a taste for LCs. She calls the youngest one Mommy's Fake Boy, so she knows he's her half brother, and she's stockpiling evidence he's gay."

"She's planning. Laying groundwork for a coup."

"She's got a supply of sleep meds. Heavy meds, liquid form, big supply. All prescribed by Oliver Huffman."

"Recruitment tool."

"Fuckers."

"Yeah, we've got the fuckers, Baxter."

He glanced at her screen and the display of the compound with its hot spots. "We're going tonight?"

"We're going tonight. I'm going to take our end of the op for a spin in a holoroom, just tighten it up where I can. Be ready."

"Oh, born that way, Loo."

CHAPTER
TWENTY-ONE

She took her spin, programmed in the other teams, the backups, the takedown, the timing. By scaling Roarke's four-minute lag to four seconds, she could run it through quickly — then have the computer calculate reality time.

She ordered and reordered priorities on each run-through.

Satisfied she'd closed any apparent holes, she briefed Whitney, and with his go, pulled in Lowenbaum and his SWAT team to handle Tribeca.

The first phase.

With Lowenbaum, she worked on the timing and movements of that area of the operation.

"A lot of kids, Lowenbaum."

He nodded as they stood in the mock-up holo of the block. She'd programmed the names of the residents and number of minors on each house.

"Understood. We'll have the Child Services reps you selected behind the line, and we'll get the kids to safety. You're sure about those reps?"

"I got them from the head of An Didean. Rochelle's solid, and she's worked with these three people. Some of the women on the block will be like the two we have at Dochas, and some will be like Barbara Poole. Even the ones who don't want to be there may resist or run. Some may not be able to run if they have the shockers on, or their kids do."

With Eve, Lowenbaum walked up and down the holo block.

"We've got the neutralizing device Roarke built us for that, Dallas. You've done all the work till now, even listing the target houses by probability of resistance. We'll handle the rest."

"Any adult males, if there, must be separated and contained. Some may have weapons, most will likely have comms. My data indicates most if not all of the male residents should be in the compound tonight. But —"

He looked at her. "Trust me and mine."

"You wouldn't be here if I didn't. I've got to get you on this because of the possibility of communication. That block needs to be shut down before we move on the rest."

As they'd worked together before, he knew her mindset. "And you're wishing like hell you could be two places at once so you could be on this takedown while you're here coordinating the next."

"Make that about ten places at once." Then she hissed out a breath. "We've got the best people, top cops on every one of the ops. So . . . letting go, Lowenbaum. Good hunting."

"Same to you. I'll keep you in the loop all the way."

She checked the time when he left. Shutting down the holo, she started back to the conference room.

She found Peabody and Roarke already setting up. "You beat me to it."

"You've been doing about six dozen things at once," Peabody said. "I figured I could get this going — with a little help."

"Appreciate it." She frowned at the device Roarke attached to the comp. "What's that?"

"A portable holo."

"We have one of those?"

"I had it brought in."

Hell, she thought, it was only Peabody in there. So she walked to Roarke, wrapped her arms around him for one precious moment. And stepped back when Peabody said, "Aw."

"Keep your aws to yourself. Lowenbaum and his team are heading out now. We've got FBI sitting just beyond the compound. Anyone comes out, they pick them up."

She started to rub her eyes, but since they felt like sandpaper, dropped her hands again. "We've got teams ready to pick up the Huffmans, Po, Harstead, Wexford, and others. We pulled from Special Victims, and I brought in Detective Strong and her partner from Illegals for those busts."

She paused when Roarke handed her a glass. "What's this?"

"It's a protein drink — and it's chocolate. Don't bitch about it."

"Fine. Rochelle gave me names of CPS reps she knows and vouches for. They're with Lowenbaum. I've got more supporting the hit on HQ."

"Dochas is prepared to take any women and children who need sheltering."

She glanced back at Roarke. "Do they have room? There could be a lot."

"They'll make room. And when and if necessary, arrangements with other safe houses. Leave that one to them. Moira knows the system, and they'll work it."

"Okay, fine." She drank without thinking about it, then had to admit: Not half-bad. "Abernathy swears their teams are solid. They'll have air and sea support, and they've agreed to hold until I give them the green. Same with the FBI on the farm team."

Now she paced and drank. "That's more problematic. It involves multiple states and locations, and it's so spread out. Lots of open land. Air support there, too, but . . . We won't get all of them. Odds are low we'll get them all."

"And they'll be running with, basically, the shirts on their backs," Roarke reminded her. " 'Things fall apart; the center cannot hold.' That's Yeats, and applies to this. There'll be no center, Eve. And the order falls apart."

But he went to her. "It's hard to have other people take control of what you can't do."

"Solid cops."

"Remember that. And here come some of your own."

Those solid cops filed in, and Jenkinson and his tie came directly to her. He held out a hand.

Baffled, she shook it. "Okay, what for?"

"Whitney stopped by the bullpen to tell us you'd put in commendations — for every one of us who worked on Cobbe. It matters, Lieutenant."

"You earned it, Detective."

"It matters," he repeated, and went to take a seat.

"It really does," Peabody added. "Thanks."

"Just take that happy energy into this briefing and beyond. Can you work the holo thing?"

"Well . . ."

"I've got it." Roarke gave Peabody a pat on the shoulder. "It won't, obviously, be full-size," he told Eve. "But it will be to scale. And since he's here, we'll have McNab run the screen."

"That'll work. I'm going to —"

She snapped to attention. "Chief."

Chief of Police Tibble came in with Whitney. Tall and lean in his dark suit, he crossed to her. "I'm here to observe, Lieutenant, and offer any and all assistance as needed. I'll be joining this operation."

His lips curved, just a little, as her face went instantly blank. "Outside the compound, with the commander, APA Reo, and other support."

"Your support and assistance is very much appreciated, sir."

"As long as I don't get in the way," he finished. "I've studied your operational plans, Lieutenant. Very bold, very thorough. Let's make them work."

Like Jenkinson, he walked away to take a seat.

Eve spotted Mira. "Jesus Christ, don't tell me you're planning to go on this?"

"Of course. Some of the prisoners may require immediate evaluation, medically and emotionally." She patted Eve's arm. "I'll be well out of the way until needed."

Let it go, she told herself. Let it all go but this.

She waited for Teasdale, Conroy, Reo, Reo's boss, and all the others.

And realized too late she still had the room's AC on her menu. Coffee flowed like a rich, dark river.

"Sit or stand, but be quiet. Inspectors Abernathy and Jonas, Interpol, are on speaker, as are Special Agents Clyburn, Reese, Monica, Rosencroft, and Paulson, FBI. We'll coordinate with them on every step.

"Lieutenant Lowenbaum and his unit are even now converging on the block in Tribeca, while Special Agent Teasdale has agents outside the compound in Connecticut to pick up anyone who leaves. This will cut off any opportunity for communication back to the HQ, the island, the farm system, or the subjects who will be picked up in New York and elsewhere.

"This is a major and multipronged operation. We're going to take it step-by-step."

She started with Strong and the other detectives on the busts, and the search teams who would follow up at those locations. She had Interpol and the FBI brief on their areas.

And stepped away to answer her comm.

She stepped back in as they wound it up.

"Thank you. The first stage, Tribeca, is complete. The block and its residents are contained." She'd expected the cheer — she felt one inside herself — and let it ride.

Teasdale lifted a hand. "Two male individuals have been detained after leaving the compound. They are being transported for questioning to FBI headquarters."

"So far, so good. Here's what we've got coming up. Roarke?"

The holo of the compound spread at Eve's feet, and got a lot of murmurs.

"Nice." Feeney grinned at it and slurped his coffee.

"McNab, on-screen."

She picked up her laser pointer. "We'll breach the walls at these locations. One team, consisting of an e-cop and a detective or uniform, at each. Roarke and I go at the gate, and if successful, I'll give the go to the other breach teams. Each e-cop will carry a hand device, which, when the code is engaged, will shut down the security system for an area of fifteen feet — not a millimeter more or the system goes on alert. It will take four minutes before the code can be resent for the next fifteen feet."

"It's down to two minutes, ten seconds," Roarke told her.

"Two minutes, ten."

And she ran them through every step, assigned teams to the breach points, to the backup, to the specific targets and takedowns.

"When we hit the targets, Captain Feeney will jam the comms and open the gate. We can't risk doing this until we're inside and in position. When he jams the comms, Interpol and the FBI get the green. The teams in New York, and elsewhere, hit their targets."

It would work, she thought. Timed right, it would all work.

"No one who is not on breach, backup, or takedown teams enters the compound until it's secure and contained. Exception for medical personnel if needed.

"I want anyone held in what we believe is a prison freed and taken to safety. I want you to look at this face. McNab, bring up Foxx. Ella Alice Foxx, who risked a hell of a lot passing me a message. They abducted her, they have most certainly tortured her, she is being held against her will. Remember her face. Remember there will be others like her.

"Questions?"

There were a lot of them. She answered, or lobbed to Feeney or Teasdale or Reo.

When the questions tapered off, she wound it up.

"Everyone — and that includes those who remain outside the compound during this operation — will wear vests. Everyone going in wears black, will have night-vision goggles. Everyone will have earbud comms and recorders. Every step of this is on record. As I said before, we don't know how many weapons may be inside. We don't yet know if they have armed foot patrols, human or droid. Stunners on medium for quick incapacitation. You're going to be fucking stealthy."

She checked her watch. "Compound teams, meet on Garage Level One at twenty-three-thirty. Be equipped, be geared up, be ready. Meanwhile, get some rack time if you can. Dismissed."

Shelby hurried to her. "You put me on the backup team on HQ."

"That's right. Do you have a problem with that?"

"No, sir!" She actually snapped to attention. "I didn't expect, with my limited time in this division, to be part of this operation. Thank you, Lieutenant."

"Don't screw up and you'll be fine."

"That'll be my mantra. I have a question, sir, I didn't want to ask before."

"Go."

"Do you think Gwen knew all this? I mean about the human trafficking, the torture, the rapes, the slavery?"

"She experienced some of the torture herself. Yeah, she knows. Nothing matters to her but her own comfort and position. We probably can't prove it, but she knows."

"I never would've thought that of her. I don't really know her anymore, but — Thank you, Lieutenant."

"Grab a little downtime. And stay sharp."

"Is that what you're going to do?" Roarke asked as the room emptied. "Grab some downtime?"

"I've got too many irons in the fire for that. And why did I say that?" Baffled, she dragged a hand through her hair. "Why would anybody put irons in a fire?"

"To keep them hot, I'd say."

"Oh." She considered. "All right, I'll accept that one. I need to keep my irons hot. I'm too revved," she added before he could object. "And I need to debrief Lowenbaum. I've got more data on Mirium Wilkey, and I need to prep for interviews with her and her father. Tonight. Hot iron — you strike then, right?"

"You do indeed."

"I need to get my gear. So do you. You need to hit Requisitions for black, and other shoes, and —"

Roarke stopped her by tapping a finger to her lips. "I'll have something appropriate brought in for both of us. I'm not wearing what I can finesse from your cop shop. Even in this, I have standards."

"That's your iron to fire."

"I'll have appropriately stealthy attire here for both of us by half-eight. I'll meet you then in your office."

"I'll be there."

Alone, she looked at the board.

"We're coming to get you, Ella. Hang in."

When she turned to leave, Lowenbaum, still in full gear, stepped inside.

"Quick work, LT."

"No weapons," he told her. "A couple of the women — Poole being one — tried kitchen knives or skillets. No injuries. Three of the women and five of the kids had those goddamn tracker-slash-shockers on. We had MTs transport one, one really pregnant one, to a medical facility.

"So." He sat, rolled his shoulders. "I'll run it through for you, and copy the recordings to you. But before we get to that, my teams want in on the HQ. We're wound up, pissed, and want in. You need to make room."

"I'll make room."

By the time she dealt with all the irons, it was after nine. She stopped at the door to her office. Roarke sat at her desk, his pricey shoes up on it, the chair kicked back, and his eyes closed.

She started to step back out, ease the door shut.

"Your stealthwear's on your miserable chair," he said. "You're late."

"Couldn't be helped."

He grabbed her hand, pulled her into his lap.

"Jesus! Knock it off."

"You'll have noted those remaining in your bullpen are doing exactly this. The others found somewhere else to snatch a bit of sleep."

"I also smelled pizza in there. Not a crumb in sight, but I smelled pizza."

"They ate, as you should. But since you've been going for near to twenty hours with barely any sleep, you need this more. One hour," he said. "Just shut it off for an hour. You'll be sharper for it."

"Maybe. Let me shut the door."

He just snuggled her in. "None of them care, Eve. Take an hour, then we'll drag those bastards to the ground."

She'd covered everything, she told herself. Gone over every step, again and again. Consulted, briefed, answered, questioned.

She could take an hour.

She dropped into sleep like a rock in a well.

When he woke her, she unwound herself, locked the door. Even before she turned back she smelled the coffee — and the pizza.

"One slice," he said. "You'll say you don't want to feel full."

She drew in those blessed scents as she stretched out the kinks. "You think of everything."

"I think of you."

She met his eyes. "I know you do."

Loose again, she ate the slice, drank the coffee. She had to admit as they changed clothes she did feel sharper.

She strapped on her weapon, her clutch piece, a combat knife.

"I assume you have your own."

"I do — and to make you feel better, Whitney authorized the stunner."

And because she thought of him, because she knew him, she eyed him. "You've got more than a stunner on you."

"Well, the stunner's authorized, so we have that."

He wore black, as she did, a long-sleeved tee, pants, thick-soled black boots. He handed her a thin cotton cap. Then put on one of his own, tucked his hair up into it.

It shouldn't have amazed her he looked ridiculously sexy.

"So this is how you looked when you robbed people blind."

"We'll say this is often how I dressed for certain activities."

She handed him a vest, took her own. "Let's move."

As she passed through the bullpen, Peabody and some of the squad walked out of the locker room. They fell in line, got in the elevator.

"Anybody else thinking breakfast beers after this bust?" Baxter slipped his hands in his pockets. "We could hit the Blue Line looking like a team of cat burglars."

"Bust now, beer later," Eve said.

"That's what I'm saying."

In the garage, it surprised Eve to see Mira in the same cat-burglar black. "You're not going in until —"

"No, of course not. But it would be foolish to wear a suit and heels at such a time."

"You're with the commander, the chief, Reo. Everyone else, into your assigned vehicles."

She got into her own, settled on one of the drop seats. Ignoring the chatter, she went over every step again on the drive to Connecticut.

She tapped her earbud. "Inspector Abernathy, we're at target."

"We're ready here."

"Special Agent Clyburn?"

"On your go" came the response.

"Breach teams, move into position."

She got out, studied the wall. "No lights on in the gatehouse. Roarke and I secure that first." She gave him a nod.

He did what he did with his device while she ticked the seconds off in her head.

"This point's clear."

To her astonishment, he scaled the wall like a damn lizard, then reached down a hand for her. "Up you come, Lieutenant."

She took his hand, and the boost from one of the backup team.

Roarke leaped down, agile and quiet as a cat. She dropped beside him. Sidestepping to the gatehouse, she waited for him to deal with the locks. Weapons drawn, they slipped inside.

In the dim backwash of the security lights she saw equipment, screens, a table, and some chairs.

Clearing back, she scanned a small bathroom, a refreshment center.

"It's clear. We move on."

"Thirty seconds more."

"Breach teams, first go. We'll be fifteen feet ahead."

Slow and steady, she thought as they moved through the dark, stayed in the shadows, thirty feet, then forty-five.

Roarke took a moment in the next timed gap, shut off their recorders.

"What the —"

"I have to say it. My Christ, what a pair we'd have been."

The absolute delight in his voice tickled her soft spots.

"You move like smoke, smoke with nerves of steel and unshakable focus. We'd have romped the globe, you and I, plucking every precious thing we wanted. What a pity we didn't meet in some lovely alternate world where you weren't a cop."

Though amused, she gave him a dour stare. "I'm a cop in all of them."

"You're likely right. And still." He sighed, reengaged their recorders. "And there's the mark. Moving on."

Sixty feet, seventy-five, ninety.

"Not a sign — not from any team — of guards."

"They trust the system." Roarke shrugged. "As really, under other circumstances, they should."

By the time they'd crossed more than a football field with their backup team behind them, Eve had the main house in view. "Lights off there, too. Off in every building so far."

"It's past one in the morning now, heading toward two. You were right to wait until midnight to start this."

"We've got teams that have reached their targets, others approaching same. Takedown teams, move in. Move into target, and hold."

When they reached the second gate, Roarke shut down the system, eased it open enough for them to slide through single file.

She could smell buoyant spring on the air from the flowers, and thought of the woman and the two girls working. We're coming, she thought as she had with Ella. Nearly there.

When they reached the veranda, she realized the humming in her head wasn't a brewing headache, but anticipation. Like an engine idling fast for a race.

In the silence Roarke worked on the locks. She used hand signals to order the teams behind her to hold.

And used them again to signal she and Roarke entered first — to hold.

He eased both doors open, barely a whisper of sound.

Nothing moved in the grand, wide entranceway.

Ahead stairs curved up, then split into a double staircase.

"We're in the main target." She kept her voice low as she moved forward. "Feeney, shut it down. Abernathy, you're a go. Special Agents, you're a go. Bust teams, go, go. All teams go. We're full green."

Air support flooded the compound with light.

She took the stairs two at a time while teams cleared the main level. At the break, Roarke split off with his team, she with hers.

He to Wilkey, she to the daughter.

She wanted the daughter.

Down the hallway she signaled cops to the left or right to clear other rooms, to take occupants into custody.

When she reached what she believed was Mirium's door, she found it locked.

"Oh yeah, this is yours, you bitch." She considered picking the lock. Then, as the first sounds — not alarms, but shouting — came from outside, she stepped back. Getting a running start, she kicked it open.

Lights flashed on in the room beyond a plush little sitting area. When Eve charged in, Mirium was out of bed and reaching into a drawer of her nightstand.

"Pull a weapon out, and I drop you. Please, pull a weapon out."

"What are you doing? Are you out of your mind?"

Eve recognized the red nightshirt as silk when she spun Mirium around to cuff her.

"Get your hands off me! Get out of my house!"

"Mirium Wilkey, you're under arrest for the murder of Ariel Byrd, for the abductions of a number of human beings who will be named in this warrant. For the forced imprisonment of human beings, for accessory to rape, and other charges that will be included in your booking."

"This is persecution for our faith."

"Faith my ass. Officer Shelby, please read Ms. Wilkey her rights, and see that she is taken to one of the wagons we have waiting."

"Yes, sir."

She rushed out, listening to the reports through her earbud.

She spotted Roarke's team dragging Wilkey out of his room. Behind them, Roarke had his arm around the shoulders of a woman.

"My girls, please. My girls."

The hat had obscured her face when she'd gardened, but Eve saw enough to recognize her. "You're safe now. They're safe now."

"He keeps them in the other wing, upstairs. The children are locked in at night. They're Cassie and Robbyn. Please, don't hurt them."

"No one's going to hurt them, or you. Your name?"

"Fiona Wil — No, no, he makes me use his name, but I'm Fiona Vassar. He says I'm his breeding wife. My God, my babies."

"We'll get them out," Roarke murmured to her. "We'll bring them to you."

"He's a monster."

"Get her to Mira. Cassie and Robbyn," she said, looking into Fiona's eyes. "I'm going to bring them to you. He'll never touch you or them again."

"I have a son, but they took him. He's two now. I don't know where —"

"We'll find him. We'll find him."

"Come now, Fiona, we'll get you away from this place. You and your girls. Come with me now."

Roarke led her away, murmuring to her all the while.

"Clear it," Eve ordered. "Top to bottom. I want e-men to start on the electronics once it's cleared."

Wilkey, wearing only a long white robe, struggled against his restraints. His eyes, feral and wild, latched on to Eve's.

"You won't bring down the order. Our faith will remain unbroken, our numbers will rise up and —"

"Save it," she snapped. "Get him out. He can spout his bullshit from a cell."

She left them to it, went outside to check on the progress.

"Dallas!" She stopped when Detective Carmichael called out. And Eve waited while she led the woman to her.

"She was pretty insistent about seeing you," Carmichael said. "We got her out of a room behind the kitchen. The shrieking hag of a bitch with her fucking stabbed Santiago."

Eve held up a hand. "How bad?"

"Opened up his arm pretty damn good, boss. MTs have him, and we got her — Gayle fucking Steenberg. I want to check on my partner, but I wanted to bring her over first."

"Ella Alice Foxx," Eve said, and held out a hand.

"You know me. You know me. You came."

"I know you, Ella, and we're here because you didn't give up."

Ella threw her arms around Eve. "There are so many of us. So many like me."

"I know. We've got you now."

CHAPTER
TWENTY-TWO

It took just under two and a half hours to fully contain the compound. It would take days, very likely weeks, to fully process all the people inside, to record or confiscate the evidence, to interview, to find shelters for those held against their will, to do medical and psych evals, to deal with the minors.

And the one hundred and six — at current count — women in various stages of pregnancy.

She toured the torture chamber — the term fit — of what had been the prison. Exam and treatment rooms held tables fitted with restraints, with two containing shock therapy devices. One room offered a sensory deprivation chamber. Locked cabinets contained drugs — legal and illegal — pressure syringes and surgical tools, test kits. And shock sticks.

On the floors above, ten-by-ten rooms served as cells. Windowless, a single steel door, a single cot fitted with restraints, a toilet, a sink, a wall screen.

She stood in one of those rooms now. She knew what this was like. Richard Troy had tied her to the bed sometimes, had often left her in the dark.

She knew what it was like to lie there shivering, helpless, hopeless.

When Roarke found her there, he put his hands on her shoulders, kissed the top of her head. She didn't bother to object.

"At least I usually had a window. The teams got nine people out of here. Six women and one man in the cells, two guards — one male, one female. The female's the Mother Catherine Gina told me about. Catherine Duplay. She grabbed a shock stick and resisted. In the struggle, she got a good taste of her favorite form of torture."

"You're a little disappointed you weren't the one to give her that taste."

"I can't deny it. We've cleared the buildings, the housing units. Most people just gave up. Sure, there was some running and screaming, but most just put their hands in the air."

"When you're woken from a sound sleep by law enforcement pointing weapons in your face, hands up is survival."

"That, and most didn't have weapons. It's going to turn out you had to reach a certain level to get one of those fucking shock sticks or a stunner. A few had knives."

"And how is Santiago?"

"Twenty-two stitches — some muscle involved there — and a couple weeks of desk duty. He's the worst of it. Some nicks, some bruises. We got lucky."

"No." It annoyed him enough to turn her around to face him. "Lucky my ass, Lieutenant. You did the job, step-by-step. This could've been a war zone. You made sure it wasn't."

"The war's not over. Abernathy reports the island is mostly contained, but mostly isn't all. It's a lot bigger than this compound. Same goes for the farm system.

"On the other hand," she added as they walked out, "the Huffmans are in custody, so are Po and Harstead, Wexford. I'm having Gwen brought in for another round. I'd really like to work something on her that sticks, but I don't see that happening. We've got the Pooles."

"You have the Wilkeys."

"Yeah, we've got the fucking Wilkeys." Her face went fierce. "Every one of them."

Outside, lights lit the compound like noon. Cops swarmed everywhere, clearing buildings, searching for hidey-holes, grid-searching the grounds. She signaled to the Crime Scene van.

"It's all yours."

"I expected to find you exhausted," Roarke commented. "And you're the opposite."

"Got another wind. I don't know which number wind this is, but I've got it. Teasdale and I worked some things out. I get to interview Wilkey before she takes him. I get Mirium Wilkey, then she'll toss in the federal charges, but I get her first. I get Piper, the Huffmans, Po, Harstead, Wexford, the Pooles, and so on. Everyone will do their federal rounds, but first they're mine."

"The FBI wouldn't have this without you."

"I wouldn't have it without them, so that's a wash. Our sweepers and EDD will work with the feds to process this place, and the facilities outside the complex. Our PA will work with federal prosecutors.

Then there's the international aspect, but right now, I'm focusing on two murders and the abductions and enforced imprisonment in my city."

Medical vans worked on-site to treat and evaluate. Police wagons loaded prisoners. Eve spotted the gate guard — in restraints, sporting a black eye — and felt another little lift to her spirit.

He spotted her, too. He elbow-jabbed the cop loading him into the van, and rushed Eve like a bull.

She didn't bother to reach for her weapon, held up a hand to stop anyone else from stunning him. And let him come.

All she had to do was sidestep the charge and trip him — but the added uppercut gave her an even higher lift.

He fell like a tree and skidded a foot or so on his face.

"We'll bury you, bitch! We'll bury you."

"You're the one eating dirt, asshole. Add another charge of assaulting an officer and resisting arrest to his slate," she told the uniforms who dragged him up again.

"Big man," the uniform snarled. "Had a stunner, and hit my partner with a stream, then grabbed his own kid — eight years old — and tried to use the kid as a shield. Kid gave him the shiner."

"Good for him."

"Her," the uniform corrected, and muscled the guard into the van.

At the gates, Eve saw Whitney conferring with Teasdale. And Nadine, outside those gates, doing a one-on-one with Tibble, with the compound, the activity at his back.

"Commander, Special Agent, the compound is secure. Joint teams are processing. At last count we have six hundred and thirty-two adults and fourteen hundred and eighteen minors moved or being moved out. APA Reo and the reps from the federal prosecutor's office, the state's attorney's office are running tabs on the number of arrests and charges. Child Protective Services is conducting interviews and evaluations."

Whitney held up a hand to stop Eve's report. "Do you wish to remain here overseeing this cleanup operation?"

"Sir, I'd prefer to call my division back into Central and start the interview process."

"Done. This was good work, Lieutenant. Down the line good work."

"Thank you, sir."

"I'll remain here," Teasdale told her. "And touch base with you later today." She paused as Conroy raced over.

"They found him. Tony — Agent Quirk. He's alive. In bad shape, but alive."

"Where?" Teasdale demanded.

"The farm system, somewhere in Iowa. They had him in a cell, shackled in a cell. Had a shock collar on him. Beaten, tortured, but alive."

He turned to Eve, held out a hand.

"That's good news, Conroy." She shook it.

"He's a friend of mine. He's got internal injuries, and the medical I talked to said without treatment, he wouldn't have lasted another forty-eight. He's alive because we pushed on this tonight. I thought it was a mistake. I was wrong."

"I've been wrong once or twice myself. I need to speak with Nadine, Commander, then I'll be at Central."

"We'll need to schedule a media conference later this morning," Whitney told her. "Kyung will coordinate with you. No good deed," he added.

"Yes, sir." She walked over to Nadine, who'd concluded her one-on-one with Tibble.

"I really need to get in there, Dallas. They won't even let our choppers do flyovers."

"I'm not in charge of that. But I'll give you a one-on-one here and now with as much detail as I'm able."

"I'll take it." Nadine angled her head, narrowed her foxy eyes. "Did you manage to grab eight hours of sleep somewhere? You look a hell of a lot fresher than you did this afternoon."

"Kicking ass is better than sleep."

"Apparently." Nadine signaled to her camera.

Two hours later, on a morning that dawned with a steady spring shower, Eve sat at her desk. She pumped coffee as she worked on her strategy.

Roarke, who'd stated — firmly — he was in for the duration, had gone off to find some quiet place to start his wheels and deals.

She'd told her detectives to grab sleep, a shower, a change of clothes, food, whatever they needed. And to report back to the bullpen by zero-nine hundred.

More hot irons to handle, she thought.

Twenty minutes before deadline, she decided to shower off the night herself and start fresh.

As she started out, Shelby started in — with a garment bag.

"Why aren't you at home sleeping?" Eve asked.

"Tried, sir. Really couldn't. I'm hoping you'll clear me to hang in Observation during some of the interviews."

"You earned it."

"Thanks. A Mr. Summerset just brought this in for you. He said Roarke asked him to bring you a change of clothes."

Eve studied the bag. "Sure he did."

She knew the bony cadaver went into her closet, but she didn't need to be reminded before interview.

"Lieutenant? I want to say my ambitions don't aim toward a gold shield. I like the uniform."

"I know."

"Oh. Well, good. I didn't want to disappoint you."

"Shelby, you're a good cop, and an asset to this division. You keep at it, you continue to work your way up to being as good, as solid, as exemplary as Officer Carmichael, you'll be an even bigger asset to this division and the department."

"That's exactly where my ambitions aim, Lieutenant."

Eve took the garment bag, headed into the locker room and the narrow closet with the piss-trickle of almost hot water that served as one of the showers.

Despite the facilities, she did feel fresher.

And when she opened the garment bag, she put aside the fact that Summerset's fingers had been on her clothes — including her underwear — and let herself bask in the other fact.

She saw exactly what Roarke had intended when he'd ordered this outfit.

Black pants, straight line, and short black boots. A white shirt as crisp as an Alpine breeze. Black vest, not a jacket, so her weapon remained visible. Leather vest, no frills, all business.

Dressed, she stepped out and saw Peabody in the process of removing her pink coat.

No pink otherwise — not even her usual boots — but a dark, murderous red shirt with a thin gray-and-red scarf used as a kind of tie. Gray pants, scarred black boots.

No jacket, Eve noted. Weapon visible.

"Got two hours in my own bed," she told Eve. "McNab bunked up in EDD. They're really slammed. I hit the espresso — just a hit. I learned my lesson there. Feel ready."

"Good, because we're having our interviewees brought up to the boxes at nine hundred." She checked the time. "So they've got ten minutes."

She turned because she recognized the familiar click of heels coming toward the bullpen.

"All the interviews will be on record," she said as Mira came in. "You didn't have to come in this early to observe."

"Eve, I went to medical school, and I raised children. It's hardly the first time I've worked on little sleep. I had an opportunity to speak with several of the women, and more than a few men, who'd been held one way or the other. I'm here because I need to be."

"Understood. Appreciated. Peabody, would you see that Observation is stocked with decent coffee and the tea Dr. Mira likes?"

"Oh, and that is appreciated."

Jenkinson and Reineke came in next. Jenkinson's tie, a flaming orange, had little red devils all over it. The kind with horns and pointy-end tails and snarling grins.

"Really? Today?"

"Especially today, Loo, because if there's a hell, those bastards are going to fry in it. But first we're gonna lock them in cages."

"Did you read our report?" Reineke asked. "One of the kids we got out was locked in his room in one of the apartments, restrained to the bed. Gay kid, and he said they were going to send him to the island for Realignment today if we hadn't come. Fifteen years old. His own parents, Dallas. His own mom and dad."

"I read it. Let me see the socks."

That made him grin as he hiked up his pants leg. Black socks with one red pitchfork-wielding devil on the side.

"Okay, just — For fuck's sake, Santiago, you're on medical leave."

"No, sir." Face mutinous, left arm in a sling, he stood his ground.

"There's no talking to him," Carmichael told her.

"Then I won't waste my breath."

She waited for the rest, including Reo and the other lawyers, the feds. Feeney and Roarke came in together.

"Okay, boys and girls, hell of a job, all around. We're going to do the same today and nail this shut. Everyone will be fitted with ear-buds. Rather than Feeney trying to catch you up on EDD's findings, and they're still coming in, you'll have an EDD officer fill you in on your specific subject, and continue to inform you as data comes in."

"My boys are humping it, and the feds aren't slackers."

"Reo and the other prosecutors will work with you on charges and potential deals if such deals help fry bigger fish. Remember, after dealing with us, and whatever deals are or aren't struck, these subjects then face federal charges. Nobody walks away from this.

"Dr. Mira will observe. Peabody and I will rotate between Stanton Wilkey, Mirium Wilkey, and Lawrence Piper. Jenkinson and Reineke take the Huffmans and Gayle Steenberg."

"Come on, Dallas. I should —"

Before Santiago got the rest out, Eve froze him with a stare. "We're charging Steenberg with attempted murder of a police officer. You're that police officer. You don't interview her."

"Got you covered, Santiago," Reineke told him. "We'll lock her down."

"Do you doubt your fellow officers can handle — what was it, Detective Carmichael? — the hag of a bitch?"

Santiago shot his partner a half smile. "No, sir."

"Good. Baxter, Trueheart, you take Po, Harstead, and Wexford. Carmichael and Santiago, the Pooles and Hester Angus, the Tribeca midwife."

"That's first round. There will be more, but this round is key. Each interview team, take the next twenty to familiarize yourself with your subjects. Consult with Mira and/or Reo if you have applicable questions. Detective Carmichael?"

"LT?"

"See that your partner takes any necessary breaks. Dr. Mira will evaluate his condition every two hours."

"Aw, come on, boss."

"That's the deal, Santiago. Take it or go home."

"I'm taking it, I'm taking it."

"Study your subjects, work out your rhythm, and report to the assigned interview rooms — they're in my notes — at zero-nine-thirty."

"Lieutenant, if I could address you and your officers, very briefly."

"You have the floor, Special Agent Teasdale."

"I received word only moments ago that Utopia Island is fully shut down. There were five casualties, two law enforcement, three residents. Any injured are being treated in the medical facilities there, as they are, I'm assured, excellent. While the farm system is not yet fully contained, we estimate it at eighty-five percent."

"How's your agent?"

"Stable condition, thank you, Lieutenant. We have amassed a great deal of data from both of these areas. We will, of course, share all of it with the NYPSD. At this time, however, I think it's important to relay Rachel Wilkey is in a coma, and has been for nine days, following an attempt at self-termination. We have records showing this is not her first attempt. Evidence and statements at this time indicate Aaron Wilkey, Wilkey's youngest son, was not part of the criminal enterprise. He has been restricted to the island for months, and has endured two Realignment procedures. He is cooperating fully with authorities."

"That's good information, thanks." Eve scanned the room. "We use it and put these motherfuckers where they belong."

She took a minute to speak with Roarke while her detectives got ready. "Appreciate the change of clothes."

"You look like a self-contained, professional ass-kicker."

"A good definition of a cop in this case. Get any sleep?"

"I bought a couple of planets instead. Better than sleep."

"You're probably not really kidding. I need to huddle with Peabody."

"I'm going to do the same with EDD. I'm useful," he said before she could respond. "And I'm enjoying it."

"I know the first, and since the second seems true, go enjoy. Peabody." She gestured to her office. "Piper first."

"I lost that bet. I figured we'd hit Mirium Wilkey first."

"You read Piper's data. How would you describe him?"

"Wife-beating, misogynistic bully."

"You don't say true believer. He'll roll. To save himself, he'll roll on the Wilkeys."

"It won't save him."

"No. Here's how we play it."

When they walked into Interview, Piper sat alone, arms folded over his chest. His knuckles, though healing well, still showed raw from beating them against his wife.

"Record on. Dallas, Lieutenant Eve, and Peabody, Detective Delia, entering Interview with —"

"I'm not talking to cunt cops."

Eve continued to read details into the record, then sat. "Mr. Piper, the record shows that you were read your rights at the time of your arrest."

He tried to stare through her.

"We're aware that you exercised your right to contact a legal representative. However, that representative has also been arrested. And your financial accounts have been frozen due to your connection with Natural Order. If you wish legal representation at this time, we can and will arrange for a public defender."

"Fuck you, bitch. You can't do that to my money."

"We didn't. The FBI did, so you can take that up with them. Do you wish to have us arrange for a public defender?"

"You think I don't know they work with the cops? You think I'm stupid?"

"My opinion in the matter of your stupidity isn't relevant. Are you waiving legal representation?"

He jabbed a finger at her. "Fuck you and fuck lawyers. I don't need a lawyer. I don't need to talk to you."

"Let the record show Mr. Piper has waived his right to an attorney. While he may exercise his right to remain silent, we don't have to. We will inform Mr. Piper of the weight of the charges against him. Detective."

"Mr. Piper, you're charged with spousal abuse, spousal assault, endangering minors — three counts — due to the locks installed on the doors of your children's rooms."

"That's all bullshit. I'm the head of the house, the breadwinner. I run my house as I see fit, so you can fuck right off."

"You saw fit to strike your wife on multiple occasions — we have the records from the Huffmans' medical facility." Good Cop Peabody made no appearance here. She continued in a cold, flat voice. "You are further charged with murder in the second degree for the beating death of your wife —"

"Six months' pregnant wife," Eve added. "The jury's going to want that information."

"And are charged with leaving a crime scene, attempting to conceal evidence."

"That's all bullshit! My wife died from complications of a miscarriage. I called her doctor, I got her to the

414

best hospital I know. Now you've taken my kids. They just lost their mother. I lost my wife. I'm going to sue your bitch asses to the —"

"They took your wife out of the house in a body bag," Eve said. "Your cleaners missed a spot, Larry, so we have her blood and yours on the wall where you beat her head in. That's off-planet, a lifetime in a cage. And with the other charges? Add another twenty. And that's before the feds hit you with accessory to kidnapping, torture, forced imprisonment. And I'm barely getting started."

"You can't prove any of it."

"I have proved it. Two witnesses, Larry, heard your pregnant wife screaming, begging you to stop. Heard you screaming at her, beating her, bashing her head against the wall."

"Lying bitches. Who's going to believe them?"

Eve leaned in. "I believe them. A jury's not only going to believe them, a jury's going to eat up every word they say. Two witnesses, blood, and forensic evidence. And guess what, Larry, your wife's body."

She watched him jerk back at that.

"We recovered it from the crematorium on the compound. Hell of a thing to have, a private crematorium — but they hadn't disposed of her yet. Her body is now at our morgue. We've got the Huffmans, we've got your head cleaner. The Wilkeys, the Pooles. We've got the island, we broke the farm system. You're fucked, Larry. And yeah, bone stupid if you think the Huffmans, the Wilkeys, any of them will protect you now."

"Hard to protect some flunky," Peabody added, "when you're locked in a cell."

"You've got one shot or we walk out of here. As it stands, you'll do life off-planet with a twenty-year sweetener. Take the shot, give us chapter and verse on the Wilkeys, on Natural Order, and we can talk to the PA about reducing the murder charge so you'd have a chance at parole in twenty-five. Cooperating witness or a lifetime plus off-planet. Up to you."

"What do you want to know?"

He spilled, then spilled some more, primarily confirming and corroborating evidence and statements she already had. But she didn't object to adding to the pile.

As he spoke, Roarke's voice came through her earbud, and, with that lovely hint of Ireland, gave her more.

"All right, Larry, I'm going to talk to the PA about reducing the time for beating your pregnant wife to death and get you that twenty-five on-planet."

"With parole."

"Possibility of parole. Then there's the twenty for child abuse and endangerment."

"What? Wait!"

She sent him a cool look. "I explained that to you, on record. Your prints on the locks, Larry. Only yours. Same deal with the illegal substances — the derivative of Whore, the date-rape drug — found locked in your office. The bondage toys? Woo, Larry, but that's a personal choice. After that, you're going to have to deal with human trafficking charges. We're leaving that to the feds, so good luck there."

He started to sputter.

"You kept really good records on your computers — at home and in the compound. You had a good shot on a solid return on your investment with Marcia. The fifty K marriage fee's steep, but you got a ten K rebate since you found her on your own.

"Amazing how they broker people, isn't it, Peabody?"

"I know I'm impressed. He banked the five K each for his three kids, and got that really nice house for dirt cheap rent as long as he kept Marcia in line."

"And had another five K in the bag, except he killed her."

"You're twenty-five large down, Larry."

"Thirty-five," Eve corrected. "The order billed him another ten for the cleaning fee."

"Right, right." Peabody shook her head. "And it didn't even work. That's what a bad temper gets you, Larry." Enjoying herself, Peabody wagged a finger at him. "Out thirty-five grand, forty-five years as a guest of the great state of New York, and that's before the feds welcome you to one of their fine facilities."

"But we do thank you for your cooperation." Eve rose. "We'll have you escorted back to your cell."

"You lying bitches. You cheating cunts. All of you, all of you worthless whores."

"Now you're getting me excited. Dallas and Peabody exiting Interview. Record off."

When they stepped out, Eve leaned back against the wall a moment. "A moron. A vicious, woman-hating, nasty-assed moron."

"He never asked for the deal in writing. You know what?" Peabody added. "He wasn't listening, not really. Because we're women. He just heard deal, and jumped."

"Yeah, well, he's jumped in a cage for the rest of his nasty-assed life. Have him taken back and have them send Stanton Wilkey up. Then take twenty, get your mind clear."

She walked back to Observation and found Mira, Teasdale, Reo, a couple other APAs, and Shelby.

They used the wall screens, she noted, splitting them among the interviews in progress.

Reo tapped her earbud off, gestured Eve back out.

"Jenkinson and Reineke finished with Gwen. You'll want to talk to them before you take Mirium. We're not going to push for prison time there. Yes, she knew, at least about some of it. Yes, she's a selfish, greedy, entitled diva who doesn't give a shit about anyone but herself. But her fear's just as real. She tossed her parents under the bus, then ran them over a few times. I can't really blame her."

"I'm not going to feel sorry for her."

"Nope, no sympathy here, either. She had choices, and she chose wrong, again and again. But for someone like her? Knowing her days as a rich socialite are finished? That's genuine punishment, and justice, too."

"I can live with it."

"Good. Po crumbled so fast we could barely keep up. We've got a lot of names, and that's going to make processing, identifying, and helping abductees easier. She's done. She'll live out the rest of her life in a cell. Same with Vince Poole — no challenge there. There's a man more terrified of his wife than prison. And more terrified of the order than his wife. They're bringing Barbara Poole up now. She'll be more of a challenge, I think."

"They'll handle her. Challenge is good."

"You didn't get one with Piper. What an idiot. I actually saw Teasdale smile when you wrapped him up."

"Did you record it?"

"Sorry, wasn't quick enough. It may happen again. Who's up next for you?"

"Stanton Wilkey."

"Good call." Reo turned back to Observation. "Oh, the coffee's appreciated."

Eve rounded up her detectives between interviews, got the highlights, shared her own.

She hit more coffee to wind up for her own next round, then met Peabody outside of Interview.

"No lawyer," Peabody told her. "Barbara Poole took a public defender, and so did Harstead. The Huffmans — excluding Gwen — reached out to what looks like a friend of a friend's lawyer. Not in the order, and not a high flyer."

"I heard. Let's see what the supreme leader has to say for himself."

She walked in where Wilkey, now in an orange jumpsuit, sat with his legs folded on the chair, his open hands palms up on his knees, and his eyes closed.

Meditation's over, fucker, Eve thought.

"Record on."

CHAPTER
TWENTY-THREE

He opened his eyes and smiled as Eve read off the rest of the data. "I'm sending pure light into the universe to push against the dark you, misguidedly, brought to so many. It must be so difficult to carry so much dark inside you. I could help you."

"How? By locking me in a room, restraining me to a cot, maybe giving my brain a few good jolts? Or just letting Mother Catherine loose on me with her shock stick?"

His smile never faltered. "Meditation, self-examination, coming to an understanding of your place and purpose in the natural order brings peace and calm to the mind, the body, the spirit."

"And if that doesn't work, a dip in the sensory deprivation tank. You've declined legal representation, is that correct?"

"I have no need. My faith and my faithful sustain me."

"Great. You should know, a lot of your faithful are already rolling on you."

"To be weak is human."

"Christ." Eve scrubbed her hands over her face. "I don't get paid enough to listen to this. You're facing a multitude of federal charges, including but not limited to human trafficking, illegals trafficking, enforced slavery, abductions, torture, ordering the performance of medical procedures against the will of the patient, the abduction, torture, and forced imprisonment of a federal agent. There will be global charges as well, including the above, and along with forced sterilization, abortions."

She paused a moment, but he said nothing.

"The international police have shut down your island, Wilkey, and have all the records your people so meticulously kept. When your insane Realignment tortures didn't work on homosexuals, you chemically castrated the men, sterilized the women."

"Such a perverted lifestyle choice cannot be allowed to disrupt the natural order of the greater good."

"If individuals of different races living or imprisoned on said island managed to slip through the cracks to form a relationship, the punishment was shock treatments followed by thirty days' solitary confinement. If said relationship resulted in pregnancy, the pregnancy was terminated and both parties sterilized."

"Of course, of course." He nodded as if they were in perfect agreement. "The mixing of races dilutes the power and light of the whole. To each their own kind, my dear. This preserves cultures, it enhances the strengths and diminishes the weaknesses in each race. It brings peace and true freedom."

"The above charges violate international laws."

"The laws of our order answer to a higher power. Utopia Island is a sovereign nation —"

"In violation of a crapload of international laws. But we'll just leave that to those authorities and focus in on

421

the multiple lifetimes you'll be doing courtesy of New York."

"You and they have no authority over me and mine."

Peabody rolled her eyes. "Which is why you're sitting here in that fashionable suit."

"Where my corporeal form resides means nothing. My spirit remains free."

"Your spirit's never going to know freedom again," Eve said. "Your wife remains in a coma after her latest attempt to self-terminate. Her chances are fifty-fifty."

"Sadly, my wife suffers from typical female weaknesses and complaints, so her mind and spirit are in constant struggle. The universe decides in these tragic matters, not I."

"But you decided, though she was physically and emotionally incapable of carrying more children, to continue to impregnate her so that she suffered multiple miscarriages."

"A woman's purpose in life, indeed her greatest joy, is creating life, then nurturing that pure spirit. A husband is duty bound to fulfill his wife's purpose and bring her joy."

"Right." Eve flipped through her file. "So her physical and emotional health, her willingness to accept your decree of her 'purpose' doesn't apply. So when your wife underwent a hysterectomy to save her own life, you then impregnated, by forced insemination, a nineteen-year-old female — recorded as Patricia Hemstead."

Eve looked back at him. "Apparently your so-called marital duty doesn't just apply to your wife."

"The young girl trod on a crooked path. We helped her find the way, and gave her purpose."

"By forcing her to become an incubator," Eve snapped back. "To fulfill your purpose. Hemstead was then kept against her will, often in restraints, forced to complete the pregnancy, after which you took the child from her. You transferred Hemstead to your farm system, just getting off the ground then — in Kansas. In the case of the male child you named Aaron, your wife was given the child to raise."

"We saved the vessel from a life of chaos and poor choices, and gave her the greatest gift a woman knows."

"And Patricia Hemstead, again according to your own records, died eighteen years ago when she slit her own wrists with a piece of broken glass."

He lifted his hands, briefly bowed his head. "We mourn her terrible choice."

"I bet. Your youngest son has spent most of his life tending to the woman he believed was his mother, and much of that in restriction on the island."

"A child is subject to his parents' will, and has no greater purpose but to honor them."

She saw the little cracks forming. His smile, not so calm now. His eyes not so dreamy. A man used to deference, even reverence, didn't care for questioning and disgust — and she made sure hers showed — especially by women.

"And keeping him on the island's handy, as it would be embarrassing for the head of Natural Order to have a gay son."

For the first time Wilkey's face tightened. "My son has not chosen to be a homosexual."

"No, he hasn't, because choice has nothing to do with it. But let's move on to your other kids. Your oldest . . . What's his name again?" Eve made a show of looking through her files.

"That's Samuel," Peabody told her. "The embezzler."

"Right, right, the one who likes to dip into the membership fund to finance his lifestyle."

Wilkey flicked a hand. "That's nonsense."

"You must've taught him something." Peabody smiled broadly. "Because he kept really good records, in both sets of books."

"I was getting him mixed up with the other one, the one who likes to look at little girls."

"That's Joseph," Peabody said helpfully. "He's got an extensive collection of child porn — a lot of little girls right from your membership rolls. Most of them with paternal permission. But we give him some credit, as for sex he hits up adults. Licensed companions."

"These are terrible lies. The weakness of women, by nature, often resorts to lies, to cunning."

"We've got the pictures," Eve said. "And what do you care? They're females. Just getting groomed for their purpose in life, right? Anyway, both of your older sons are going away — we'll be talking to them for a long time. It's a Wilkey family affair."

"We can't leave out the daughter."

"Sure can't," Eve said with cheer. "No embezzlement there, no sick taste for ten-year-old girls." Eve sat back. "She's just a murderer."

424

"More lies." But his soft hands balled into fists. "No one will believe your lies. How I pity you, how I will pray for you."

"You can save the pity and prayers for yourself. This is truth, and your faithful as well as the world in general are going to get a whole crapload of truth. And a lot of those faithful will suddenly turn faithless and roll all over you and the rest. And the rest of the world? They're going to stop seeing you and your sick order as crazies or bigots and see just how unnatural you are."

"The true flock will never turn away."

More cracks, deeper cracks. Eve smirked at him, pushed harder.

"Keep thinking that. And just an FYI, if you're thinking that Congressman — Jeez, what the hell is his name? It's been a long few days."

"Congressman Orlando, Oklahoma," Peabody provided. "And there's Senator O'Connell, Kentucky."

"Right — what would I do without you? If you're waiting for either one of those gentlemen — and I use the word loosely — to come to your defense, strike up the fucking band, forget it. They should both be in custody about now. Bribery — accepting and making — conspiracy to defraud the United States of freaking America. But you don't need to hear about their problems when you've got so many of your own."

"Freedom of faith, my constitutional right, protects —"

"Don't you begin to speak to me about rights." Eve slapped the table, lurched up. "Let's talk about Fiona Vassar's rights. Abducted, drugged, tortured, forced to go through a bogus marriage ceremony to become your breeding wife. Raped by you repeatedly, restrained, forced into servitude."

She paused a moment, pulled herself back. "Her children are with her now. Cassie, Robbyn, and Seth — that's the name she gave him before you had him sent to what you called the Nursery — with several other kids."

Berenski at the lab had come through with the DNA match there, Eve thought. Sometimes Dickhead didn't earn his nickname.

"They're all together now, safe from you now."

"So are the others you designated as breeders," Peabody snapped out. "You perverted fuck."

"Ella Alice Foxx," Eve continued, "abducted, drugged, tortured, forced into servitude, and held against her will. You'd already banked payment of a hundred thousand — she was a prime one — for her forced marriage, to take place next week — you had the date marked."

She reeled off names, no need for the file now, no pretense, of women taken — the ones he'd kept, the ones he'd sold.

"They have stories to tell, you pathetic excuse for a human being, and they're telling them. Your block on Tribeca's done. Your jailer there's in custody. The Huffmans are in custody, your recruiters — what a tame name for a vicious practice — are in custody."

Now his voice roared out, a fanatic in the throes of persecution. "You, the unworthy, the unnatural, attack our faith. Our faith will stand and spread and triumph over your vicious and unholy attacks."

426

But his face had paled, and the knuckles of his folded hands went white.

"Not a chance. The judges, the cops, the lawyers, and all the rest on your rolls — in custody. Some of them will flip hard on you and yours to save their own asses. You're done. And you know why you're done, why your cult is finally broken? Because your daughter's been planning and plotting how to take over, and she killed rather than risk a hitch in those plans.

"I'm betting you were on her list of disposables."

His face relaxed again. So sure of himself there, Eve thought. So sure a daughter would remain ever loyal.

"You lie. You lie to test my will, my faith. Mirium would never betray me or the order."

Eve leaned forward, spoke softly now to give each word import. "She despises you, and because I know that, I'll turn her. She knows everything there is to know, your personal assistant, your recruiter."

"Mirium is blood of my blood. She is fruit of my seed. She will never turn against me. If you make a martyr of me, the faithful will rise up."

"Nobody's going to mistake you for a martyr. Did you authorize and finance the abductions of selected individuals in New York City? Deny it," Eve invited. "Because every one of them deserves their day in court recounting what you did."

"I saved their lost souls."

"You don't deny the abductions?"

"I deny nothing. I am shepherd to the lost sheep."

"Did you authorize the restraint, imprisonment, the use of shock devices, forced feeds, sensory deprivation, physical beatings on individuals abducted from New York City?"

"We trained them, educated their minds and their spirits. We saw that they had proper nutrition to cleanse their bodies of the toxins of your secular world."

"Were the instruments and procedures I just named used in this training?"

"Yes. The dark and the false freedoms must be burned out to free the spirit."

"Did you sell and profit from the sale of human beings abducted from New York City for the purposes of forced marriages and for impregnation of the females abducted?"

A bead of sweat trailed down his left temple, and that was fear. His eyes burned into Eve's, and that was hate.

"You are an unnatural creature."

"Okay. Do you need me to repeat the question?"

"A woman's purpose is to serve at her husband's will, for a woman's will is fragile and fickle. It is her purpose to bear the joy and pain of childbirth and bring life forth."

"And with this in mind you abducted, trained, then sold women to men who would pay the fee."

"A man must invest in family."

"So yes. Did you authorize and provide — at a fee — trackers with shock options to be utilized by these husbands on wives and minor children who they deemed required them?"

"A man is the head of the household, and a woman is duty bound to obey. You have a sickness, a terrible sickness enhanced by the perverted freedoms and laws you cling to."

Eyes flat, Eve just stared back at him. "So another yes. Did you authorize the removal of Marcia Piper's body, and the contamination of the crime scene after she was beaten to death by her husband, Lawrence Piper?"

"I regret his methods reached that extreme, and he will be punished by the order. But she disobeyed him. My people didn't contaminate the household. They purified it."

"Okay then."

She rolled through more charges. She could read the fury in his eyes now, and the spread of real fear. But he remained stubbornly adherent to his tenets as justification for all.

"That wraps up this part of the program. You'll be escorted back to your cell, have a break before the feds get their shot at you. After them, Interpol. I almost hate to send Mirium to Omega, seeing as she started this ball bouncing. But duty calls."

Eve rose, and now his eyes looked at her, fevered, fervent.

"You'll never stop the order, its righteousness. Our spread is wide, our roots are deep."

"Wide maybe." Peabody shrugged. "Or it was wide, but those roots can't be more than an inch deep. Otherwise, they wouldn't have been so easy to rip out."

Because Eve smiled at her, Peabody shrugged again. "Dallas and Peabody exiting Interview. Record off."

"Nice parting shot," Eve told her when they stood outside. "That's a gardening thing, right?"

"Yeah. Jesus, I need another shower after that."

"Take an hour."

"I don't need that long to shake it off."

"Take an hour," Eve repeated. "Get some food, take a walk. This was the worst of it. The daughter's more your normal greedy murdering bitch."

"And we eat them for breakfast."

"Every day. Twice a day."

Peabody laughed. "Can't eat that much. New pants."

"Take your new pants and have that sick son of a bitch taken back to his cage."

She started toward Observation, but Mira, Teasdale, and Reo stepped out.

Eve looked at Mira first. "He's legally sane."

"Yes. He's a fanatical bigot with a messiah complex who may believe a good deal of what he said in there — not all, but a good deal. And legally sane."

"Good." Now at Reo. "No deals."

"Not even a tiny one."

"Good again. Special Agent."

"I'm going to ask what might be considered a favor, but what I hope will be understood and prevent any friction between this department and mine."

"He took your man, he beat your man half to death. You want Wilkey first."

"Yes. You've more than laid the groundwork for the federal crimes we'll charge him with. I want you to agree not to fight me on him serving his time in federal prison before your charges kick in."

"Done."

Teasdale opened her mouth, then closed it, nodded. "You say that understanding he won't live to pay for what you charge him with here."

"He's going to die in a cage. Why would I care what kind? Except sometimes I do," Eve added. "Mirium Wilkey."

"Is yours first, no question. Not from my end. I'm about to confer with Interpol. Hopefully they'll be as cooperative as you."

"They'll have the upper echelon from the island. Whoever ran the day-to-day, brought people in, did the torture, and so on. They'll take that. Everybody gets a share. Is it Abernathy you're meeting?"

"No, someone a bit higher up."

"Good luck. One question? Are you looking at higher up? The lateral move from Homeland to the FBI."

Teasdale offered a very slight smile. "Opportunity knocked. I'll speak to you again."

Eve stopped in the bullpen for a quick roundup with whoever was between interviews. Santiago sat at his desk using voice command to write his report.

"You gave us the easy ones because I got dinged."

Behind his back Carmichael rolled her eyes, but Eve stepped up to his desk.

"My take? You're feeling bitchy because the crazy woman got a little piece of you."

He shrugged. "That's fair."

"I respect that. Did you nail them all down?"

"Yeah, the APA and shrink assigned signed off."

"Good. The next two won't be so easy. Call up Phiffer. Head cleaner, Piper homicide. He dug up a lawyer. And pick one of the cleaning crew — they're in the file. Take the lower level guy first, squeeze him, flip him, and take down Phiffer."

"We can do that." Considerably brightened, Santiago turned to Carmichael. "We can do that."

"Yes, we can."

Satisfied, Eve went to her office, and found Roarke.

"You were in my ear twenty minutes ago."

"Now I'm here." He pointed to the covered plate on her desk. "Cold pasta. Eat something."

"I need to prep for Mirium Wilkey."

"Tell me you're not already fully prepped and ready for her."

Since she couldn't, Eve sat, lifted the cover. Cold pasta — with vegetables, of course, because Roarke.

"Data's coming in so fast. EDD's a machine today."

"I can say the same for your division. And as I'm no longer quite so useful, I've found a place to catch up on some work."

"Your office — home or Midtown — would work. You've given this a hell of a lot of time."

"I'm invested."

With his hands in his pockets, his fingers found the button, Eve's button, and rubbed it.

"Dochas has taken in ten women and eight children. Women who were already sheltered there volunteered to double up. That speaks to me. And when you've closed this down for the day, I'd like to take your squad and EDD out for drinks and a meal." He held up a hand before she could object.

"Things moved fast after Cobbe and Ireland, and I'd like to show my appreciation in a tangible way."

"You hauled them to Ireland and back in a private shuttle, your family fed them like an army on leave."

He simply walked to her, ran a hand over her hair. "I'd like to do this."

Needed to, she realized. Maybe needed to so he could — so they could — shut out some of the misery they'd seen for just a little while.

"You want to blow a good chunk of your fortune on a bunch of cops, fine with me. I'll pass the word. But that's a hell of a lot of people on short notice."

"Happily I own a very fine pub not far from here. It'll be closed tonight for a private party. I'll do that catching up now so I can observe some part of your evisceration of Mirium Wilkey. I'd wish you luck with it, but you don't need it."

He leaned down to kiss her. "Make her pay," he murmured, "for all of them."

She would, Eve thought. She'd make Mirium Wilkey pay for Ariel Byrd, for all the rest. And for putting that hint of sadness in the eyes of the man she loved.

Because, she knew, he saw her in Ella Foxx, in Fiona Vassar — and all the others.

When she walked into Interview with Peabody, started the record, Mirium sat in her jumpsuit, back straight, hands folded.

"So, Mirium, I'm told you've been informed the lawyer you attempted to contact for representation in these matters is unavailable. Due to being charged with multiple crimes also relating to these matters. And you've opted not to engage or request other legal representation."

"I'm capable of defending myself."

"Good for you. We'll get started. Gina Mancini, Ella Alice Foxx," Eve began, and read off a long list of names as she laid their ID shots on the table. "You may be surprised to see some of this official identification, as you played a part — that computer science degree — in wiping their official records."

"I don't know what or whom you're talking about."

"Oh now, Mirium." Shaking her head, Eve offered a small pity smile. "If you think capable of defending yourself equals starting off with easily debunked lies, you're heading down the wrong road. We have statements from every one of these women, who all identify you as their abductor. We also have statements from three — so far — of your accomplices, Jane Po and Michael Harstead and Denise Wexford, corroborating that. They also gave complete details on same, like the drugs you used, the vehicle you drove, the payments you made in exchange for their assistance."

Mirium barely missed a beat. "I did what I had to do to protect myself."

"You drugged and abducted these women — some minors at the time — and delivered them to the compound in Connecticut — thereby crossing state lines — to protect yourself? These women threatened you?"

"Not them. My father, my brothers, the people he controls."

"Your father threatened you?"

"Every day of my life." She worked up watery eyes that to Eve looked more like an allergic reaction than tears. "You have no idea what he's capable of."

"Oh, we've got some clues. What was the nature of the threat?"

"If I didn't do what he ordered me to do, he'd have me taken to the island, keep me there, or worse, he'd sell me to one of his faithful."

"Like you helped him sell the women you abducted for him?"

"I'm not proud of what I did, but I feared for my life. Every day. If you question Stanton Wilkey, the repercussions . . ." She trailed off as she pressed her lips together, stared down at the table. "I could be locked in my room for days on his whim."

"How terrifying." Peabody widened her eyes, blinked them. "Locked in a suite of rooms, Dallas, with a big, soft bed, an entertainment screen, an AutoChef, a spa-like en suite. The horror!"

Mirium cut her gaze to Peabody, and the heat in it burned away the fake tears. "The man's a monster. He could have me beaten."

"Should've led with that," Eve commented. "Most people would. So, in terror of your monster dad, you traveled freely from the compound to the city, had meetings, often stayed at the — you called it a pied-a-terre, deceived young women by posing as a recruiter for employment, then drugged them and transported them back to the compound."

"All under duress. I had no choice."

"Right. And in all those hours, sometimes days, away from the compound and your monster dad, you never once considered going to the authorities with your fears and desperation."

"I was afraid to. I truly believed he was invincible. Now I have hope, but I'm still afraid."

"Uh-huh. And those fears traveled with you when you visited the farms and ranches out west, or shuttled to Europe, the island, when you banked your recruiter's fees and so on."

"The fear of the Time Out, Dallas. It can't be overstated." Peabody snickered, then chuckled, then threw up her hands and broke into giggles.

"Don't you dare mock me, you stupid bitch!"

Mirium shoved up and, since Eve had — deliberately — had her brought in without restraints, lunged.

Since Peabody timed it well, Eve let it play out. Mirium's shove, Peabody's grab and spin.

"That's assaulting an officer," Peabody snapped. "Sit down, stay down, or I'll put you down."

"Said charge is added to the record." Eve spoke mildly as Peabody put Mirium back in the chair. "And if you don't want to be mocked, don't be so damn mockable. Because everything you said is bullshit."

Because, despite all of her planning, Mirium Wilkey hadn't planned on this.

Now Eve shoved up, slapped both hands on the table, and leaned across and into Mirium's face.

"Bullshit, and every single one of these women, all your accomplices, every woman who worked in that house in the compound will testify to the bullshit. You ran that household, Mirium, treating these women like your personal slaves, happily ordering physical punishments if any of them didn't move fast enough to suit you. Fucking tyrant, slapping Ella Foxx because there was too much goddamn pulp in your fresh OJ."

"They'll say anything to get back at my father. I had to maintain strict discipline in the house or —"

"And when you decided to assign Fiona Vassar to clean your rooms, scrub your toilet, make your bed and she didn't fluff your pillows to your satisfaction, you slugged her? How the hell would your father have known? You ruled that house your way because you fucking enjoyed it."

Eve sat back again. "You're your father's daughter, Mirium. If you want to play the victim tune, be my guest, but it sure doesn't sing."

"You can't know what it's like to be raised by a monster, to do his bidding because it's all you know, and he's everything you fear."

Everything inside Eve tightened, twisted. And she used it, let it burn through her.

"I know you made your own choices. You weren't helpless or beaten down. You weren't locked in and defenseless. You wanted the life, the money, the travel, the power. You killed Ariel Byrd to gain and protect that power."

"That's insane! I told you before, I didn't even know the woman. I was on retreat, in the compound."

Rounding the table slowly, Eve leaned down, spoke quietly. "Do you really think you and your e-crew are better than me and mine? We have you leaving the compound on the evening of the murder, zipping out the gates in the same SUV you habitually used to abduct women. We have you entering the residence downtown. We have you leaving the residence twenty minutes before Ariel Byrd's time of death. And we have you coming back with blood — her blood — on your shirt."

Eve strolled around the table again, tossed evidence bags on the table. "We have the copy of Byrd's key card — you should've ditched that. We have your recordings from the device you put in Gwen Huffman's 'link."

She tapped a bag with a tiny chip inside it. "Didn't think to seal up when you made that, installed it."

A risk, Eve thought, as they'd only found a partial. But she saw from the flicker on Mirium's face, it had been a risk worth taking.

"You heard Gwen and Ariel argue, and Ariel in the heat of the moment threaten to expose Gwen. Couldn't have that, could you? You'd gone to so much trouble, had such an investment. It went all the way back to that summer in the Hamptons when you saw Gwen with another girl and outed her. Off to Realignment with her, and that was power. It must've tasted so sweet."

She sat, pulled Ariel's crime scene shots out of the file.

"So you kept tabs on her, all this time. You knew the Realignment was bullshit, worse, torture — you're an educated woman — and you knew Gwen continued to have relationships outside the rules of the order. But you bided your time there. Money and power on the line. You wanted her to meet the terms of her trust as much as she did. You're the one who pointed her toward Caine."

"It was going so well, too." Peabody picked up the rhythm. "He falls for her, they're engaged. And then she screws it all up with this artist. You need her to get that money — marry the rich guy, have a kid, get the big pot of money. Then you can blackmail her."

"A nice side income. Sure, she can play her game out, divorce him for cause, move on, but she'll pay, she'll keep shelling out to keep you quiet."

"You can't prove any of this. It's nothing but wild speculation."

"Sure we can. Have proven the bulk of it, and the rest follows." Eve kicked back. "You plan things out, Mirium, you organize, arrange the steps. But that temper messes you up. You should have waited Ariel out, but you beat her skull in because she would dare, dare to threaten your payoff. You'd have Gwen and her money — or her family's money — on the hook forever. You know her well enough to be sure she'd pay to protect her image, her status, her fortune."

"We've only known her for a few days," Peabody added, "and we know she's a shallow diva who only worries about herself. Golly." Peabody blinked her eyes. "She's a lot like you."

"Yeah, they're sisters under the skin," Eve agreed.

"We're nothing alike." Mirium hissed it out.

"Well, you're some smarter, and get some jollies over violence, but otherwise . . . You'd handle Gwen, right, Mirium, pull in that steady income? Then all you have to do is deal with your father. He's getting older, he's vulnerable — too many risky predilections now — and you know where all the bodies are buried. You've made sure of it. Your brothers? You can take care of them the same way. You take over, give it a little time. Maybe enough time for the Huffmans to have a fatal accident."

Eve touched a finger to Ariel's photo. "All that planning, all that investment, all that patience, that time, all blown to shit because Ariel Byrd fell in love with your pigeon.

"Oh yeah." Eve held up a finger. "You didn't have time to get your bloody shirt to the cleaners. Should've gotten rid of that, too, but I guess you really liked it. Shoving it in a laundry bag doesn't take care of the blood. Ariel's blood. So play victim all you want if that blows up your skirt, but you're going down for murder, for her murder and all the rest. And Natural Order is finished."

Now Mirium leaned forward. "Do you think I give one small fuck about the order? A means to an end, nothing more. I had to listen to those rules, that rhetoric, that insulting crap all my life. Born female, I was less, always less. Good for nothing but running a household, pushing brats out of me. He set a deadline. I had less than two years before he married me off to the highest bidder. What do you think about that?"

"I think you should have made other choices. You could've walked out."

440

"And into what?" Visibly incensed, Mirium threw up her hands. "I was entitled to my inheritance, entitled to be in charge. Jesus Christ, two of my brothers are morons and the half-bastard's gay. I'm smarter than all of them, and I'm relegated to making sure the furniture's dusted."

Eve went with a hunch. "So you asked to recruit."

"I showed him what I could do, how much I could bring in. God knows we needed it the way these idiot men spend and buy and squander. And still, after all that, he tells me it's time to do my duty as a woman. I convinced him to give me time, but it was running out."

"And you already had the Huffman plan in your pocket."

"Sex is Gwen's drug of choice. I saved her sorry ass from exposure countless times. I got sick of it. Who wouldn't? I was so close, and that slut of an artist thought she could ruin things."

"You showed her," Peabody murmured.

"You're damn right I did. I protected myself. And I protected Gwen. Again. When I headed over to that loft, I thought about talking her down. I'd done that with others. I thought about paying her off. I'd done that with others. And I decided the hell with it. I'm sick of it. I heard the music, knew she was up there, and had all those tools up there with her. Just end it, and maybe when Gwen hears about it, she'll get scared enough to behave herself until she's married and pregnant."

"You used the copy of the swipe. You'd gotten it from Gwen's purse, made a copy."

"The same time I bugged her 'link. I went in, went up, picked up the hammer, and did what I had to do. I've waited my whole life to take what I'm entitled to. Waited, hearing how I'm to serve, to be weak and fertile and obedient. I'm entitled to be who I really am."

"Yeah, I'd say you crossed that line awhile back."

"I'm willing to deal." Mirium folded her hands again. "I want immunity."

"I want a big glass of dry red wine and twelve hours of sleep." Eve shrugged. "I'll get mine eventually. You don't have a prayer on yours."

"Immunity." Mirium twisted her lips into a smile. "And for that I give you everything. Names — I'm talking high-level politicians, judges, cops, celebrities, and more. I'll give you details on my father, my brothers — the real ones, not Mommy's Fake Boy, because even my father didn't trust him enough to bring him into the business. I'll give you details on the inner workings of the order, financial data, training centers. There's nothing I don't know. I made it my business to know all the details."

"I bet you did. I respect that. Especially since we've made it our business to know and find out all those details, those names, those locations. We have it all, Mirium, and don't need you. But thanks for the offer."

Eve rose. "You've just confessed to first-degree murder, to multiple abductions feeding into human trafficking, to assault, and so on and so on. You can try the victim tune again, but it's all on record now. You're going to learn what it really means to be locked in a room. Or in this case, a concrete cage.

442

"Dallas and Peabody exiting Interview. Record off."

"You can't know it all! You can't! I'm entitled to protect myself, my birthright!"

Peabody blew out a long, slow breath when Eve shut the door.

"If I needed a shower after Wilkey, I need the fume tube after that. She's worse, Dallas."

"She's a lot worse, and she's finished. Good job in there, Peabody. Good job with all of them."

"Are we really going out for that big glass of wine?"

"That's the plan. Any interviews still in progress should conclude, then we shut this down for the day. Hell, we're still going past end of shift. My overtime paperwork is going to suck balls."

She shook it off. "I'm going to talk to Reo, to Mira. Go ahead and write this up. We can close the book on Ariel Byrd's murder."

She talked to Reo and Mira, and found herself telling them both to join the damn pub party. Then she went into her office, sat, and contacted Ariel Byrd's mother.

She hoped by letting the woman know they'd gotten justice for her daughter, she'd find some comfort.

When she finished, she sat back, looked at the photo on her board of the woman who'd started it all.

"Too high a price," she stated. "You paid too high a price. And still, without you paying it, who knows how much longer, how many more."

She rose, intending to go out to the bullpen and check on progress. Roarke stepped into the doorway. She hadn't heard him — she rarely did. He moved like a cat.

She gestured him in. "Close the door, will you?"

When he had, she moved straight to him, wrapped around him, pressed into him.

"Hang on to me a minute, okay?" She shuddered once. Only once. "Just hang on."

"Always. It's all right now, baby. It's done now."

"She said — she said I couldn't know what it was like to live in fear of a father, and I thought — God! She was never afraid of Wilkey. She never was afraid."

"I know."

"I just need a minute. Just need you for a minute."

"You'll have me a lot longer than that. And we two? We'll have an evening with a lot of the very good men and women who helped end this madness."

"Always more madness," she murmured.

"True enough, but you know to take victory when it's in your hand."

"I do." She breathed out, held tighter for a moment, then stepped back. "I do. So we're going to go eat and drink with those good men and women. Then we two? We're going home and having a whole bunch of really good sex."

"That's a fine victory lap, isn't it?"

She started out with him and glanced back, just once more, at Ariel Byrd. Love, she thought, doomed some — she saw it nearly every day.

But . . . And bullpen full of cops or not, she took Roarke's hand.

Some, love saved.